STEPPING ON THE CRACKS

Chris Carter

Matador
9 Priory Business Park
Kibworth Beauchamp
Leicestershire LE8 0RX, UK
Tel: (+44) 116 279 2299
Fax: (+44) 116 279 2277
Email: books@troubador.co.uk
Web: www.troubador.co.uk/matador

ISBN 978 1780881 553

British Library Cataloguing in Publication Data.
A catalogue record for this book is available from the British Library.

Typeset in Aldine by Troubador Publishing Ltd
Printed and bound in the UK by TJ International, Padstow, Cornwall

Matador is an imprint of Troubador Publishing Ltd

I would like to thank:

*All my family and friends, too many to mention, who supported and
encouraged me to publish this story. But a special word for the artist Kevin
Cocks and the legend that is Fergie, to Pete Elford, to Ben Hewer for his
unwavering optimism, and of course, the ingenious cover design. To Ness
for her patience as I spent too many nights trying to make sense of it all.
And a special thanks to the brilliant writer and author, Mary Rensten for
all her hours of time, help and encouragement, but most of all for believing
in me.*

This book is dedicated to my brother, Gary.

CHAPTER ONE

July 1973

'Dave!... wait up! I've gotta get a can of Coke or something, I'm gasping.'

We were making our way along the Hammersmith Road in the dying embers of a warm July afternoon. It was still hot and Dave, his hair the colour of clay, dragged me along in his wake.

I must be mad! I thought to myself. For I had rushed like crazy to meet him from football training. Hadn't even gulped down a glass of water or anything, had just dressed quickly, left my kit bag with Billy, making him swear on his life that he wouldn't fill the damn thing with left behind jockstraps or stuff the fingers of my goalkeeping gloves with soggy balls of bog paper. And then, with the shuttles and jumping for endless crosses still heavy in my legs, my unbuckled belt flapping round my waist and the Bowie T-shirt that Dave had lent me in my hand, I had pelted down the high street after the number 7 bus and caught the back rail just as my legs had been about to give out on me.

The conductor had lent precariously against the rail and grinned at me as I had plonked myself, gasping for breath, on the bottom stair.

'Gotta be quicker than that, Johnny, if you're gonna be England's new number one now Banksy's gone,' he'd smirked, tipping the peak of his cap back the way he must have seen old Reg Varney's sidekick, Bob Grant, do a hundred times before on *On The Buses*. I rolled my eyes, thankful that I hadn't recovered enough to have to answer the cocky git. I sat and waited for the breeze to dry me off enough to put Dave's T-shirt on.

And then I was like some capsized water-skier as Dave weaved along the pavement at breakneck speed, the coolest kid in town picking his way through the crowds, and just when it looked as if he had been about to career head-on into some innocent passer-by, he glided around them like a cloud of smoke, picking his way effortlessly towards his destination… the Hammersmith Odeon.

It was the last night of David Bowie's British tour and Dave was determined to see it. 'Da-ve!' I called out again but he hadn't heard me. If anything he picked up the pace through a wall of people, like water following the path of least resistance.

'Dave! Bleedin' 'ell!'

And then he stopped sharply, straightened his lithe body and spun round with that look that I'd seen ever since I can remember. That ever so slightly perplexed expression; amused almost, as if he couldn't quite believe the incompetence of the people that life had dealt him, and then that thin smile creased his face.

'Something big is going to happen tonight, Johnny, I can feel it.' He gave my shoulder a firm pat as if it had slipped down and needed replacing. 'Come on,' he told me smartly, 'we've got to go.' And even though the time was only approaching five and the damn thing didn't start till eight o'clock, I took a deep breath, shook my head and smiled admiringly at the sheer enthusiasm of my friend, and fell obediently into line.

The white oblong above the doors read:

FROM 8PM WE'RE WORKING TO-GE-TH-ER WITH
DAVID BOWIE

Already the crowds had gathered. A sea of shoulder-length hair with clusters of denim wherever you looked. The faces of Bowie and Bolan stitched onto backs; lapels peppered with badges like twentieth century pearly kings and queens. It felt odd, dreamlike almost; the atmosphere a blend of calmness and excitement.

Even the policemen appeared relaxed, many of them jacketless, the sleeves of their aqua-blue shirts rolled neatly up around their elbows added to the holiday air; no one was there for trouble. They were there to see Bowie... *Ziggy*... his rock star creation. What had Dave called it? 'Life imitating art?' 'Art imitating life?' Well it had been something typically "Dave" anyway.

Bowie: they called him a rock star but to me he seemed more like an actor, but what did I know? He was extravagant, wild, unpredictable, but above all, cool. Much the same as Dave, he could be anything he wanted to be, I reckoned. Good at everything: football, running, all sports, reading, writing, fighting. Could write his own headlines but all he wanted to do was write Bowie's.

A denim-clad teenager lumbered up to a group of coppers. The faintest flicker of alertness registered beneath their helmets.

'Don't need you all here man,' he drawled as if he were from San Francisco not South Croydon. 'Don't need the heavy scene, we're all here to-ge-th-er.' And he stuck a thumb up in the direction of the billboard and smiled with heavy eyes. 'We're here to worship.'

Two or three of the policemen rolled theirs but most returned his smile, enjoying the sheer innocence of it all. And then, right on cue, as if someone arranged it to justify their presence, news of an incident crackled over a radio... 'A gang of skinheads ...'

They were the talk around school, the skinheads; gang going around gouging crude markings into people's flesh and filling them with Indian ink.

A car pulled up and a crowd quickly formed around it, like ants converging on spilt ice cream. Girls screamed, excitement heightened but then dropped a level when Angie, Bowie's wife, stepped out of the car. A Bowie but not quite the one they had been expecting. But still, the sight of her commanded respect and bouncers and police joined forces and cleared a path for her as people reached out for the slightest of touches, as if she were some sort of magical healer or something.

She looked every inch the American rock beauty with her short bleached blonde hair whipped up around her head and stripy red pirate top, as if she had just stepped out of some chauffer-driven, futuristic, fashion time capsule. She stopped and began to sign some autographs and was quickly caught up in a web of outstretched hands holding pens and programmes. She interacted with the crowd, nodding and smiling politely; she appeared at ease but at the same time a little shy, awkward from all the attention. She handed a pen back to some starry-eyed girl and made to continue up the steps of the Odeon when all of a sudden she spotted Dave loitering at the back of the crowd.

She squinted for a moment and then smiled sweetly. 'Hell-o,' she said in that squeaky American accent of hers, and for the briefest of moments it was as if they were the only two people there.

'Hi.' Dave nodded casually, as if he was greeting a well-wisher in the corridor at school.

They held each others' gaze for a moment longer and then she cocked her head to one side, like some tiny bird, and was gone; the crowd around her followed like slivers of metal following a magnet.

I turned to Dave and, not for the last time in our lives, looked at him as if seeing him for first time.

'Have you met her before?' I asked in wonder.

He nodded casually. 'Once or twice, yeah.'

Words failed me.

He lifted his chin in her direction. 'She make's a lovely cup of tea.'

The first thing that hit me was the heat; the atmosphere inside the Odeon seemed to be approaching boiling point. Dave had seen

Bowie before but even he said that he had never experienced anything like it. Beethoven's "Ninth Symphony" filled the auditorium and I felt as if I was about to go to war or something. I felt a chill run the length of my spine... and then everything seemed to happen at once: the lights went down, the crowd roared, the lights exploded back into life... Bowie was on stage, Mick Ronson's guitar opened up like a machine gun raking the stage, firing the first notes of "Hang onto yourself"... and although it would never mean as much to me as it did to Dave, I could forever say that I was there.

The next evening Dave dragged me up town again, this time to the Café Royal in Regent Street, where Bowie was having his farewell party for *Ziggy*. Once again there was a crowd, although not as many people as outside the Odeon. These were the hardcore fans, the infatuated, the ones who ate, slept and drank Bowie. They hovered round the entrance but were kept at a respectful distance by the doormen and bouncers. The biggest names you could imagine kept on sweeping through the doors: Mick and Bianca Jagger, Paul and Linda McCartney, Cat Stevens, Lou Reed, Keith Moon, Ringo Starr, Lulu, even Barbra Streisand was there! My jaw felt permanently slack but Dave had appeared unfazed; he had eyes for only one of them. But we had to wait some considerable time for Bowie to arrive, long after most of the fans and the press had gathered.

Bowie stepped from the car, Angie following, and a handful of cameras flashed in his face. He seemed not to notice. As he made his way to the door Dave suddenly called out, 'David!' Bowie turned towards us; a mutual smile for the cameras and crowd played instinctively on his face. But then he saw Dave and stopped and turned.

'Oh hello again.' He smiled, was no more than two feet away: David Bowie! He was just a little taller than Dave, but his spiky flame hair created the illusion that he was bigger. He was dressed in an ice-blue suit and had some kind of flower in his hand. It was hard to take the moment in, what with the constant white flashes exploding from the cameras.

'Hi,' Dave replied, and it was the closest I'd ever seen him to flustered. For once he actually looked like a child, this foolish great grin on his face. But then it was gone, and he was his composed self again.

'Did you enjoy last night?' Bowie asked. Not 'Were you there last night?' as if it was obvious where he'd have been... which I suppose it was.

'Yeah, great.' Dave nodded, fished inside his denim jacket and pulled out a Manila envelope and held it expectantly to his chest.

'More writing?' Bowie asked, taking the envelope and half pulling out sheets of A4.

'Bits and pieces,' admitted Dave sheepishly. 'And some other... *stuff*,' he added.

Bowie looked across at Angie by his side.

'The kid who came round to Beckenham, the *wordy* one,' he explained, whilst he casually flicked through Dave's work.

'I know darling,' she drooled. 'Met last night, didn't we hon?'

Dave ducked his head, a little smile forming on his face. Bowie nodded thoughtfully.

'Looks good,' he said, 'although you've spelt "flamboyant" wrong.'

And then something fell from between the wad of paper and fell to the ground. A quizzical, almost mocking expression played across Bowie's face.

'A fan letter!' he exclaimed, as Dave hastily scooped up the small white envelope. 'Wouldn't have thought that'd be your thing.'

'Err, not quite,' Dave muttered, tucking the thing back under Bowie's arm for him, me invisible by his side.

'I'll have a look at them but I gotta go now,' and that shy, almost effeminate grin played upon his face. 'Big night ahead!' And with that he turned back into the maelstrom of flashlights and clicking cameras.

And that was life with Dave, the utter privilege of being the best friend of this enigma of a boy. Except, of course, he was never truly a boy at all. He was the cool kid in town, there was no denying it, and he was my best friend. And of course the less he tried to *be* cool, to just be himself, the more mystifying the legend became. We suited each other Dave and I: the lazy, quiet, mysterious kid who, in the blink of an eye, could run like the wind and articulate like a teacher, and the stereotypical boy, open as a book. We just seemed to fit.

I thought of Dave, the Dave I had grown up with, travelled with through the changing seasons of childhood, through the confusing minefields of our teens, until we blindly stumbled into the boundaries of adulthood.

There was a different side to him. He didn't show it all the time, but it had been there, always when you needed it. He simply grew up quicker than the rest of us, realised that he'd had no alternative really. His mum struggled against the tide of each day, some days she hadn't even tried, never rising from the safety of her bed, cocooned in her own world. She had been a sickly, fragile woman. Mousy, lank hair stuck to the sides of her gaunt white face. Life had been all too much for her. Sometimes when I would knock for Dave, she would just look down at me, like Dave, tall and wiry, but with dull, lifeless eyes, sunken into the sockets, like the colour of the fume-stained walls leading into town. She would never say anything, just step aside and let me climb the narrow stairs behind the door that led to Dave's tiny room. Dave wasn't meant to happen. "A mistake" was how his old man had explained his entrance into the world, and he had never seemed to hide the fact from him.

I had never known my dad. Billy, who, as much as he hated to admit it, mirrored his own spitting ball of aggression for a father, who would beat the shit out of him whenever he was home, drunk or sober. But to me, Dave's old man was the worst. Mental abuse, it leaves no visible scars, no traces of damage, but deep down Dave's dad must have left plenty. Although he also carried his own scars, tangible wounds from a destructive childhood spent fighting Mods up and down the streets of London. But then he was just this ageing rocker refusing to bow to the responsibilities of parenthood. The last, precious years of carefree rebellion had been cruelly snatched from him with the pregnancy of the tall, pasty-looking girl from the bank. And Dave had been an anchor weighing him down to the decks of fatherhood. He'd walked out on the pair of them more times than I could remember. But he would always return after a few weeks or months, and everything would just carry on like before. It hadn't been through any sense of loyalty that he kept returning, the stark truth was that what or whoever he had left the pair of them for, had come to an end and he'd simply had no other place to go.

We had been so close, me and Dave, there had always been this unspoken understanding hanging in the air. We hadn't needed to talk about all the crap with his old man or the lack of one in my life. Just hanging around together, kicking a ball or playing records in his bedroom was always enough. Simple, seemingly empty things, helped to fill one another's voids. Killing time helped us to kill each other's demons.

I only ever asked him about meeting Bowie the once, I can still remember it as if it were yesterday, the pair of us sitting on the swings in the park, in the summer of '73, just days after the Hammersmith concert when Bowie had brought the curtain down on *Ziggy*. The sun bleaching the grass dry, heating up the playground as if it were caught in the eye of some giant blow torch, the bars of the climbing frame and shiny aluminium of the slide too hot to venture on. With their backs to us, sticky, sweaty kids had queued impatiently at the ice cream van, irritable from the heat, heads boiling in mops of long hair. From our position sitting idly rocking to and fro on the swings, it had been impossible to distinguish the boys from the girls.

And he had squinted at me in that easy way of his, as if he were struggling to keep his thoughts from drifting off. Sometimes I would think that his mind was already in the next day, as if he were bored and impatient to move on, like one of the kids in the ice cream queue, only to find that when it has his turn to be served, they didn't really have anything that he wanted anyway.

'So when did you meet Bowie?'

'A year or so ago.' He'd shrugged. 'Won't be going back though,' and he had pushed off with one foot and swayed past me.

'Why?' I had asked. 'Cause you can't spell "flamboyant"?' I'd smiled. It wasn't often I got to rib Dave.

He raised an eyebrow, the way a grown-up might. And with a tap on my head, the balance was restored.

'No, nothing like that,' he'd said, 'It's just... ' He pointed his toes to the sky then tucked them beneath his seat, flying high.

'*Just* what?' I'd demanded. But he'd disappeared into the glaze of the sun; higher and higher until I felt sure that his momentum would carry him over the framework.

'Just... WHAT?' I screamed blindly into the sunlight. And then he had rushed past me, swooping backwards like some great bird in reverse.

'Cause I don't want to lose the thrill of being... ' His words had trailed off and I'd assumed that I had lost them in the rise of his swing. But then he'd come into land, scuffing his feet across the tarmac to slow himself. 'You know when you're coming to the end of a sticker album, right?' He'd settled himself back beside me and wrapped his arms high around the chains so that his hands had hung loose. He looked for all the world like James Dean in *Giant*, the bit when he has his arms draped over the rifle across his shoulders. I could see one of his deep analogies coming my way.

'Riiight,' I said cautiously.

'You know when you've only got one or two left?' He'd nodded, willing me to keep up.

Actually I had always found that bit more frustrating than fun, the fruitlessness of spending all your pocket money on what were nearly always swops. But I understood what he meant.

'And then the moment comes when you finally get your hands on that last sticker.' He had that glassy look in his eyes then, the way he often would when he would try and explain things to me and Billy, as if he'd been hypnotised by his own thoughts.

'You peel off the backing, line up the edges, nice and neat, and… ' He fell silent, lost somewhere, gazing at the viaducts in the distance. A high-pitched scream from two girls who had been sitting on the nearby roundabout sucking their ice lollies had pierced the air, as Donny Osmond had come over the tiny transistor radio that hung from one of their wrists.

He'd sighed heavily before continuing. 'And that's it… all *over.*' He shrugged his shoulders at me; explanation complete.

I had wanted to understand, had thought I *did* understand; could get my head round the fact that he hadn't wanted his relationship with Bowie to end, but surely as a fan, a fan who had been welcomed into his idol's home, you would have grabbed every opportunity that you could to visit. But there was Dave, the biggest, most knowledgeable Bowie fan you were ever likely to meet, and he was… was *ending* their relationship!

Donny Osmond had finished declaring his "Young Love" by then and ironically Bowie's "Life on Mars" had begun to play, tinny and slightly distorted; two songs from that summer that couldn't have been more different. And then from nowhere, as if to fit the shift in mood, a solitary cloud floated across the sapphire sky and blocked out the sun. And for the briefest of moments goosebumps had peppered my skin, as if I had bitten through my own ice cream with my front teeth. Dave had peered up at the cloud before the sun had slipped from beneath its cover and muttered something, talking more to the sky than me, his words sounded something like, '... *And what then?*'

And then the ice cream van had started up, its manic jingle drowning out Bowie, as it made its way slowly down the path and up the main road. I could see groups of kids converging by the park gates, praying that he hadn't run out of Fabs and 99s. And when I had turned back towards Dave's swing it had been empty, rocking gently as if he had never been there.

'Come on, Johnny boy!' he called over his shoulder without turning round. 'Race you home, and bet I beat you!'

And the moment had gone, evaporated like a 99 left in the sun.

'Never!' I'd cried, leaping off my swing and flying past him.

'Hey, don't forget the rules!' he'd called after me. 'No stepping on the cracks!'

CHAPTER TWO

May 1974

Dave rummaged through his school bag and fished out his Munich '74 sticker album. Brushing away the covering of salt, pepper and sugar carelessly spilt across the table, he tore open the two packs of stickers he had just bought, and laid them down in alphabetical order: Argentina through to Yugoslavia.

'It's not the same though, is it?' remarked Ketchup, as he dunked another chip into the mountain of tomato sauce that he'd piled on the side of the communal plate; the boy really lived up to his nickname!

'There's always Scotland,' I shrugged, more interested in the faces that Dave had spread out before him.

'Fuck Scotland!' snapped Billy

Dave, Ketchup and I glanced over at Lui, the café owner, hoping he hadn't heard what Billy had said.

Lui's was no more than a greasy spoon café on the end of a small parade of shops that consisted of a newsagents (the sweet shop to us), a laundrette and a bookmakers. Its clientele consisted mostly of builders and truck drivers, but Lui couldn't abide swearing, although it was very rare that you would find anyone to be offended by it.

At Lui's you had the choice of a red, yellow or blue Formica-topped table, each one peeling and chipped at the edges. And the option of a creaky, plastic-covered chair of the same colour, worn smooth and shiny from the years of use. It was the only place in town that tolerated the four of us loitering over one plate of chips for an eternity.

And he liked kids, Lui; pretended to be annoyed, to be tough, would have a little moan about our taking up space that paying customers could fill, but it was just an act. He understood kids, the boredom, the unspoken pressures and the bottled up angst. Especially boys like Dave, ones who had pretty desperate backgrounds.

'My dad says the Scots hate us,' Billy continued as he lent across the table, snapping up a sticker of Scotland's Joe Jordan from the freshly opened packs that Dave had lying in front of him. 'So we should fucking well hate them back,' he added, before tearing the picture of the Scot in half.

Dave looked up at Billy and sighed. 'Shut up, Billy,' he said. 'What if I'd needed him?' Dave added, motioning his head towards the two halves in Billy's hand.

'Tough, I suppose!' He smiled cockily, but he knew as well as Dave that we had all completed the Scotland team and we only needed a handful between us to complete our collections. I was nearer than the others; the Brazilian Marinho my only blank space. And Dave needed him as well. Of course, Billy had him! Forever going on about it, folding his book open to the page, flashing it in mine and Dave's faces, pretending to peel it out of his album for one of us. 'Who wants it? Who wants him the most then? How much, eh?' That cocky grin spreading across his face. And I would laugh despite myself. You had to know Billy, you really did otherwise he was just too much. I was more annoyed that he messed up his book, bending all the pages, ruining his stickers, but Billy didn't care. In fact I was surprised that he kept at it as long as he did. Spending your money on one or two packs whenever you could, the meticulous scrutinising of swaps in the playground with kids you wouldn't usually even nod at. But he couldn't bear to be left out.

Ketchup had Marinho too, and it was beginning to drive me mad, it really was. The fun had gone out of collecting, faced with the overwhelming odds to finding one solitary sticker. Every opened pack disappointed instead of thrilled. To see strange, mysterious faces staring back at you. Unlike the domestic Football League stickers you would get every season, with all your favourites, and where you would know every player from every club, from Arsenal to Wolverhampton, the World Cup collections were different; unpronounceable names from far away countries.

The chiselled faces of the Italians, dark and brooding; Germans, East and the West, ridiculous-looking in sky-blue button-up jackets, complete with pocket. What could they possibly keep in those breast pockets that they would need on a football pitch? Half a page dedicated to the Haitians, only one white face among them, the rest black like big Kenny Dennis, the kid at Bishop's Walk School who'd come over from some place in Africa. And so it went on, the bright orange of the Dutch, the Swedes, Poles, Argentines; but it was the Brazilians who fascinated me, the world champions. Those famous yellow shirts with the green hoop around the neck; they just *looked* like footballers. No Pele but still a page of famous names: Rivelino, Jairzinho, Carlos Alberto and of course, Marinho: my football nemesis. And I was beginning to hate him, this mop-haired blonde Brazilian, and when did you ever see a blonde Brazilian? Oh I knew that I could send off for him, complete my collection that way and be done with it, but that seemed too much like hard work, and besides, it defeated the whole object of collecting and swapping.

Lui appeared at the head of our table, the buttons on his white shirt straining over his belly, dishcloth draped over his shoulder. 'You-ah alright boys? Want-a-some more chips, eh?' he asked.

'No thanks, Lui,' said Dave, answering for the four of us.

'Okay.' He smiled, placing his hands on the table and leaning across. He was barely taller than most of the kids who came into his café and Dave towered over him, nothing like his rugged countrymen who filled my book.

'And you watch your mouth, eh?' he whispered to Billy and turned back to his counter.

Something flashed in Billy's eyes. 'Fucking wop,' he sneered. But it was under his breath and didn't carry the usual malevolence. Billy was like Marinho, I thought: stocky, scruffy blonde hair, unable to pin down.

I'd known Billy for as long as I could remember, as long as Dave and Ketchup. There was a bond between the four of us. There was the thing with our dads, but there was also the football. Every team we played for, we had all played for together.

As for Billy's dad, I could just imagine him saying that thing about the Scots, he seemed to hate everyone. A short, muscular man with beady eyes that bore right through you, they were so dark and narrow that barely a glint of white could be seen. The sparks had certainly flown one Saturday afternoon the previous year, when Dave and I had gone back to Billy's flat. We'd played for the school in the morning, winning six-nil. I used to hate those games, an easy Saturday morning for everyone else but I would be bored stiff. Fingers and toes numb from the cold, jogging up and down in my penalty box to keep warm.

The three of us ended up back at Billy's playing records and reading comics. Billy always seemed to be left alone in the flat. Often he would scurry into class with some lame excuse, his mum was sick or her alarm had failed to go off, but we knew it was because no one had come home the night before and Billy had been up all night watching horror films.

And there we were, comics all over the floor, The Sweet's "Blockbuster" turned up full volume, arm left over on the record player so that it repeated again and again. Then the front door banged shut and this angry barrel of a man stood in the doorway and we saw Billy in years to come. He chased Billy all around the tiny front room, plates, vases, records and comics flying all over. Round the dinner table and over the grubby brown settee that Dave and I tactfully chose never to sit on. He caught Billy just as he reached the door and hit him so hard across the top of the head that we couldn't believe that he didn't fly down the hallway. If it had been me, they would still be picking bits of me out of the wall, but Billy had his dad's genes. He just rubbed the crown of his head, as if he were troubled by something. The old man told Dave and me to fuck off and to go and piss our own parents off. And as we hurriedly grabbed our things and made for the door, I can still see Billy grinning stupidly at Dave. 'See,' he said casually, 'told you my old man was a bigger tosser than yours.'

The Wednesday before the '74 World Cup final we had a final of our own, The South London District Schools' Cup for under 14s. It was played down at the park. And it seemed as if everyone that we knew was there, both schools demanding that all pupils from the year attend, in full school uniform. It was amazing how many did, considering that it was the holidays and all; and some even brought their school bags. And I can still remember that feeling as we ran out from the half-derelict pavilion and onto the pitch, our P.E. teacher, Mr Brown, trying to assemble us into some kind of a straight line, all professional-like, with Dave, our captain, standing there, waiting patiently. He was cool and unflustered, ball tucked under his arm, while the rest of us couldn't keep still. Billy was skulking in and out of line pinching the backs of legs or trying to inflict dead arms on the rest of us, pretending that it was all a laugh, that he wasn't bothered.

There wasn't a gap in the crowd. The whole pitch surrounded by cheering school kids, teachers and over-excited relatives. There were a few scouts among them, maybe not from the top London clubs, but still pro clubs: Brentford, Orient, Fulham, Southfields and maybe a couple more.

Dave was brilliant. All the grown-ups said that he had a wise head on young shoulders. They called him "Our Bobby Moore".

He gave me my first touch within seconds of the kick-off. Could have knocked it up-field, started an attack, anything, but he just rolled it back. Knew I liked to get a feel of it, to hold it in my hands and bounce it around my box. I loved that feeling, the game in *my* hands, when I dictated the minds and movements of every other player on the pitch.

It's strange how childhood memories stain the mind, seep in like the ink of a tattoo. Each one of us always remembered that game. From all the hundreds of matches that we must have played together, finals, league winning games, district and representative appearances, trials and debuts. Through all the years and all the teams, the four of us: me, Dave, Billy and Ketchup, could remember it as if it were yesterday.

Old Ketchup, out wide on the left, would trot up and down, never exerting himself. If you didn't know him you would have thought he was lazy, but he was a clever player, shrewd. Then someone, usually Dave, would feed him the ball and it was as if someone had switched him on, and off he would go making the opposition look stupid. It wasn't pace that Mickey was blessed with, if anything, he was a bit tubby, drowning everything with tomato sauce. It was timing: balance and timing. Down the left and delivering what always seemed to be pin-point crosses.

Billy was… well, Billy. Some boys I knew would change the minute they pulled a football shirt over their heads, quiet, unassuming kids, transformed into thugs. But Billy didn't need to hide beneath a uniform. He played football like he played everywhere, pitch or playground, it was all the same, always with an edge of malice. He was a destroyer, wherever we played throughout our childhoods, that was the responsibility that every manager bestowed upon him and he would set about it with a diligence that he never showed in any other aspect of his life. And it wouldn't matter to Billy how big or small a player was, he treated them all with the same amount of contempt. If you wore a different coloured shirt from the one Billy was wearing on the pitch, you weren't safe from his attentions, he seemed to take it as a personal insult. He was a great tackler, could take the ball as well as the man, when he had the mind, but as always with Billy, he would usually go too far. I've seen him do some terrible things on and off the ball: kicking, stamping, punching even. If his blood was really up, it wouldn't cross his mind whether or not the ref could see.

Dave at the back, playing the game as if it were a film and he knew what was about to happen next. He wasn't ungainly or awkward on the eye, the way kids of his slight build could be. He would glide majestically across the pitch, intercepting passes, heading away crosses, snuffing out danger just as it was about to erupt.

And then there was me: goalkeeper. I don't think any kid really starts out with the dream of being a keeper. Nine times out of ten it's something that just happens. I think it was probably because no one else wanted to, to prove I could, that I wasn't scared. The individuality of it, wearing a different shirt to the rest of the team, being able to do something that no one else, other than the other goalie, could do. To use your hands. I never let on but I secretly loved the rumour that to be a goalkeeper you had to be a little bit crazy. The reputation cast around me like a giant shadow, elongated and distorted; a trick of the light.

I soon realised that I was good. I mean, I don't think I possessed a kind of natural, God-given talent, like Ketchup and his ball skills, but I would do things that other boys wouldn't. I learnt from having Dave in front of me. I watched him watching the game. Most kids would stand around bored when the action was up the other end of the pitch, but I learnt to read things, to anticipate the next move and position myself accordingly. Crosses were my strong point. Couldn't understand the reluctance of other keepers to come out for crosses, you had this huge advantage of being able to reach up and use your hands. I found it the simplest thing, but other boys seemed to be afraid of dropping it, or arriving too late or being left unguarded, like a soldier deserting his post.

And there we were, nil-nil with ten minutes to go. Just a handful of opportunities at either end the entire game, no more than half chances really. I had tipped one over the bar from Kenny Dennis, the giant black kid who was the heartbeat of the Bishop's Walk side. His kick was a real pile driver, but it had looked more dramatic than it was. Nothing between us, never was, them and us; the best two teams in the South London.

With the exception of Dave, the occasion had got to everyone. The surge of enthusiasm and energy stifled, neutralised by nerves. Uncapped potential gushed all across the pitch like a newly-found oil well.

There wasn't a boy on the pitch who wasn't represented by mums, dads, uncles and even aunts. Except the four of us, that is.

It really didn't matter much to me. I knew Mum would have been there if she could, but she had to take the shifts when they were available, overtime and all. She had come to watch me a couple of times but she couldn't understand why I wanted to stand there, all alone, while all the other boys raced around the pitch, kicking the ball, yelling and screaming at each other. At first she had thought that I was being punished, banished to the corner of the room. And of course there was always Mum's "friend" Derek.

Extra time loomed, and I was roasting in my thick woollen goalkeeper's jersey. Then, as the heat of the day had begun to relent and with five minutes to go, Dave's dad turned up. Dave had just made this fantastic last-ditch tackle, took it right off the centre forward's foot, just as he was about to shoot. I had come out but it was a gamble really, luck in or out, and then Dave just poked it off the lad's toe. The boy went tumbling as he connected with thin air and there were some half-hearted shouts for a penalty, but as I had picked up the loose ball nearly everyone there was applauding. And that's why I had noticed him, Dave's dad. On the touchline he looked out of place, cigarette jammed between his lips, the only one not clapping. Just standing there, all faded jeans and leather jacket; greying hair greased back with this sad Bill Haley kiss curl hanging limply over his knotted forehead, something close to jealousy gleaming in his eyes.

But Dave had seen him too and his self-belief, his self-assurance, fell away like a cloak off his shoulders.

It was one thing to have parents like Billy's, aggressive and mostly drunk, but to have a father like Dave's was quite another. Filled with resentment, as if you were a slice of bad luck, something that disrupted your life. I'm not saying it's easy for the likes of Billy, but in a way they don't realise that things are any different. Billy was an extension of his parent's personality, a smaller replica... a bit like Russian dolls.

Dave retreated to some dark corner of his mind and was replaced by an impostor. My feelings curdled like milk, making me feel sick. To me, it looked as if he was trying too hard to look like he wasn't trying *too* hard; didn't want his dad to think that he was trying to impress him. So he turned and rolled this ball back to me, nothing flashy in opting for the sensible safe choice, giving the ball back to your keeper. But it was too casual, lazy and under hit, the pass of a tired player, but Dave had expended less energy than any other outfield player, what with his timing and vision. What it was, was the pass of an uncertain player, confidence leaking through the punctured holes of his concentration, pierced by the appearance of his father.

But I had seen it coming. I knew that he wasn't the same player, the same boy. And I was already off my line, making my way forward. But the Bishop's Walk forward had seen the transformation as well, and he was quicker than me, quicker than

20

most, one touch and he was there, bearing down upon me.

I met him on the edge of the area, covering all angles. I knew that the fast kid was left-footed. He had scored enough against me, so I fell away to my right, his left… *luck in or out*. And at that moment he took the ball the same way, with the outside of his boot, trying to go round me. And it was easy really, just looked much harder than it was. I fell across the ball, smothered it safely beneath my body and into my arms.

I could hear Mr Brown yelling across the pitch, telling Dave to 'wake up'. I looked over at Mr Brown, hands cupped round his mouth, sweat running down his face, his black locks plastered to his head. I wondered, vaguely, why he didn't take off his top, but thought he probably didn't want to ruin the affect of the new tracksuit. He was aware of Dave's old man and knew the story, but the moment had got to him. I tried to catch Dave's eye, wanted him to know that it was all right. Dave wasn't looking at me, but over to where his dad stood, but his old man had gone, as if he had never been there at all. Just rows and rows of cheering school kids and the other mums and dads: the normal parents.

It was those things that messed Dave up, the not knowing. Trying desperately to swim against the tide of natural instincts that swelled inside, instincts that made him want to impress, to make his dad proud, instead trying to make him think that *he* didn't give a toss for his approval or admiration, and in the end he would achieve neither. Left treading water, stranded in a sea of uncertainty.

Then it was our turn. I could feel something was about to happen the minute Ketchup received the ball, although this time not from Dave, who was still standing, trance-like, on the halfway line. Mickey was off, down the left as usual, socks around his ankles, left foot like a wand. But for once his cross was poor, it wouldn't have beaten the first defender if the kid hadn't had panicked, swinging at it wildly, slicing it straight into the path of Danny Beavis, our centre-forward.

And that was Danny's game, in the box. Feeding off scraps, like a bird of prey. He took a touch. I remember that split second feeling of excitement before, knowing that Danny was about to score. A winner's medal, another step in what was surely going to be a glittering career.

I could tell by the other goalkeeper's dive, stretching full length, desperately down to his left, that it was going in, going in all the way. Could tell by the way Danny had shaped his body that he had placed it just right, inside the post. From my view straight down the pitch, it was just a matter of waiting for the net to bulge out at the side, the ball nestled snugly inside.

But the net didn't bulge. Instead the ball just kept going, past the post and into the crowd. There was no cheering from our sets of supporters, just the audible rumble of groaning disappointment. Mr Brown held his head in his hands, as if he were trying to stop it exploding. I stood there, frozen in mid-celebration, arms held out at shoulder height, a goalkeeping scarecrow.

My first thought was that the net must have become untied from the post, worked itself loose during the game. They couldn't have seen it properly, the ref, the linesman, the crowd. They didn't understand! Danny just *didn't* miss. He had played for Fulham youth and there was always someone, a scout from one or other of the London clubs, there watching him.

But I was wrong. There was no hole in the netting and the Bishop's Walk goalie was standing behind his post, tapping the toes of his kicking foot into the rock hard earth, just like he had seen all the professionals do on *Match of the Day.*

Kenny Dennis had the ball now, a menacing sight. An alarm bell rang in my head. That was his advantage in life, the sheer size of him. He frightened everyone, even the older kids. In all the time I knew him he had never had a fight. But his reputation slowly grew, like the young trees planted beneath the viaducts.

He was moving forward now, this giant of a boy, fully six

inches taller than any other kid around, and with the sweat on his black forehead glistening in the sun he looked even darker, dressed in the contrasting white strip of his school. And he was shaping to shoot now, moving into his range, twenty, twenty-five yards out, only Dave in front of him, the other defenders still in dream world. I knew when Kenny hit it that it would rise... and keep on rising, like a plane taking off. It would be above me somewhere. A top corner probably. I was prepared, bouncing on my line, ready to launch myself in the direction that it flew.

If it had been the real Dave out there I would have stood a better chance. The real Dave would have closed him down, forcing Kenny onto his left, his weaker foot, by shielding his right-hand side.

But Kenny was closer now, could even afford an extra touch, probing forward to the edge of the "D" on the penalty area, and Dave remained rooted to the spot.

And then Dave came alive. Maybe it was the voice of Mr Brown penetrating the clouds of his muddled mind, or Dave dragging himself back to life. He moved forward but he was too late, Kenny had already pulled the trigger, and as his bullet rose, it caught Dave on the top of the shoulder, and just like in the old westerns on a Saturday night, sent him spinning, dumping him in a cloud of dusty, dried earth. The ball was heading skywards, flying through the air at some crazy angle. I knew I was in trouble, even before I had lost its flight in the sun. I was only a yard, if that, off my line, and had deliberately taken up that exact position to give myself every chance. And then I saw it, falling like a blazing comet from the sky. I clawed desperately at the space behind my head, the few inches that seemed now like a yawning chasm. I tumbled over backwards, off balance, legs passing my head, feet tangled up with the ball in the netting, I felt the burning pangs when you know, deep down, that there really is no solution, when belief simply is not enough.

Back in the changing rooms, Mr Brown muttered something about 'not taking our chances' as he shovelled the kit, thrown from all corners of the room, into a great big canvas sack.

He stood back up, kitbag slung over his shoulder. His face was bright red, as if all the blood in his body had gathered there. It glowed through his fluffy sideburns. Mr Brown had modelled himself on George Best. Had probably thought that he had a head start on account of his dark hair, thick and scruffy looking, falling lazily on his shoulders, but he couldn't have reckoned on his sideburns. Most of the lads in the fourth and fifth years had stronger growth than him. He really believed that we were going to win that day. He was a decent bloke, unlike most of the teachers. He had time for you, you could talk to him if you had a mind. I don't think many boys actually ever did, wasn't really something that came easy to us, but knowing that you *could* was help enough. And he would have a joke with you, especially out of school, away games and stuff, like the final. But no one was joking that day.

Of course Mr Brown could have been talking to himself, but you didn't have to be top of the class to realise that his comment was aimed at Danny. Mr Brown would never usually have a word said against us, "his boys". But he'd tell you if you were doing something wrong and he would explain *why*, not just bollock you in front of the rest of the team like some managers did. But that day, like the rest of us, he just couldn't believe that Danny, of all people, had missed such a simple chance.

Poor Danny was absolutely crushed, just sitting there in his pants staring at the floor as the rest of the lads shuffled slowly off home, muttering 'See ya' and 'Bye'.

Billy tried to ease the tension in his usual crude manner, just like he had done when we had been nervously waiting to step out onto the pitch from the narrow corridor of the pavilion. Pretending he didn't care, feigning insouciance, like it was all a joke. Moaning about the poxy little runners-up medals that we had received and that he was the unlucky one as the base of his presentation case was a kind of gay pink and not red like the rest of the team's.

Danny told him that he could have the whole flippin' thing, nodding in the direction of the shiny red box on the bench beside him. Edging away from it, as if the very sight of it offended him, like being told to sit next to one of the gimpy kids in class.

Billy told him not to be stupid, that it was nobody's fault and he went over and sat next to him and gave him a playful nudge, shoulder to shoulder, nearly knocking Danny off the bench.

'In fact,' Billy said, 'let's all blame Chalmers.' He made his way back over to his kitbag. 'I mean my fucking granny could have saved that!' he said, out of Mr Brown's earshot.

I didn't mind, knew that he didn't mean it. That Billy was only trying to lift Danny's spirits. Billy wasn't usually one for thinking of others, but football was different. The lads all together, united, us against them, the rest of the world. The adrenalin had left our bodies and on its way flushed everything with it, a giant pool of energy and emotion, mixed with the dying bubbles of shampoo and soap. I wanted to say something to Danny, comfort him a little, maybe put an arm around his shoulder but I wasn't really like that anyway, not with mates, or Mum. But to witness this from Billy, to see him snap the brittle atmosphere like a dry twig, really showed how much we all meant to each other. We didn't need the complicated refinement of explanation. We all knew what Billy was doing, something that even Mr Brown, with all his fancy education and experience, couldn't do. A bit like watching *The Magnificent Seven* with Mum on a Saturday night, only this time with the volume turned down. Didn't need the words to know what was going on or what the good guys were trying to do.

A smile crept across Danny's face, a thin, weak smile, but a smile nonetheless, for he appreciated what Billy was trying to do, for caring. Although, when Danny picked up his medal and stuffed it deep inside his bag, I noticed that the case was now a light pink, not the red one he had before.

CHAPTER THREE

May 1974

We stepped out from under the gap in the railings and followed the traffic, lighter now in the late afternoon, into town. Both of our houses were only across the road. Just one of many rows of terraced houses, like lines of dominoes, all joining up with the main road that led from the Thames and through into town; flowing veins linking up with the main artery, pumping through the heart of London.

The sun had been dulled by the late afternoon, the sting taken from its glare as it slipped away somewhere behind the tower and office blocks in the distance. It seemed to melt like butter, smearing the horizon with a golden-yellow. We walked past the line of old Victorian cottages opposite the church. It wasn't just for the obvious reasons that I liked summer. The school holidays, good telly in the mornings, warm, sunny days spent kicking a ball about the park, playing beneath the viaducts, stretching the days into evenings, ringing out every last drop of daylight. It was mostly for the explosion of colour, daubed like paint across the greyness of town, lighting up the concrete skyline. The clothes that people chose, vibrant, lurid images moving through town like a kaleidoscope. Fashions influenced by the pop stars and music of the time: Gary Glitter, Slade, Sweet, T-Rex and, of course, Bowie.

Lui's was just the other side of the bridge, like walking through a time tunnel: on the one side, yesteryear, and under train tracks, into the beginning of the sixties' suburban uprising. As we stood outside I wallowed in self-pity, the black coal truck parked outside the bookies fitting my mood, and half-heartedly tried to work out the up-side down faces, as Dave thumbed through the stickers he had just bought.

'Who have you got then?' I asked with no interest, as Dave tore open the two packs of stickers he had just bought from the sweet shop. I just couldn't get the goal out of my mind, kept imagining the ball dropping over my head, if I had stayed on my line, would I have reached it? Probably, but then again…

'What you got there then?' spat a voice from behind my shoulder. 'Football stickers!' The voice exclaimed in disgust. It belonged to a wild-eyed skinhead with blue-black markings over his face; a cross on his forehead, two blobs beneath an eye.

'Got any money on you?' he ordered, motioning towards Dave's blazer pockets. Dave's eyes narrowed and for a heart-stopping moment I thought he was going to say something but then he just gave a slight shake of the head, sighed and fished for the loose change.

'That it?' the skinhead screamed in disgust. He towered over us, maybe a year or two older.

'That's it!' Dave shrugged as he held out the nine and a half pence.

'Prick!' he sneered as he slipped the change into the hip pocket of his jeans before turning his attentions on me. I felt a sharp pain explode in the right cheek of my behind, literally lifting me off my feet. I wondered what the hell had happened as I gasped out in shock. And then I saw the other two. Stupid grins fixed in round pink heads. They stumbled past behind us, half wrestling with each other, and I realised that it had been a ten high DM boot that I had felt up my arse.

'Well… fuckhead!' the leader demanded impatiently. I could smell the glue on his breath, in the air that surrounded him. I could taste the musty vapours seeping into my throat, clouding my senses. My eyes began to sting slightly and I blinked and wiped them with the back of my hand.

'Look at this boys… he's crying!' The other two were too busy harassing some old boy, asking him for any loose change, and when the old man told them to 'bugger off and find a job' they nicked his trilby hat, laughing and posing, trying it on and throwing it to each other as if it were a frisbee.

'I'll give you somethin' to fucking well cry about unless you give me your money, you little prick!' he spat, glaring down at me. He wavered slightly, adjusting his feet to keep his balance.

The stinging in my buttock was replaced by a jabbing pain that shot up into the right-hand side of my back. It crept into my guts, and I could feel the bile rise to the back of my throat. I shrugged my shoulders and held out my hands as if to say sorry. I wanted to speak, to tell him that I didn't have a penny on me, but I knew if I opened my mouth I would be sick. He pushed me out of the way and rummaged through my kit bag and came up holding my medal, turning the tiny red box over and over in his hand.

'This will 'ave to do.' He shrugged and turned to join his mates. I grabbed at his arm, pulling him back round. The glue had shrouded his coordination, and he stumbled to the floor. His eyes darkened, pupils twisted like marbles. He had two dark blobs on the side of his face. Teardrops, not the work of a professional tattooist but made with the point of a compass that had jabbed away at the skin, before one of his mates had poured in Indian ink. And I knew if I wasn't careful that I would soon have one, branded like a piece of cattle. But I couldn't let him take my medal. A runners-up medal: in a sense a sign of failure, and it wasn't as if I didn't have others, ones that celebrated victories. But in a sense, they had all come too easy.

I knew as he bore down that he was going to hit me. The punch landed somewhere on my shoulder, wild and exaggerated, his brain unable to connect with his limbs.

The first thing that I remember was kneeling on the floor and throwing up; liquid mostly, squash taken after the game and bits of orange from half-time, the acid burning my throat, bitter and aggravating. The giant skinhead jumped back as the sick splashed across his boots, a skinhead's prize possession. I looked up and his face was darker than thunder. I could see his mates coming over now, moving into focus behind him. I wanted to stand, to try to protect myself, but my legs were useless hollow stumps. I turned round on the floor like a wounded bird, and he circled me like prey. And as he ran, ready to kick the crap out of me, Dave, all of a sudden, did the simplest thing. Stuck a leg out and sent him tumbling like a drunk across the pavement, and he just lay there, talking to himself, as if he couldn't understand how he had got there. *A chance to escape.* But it wasn't over; there was still the other two. I wouldn't forget the leader, his face, the leanness, the way he carried himself… it stirred something but I didn't know what and I didn't have the time to dwell on it. I imagined that when he wasn't so wasted, it could have been mistaken for a kind of arrogance. But the others all looked alike to me, the shaven heads robbing them of character. The other two were only divided by the colour of their T-shirts, like negatives, one in black, the other dressed in white. The black one had Dave by the hair, dragging him down, as if his head were made of lead, whilst the other rained in kicks and blows. I flung myself towards him but landed somewhere below his waist. I could smell the cigarette smoke and the cider stains engrained in the fibres of his jeans, but at least he couldn't kick Dave anymore. I didn't look up, didn't want to catch one of his punches full in the face. I was aware of movement from the corner of my eye, shapes appearing. Finally I was thrown clear and spun across the floor, landing in my own sick. And then there was Lui and two giant blackened monsters beside him, coalmen from their flat caps to their boots. They grabbed a skinhead each, huge hands like diggers scooping them up, leaving black hand prints all over their arms. White skin tried to put up some kind of a fight, David versus Goliath, but without the sling. 'Fuck off!' screamed the pink blob.

'You like tats, do you?' said the coalman. 'Here's another.' He rubbed his giant hand across white skin's head, leaving a giant print, like a shadow, across his skull. And they were still laughing, the coalmen, great booming laughter, as the skins made their way into town, cursing and spitting threats into the fading summer light.

All was quiet again by the time we walked back up our street. Lui had fed us sausage and chips, and a couple of glasses of Coke. Told us nothing happened outside his café that he didn't know about and that the coal boys were regulars of his.

Despite what had happened I couldn't stop thinking about the winning goal that had dropped over my head, but no matter how many times I replayed it I still never got to it.

'I mean, you'd think he would have celebrated the goal, jumped all over Kenny or something first,' I moaned, 'but to run straight over to you and tell you it was "your" own goal.' I shook my head wearily. 'You must have really pissed him off with that last ditch tackle... what's his name?... *Shelly* or *Sheelly,* something like that.'

'*Shit* head, I think,' smiled Dave. 'You alright... not going to bring your chips up are you?' He joked.

'Naah... fine now.' I shrugged. It was still just light, but fading fast, that time of the day when you can see the darkness close in by the minute. I gazed back down the street, jumping in my mind across the rooftops of the houses on the other side, as they descended like steps to the bottom.

'Been quite a day, eh?' said Dave, as I looked over to where the park lay below the line of railings and bushes.

We stood outside Dave's front gate as he looked at the light in the front room and sighed.

'Better go in I suppose.'

He had a bald patch on the side of his head where the skinhead had torn out a clump of his hair.

'Oh, I nearly forgot,' and he began digging around in his blazer pocket.

The birds were in full chorus, perched upon the chimneys and TV aerials, silhouetted against the red smear of sky. Their evening song hung heavy with me, for as a kid it always spelt "time to go in" but that evening it came as a relief. I just wanted the day to be over, a massive disappointment followed by a beating. I longed for my bed, to snuggle beneath the sheets, dream up secure, private thoughts, silly, stupid things. Like playing for England at Wembley, and in my dream I would still be a thirteen year old, it didn't matter to anyone, it was, after all, my dream, my world; where things like today never happened. Maybe I would conjure up thoughts of Debbie, maybe we would kiss or hold hands, just something simple, something that didn't scare me.

'Here we are,' he said, holding something out in his hand and dragging me back from my dream plans.

'What's this?' I asked as I took the piece of paper from him. It was a football sticker… a little crumpled, but entirely usable.

'It was in the pack I opened just as that nutter turned up… you might as well have it,' he explained.

'But… ' I stared disbelievingly at the face in my hand. 'You need him as well.' It was the face of Marinho, the blonde Brazilian.

'Well, you've finished your album now, haven't you? I'll see you tomorrow.'

And I knew there was no point in arguing, knew that he wouldn't take it back. It was just a small part of what made Dave special. He was more than just a great mate, from rambling on about their centre-forward, taking the piss out of him, to this, knowing that it was unlikely that he would come across another Marinho. *He* was the one who had scored an own goal, the one who had lost it for five crucial minutes during the most important match of our lives, and yet, *he* had dealt with it, at thirteen years old, put it down to experience, without anybody's help or guidance. And instead, concerned that it wouldn't shatter *my* confidence, thought only of me.

I wondered yet again at the enigma that was my friend Dave, at how a boy my own age could be so self-assured, but yet seem so lost; could know me so well and appear not to know himself, for there had been something there that night, after the run in with the skins. He hid it well and maybe no one other than Billy and I would have been aware of it. It was in the gentle arch of his eyebrows, the faintest crease, no thicker than a strand of hair, upon his forehead, the merest flicker in his eyes… as if his mind was conjuring up memories that he'd rather not face. I was just about the luckiest kid alive to have a friend like Dave watching over me, but that was until *The Kick In* happened.

CHAPTER FOUR

November 1977

'Do you think we'll play tomorrow?' I asked, gazing out of Dave's bedroom window, out over row upon row of identical rooftops.

'What? Er… dunno… maybe,' mumbled Dave. He was kneeling on his bedroom floor, flicking through one of the many rows of albums stacked against the wall. He owned so many that the floor was the only place that he could store them without committing the ultimate sin for a record owner, which would be lying them flat, piled on top of one another, where they would eventually warp.

I didn't know why he bothered thumbing through them; I knew he would return to the select few, the ones leaning against the record player for easy access.

The haunting sounds of the Bowie album *Low* slowly drifted through the tiny room. 'Surprise!' I exclaimed sarcastically, as I followed the zig-zagging path of a raindrop down the window. Outside the sky was as dark and sinister as Bowie's eerie vocals, as the record moved through the track "Warszawa", clouds as black as coal floated by, scraping the tops of the swaying trees in the back alley. In my mind this was by far the weirdest transition of Bowie's musical career. He had shed the skin of *Ziggy* and fallen into '75, '76 and '77 in a haze of drug-influenced, synthesised songs, like nothing I had heard before. He was no longer in Beckenham, had lived out in Los Angeles, starred in some weird alien-orientated film and, according to Dave, was in Berlin now. And it seemed to me that he had taken a part of Dave with him.

The music scene had changed dramatically. Pop music had collided head-on with an angry, disillusioned new generation. Struggling to believe in anyone, anything. And like some bizarre laboratory experiment, punk rock was the result. The kings of glam had been overthrown, and with the death of Marc Bolan in a car crash, the shiny clothes and glitz of the early seventies had faded, and a new voice rang out for the non-conforming youth of the day.

Although, in truth, it was simply a natural progression, taking rock 'n' roll to the next stage, evolving like ape to man. And the rock influence was there, brimming beneath the surface, just that the edges were left untreated, ugly to look at and sharp to the touch, just the way it was meant to be.

And, of course, the kids loved it. It wasn't as much a breath of fresh air as a hurricane, ripping through the hard urban streets of London and inner cities the length of the country, whipping up hundreds of bored, stagnant teenagers and spitting out a generation who could finally identify with something, themselves, each other, and of course, the music.

And we were caught right up in the middle of it all, in the eye of the storm. London positively hummed with a fresh, new kind of malcontent. Kids with attitude flocked to the King's Road and the notorious SEX shop where it had apparently all begun with the birth of the Sex Pistols. And we loved them all: the Damned, the Clash, thumping out influential punk anthems with raw energy.

But Bowie was still cool, reinventing himself literally every year. Dave had immersed himself in the characters and images that he portrayed. And Bowie's two albums of the year, *Low* and *Heroes*, following on from *Stationtostation* the year before, were deeper than just about anything I had ever heard. The haunting sounds and the darkness of the music seemed to fit Dave's personality. He was so much more withdrawn, pensive, lost in the world of his own thoughts. Sometimes I would go round and find him just lying there on his bed, Bowie's voice filling the room. I couldn't hear his songs anywhere now without thinking of Dave's bedroom, it was as if that's where they belonged, anywhere else and it felt wrong, like replacing an album in the wrong sleeve.

He seemed to be forever lost in his own world lately, content with his own company; reading, writing stuff and playing his records. At times it seemed as if he had already shed the skin of his childhood, outgrown it all long before the rest of us.

Even football had lost its edge in Dave's eyes. I knew he couldn't have cared less if we played on Sunday or not, never mind if it was a big top of the table clash. It was widely known that top London scouts were to be there. But what did Dave care? They all wanted him anyway.

'Fancy a kick about down the park?' I asked, full of sudden enthusiasm as the idea grew on me. 'I want to practise some low shots… especially if it's going to be this wet,' I added.

'What, in this!' Dave nodded at the window. 'You'll be all right… you're good on the ground anyway, you know you are…' Dave continued, trying to justify his reluctance.

'S'pose,' I sighed.

'Anyway, I've got some stuff I want to do…'

I pressed my left temple to the window and could make out the back of our tiny patch of garden, swimming out of focus through the rain.

'I'll go then,' I said, struggling to my feet. My legs ached with boredom, and I wondered if I even had the energy to play football.

'You can stay if you want,' Dave interjected. 'It's just some writing stuff, it's just that I wanted to get it done before he comes home, that's all,' Dave explained, meaning his dad.

I stopped mid-stretch, considering Dave's invitation. 'Nuh, it's all right,' I decided. I knew he wouldn't have minded, wouldn't have felt that he had to talk or anything. I could just hang about, put a record on, flick through a football book or two, both comfortable within the easy silence that comes from being close friends.

But as much as I loved the cosiness of Dave's bedroom, crammed to the rafters, a kind of organised chaos, with its book-laden shelves and neatly pinned up pictures cut ruler-straight from old magazines and its row after row of albums lining the walls, I knew that he would be more creative with whatever it was that he intended to write if he were alone. Probably a letter to some music paper, he had had a couple printed, or words to a song that he had jangling around in his head like a pocketful of keys. He could never seem to settle until he wrote it down, became more reticent until he had spread it all out before him and unravelled the twisted lines into something tangible, in black and white.

Dave had grown deeper into his world of writing. He had always jotted things down, written lyrics, lines or verses of songs, Bowie's mostly, just like other kids would scrawl the names of football teams or pop groups over exercise books and school bags.

But something had changed in his writing lately, although I didn't understand half the stuff he wrote I understood the gist of it, the theme that threaded its way through every line. Whether or not it happened to be about Bowie, there always seemed to be something about isolation, of not belonging, of somewhere along the way, losing your dreams. I could see that he was writing about his own life, sort of holding a mirror up to his soul and turning what he saw into words, but I didn't really think about it too much. We all kind of had something missing, what with the dad thing, like living in a house that only had three sides, but it didn't really matter that much; or at least we never seemed to let it.

'Da-a-vid…' his mum's voice lightly filled the air as I reached the foot of the stairs, like shattered glass rattling inside a tin.

'Pop down the chip shop for me, will you… your father will

be home any minute and I haven't cooked a dinner… there's a good lad.' I peered round the door to let her know that it was me not Dave that she was talking to. The room was in darkness, except for the glow of the television set lighting up her face which was surrounded by blue plumes of cigarette smoke, like something from a horror film. 'Oh… it's you,' she sighed, 'didn't know you were here… did I let you in?' she asked in that sad, weary tone of hers, as if the very act of speaking was all too much. 'Don't suppose you'll go, will you?'

There was a time, I thought to myself, as I changed into some football kit and stepped out the back door, when Dave would have kicked a ball about with me in any weather, the rain had just been a suitable excuse. Still, it *was* hammering down, thudding against the old coal shed roof.

I thumped a ball against the back wall, being careful to keep it low before bending down to save it. Knees together, side on, letting the ball zip along the narrow stretch of grass, before coming down to meet it. It was one of my greatest fears as a goalkeeper, letting one through my legs. Ever since Ray Clemence had let the softest of shots slip through his hands and legs up at Hampden Park the year before. Honestly, all watching England ever did was break my heart!

It had been a strange, confusing year. Nothing appeared simple anymore, the insouciance of youth fading, as the slow metamorphosis of child to adulthood progressed. Everything seemed to have changed since *The Kick In*. That's what it was known as, whenever the topic came up, when it was mentioned in the classroom or playground; it was legendary, infamous.

Before then, everyday that I could remember was either black or white, good or bad. Never thought much further than that really. But since that day we had all passed our sixteenth birthdays and it wasn't at all like being thirteen, fourteen or even fifteen. It was as if my childhood, the innocent floorboards of youth, had fallen away, and I was left stranded, floating in that space between boy and man.

It was a year full of beginnings and ends, all hovering weightless around me, but I couldn't seem to grasp any. Pivotal moments popping up like molehills in my mind, those crucial landmarks of life. The blacks and whites had slipped into one another, and now everything was a murky grey, and I didn't know what was what, for the worst or for the best. I wasn't ready, or wasn't prepared, to move on.

We were leaving school, getting jobs, the clever ones staying on for another year or going to college, their future all mapped out for them. They couldn't wait to step out into the real world and join in the race of life. But not me, my future seemed less clear, like one of those difficult mazes you give up with in frustration in the end. The ridiculous ones you would find in a Christmas annual with three or four kite strings all tangled up and you've got to trace the path through an impossible jumble of black squiggles.

I didn't want to join the race, it would be more like stepping onto an escalator that was moving at twice its normal speed, and I knew I wouldn't be able to keep up, would stumble and run flat out just to stand still.

School was safe. Dave had taught me that a long time ago. Like he said, nothing could really hurt you there, like butterflies in jars, but now we were being set free, into the savage winds of reality.

Everything was changing, like shifting clouds on a stormy day. Life away from school had moved on too. Though not consciously, hanging around down the park or at Lui's were slowly being replaced by nights at the pictures with dates, weekend parties and, when we could afford it, nights at one or two of the pubs in town that would let us in. But football was always there, something to believe in.

And what was I going to do if I couldn't make it as a footballer? I was sixteen now and if I was to stand half a chance I should have been signed up as an apprentice long ago. The same as big Kenny Dennis up at Birmingham City, or Danny, who had finally been taken on board by Fulham... *Fulham!* The lucky sod! Danny was my inspiration, it was literally his trials and tribulations that kept the flame of hope flickering inside of me, when lonely, dreary days in the rain threatened to extinguish it.

Fulham had let him go, not once but twice, but eventually they had signed him up. That's why Sunday's match was so important to me. I knew there would be a few scouts there, as always with the big games that took place in the area. My arm was healing nicely now and it felt stronger each day. And the confidence was there again, that was the crucial thing for me. I wasn't afraid to land on it, or take a kick from diving at some forward's feet.

Breaking my arm in *The Kick In* last spring could not have come at a worse time, what with my trial only a week away.

It had been just another game, some grammar school in Croydon. It had been freezing, I remember that, late March near the end of our season, the tips of my fingers ached from the cold. I had noticed this tubby bald bloke standing with Mr Brown, late in the second half. I had thought it was odd as old Brownie didn't like to talk to anyone during a match, claimed it broke his concentration. But he was deep in conversation with the fat man, and every now and then I could sense that they were looking over in my direction.

After the final whistle, Mr Brown had called me over and I knew that the bloke was a scout, and suddenly I couldn't feel the cold eating through my bones, could only feel my cheeks glowing with anxiety from the attention, and I hoped that it didn't show as I walked over, trying to act like I didn't know who he was, when all the time my arms had gone all tingly.

'This gentleman would like a word with you, John,' Mr

Brown explained, and I could see the pride in his face; he tried to hide it but it sparkled in his eyes. His sideburns had gone now, his face was a little rounder. 'We'd like you to attend a trail with Southfields…' explained the fat man. 'Two weeks today… call me by tomorrow evening if you're interested,' and he handed me a card with his name and telephone number on it. *Southfields Football Club* in big red letters.

'Would you like me to come with you, Johnny?' asked Mr Brown, all chuffed, as we made our way back to the school coach. It was like one of my mates asking me something, not our P.E. teacher, but I knew that he was simply excited for me.

' I dunno sir… I guess…yeah… thanks.' He had told me not to tell any of the lads yet, for my own sake, just until he had checked a few things out with the club. I was in too much of a daze to object. As I climbed aboard the coach, my legs felt playground-fight wobbly, but when I had taken my seat next to Dave he was grinning, that all knowing smile stretching from ear to ear.

But then *The Kick in* happened and life had never been the same since, not for anyone, it seemed.

'We'll look at you again… when you're back playing,' the youth team coach had told me when I turned up at Southfield's training ground with my left arm in plaster. 'Thanks for letting us know… Chalmers, wasn't it?… the goalkeeper… I'll make a note of it.' I doubted he would even remember that I had come over, let alone a week early to let them know, not wanting to let anyone down. I only had the fare for one-way, had to bunk the buses back home, jumping off when they caught me, not easy with one arm. So I hoped, desperately, that I could pick something out from the year, find some kind of hope among the ashes of *The Kick In* that still burned, among the debris of a failed relationship and O levels that I hadn't even bothered to sit. Something like the promise of a trial, that would be all the hope I would need, something real to aim for. For what else was there?

And as I lay in the bath, soaking the dirt of the back garden from my knees, with the rain drumming like a demented soldier boy on the windowpane, I wondered if anything would be the same ever again. It seemed as if everything changed after *The Kick In*.

There was Dave, turning to himself more and more, self-absorbed with his Bowie albums and his writing. Billy, it seemed, was never more than one step from oblivion. And Ketchup had moved away.

His old man had taken them, Ketch and his mum, back up to Scotland with him, to be a proper family again. His old man had been watching him growing up in the pages of letters and photos instead of before his own eyes. Ketchup was desperate to go, to be with his dad no matter where it may be, but you could see the pain ingrained in his face, having to mentally drag himself into the car, leaving behind his friends, his home, everything he had ever known.

Even Billy had changed. It was as if his very spirit was slowly draining away a little more each day. But there was still that undercurrent of evil, hovering beneath the surface, like a deadly loose wire. It was a mixture of guilt and revenge, stewing inside his head.

It was as if they had kicked our world inside out that day. Beat the child out of us. And when we had picked ourselves up, amidst the cuts and broken bones, limping through pools of our own blood, each of us was left with scars, buried deeper than the ones they had tried to inflict upon us.

After that day the world changed, moved on into another time. Everything was more vivid, starker, the noise of everyday life sharper. I couldn't put my finger on what it was, but it was unnerving, cynicism hung in the air like rumbling thunder. I don't think the others really thought about it at the time, not even Dave. As if the alley had been some kind of time tunnel, but I knew that we could never go back.

CHAPTER FIVE

November 1977

There was nothing new about them failing to answer the front door at Dave's house. Sometimes I would be standing there for ages, rattling the knuckles of my fingers against the faded wood until they were red. Then, upstairs, Dave's record would end or be in between tracks, and he would hear me. His mum ignored it most of the time, same with the telephone, answer them if she was in the mood and could be bothered to drag herself from the pits of her armchair in front of the telly. I could see her there now, a dark silhouette barely visible through the camouflage of the net curtains. But this time she couldn't have even heard me, not with the sound of Elvis thundering through the house at full volume, shaking the slim arches of frosted glass in their front door frames. I knew it was because of her old man. He had been gone over a week now, it wasn't the first time that he had buggered off, and he always came back. When the barmaid, or whoever it was that he had shacked up with, had had enough of him and kicked him out, and she never did or said anything, Dave's mum, not a word, just sat there in her chair and simply replaced the TV with the old man's Elvis records as if the sound of the King's voice could somehow reach out and call him home.

It seemed poignant, somehow, with Elvis having died earlier that year. I can still remember the headlines in one of the papers: *ELVIS IS DEAD*. It seemed so cold, so final; almost rude, like there was a lack of respect. All the older kids, the punks in the pubs and that, all laughing, telling jokes, "Heart-attack Hotel" and that kind of thing, but even though I had never been into his music, or any of the rock 'n' roll scene, and I had thought that I would feel nothing but a kind of apathy, but to my surprise, I felt a familiar kind of emptiness. I could only put it down to feeling sorry for Mum. Like all the parents and grown-ups, she was pretty upset. 'Part of our childhood,' I overheard Mr Brown discussing it with another teacher at school and I could see it then, that their generation didn't have the diversity, the choice in music that we had and that he truly was their King. It was just another part of everything that I knew, took for granted, like the sounds of the trains in the distance, rumbling and rocking me to sleep.

'He's out,' came the sound of the dull, lifeless voice from somewhere behind the window.

'Do you know where, Mrs Connelly?' I asked, peering at the net curtain.

'Just *out.*'

I couldn't remember the last time I had such a spring in my step, as if I were bouncing between the cracked, grey pavements the way I always did, like the feeling I would get tingling up and down my legs after a thorough warm-up, stretching and loosening the muscles until they felt supple and relaxed, all the heaviness ironed out like the creases of a shirt.

The world seemed a brighter place too. The contrast dial of my mind had been adjusted, and I could see colours that weren't as clear before, could see past the slate-grey skies into the promise of a blue sky, and from the corner of my eye, streaks of deep green as I passed the bushes hiding the park below. The lines of concrete buildings and tower blocks in the distance appeared less forbidding. Cars and lorries passing by, in and out of town, usually resembled paths of working ants, but even they seemed to be in less of a hurry.

I knew that it was just me, that nothing had really changed, that the sights and sounds of suburbia were as bleak and oppressive as usual, like yesterday and the day before, but I didn't care, I was more than happy to let the joy of being offered a contract, an apprenticeship, spill into my world.

It was as if I had been sleepwalking through my life, but now I couldn't even feel the cold, the blood was racing through my body so fast I could actually hear my heart pounding, echoing through my chest. It was a crisp, late November morning and I had received an early Christmas present. The only thing that I had wanted, the kind of present that couldn't be bought in any shop, that couldn't be bought at all, for any price.

Compared to most of the other kids that I knew in the same boat, it had taken a while in coming but it was here now, that's all that mattered. That rainy Sunday morning last month, I would never have believed it possible, had thought that another chance had passed me by, slipped through my hands, and I couldn't have felt worse if it had been a football creeping through them.

The whole thing had been a complete farce. Parts of the pitch were actually underwater, clear pools of rainwater lying on either side of the pitch but as they were only out on the wings the pitch was deemed fit and the game went ahead. I reckoned that they didn't have the nerve to cancel it, what with it being a top game and some important people there and all. By half-time they had had no choice. I was surprised the ref had even allowed it to go that far. Maybe he was under instructions, who knows?

As we had trudged off at the break, 2-0 down, the entire pitch was nothing more than a brown, stinking mess. A giant mud bath, every step you took slipped and squelched beneath your feet. One lad, their centre-half, had even lost his boots at one point, jumped to head a ball clear and left his boots glued to the edge of his penalty box, like a cartoon character blown out of his shoes by a cannon or something.

They had scored two early goals, when the pitch had still resembled one that football could be played upon. It wasn't until we had got out there, the mud and rain splattering up the backs of our legs as we warmed-up, that we could see the amount of surface water everywhere, hiding like jellyfish on a beach. And they had been a different class, Riverside. Had no less than five boys who had already been offered apprenticeships at pro clubs, all ready for when they left school. They were staying on in the hope that they would be selected for the England schoolboys, they were that good. The first goal was a one on one. I came out, stood tall, forcing him to make a decision, but he just dropped a shoulder, sending me the wrong way, and drifted past me all casual, and walloped the ball into the empty net. I should have learnt from that, but I thought he was just being bigheaded, all cocky. Flash git, I had thought to myself as I looked over my shoulder, down on one hand and knee, left stuck in the mud like a right prat.

But after the second goal, I realised that he was just making sure that the ball didn't get stuck too, making bloody sure it went in. It was a shot from the edge of the box that skimmed like a pebble across the pitch before suddenly hitting a pool of water and stopping dead. I was already well on my way down, their centre-forward was already upon it, like a cat on mouse, the simplest of goals, a dead ball in the middle of the penalty box, and the keeper stranded on his knees, as if the mud had claimed me, pulling me down into the pits of hell. And at that moment I wished that it had. I flailed my arms hopelessly as he lifted the ball above me and into the net, but I knew that it was only a gesture.

I couldn't help but blame myself for that one. I tried to reason with myself as we walked off at half-time, that I couldn't be expected to know that that would happen, but I did. After all, the boy who scored the first goal had accounted for the state of the pitch, why hadn't I?

I had reckoned abandonment was my only hope, as we stood

around sucking pieces of orange and sipping hot tea from plastic cups that burnt your hands unless you held them by the lip running around the top. Both the managers and the ref were back out there, wading through the quagmire, inspecting the pitch. 'What the 'ell are they lookin' at?' exclaimed one boy. 'Frigging obvious it's unplayable!'

'It's ridiculous,' moaned another.

'Got to be seen to be doing their job,' said Dave. And there was this bloke hovering about, a scout from Orient or QPR, someone like that, I had seen him before, we learnt to recognise the scouts just in case, and he approached Dave all sneaky and put an arm around his shoulder like he was his best buddy. You couldn't hear what he said, mumbling under his breath as if he were telling Dave a big secret or something, but I could see Dave shrug his shoulders and shake his head, as if to say 'Sorry'.

'It's off, lads,' said the ref, sliding his feet along the side of the pitch, inside and out, trying to wipe away the wedges of overlapped mud from his boots.

'Thank God for that!'

'About time!'

I was walking behind most of the lads, languishing behind, trying to make out who was who. The lads were caked so heavily in wet clinging mud it covered the numbers of their shirts. My own jersey was so heavy it felt as if someone had slipped some weights into the hem, like a jockey's saddle.

'Hello Johnny… how's your arm now?' It was the fat man, the scout from Southfields. I hadn't seen him among the crowd.

'Fine thanks,' I replied in shock, wondering where the hell he had sprung from.

'Good… still got that card I gave you?'

'Yeah… yes … at home.' I could picture it now, lying on my bedside cabinet, must have looked at it a hundred times since he first gave it to me.

'We'd like you to do a bit of training with us… see how you are coming along… Wednesday night, six o'clock,' and he produced from his pocket a piece of paper with the address on. 'Let me know if you can't make it… have any difficulty getting there… my number on the card.'

'Right… fine… I mean… there'll be no problem,' I said, thinking that I would walk there if necessary. And then he was gone, hands buried deep back in the warmth of his pockets, melting back into the drizzle like a shadow with the fall of the sun.

I had loved the training, absolutely loved it, it was proper training, practising everything that a keeper needs to: low shots, long shots, reflex stuff, crosses, endless crosses…from both sides and, of course, that eased my nerves, because as I said before, if I had a strong point, that was it. Even the physical stuff didn't faze me. The running and that. In fact I think they were quite surprised how fit I was for a goalkeeper. But I had never minded all that, to me it was all part of it, being one of the lads, I had never wanted to just sit by while the rest of the lads ran themselves into the ground.

During the next few weeks, boys came and went. Some asked not to come back, some offered something more permanent by other clubs and a few who simply couldn't handle it. The training; like nothing that they had ever experienced, not just the kick about that they were used to.

So I wasn't overly surprised when they told me that I should expect a letter soon, for a meeting with the boss to discuss apprenticeship terms. It wasn't that I wasn't thrilled or that I had grown bigheaded or anything. It was just that in the past few weeks that I had been training, so many faces had changed that you came to realise that they were keeping you there for a reason.

Nothing else mattered anymore. I could see a purpose in my life, it was like everything had jumped back into focus. I didn't think of Debbie, I couldn't hear the distant resonance that still rumbled on from the aftermath of *The Kick In*, the noises that still resounded like prowling thunder overhead. I simply lived for the training.

I couldn't even muster disappointment when England missed out on the World Cup finals again, despite beating Italy 2-0. I had seen it all along, ever since they had looked hopelessly out of their depth in Rome last November. I had done all my grieving back then. I remember sometime in the summer, when a few of us were unloading tables and chairs from the minibus, leant to the community by the school. And this teacher we were with was filled with this sense of national pride. 'Wouldn't happen anywhere else in the world, you know...' he'd said, chest all puffed out like a robin, talking about the street parties that we were helping prepare, in celebration of the Queen's Silver Jubilee. And I remember ours, rows of children sitting along the lines of tables, all squashed neatly together, and covered with paper tablecloths and plates. Everything stacked on them from cakes and jellies to sausages, and cheese and pineapple chunks on sticks, sitting on the tables like giant porcupines. And above a canopy of bunting, hundreds of tiny Union Jack flags fluttering in the sunshine, secured round lampposts and peeling guttering, criss-crossing the street like camouflage.

'... And we'll win the World Cup next year too, you see... right under the nose of the South Americans...' the teacher rambled on, and I thought to myself that *I* was meant to be the daydreamer, I had always been accused, by teachers like him, of walking around with my head in the clouds.

But it didn't bother me now. Not when I had something very real to pour my dreams into. And just before I was told about the imminent apprenticeship, a landslide of boys fell by the way side, a mass clear-out, washing away their dreams and crushing spirits. Their only solace that maybe another club would take them. At least I had the security of knowing that, as a goalkeeper, there wasn't as many of us around, and we were supposed to have a longer shelf life... or so I thought.

CHAPTER SIX

November 1977

'Hey, Johnny... how-ah are you?' asked Lui as I closed the door behind me; shutting the cold outside. The smell of sausages and bacon filled my nostrils and the cosiness of the café washed over me like a warm shower, steaming up the windows like the school minibus on a rainy day.

'Fine thanks, Lui,' I smiled. It was quiet for a Saturday, just a gang of builders sitting over the far side, around a table piled high with plates of toast and steaming mugs of tea. Lui appeared from behind the counter, trusty tea towel slung over his shoulder, carrying five plates full of fried breakfasts, balancing one in the crook of his arm, as if he were rushed off his feet.

'Tea?' he asked, plopping the plates in front of the builders.

'Please, Lui... when you're ready.'

'I'll bring it over... He'll run-ah that pen out in a minute,' he remarked, motioning towards our usual spot in the far corner. Dave was sitting by the window, hunched over a notepad, his tea cloudy from neglect, scribbling away furiously. He hadn't even noticed me come in. I picked out my faithful yellow chair and sat opposite him.

'Johnny!' Dave exclaimed, looking up from his notepad. 'I was going to call round later... just had something to do,' he nodded at the writing in front of him. 'She's gone all weird again... banging out his old Elvis records... you know.'

I raised my eyebrows to say I understood; words not necessary.

'Have you heard anything yet?' he asked, before taking a sip of his tea and realising that it was stone cold.

'Yeah, got a letter this morning… they want me to go up there next Tuesday, with Mum, and talk about signing an apprenticeship.'

'Johnny that's brilliant!… Brilliant! You wait, it won't be long and you'll be full pro!' It was the most animated that I had seen him since… I couldn't remember. I had pictured myself bursting through the door, wading past the tables and chairs, squawking like a kid at Christmas time, *'Guess what!… You'll never guess what?'* But there was something about Dave, something deeper than usual that seemed to deflate my enthusiasm. Something there, lurking behind his eyes, playing on his mind. I was half-expecting a "but", as if he were about to warn me not to let myself get carried away; keep my feet on the ground. But I knew that wasn't really it. We had discussed all that, and besides, Dave knew me better than that. It was something else, something bothering him. His lips rocked from cheek to cheek as if he was chewing gum, and the words in his mouth were struggling to come out. His brow wrinkled, distorting the scar in wavy forehead lines. And I suddenly had this stupid picture in my head, that behind the scar, deep inside, there was this conveyer belt whirring round and round his brain, trying to select the appropriate way to tell me whatever it was that was troubling him.

Lui arrived with my tea. 'How's England's future goalkeeper eh?' he winked, patting me on the shoulder. He had become even more protective of us since *The Kick In*, had even blamed himself for not going to the police and reporting the skinheads after the first incident outside the café after our cup final.

'Fine thanks, Lui,' I smiled. He could never do enough for us now. And it wasn't like before, when he simply felt sorry for us, someone who sympathised and understood the restless malcontent of teenage boys. No longer children but not yet men. And it had become a little overbearing, too much really. It wasn't just a cup of tea and a plate of chips that he was more than happy to let us have, it was anything on the menu; from a full fry-up to his speciality, "Lui's homemade Spaghetti Bolognese". And he would never accept any payment, not a penny, even when we had a few quid.

We had tried to tell him that it was nothing to do with him, that he couldn't blame himself for what had happened that day, that they were nutters, the Bovver Boys, and that they probably hadn't even recognised me and Dave from that day when he had recruited the coalmen to rescue us. But I don't think he ever believed us, so we gave up trying in the end. Maybe it was one of the reasons that we didn't go to Lui's so much, who knows? And I must admit, I couldn't blame him for not believing the part about not recognising us. Not that I did blame him in any way, it was just that I didn't really believe that part myself.

I raked my fingers up and down the inside of my arm, from just below the elbow to the wrist and back.

'Arm playing up?' Dave asked

'What?... No, no it's fine.' It was a nervous thing, like a facial tick or twitch, which had stayed with me since the plaster had been sawn off my mended arm. Whenever I was nervous or edgy about something, my arm would begin to itch, as if the plaster were still wrapped around it. And it used to itch like mad then. The only way that I could ease the irritation was by slipping a ruler down the side and scratching, furiously away until the skin was sore. And now I was left with this phantom itch. I tried to ignore it, when I could feel the tingling begin, tell myself that it was all in my head, but it was no use, it felt as if something were scuttling across my skin, like hundreds of tiny spiders were crawling up and down my arm.

'What about you, been up to anything?' I tried to ask all casual, as if I weren't trying to prize something out of him, be dead subtle. But then he smiled that thin, knowing smile of his. And I might as well have shoved a giant shoehorn or something down his back. He knew that I knew something was up. I should have known better really.

'Well yeah.' He dipped an ear on his shoulder, as if he were trying to break some sad news to a child. 'Now you come to mention it… It's to do with this letter that I'm writing.'

CHAPTER SEVEN

December 1977

'Your round, J,' Billy burped, slamming the empty glass of his third pint on the table.

'Jesus, Billy! Slow down a bit!' I still had over half a pint left and Dave and his flat mates had barely touched theirs.

'It's not me who's drinking like a fucking poof, is it?' He smirked, typical Billy.

'Well you'll have to wait a minute,' I told him. But I started to drink up despite myself, trying hard not to let it show.

We were in a pub somewhere behind Baker Street, not far from the flat where Dave lived. This was Dave's world now. And it was a melting pot of cultures, music and fashion. Where the pubs and bars hummed with life like a swarm of bees buzzing through your head, where live bands played, lots of angry young punks just waiting to be discovered. Screaming Johnny Rotten look-a-likes, jumping around the tiny mock stages like fallen power cables, fizzing with a dangerous energy. Or they were fronted by braless young girls, drooling suggestively over their microphones, trying to turn the boys on, in their ripped fishnets and string vests.

And he looked as if this was where he belonged, Dave, completely at ease. The lifestyle, living in town, away from the destruction of home, and now he was living his dream… the same as me. He fitted perfectly into the environment, finger on the pulse of the music scene; this fabulous new job, building quite a reputation for his gig reviews and the curt, black-humoured paragraphs he used to write up the new releases whenever they gave him the chance… *caustic* was the word one of his flatmates used.

But the worry lines had faded from his face, lifted like a stain in the wash. Those lines that had sunk into his brow and crept around his eyes, visible debris from *The Kick In* ageing him before his time, as if the air of maturity that had always surrounded him had finally caught him up.

And I knew that it was the desired affect, the ghostly-white look, like Bowie's recent invention: The Thin White Duke. And of all the Bowie creations this one actually suited Dave the best. And he had the flame-red hair too, complete with dark roots showing through, all swept back over his head like a pair of stage curtains. I wondered if he was going to continue to re-enact the pictures on Bowie's album sleeves. I wanted to ask him if we would be up at the crack of dawn, or waiting around until dusk, until the sun melted away into watery colours of orange and red. And I would snap away with Dave's old camera, trying to capture his profile against the backdrop, just like the cover from the album *Low*.

I wanted to ask him, but I knew that I wouldn't. Not in front of his two flatmates, Ronnie and Stuart, who were also his work colleagues. And I could tell that they were already wondering what the hell they were doing spending their Saturday night with a couple of boys, just out of school.

With Dave things were different. He was never our age, not really, not in mind or in body. That "wise beyond his years" thing again, could hold his own in any grown-up circle, the adult world, it was how he had found himself in his new job.

Working for a music paper! They had been so impressed with the material that he had been flooding them with: letters, articles, reviews of albums and gigs that he always managed to bluff his way into. And suddenly there he was, sharing a flat in the heartbeat of London, with a pair of young professional journalists, and following his dream.

We both were. Dave immersed in his world of writing and music, and me with my football. It didn't seem possible, it really didn't, that maybe, just maybe, I really could make it, and Mum had been thrilled, so proud, and everyone was great about it, wishing me well and that. But to be honest it wasn't such a big deal round our way. There was just so many good footballers in the borough, popping up like daffodils in springtime, kids being taken on, signing for this or that club, and occasionally one or two would be signed by the really big clubs, the Tottenhams, Arsenals or even Chelseas of this world.

'Fuck it, give us the money, J… I'll get 'em myself.' Billy was wriggling with impatience in his seat. 'Same again, is it?'

'Not for me,' said Ronnie, stifling a burp.

'Nor me thanks,' added Stuart.

'Suit yourself,' sniffed Billy. I handed him the money and watched him breeze up to the bar, puffing out his chest, trying to make himself look older, but he needn't have bothered. It was so busy, a typical Saturday night up in town, that no one was going to bother about some kid a few months under age. If there was one person who could look after himself in this world it was Billy, the last person you would have to worry about. But, strangely, I did. For Dave and me everything was beginning to fall into place, fit together like the pieces of a jigsaw. Somehow, against all the odds, against all the shit that we had been through, everything had miraculously opened up for us. But Billy just existed, aimlessly from day to day, under age and spending virtually every night, pissed in the pub. He was turning into his dad. He looked constantly tired, haggard, and in a completely different way to Dave, older than his years. He was labouring on some building site over in Acton. Lugging bricks and filling skips all day. His hands were the hands of a fifty year old, rugged and cracked like old leather. I had suggested that maybe he could do a City and Guilds, one day or night a week, learn a trade, bricklaying-plasterering or something. But he wasn't interested. 'It's all bollocks, J,' he had said. And the most depressing thing about it was that he sounded like an old man, someone who had seen more than enough crap in his life to care anymore. And he was drinking far too much. Out every night drinking with men nearly twice his age, builders, labourers, navvies. And he was always in debt, and often in trouble, seemed to attract it like a magnet. The aggression was always there with Billy, bubbling inside, like a smouldering firework, ready to ignite at any time.

And Dave's flatmates, this Ronnie and Stuart were making up their excuses now, explaining that they had to be somewhere. And Dave just nodded and smiled, told them that he would see them later and that we'd try to be quiet when we came in. And I think he was relieved really, and I suppose I couldn't blame them. I mean what did the likes of Billy and me have to talk about with a pair of hip, young journalists from town? And it had been obvious from the start that we were totally incompatible the minute Billy and I had met them all in the pub, probably curiosity more than anything that had brought them along. Wondering what their new flatmate's friends were like. And Ronnie, all casual in his denim jacket and jeans, mid-twenties I reckoned, had taken in Billy's spiky blonde hair and earring and asked him if he thought 'punk was just a vehicle, a suitable excuse for rebellion against the establishment, or really about the music.'

And Billy had just stared at him, pint hand frozen in mid-air as if this Ronnie had just spoken to him in Dutch or something. And I had wanted to laugh, but I could tell that Billy was trying to work out if this Ronnie was taking the piss out of him or not. Billy looked from me to Dave, searching for the answer in our eyes, like a nervous child in the school play looks for encouragement from their parents in the audience. And he could see the humour twinkling in them, and I could almost hear Billy's voice in his head, working it out, hear him saying to himself, 'It's all right, they're just Dave's workmates, a bit poncy, but all right.'

And Billy had swallowed a huge mouthful, nearly half a pint in one go. And he wiped his mouth with the back of his hand and sniffed 'Dunno…both I s'ppose,' and whether he realised it or not it was probably the best answer that he could have given.

I didn't want to feel as drunk as I did when we made our way along Baker Street on the way back to Dave's flat. But then I never did, once the night was over. It hadn't been until we had stepped out into the cold December night that it hit me, blowing away the fuzzy warmth of the pub like the feathery seeds of a dandelion stalk in summer.

The drizzle settled on my coat; morning dew at night. It was so fine I could barely feel it, more a dampness in the air, the kind that finds its way through your clothes and seeps into the pores of your skin.

And the next year, every time I went to visit Dave the words from that song would play in my head, over and over, and I couldn't seem to turn it off, my minds' jukebox continually selecting the same track.

"… *Winding your way down on Baker Street, light on your head and dead on your feet…*"

And I remember Dave said that it used to happen to him all the time as well, that he couldn't help doing it himself, nearly every day on his way home from work or a night out. But never on his way out. He had wondered why that was and had finally concluded that it just felt like "an on the way home kind of song". But he didn't mind, said it was a good song, and that he admired the singer, songwriters, and that he was glad that it hadn't reached number one. That Gerry Rafferty should be "grateful" for Abba's

"Take a Chance on Me" that avoiding the top of the charts took the "pop" edge off it.

'The best songs never reach number one,' he had said, but I wondered if old Gerry would have seen it that way.

Music, it was all that Dave was interested in now, he didn't even play football anymore. But it did feel good, the three of us together, hanging out, messing about on the streets again. Different, unfamiliar streets, but then, things were different. Ketchup had gone, and we no longer filled each others' days anymore. A world of towering office blocks, football pitches and building sites divided us now.

I suddenly felt a pang of insecurity shoot through me. The realisation that maybe we really *were* going to drift apart for good. Not intentionally, but slowly, dragged by the currents of circumstance. And it wouldn't be until one day in the future that we would look over our shoulders and see just how far we had distanced ourselves, like waking up and gazing back to land aboard a drifting lilo.

I suddenly saw myself, through the drunken haze of my mind, fifty, sixty years ahead. An old man, hunched over, a walking stick by my side, looking frail in a thick overcoat and tatty old chequered scarf. And there I was, sitting aboard a train, passing over the ancient viaducts, with the park stretched out below, a giant green canvas. And through tired, lifeless eyes I painted memory upon memory across it; splashes of Dave, Ketchup, Billy and I, until one moment in time crosses into another, the colours of the past all blending into one, until I could no longer distinguish one from another.

And then the sight of Billy racing past me and Dave, wrenched me back onto Baker Street and the moment. 'Leg it ! *Knock Down Ginger!*' He laughed over his shoulder. And I looked back over mine and saw the windows in the posh terraced houses and porches light up, illuminating the old Victorian steps and railings. And some people were already in their doorways, cursing and shouting after Billy, before he had finished knocking on doors and ringing bells as he went. And we ran after him, not because we were scared or worried about getting caught, but because it could have been back then, after school, the four of us. Knocking on doors, clomping down the road in our beetle crushers, to Lui's or the sanctuary of the park, our long hair falling in our eyes, flowing wildly, flapping like our school ties in the wind.

'What's this crap?' snorted Billy as he returned from the toilet and slumped, exhausted from the combination of alcohol and exercise, into a buckled old armchair. Neither Ronnie nor Stuart had returned and Dave had taken the opportunity to slip a record on. Surprisingly, not Bowie this time, but a kind of meandering folk music. The singer's voice seemed as delicate as a feather, floating around the room.

'It's Nick Drake,' said Dave on his way to the tiny kitchen. 'I'm starving… toast?'

'Not for me,' I said. I could have fallen asleep there and then, could feel the lids of my eyes grow heavier. And the old sofa seemed to be pulling me down, deep into the faded, sagging upholstery, while the worn cushions moulded themselves around me. I could imagine how uncomfortable it must usually have been, to try and watch TV there. It seemed like someone had removed every spring, and that you were constantly sinking, like struggling in quicksand. But right then it seemed the most comfortable place in the world, and I just wanted to lie down, let it swallow me up, and sleep for hours.

Dave reappeared with a plate of toast and three mugs of tea balanced in his hands.

'Fucking 'ell… it's Lui!' laughed Billy. 'It's hippie shit anyway, whoever it is,' he spluttered through a mouthful of toast and waving his mug in the direction of the record player. 'Should be shot, the lot of them.'

'A bit difficult… he's dead,' said Dave, in that tired voice that he always used to save for Billy and his crass comments. But that was Billy, anything that was sweet sounding, a bit thoughtful, was considered "hippie". And besides, he loved to wind Dave up.

But the music seemed to fit the mood. Lethargy had begun to cloud the room like fog. That "back home" feeling after a night out, the weariness that hits you once you close the door on the evening, and your limbs ache from the alcohol, energy draining away like bath water. And it was just a voice and a guitar, both as smooth as honey, slow pouring, wandering cautiously through the room. And he sounded like some shy school kid; I imagined him on a stage, only the wrong side of the curtain, reluctant to play his songs for anyone other than himself.

Tiredness closed in and the conversation began to wind down, like a slowing windmill. Until then it had spun constantly, blowing us from one topic to the next, friends, girls, football, music, spinning round and round in a frenzied wind of exuberance. But now it was just the three of us, away from the crowded pubs and the bustling city streets. And it seemed like something was missing… or someone. And it was as if the haunting, folk-like tones dripping from the old record player were a lament for Ketchup's absence.

'Do you think Ketch will ever come back?' I said. It was more of a thought tossed into the room than a question. Neither of them wondered where it had come from, or thought it out of place; it was just lying there, intangible but prominent. Ketchup had gone, was playing truant, absent from our class, and all three of us felt it probably more at that moment than at any other time since he had left. Growing up had simply got in the way, the world away from school trying to remove the innocence of childhood, like walking a tightrope without a safety net.

'What's he got to come back for?' yawned Billy, from the depths of the armchair. He looked as he had been fired there from some giant cannon, landing with a splat, arms and legs sprawled across the seat. 'I mean, there's only us! And I wouldn't come back just to see you fuckers.' He grinned, with eyes half closed. 'Besides... he's got more chance up there,' he added. 'Stands to reason, don't it... less people and all that.'

We had talked about this earlier, in the pub. What he was doing, whether or not he would take the next step, find a club. But the conversations hadn't been anything heavy, just skimmed over them like flattened stones across a pond, nothing to sink the mood of the evening. But now that we were just passing time, unwinding in the tranquillity of Dave's flat, it felt strange without him, three instead of four.

'Yeah...' Dave sighed. 'Less people, but also less clubs... less opportunity.' Why didn't Billy or I ever think about stuff like that?

'Well it don't matter does it... he ain't gonna turn pro or nothin', is he?' Billy shrugged. And he wasn't putting Ketchup down or anything, it was just that the higher the level we played, the more players like Ketch were considered a luxury. I could never see it myself, I mean a player like Ketch, they could win a game for you, create something out of nothing. And it stands to reason that if you're playing out on the wing you're not going to be as involved as other players, you rely on them to provide you with the ball, can't do a thing without the service.

'Anyway,' continued Billy 'He was never the same after it all, was he?' He was fully awake now, so were me and Dave, jolted back to full consciousness by Billy's remark. I turned to Dave, trying to deflect Billy's bombshell before it had time to land. He was referring to *The Kick In* of course. But the thing was we never talked of it. Not the three of us together, the main victims. But it was always there, a part of us, it had seeped into, the pores of our skin like dried sweat.

I began to scratch the imaginary itching crawling up my arm. It was often talked about, especially by the younger ones, the kids

Dave had virtually sacrificed himself for. But we never discussed it with each other. And it was easier that way, to leave it alone. It was like picking a scab that wasn't ready to come off, still red raw underneath.

But maybe we were past it now, the wounds healed. I certainly didn't think about it as much, now that I had something solid, a goal, literally, to aim for.

I know that it had messed Billy up, even if he didn't acknowledge it. It had eaten away at him. It had been the sense of vulnerability that had gnawed at his insides until there was nothing left but a kind of hunger. A hunger that would only be satisfied by revenge, and he felt like we all did, that we owed Dave, this huge debt that we could never hope to repay. At times I'm sure that he wished that something like it would happen again, someone start on Dave, just so he could step in, crack a few heads, purge his guilt on some kid's face.

And as for Dave, I hoped that maybe he had finally begun to put it all behind him now. After all, like me, he had managed to transform his dreams into reality. And it was an amazing feeling, kind of like turning your head inside out and bringing all your thoughts and wishes into the real world. The only difference was that even Dave's dreams had a touch of maturity about them, more substance than just being a football hero. It wasn't just listening to music and writing about records with Dave. It went deeper. It was the inspiration behind it, his insight, the lyrics, the reviews, reading between the lines. And he seemed to really connect with the singer and songwriters, tuning into the creativity behind it all.

But maybe it was all just a cover, an excuse to hide behind something new, something unrelated to his world. After all, he had moved away, distanced himself from the whole scene. And he didn't need much of an excuse to leave home, now that he was old enough. And it was only a glimpse of his new life that I was catching, like splintered light through the branches of a tree, but I could understand how distorted his life back home must have looked.

And you had to know him well to see it, for it wasn't instantly visible. There was still the easy smile for a friend, the quiet, calm manner that seemed to warm him to everyone in his presence, kids or adults. But the likes of me and Billy were aware of it, his mood was slightly darker, toned down around the edges, and he often seemed somewhere else, with us in body but his mind had slipped behind a door, into a room that we couldn't enter. The job and the opportunity to move up town were more than he could have wished for. That day at Lui's, when I had told Dave about my contract, and he was busy writing a letter of confirmation about the job at the music paper, I hadn't seen him that enthusiastic about anything for so long, it made me realise how much he had changed. I had tried to kid myself that it was just youth slipping away, the changes that occur in the minds of young men, but I knew that it was more.

Maybe if we had discussed it earlier, the three of us, talked it through, exorcised our demons, purged the poison from our minds, but the truth was it had all been so unclear at first. And then it simply became easier not to mention it, to even think about it. But, of course, you can never leave it behind, not if your mind won't let you.

But Billy had been right. Ketchup had never been the same either. He couldn't shake off the web of guilt that he had walked blindly into. I remember Dave telling me that Ketch had actually had tears in his eyes when he had gone to see him at the hospital. Had taken one look at Dave's face, swollen and covered with bruises of all different shades, yellows, blacks and purples, streaked across it like a winter sunset, and had sat down and cried. And Dave had said that he hadn't been able to take his eyes off the marks dug into his forehead, that Ketchup had just sat there, didn't say a word the whole time, just sat staring, snivelling like a child. And Dave had wanted to tell him not to worry, that he would be okay, that there wasn't anything he could have done, not a thing. But he couldn't, for the stitches inside his mouth, and the ones that ran along the tip of his tongue where it had split in two, like a snake's, made it hurt too much to talk.

And it had shown just how ingrained our friendship was, that Ketchup couldn't forgive himself for *not* being there.

I finished my tea and put the cup down beside the sofa. I felt so tired and the beer weighed heavy in my limbs. Had that day really affected us that much? Changed us irreparably inside, somewhere deep in the recesses of our minds? In places that we didn't even know existed and ways that we didn't understand, so that none of it was instantly recognisable to anyone, not even ourselves?

I looked over at Dave, pale and thin; he really did look like the Bowie of the time. And he was staring pensively into nothing, somewhere above Billy's head, eyes narrowed from the concentration of thought. Where *was* he now, I wondered, back in the alley way perhaps, lost in his own private hell? I knew then, like I always had I suppose, that we weren't over it, none of us, nowhere near. I sighed heavily. Would it always be like this, I wondered; the slightest remark, the faintest memory flickering back and the whole dreadful nightmare erupting again?

I tried to push it all from my mind, didn't want it to be my last thought of the day, for I couldn't fend off the drink for much longer, my eyelids felt like steel shutters. But it wouldn't dislodge, stuck like a fishbone in my throat, choking my will. And the next thing that I knew I was lifting my head from a pool of my own dribble that had formed on the arm of the old sofa, while outside the fog smothered the sickly, pale light of morning and dulled the chirping morning song of the birds. But it was no use, it still sounded like shattered glass in my head.

THE KICK IN

July 1975

Whenever the thought of it enters my head, pours like lava through the burnt out chambers of my mind, I see Bowie's *Young Americans* face, misty and angelic, looking up at me from the gutter. The vinyl balancing crazily against the wall a few feet away cracked and chipped, rocking gently to and fro as if it had been carefully placed there.

I can picture it all so clearly, the patterns of Dave's blood upon the album sleeve, splattered across the image of Bowie's clean cut face as if an artist had administered it as some sort of bizarre and twisted final touch from the flick of his brush.

But of course none of it was intentional, it was just a prop for the sickest show on Earth. One memory veers off into another, like London waterways, and I recall when Dave posed for the cover, borrowing a clutch of silver bracelets from Debbie and her clicking her tongue and rolling hers eyes in that way of hers, but without the dissatisfaction that it held when it used to be directed at me. Even after the nightmare of the *Aladdin Sane* night, when we ended up immersed in the icy darkness of the church, we had ended up giggling at the sheer absurdity of it all.

But the terror of *Aladdin* is nothing compared to that of the *Young Americans*.

The flow of my thoughts leads me back to the brewing storm of that side street where we watched, penned in and useless against the wall, whilst Dave stood out in the street facing the tall skinhead, facing the leader of the pack… facing oblivion.

They stand like gunfighters from some western, but the thing is only one of them has a loaded gun, and as we watch helplessly like sheep behind a barrier of skinheads, he looks over and smiles, that easy grin flickering in the corners of his mouth, telling us that it's going to be all right. I see it and I'm sure that Billy does too, despite the water overflowing from his eyes and his foetal position on the floor, but the youngsters behind us probably don't even notice, too busy sobbing and shaking, scared out their wits; never before have they seen such violence or witnessed such a macabre scene.

I feel an almost parental urge to protect them, the way Dave protects us. But of course he is doing so much more than simply transforming himself into a human shield, what he is doing is offering himself up for sacrifice.

Something in my face alerts him to turn his head just in time to avoid a wild haymaker of a punch, the momentum of which carries the skinhead toppling into us. The youngsters behind me fly everywhere, like skittles, before regrouping, each trying to hide behind the other as the giant skinhead jumps back to his feet, fists at the ready and snarling with anger at being shown up. He closes in on Dave again, only this time with more caution, prowling, stalking, and I wonder how the hell Dave is going to get out of this? For there is no way that he can win… even if he wanted to, for if he were to beat the great brute, which I believe he probably could, then his army would surely annihilate the rest of us.

I berate myself, over and over: Why did we ever let the kids come with us? Why did we ever let the kids come with us?

'Oh go on-n Billy! Let us come!' the leader of the little pack had pleaded on behalf of his mates. 'We won't be no bovver, honest!' Billy had rolled his eyes and looked completely lost for words. He had looked over at me and Dave for some guidance and help but I had just shrugged and stifled a smile, enjoying his discomfort. He was not used to such hero-worship and watching him squirm from the attention was just too amusing not to prolong. They were the kids from his high rise and Billy had known them all since they had been in nappies and they regarded him as a kind of surrogate older brother. Proud of his reputation and sharing the same tower block gave them licence to travel on his coat-tails

It was the school holidays and Billy, Dave and I were on our way up town for the day to just hang out. We had no plan other than to piss about jumping on and off of buses and just see where the day took us, although I had no doubt that at some point we would find ourselves miraculously in Heddon Street, only Dave had an agenda and that was to take us to the giant record store on Oxford Street so that he could finally get his hands on a copy of Bowie's latest album, *Young Americans*.

When he saw that he was going to get no help from either of us he simply gave up. 'Oh for fuck's sake! All right.' The boys jumped up and down, pumping their fists and exchanging dead arms with each other. The oldest was twelve if he was a day I reckoned and one or two of the smaller ones looked to be not much older than nine or ten!

'But… ' he added sternly with a pointed finger, 'if you fuck us about, you're on your own!' At the sound of his raised voice they calmed down immediately. I had to admit I was impressed, this gang of seven or eight young tearaways nodding their heads obediently at their master. Maybe it wasn't going to be so bad after all.

It had been a good day, the sun shining like a demon, as if the heaving crowds moving up and down Oxford Street were melting in the heat. It was simply too busy to be caught out at anything, Billy had nicked a couple of T-shirts from various stores and it emerged that some of the youngsters were hardly novices when it came to shoplifting either. But if it even looked as if they were being watched they simply dissolved into the crowds with the dexterity of some Victorian street urchin. We bunked bus fares and scammed four extra hamburgers in McDonalds by sending up a different kid to different members of staff with crocodile tears in their eyes and tales of how they had dropped their burger. They even offered to get Dave his copy of *Young Americans* for him as a token of their appreciation for allowing them to tag along.

He had gazed down upon them, that thin smile playing on his lips, like some soft-hearted primary teacher and shook his head.

'Jesus, Billy,' he grinned. 'What have you done to them?' Billy said nothing and just shrugged his shoulders, absolving himself of any blame. 'I feel like I'm in a scene from *Oliver Twist*!' he smirked before telling us *all* he would meet us at the bus stop. Shopping for Bowie was a serious business.

Billy is still on the floor. When they had first jumped us it had taken four of them to pin him against the wall while another had used his guts as a punch bag. He was up on his knees now but would still be severely handicapped if, heaven help us, we had to protect the younger ones, and as for the kids… well we couldn't leave them and I truly believed him when he had threatened to kick the shit out of them as well. It was no bluff and we all knew it, it hung in the air, as tangible and oppressive as the heat.

No, there could only be one possible conclusion to this "fight". If the skinhead had suddenly pulled a gun from somewhere beneath his braces and shot Dave point blank between the eyes, it couldn't have been any more one-sided.

The next punch catches Dave full in the face, more of a straight jab. Obviously not carrying as much power as haymakers but enough behind it to knock most people down, but Dave sees it coming and rolls with it. Two or three more follow with Dave riding them as much as he dare but once his aggressor realises that nothing is coming back he steps up the pace, pulling his arm back further… smash, smash, smash… until it becomes impossible for him to draw the sting from every one.

The boys behind me are sobbing uncontrollably now, one even reaches

68

out and grabs my arm, the way a small child clings to a parent, and it could be just the stench from the gutter or something wafting out from the overflowing bins but from somewhere the overwhelming stench of piss fills my nostrils.

Dave's face is a bloody mess, leaking from his nose and his mouth but still he remains on his feet, constantly on the move, round and round, backwards, sideways, ducking a little here, diving a fraction there, like a boxer, with his arms strapped to his sides, taking all the punches but never quite all the full force, hoping in vain that the skinhead will think he's proved his point and grow disinterested at the lack of competition.

But if anything it was the reverse; the sight of Dave's blood splattered and dripping from his face, seemed to send the skinhead crazier, like a shark his senses heightened by the scent of blood.

Dave starts to protect himself now, left with no choice for the punishment is beginning to take its toll. He raises a forearm here, an elbow there, in an effort to deflect some of the bigger blows from reaching their destination. And at one point Dave actually hits back! Nothing too vicious just two lightning jabs to the face but they carry enough to stop the great brute in his tracks. For more by luck than judgement he manages to trap Dave in a corner. The fact that Dave has allowed himself to be hemmed in is concerning enough, there is a disorientated look swimming in his eyes, and with nothing but a graffiti-stained wall behind him, he takes the only action open to him. It buys him enough time to step out of the shadows and back into the safety of the sunlight. But of course there is no real escape and Dave knows it… we all know it. Me, Billy, Dave, his nemesis and his baying cronies, even the snivelling lads behind me I reckon have grasped the enormity of what Dave was doing, of the sacrifice he was making. I wonder if they realise though that Dave could probably have defeated the giant skin with one hand tied behind his back, the way he lurched forward, his guard down, arms hanging by his side like a demented ape. With his deadly accuracy and range, Dave would have picked him off at will, toyed with and tormented him until he'd pleaded or simply passed out.

Although what then? What if Dave had kept jabbing away keeping the

*ape at arms length the way I had seen him fight in the past whenever he had
needed too; calm and controlled. What would have happened to me and
Billy, and, more importantly, the kids?*

*There were simply too many of them. I hadn't counted how many
exactly, although I was sure Dave had a pretty good idea, but I could tell
that even if Dave and Billy took on three each and if I even managed two of
my own, there would still be too many. They seemed to be everywhere, lined
round the walls, across the entrance blocking our only means of escape,
encompassing the whole street. And they are edging closer, the ring of menace
decreasing like ripples on a pond. The thought of their response if Dave was
to suddenly fight back runs through me like ice. No doubt they would take
their revenge out on us three, but what about the youngsters? Would they
pour their venom upon them? Dissolve them like acid?*

*The sun beats down, wrestling with the shadows cast by the buildings
for control of the side street, one moment the pair are moving through the
gloom and the next they are stepping out into glorious sunlight. There is a
deep colouring forming under Dave's left eye now and a lump the size of a
very large egg above his right, forcing the corner to droop. A ridiculous
thought considering the enormity of the situation, but I can't help but think
it makes him look sad. Dave is standing sideways on now, he can longer see
the punches coming. I realise this as another volley land in his face with no
attempt to block them. And another crashes into the swollen flesh above his
right eye splitting the skin like a ripened tomato… and suddenly I realise
that it's not going to be enough; that his sacrifice isn't going to save any of us,
not even Billy's young disciples, that we are all going to be pounded into the
dirt, the piss and the dust of the street.*

*'Go down you little fucker!' the skinhead screams, frothing at the
mouth. His fists are covered with Dave's blood, as if he's dipped them in a
tin of red paint. Will Dave's blood always be there, I wonder? Will the
stains ever lift or will it forever lie there, etched into the cracks of the street, as
permanent as a watermark through a pound note?*

*'The quicker you go down the quicker it'll be over!' but still Dave does
not go down, instead he carries on moving from side to side. He resembles a*

drunk now, shuffling awkwardly from left to right, all his effort just to stay on his feet. It is too much to bear.

Two more haymakers crash down into Dave's face, they are so wild it's as if they drop from the sky. But Dave doesn't even see them. He totters from one foot to the other and for a moment I think he's going over but then he is upright again and I can't believe what I'm seeing, for he is smiling. Dave is actually smiling! That lazy, laconic grin spreading thinly across his face; it might lack some of the contentment that it usually holds, in fact it looks almost absurd, the contours and the cracks in his lips covered in crimson like some demented clown, but still it is there, that unmistakable amusement with life. Look at me, it seems to be saying. You can beat me but you can't beat me.

It is too much for the giant skinhead, something close to bewilderment plays across his face but swiftly turns to anger and he turns and signals his troops. They need no second invitation and like unleashed dogs are upon Dave within seconds, pulling him to the ground like a felled tree. By the time I break rank and am halfway across the street they have him pinned and staked out like a star, two or three to each limb with the leader straddling his chest. From just out of my sight I sense Billy drag himself to his feet, from the corner of my eye I see his arms waving, shooing the youngsters away while they have the chance. They scatter like sheep in the direction of the main street. But I am focused on only one thing: the giant boy on Dave's chest. For he is holding something in his hand, it twinkles shiny in the sunlight and panic rises with the fear that it is a knife. But then the skinhead leans forward, concentration etched in his face, his hand going to work on Dave's forehead like an infant learning to write. He sits up, cocks his head and surveys his handiwork, as he continues with the compass he holds out an open palm. The short distance I have to cover suddenly seems to open up, those abominable dreams where you can't run race across my mind. His tattooed hand closes round a bottle of blue-black ink and he rests his compass upon Dave's chest, scarlet rivers running over his temples, filling his ears with the sound of his own blood. He has the top off now, spilling some down his hand and onto Dave's chest. He has the bottle poised over Dave's head and says something I can't make out, all I can hear is my own blood pumping in my ears. But he is grinning like a demon, enjoying, savouring every second of the humiliation he is about to administer.

And it is all I need, that fraction of hesitation before he starts to pour, and I am upon him, flying horizontally through the air like I have a million times before. Only this time there is no ball for me to reach for and save but instead Dave, from an indelible branding that he would carry through life.

I land somewhere round the skinhead's neck and with a great OOF of expelled air find myself on top off his prostate body next to Dave.

'What the fuck!' the skinhead cries from beneath me. We are covered in ink the both of us, I can feel it cold and clammy running through the back of my hair and down my neck. The bewildered thug pushes me away with one giant sweep of an arm and sits up; it's as if he's bleeding blue, the ink running in rivers down his face. He leans over and spits great globules of navy saliva into the street. All of a sudden the air is rushing out through my body as a DM boot lands in my side beneath my ribs. I am on all fours gasping for breath as more boots fly at me.

Billy arrives behind me like a whirlwind, flattening two skinheads with brutal efficiency within the blink of an eye, but then his element of surprise is lost forever and he disappears beneath a wave of bald heads and raised fists. I turn my head and the backstreet spins around before me, I can just make out Dave up on his knees, his face a grotesque mask of purple lumps and a great bloody, raw mess in the centre of his forehead, before he begins to slide out of view.

I roll myself into a ball, tucking my knees into my chest and cradling my head in a vain bid to protect myself as the boots begin to find their target more and more. It gets to the point where they no longer hurt, I am just aware of the sensation of my body rocking to and fro, as if I'm drifting in a lifeboat. In a crazy way it almost feels comforting, lying in the warmth of the sun bobbing this way and that. And then before I even realise it they are gone, scattering this way and that, knocking over dustbins, scrabbling over fences and walls as the deep gravelled voices ring out and the sound of policemen's boots thunder down the road. And now my body begins to hurt, *it's as if there is the ghost of a dervish trapped within me raging around and trying to escape. But it is not until I try and actually move that I feel the searing pain, deeper and more intense than the abuse to my body. This takes my breath away, makes the bile rise from my guts and it takes a while to trace its origin to my forearm. Moans and cries ring out in the back street. I hope the kids are okay, I think to myself. I thought they had all escaped... and then it hits me, as the white light flashes through my brain, that the whimpering and sobs are not coming from any of the youngsters, that the misery ringing in my ears, the sound of pain resonating through my head, is the sound of my own voice.*

CHAPTER EIGHT

March 1978

Every morning, I would look up at Dave's house as I passed by on my way to the bus stop at the end of our street. Just one of those things that you naturally do, don't know what I expected to see, certainly not Dave. I hadn't seen him for nearly three months now... Three months! Three days wouldn't have passed between us as kids. I would find myself imagining his bedroom, what it would look like now, cold and empty. And that kind of thing would upset me, the stupid, silly things. Picturing the cleared bookshelves, pictures, bleached by the sunlight, peeling off the walls, the carpet bare, still all-new looking and colourful, where his stacks of records had once been. It wouldn't have felt so bad if they had all just moved away, and someone had changed the look of the place, given it a new personality. But it was still the same, just like it had always been: the old gate, with its white paint flaking, frosted glass rattling in the front door, the tiny, neglected patch of grass beneath the front room window, nothing but a patch of weeds really. But there was no Dave. The whole backdrop of his life was there, only he wasn't, like gazing across the London skyline and seeing that someone had removed the Post Office Tower or something, leaving just a huge space where it would have once stood. I tried to imagine that the house was dead, rotting and decaying like a black tooth. But it was no use, Dave may have gone but his presence still lingered, it couldn't be extracted, not while everything about the house remained. And there was still his mum inside, shuffling about from room to room, in a cloud of lifeless confusion and cigarette smoke. I didn't know if his old man had come back, I wondered whether he even knew that Dave lived up in town now.

I couldn't wait to get to training every day, to be part of something I identified with. Things just weren't the same around town anymore. On the surface everything appeared the same. Structurally, nothing had changed, still the park at the end of the street, the town, a cluster of buildings in the distance, like a concrete pincushion, the church, school, Lui's, everything where it had always been. It just didn't seem like "our" town anymore. There was no "our" anymore, no Dave, no Ketch and I was lucky if I saw Billy once a fortnight. He would phone, maybe once or twice every other week, ask me to come out, meet him for a drink somewhere. I knew that I should make up some excuse to do with football, tell him that I had a match the next day or that maybe I had to be in early the next morning, clean the first teams' boots or something. But I don't think he would have believed me. It wasn't that I didn't *want* to see him, quite the opposite, I *needed* him. It was just that I knew the night would be immersed in alcohol, and if, maybe someone were to look at him in the wrong way or hold his gaze for a split second too long, it would probably end in a fight as well.

I felt like a stranger in my hometown. It was as if I were somewhere very familiar, like returning to the same place on holiday, year after year, but the people, the faces were never the same, always strangers. When had everything changed? And why hadn't I seen it? If I looked back, dissected the past, I could remember everything major, vividly: leaving school, Ketch and Dave going, my football, whatever. And often down to the tiniest detail. Could match each separate event to a year, a month, even match a song from the time to accompany it, provide the picture show in my mind with its own soundtrack.

But put it all together on one giant reel of memories and it was hard to remember any particular turning point, any one defining moment when I realised things had moved on. Of course, there was *The Kick In*, that changed everything, but that was a personal thing, gnawing away at three of us from the inside out, like a poisoned tree. And it would have been funny if it hadn't been so sad. But we had tried so hard to escape the clutches of childhood, run away from it so fast, that now that we had finally left it behind, I realised that we were never really a part of it, that we had never really fitted into the cosy circles of adolescence, not like the other kids. That they had all been wrong, teachers, parents, the gimpy kids, even "sensible" Debbie. Assuming that we were childish, immature, unwilling to learn, to face up to the responsibility of adulthood, that the likes of Billy and I might drag Dave down, to the depths of our level. But the truth is our circumstances had robbed us of the innocence of youth. We used it only as protection, life's wild card, drawn upon only when needed.

It had hit me a few days after my seventeenth birthday, when I saw Debbie's friend, Jenny Hargreaves, and a few of the other gimpy kids from school. I was out with a couple of team-mates and their girlfriends. We were celebrating my birthday, and, more importantly, me signing a two year full pro contract. It was no guarantee that I would make it as a footballer. I mean, I was still in the youth team, and the money wasn't great, in fact it was pretty poor, and besides, they could let me go after two years, and I might not find another club, and that would have been it. Washed up and finished at nineteen. But it was a giant step, and sometimes I would get to train with the reserves. And besides, I could pay Mum a half decent rent.

It was over Peckham way, at the bowling alley; an innocent pastime, something that wouldn't offend, where you couldn't really land yourself in trouble with the club. And I was with a girl too, Julie, one of the girlfriends' friends. I had been out with her a few times, maybe three or four. The pictures, a drink, even a meal, treading awkwardly inside circles that I wasn't used to, that I wasn't comfortable in, the ultimate square peg. But I realised the necessity of belonging, of being one of the team, a part of the club. I looked upon it as part of the job, just like all the teams that I had been involved with, to strengthen the collective bonds between players. But making new friends was the hardest thing about it all for me. The training, playing, even the tiresome little things like the journey in every morning weren't as difficult as going out in these social groups. It had always just been me and my mates, me Dave, Billy and Ketchup, like petals from the same flower, we knew each other's ways, what we liked or disliked, where to hang out, where to be found. On the pitch it was fine, all as one, but I found the social side a little daunting, and I knew I was only with Julie because we had been set up, because all the lads seemed to have birds. And it wasn't her fault, there was nothing wrong with her, in fact she was a very pretty girl, blonde hair, blue eyes, but it just wasn't right, her face didn't fit mine.

And I hadn't thought about Debbie in what seemed such a long time. But every time that I looked into Julie's twinkling blue eyes, I wished that they were green, and her fair hair may have flowed like a fountain down her back, but it just didn't smell right, not unpleasant, but I would forget the fragrance the moment I would turn my back. It didn't linger, float through my head, didn't wrap itself round my senses, like a blanket in my mind. Not like Debbie's had done, and that was it, she simply wasn't Debbie.

And I was sitting there, trying to muster up a show of enthusiasm for the evening, gazing idly across the rows of bowling lanes, spread out like fields of corn. People watching, the blokes taking it all too seriously, all deep breaths and concentration, tiptoeing on the spot, bowling ball cradled close to their chests as if they were holding a baby. And the girls, more light-hearted, laughing at the finger hole face, giggling as they struggled to pick the thing up, as if it were a cannon ball.

And a voice dragged me back. 'Still daydreaming I see, Johnny.'

I smiled at the sight of her familiar face, genuinely pleased to see her. I had forgotten what a kind face Jenny Hargreaves had. 'All right, Jen?'

They were occupying the lane next to ours, Jenny and some of the gimpy kids from school, and I hadn't even noticed them. Or maybe I had, but it hadn't really registered, because that's where I expected them to be, at the desk next to me, familiar faces surrounding me, subconscious unable to leave the classroom, mind in permanent detention.

And we chatted easily, about friends, and what we had been up to, stuff like that. And I wanted to ask her about Debbie, did she still see her? What was she doing now? But I couldn't bring myself to, scared of what I might hear I guess.

And I looked over her shoulder, as the conversation began to dry up, touching the rocks of awkwardness, nothing left to say. 'Alright?' I nodded to a couple of the gimpy ones that I recognised from school. And they both looked at me as if I had two heads or something. And I couldn't blame them I suppose, for as far as I could remember I had spent my entire school days without uttering a single word to them.

And I had to stop myself from laughing, stifle the smile that I could feel creeping from the corners of my mouth, didn't want my face to betray what I had been thinking. I kept imagining Billy, what he would have made of me chatting away with the likes of the gimpy kids. And they were soon in full flight, after they had overcome the initial shock, chatting away as if I were an old friend. And they seemed to know an awful lot about me, considering. About my football and stuff, and they remembered things that I had completely forgotten. Like back in the third year, for instance, and me, Billy and a few of the others throwing rubbers at the back of their heads. Although I *did* remember the time Billy flushed one of their heads down the toilet, even though I pretended that I didn't.

But they didn't seem to care, weren't after belated apologies or anything, wondering if the real world had washed away the mask of immaturity that we had worn like war paint. They seemed to accept it all, as if they didn't have the right to take offence. The price paid for being one of the clever kids. And the irony of the whole thing hit me, bowled me over like the flying skittles at the end of the shiny wooden lanes. These were the sort of boys who had always seemed to be more of a threat than the kids we would fight or play football against, because we hadn't understood them, we were frightened of their ability to learn. But really it had been jealousy. And seeing them then, hovering around me, like I was someone worthwhile, special even, made me realise that they had been jealous of the likes of me!

And they had nothing to talk about apart from school, nothing to say, because it was all that they knew. But it wasn't a place that I recognised now, a school where boys like these ruled the roost, sixth formers, top of the pile. And there they were, twittering on about how great it was not to have to wear school uniforms now and that I'd never guess what, old Mr Brown had left his wife for Miss Hall, and so on. Empty, trivial things, spoken in the language of a child, things that meant nothing to me now, didn't even mean much when I had been a part of it all.

Jenny and I shared a look, stealing a glance as her friends twittered on, and she rolled her eyes as if to say *sorry*. But she had nothing to be apologetic about, it was all quite flattering in a strange, distorted kind of way. But it was certainly good to see her, especially then, with me feeling so lost and out of place. Just then Julie appeared behind me and laid both hands, one on top of the other, upon my shoulder. But I felt no affection in her touch, if anything it irritated me.

'So,' she chirped, 'are you going to introduce me, John?' And before I had a chance to answer, she held her hand out across the back of the seat as if she were offering Jen the hand of royalty. 'Hi.' She smiled a little too falsely. 'I'm Julie… John's *girlfriend*.'

Jenny accepted her hand with the good grace and manners that she had been bred with. 'Hello,' she nodded, 'Jenny… Johnny and I were at school together,' and I caught her eye again and there was something in it. Her whole face was a comfort, a buoy of reliability and reassurance bobbing gently in a vast sea that, as the night unfolded, was gradually dragging me out of my depth. And she could see that I was struggling, was pleased for me but could tell that I didn't belong.

CHAPTER NINE

March 1978

It was raining the night that I arrived home on that fateful evening. For ages I thought that would be the breaking point, the weight of circumstances that would finally pull Dave down. But I was wrong.

I think I knew that something wasn't right, even as I sat on the bus. Could sense the prickling begin in the calves of my legs, anxiety boiling, could feel the itching burning away at my arm. I pressed my face against the window of the bus, peering out into the gloom, hands shutting out the light. But there was nothing to see but the inky blackness of winter; I couldn't even make out the trains, identifiable only by their windows, tiny boxes of light flashing by like tracer fire in the night. And it was as if it were there, staring me in the face, the second that I stepped off the bus, as plain as day, but I couldn't see it, not through the curtain of rain that fell, draping itself around me, leaving my senses dull, overcast.

But as I darted across the main road, as it shimmered like black ice in the glare of the car headlights, the feeling grew stronger. And I knew that it was going to be something terrible, something disastrous. And as I turned the corner I saw the blue light flashing, reflected off the windows from the houses opposite, blinking in the puddles on the road.

The police car was parked about halfway up the street. But even from where I stood I could tell that it hadn't stopped outside my house. I knew how many lampposts there were from my house to the main road, knew every crack in the pavement, the exact place where the tarmac had been re-laid along the pavement, like a scar across flesh, the result of the burst water pipes two years ago. And then I had counted eight street lamps between me and to the blue light: Dave's house.

I couldn't remember the last time Dave had looked so much like a child to me. Hands buried deep in the pockets of his baggy black pegs, nodding obediently at the policeman towering above him, who had placed his giant hand upon Dave's shoulder, comforting him.

Despite the fading rain I could still feel the chill of the evening, could still feel the warmth irritating the hairs on my arms and legs, nervous sweat prickling the pores of my skin, like brushing against the needles of a Christmas tree. It felt as if I were moving in slow motion, like the dreams that drag you down, running in a kind of sea of glue.

They turned towards me as I appeared. 'Johnny...' Dave smiled that thin, easy smile, but there was nothing behind it, an empty, hollow smile, as if it had been painted on the face of a shop dummy.

'Okay then, David,' the policeman had said, happy now to leave him and go about his business, now that Dave was in the company of someone he obviously knew. 'Now you're sure there's nothing that you need inside, before I lock the place up?' asked the policeman.

'No, no... ever was,' murmured Dave.

'Well we'll be in touch soon.' And as he turned to rejoin the other uniforms hovering up and down the path of Dave's house, he turned to me and said, 'Look after him, son.'

We stood there, the two of us, outside Dave's front gate, shrouded by the gloom of early evening, like a thousand times before, only it wasn't really, not like anything that had ever gone before.

'What the hell's going on, Dave?' I gasped.

His voice was a whisper, barely audible. 'It's Mum,' he gazed back at the house, his eyes as black as night, 'she's dead.'

We sat opposite each other, in our usual seats, as Lui arrived with two steaming cups of tea. He had been all ready to shut for the day and was in the middle of mopping the floor when the wind and rain had swept us through the door.

'Boys! For me it is nice to see you,' he'd exclaimed. It had been a few weeks since I had been in, and as far as I knew Dave's last visit had been before Christmas, that odd time when we had exchanged the good news about our future prospects. But Lui had known that something was up the minute he had seen our faces. Heaven knows what we had looked like, I felt sick from the shock, and Dave hadn't even seemed to realise where we were, hadn't said a word or even looked up, had just drifted over to his chair, on a kind of auto-pilot, dripping with more than just the rain, emotionally drenched through, and his complexion had turned paler than usual, like cold ashes.

We stared out the window, nursing our teacups in silence, watching the car headlights swimming by, distorted by the steam on one side of the window and the rain on the other, as if the world outside was underwater. I didn't know what to say, didn't want to push him; I would let him tell me in his own time. I had these visions running through my head, of his old man finally returning, angry and bitter, blaming her for the circumstances of his life, and standing there towering above her in between her faded armchair and the TV.

Unsteady and fuelled by drink, turning the tables on the situation, the accuser not the accused. And perhaps he had gone too far this time, had maybe hit her too hard or given her an extra slap for good measure.

I sipped my tea and didn't say a word as Dave, lost in his own world, began to trace the arcs wiped across the table from Lui's cloth with his finger, over and over like a painting of rolling fields. I could see him trying to organise the mess in his head, shuffle the facts around into some kind of order before he began. He pulled a packet of cigarettes and a box of matches from his trouser pockets and lit one up as if it were the most natural thing in the world for him to have done. I looked over to where Lui was standing behind his counter, scrubbing his grill clean. And I could tell he was thinking the same thing as me, *Since when did he start smoking?* But it was just another side to him that I hadn't seen before, another link in the chain that had dragged him from his roots... from me.

I watched Dave pull deep from his cigarette and return to the abyss outside the window, and for a moment, as I waited for Dave to collect himself, I found myself thinking of the time beneath the viaducts when we had each tried, and failed, to start smoking. Dave had tried far less than any of us, three of four puffs at the most before he had thrown it away in disgust.

'Why the fuck do I wanna look like my old man anyway?' he had said, face all wrinkled. And you hardly ever heard Dave swear, but the realisation of what he was trying to do, the impression he was trying to create by smoking, suddenly hit him. And if ever there was an excuse to give up before you had even started, then Dave had found it.

And there we were, sitting in Lui's, the smell of bacon and eggs still lingering, long after the grills had been turned off. The shiny, plastic chairs moulded against the backs of our legs, squeaking with every move that we made, condensation slowly clouding up the rattling window like an early morning mist. Surrounded by everything that we had ever known, as familiar and comforting as the view from your own toilet seat or the smell of your mum's washing. And yet there was Dave, flicking ash, nonchalantly, as if it were five or six years earlier, and he was simply flicking screwed up backs of peeled football stickers into the plastic Pepsi ashtray.

He looked up and caught my eye, read my mind, as usual, and said, 'I'll tell you about it later,' and, I felt quite guilty for even letting my surprise show, it hardly seemed important then, not in the great scheme of things, not with his mum lying dead in the back of some ambulance; the worst kind of ambulance, one that wasn't in a rush to get anywhere. That would always stay with me, that thought. Whenever I saw an ambulance driving by at a regular speed, no flashing lights or sirens wailing, I would always think that it was carrying a dead body, someone that they hadn't managed to save. For what was the point of tearing through the streets for a dead person?

I looked at him, gazing back out into the rain. At this mass of contradictions, calm, unflustered Dave, who should have been crying on my shoulder or into his cup of tea, a total wreck trying to hold himself together. If you didn't know him you would have thought that he was in a state of shock, that it hadn't sunk in yet, the sudden loss of his mother. Or that maybe he was just some cruel seventeen year old thug, a yob who didn't give a toss.

But it wasn't that, I knew it wasn't that, he cared, you could see it, the hurt chasing away the life in his eyes. It was just how Dave dealt with things, calm and collected. But he was suppressing *something*, I could see him struggling to keep it in, he was betrayed a little by the jutting of his jaw, by the depths of his sighs. And he continued to stare out into the night, as if he could see something, something that I couldn't, beyond the rain, on the other side of the darkness.

And it was anger, seething inside of him. And when he spoke it was through clenched teeth, as if he could no longer hold it in and it was escaping, as potent as gas leaking through a burst pipe.

' I don't know how many times I told her... take them like the doctor told you, as prescribed... but she would pop them in her mouth like bloody Smarties... wash them down with whatever... tea, coffee... gin mostly.'

Apparently they had thought it had been suicide at first, an overdose. But it was the little things, there had been no note, a pie still in the oven, a lit cigarette in the ashtray left untouched, allowed to burn down to the filter. None of these added up to suicide.

'You thought that it was *him*, didn't you?' Dave asked. I didn't answer, simply shrugged. It wasn't like I had offended him, I couldn't insult his dad in Dave's eyes, he didn't have a sense of loyalty buried deep inside, just an empty space where a father should have been. He shook his head as he ground his cigarette into the ashtray like an old hand. 'No,' he grimaced. 'Had thought something, but not *hi*m.' I didn't know what to say to that, simply put it down to the confusion of the evening.

'I know you're a big footballer and that now, but do you fancy a drink?' he asked. And that thin, inoffensive smile touched the corners of his mouth.

Mum was up by the time I finally got home. I knew that she would be. I hadn't phoned her at work to tell her that I would be late, that I wouldn't be home for the dinner that she would have left for me. And that wasn't like me at all, I would get the piss taken out of me a lot for that, but I didn't care, I would always phone her, after all she never stopped me. I had just assumed that she would know where I was, that it went without saying. But as I shut the front door behind me it all of a sudden occurred to me that maybe she didn't even know, that she might well have missed the sordid pantomime that had been played out earlier for the whole street. That when she would have arrived home, half-dead from her shift at the hospital, everything would have seemed just the same as before, just as cold and damp as every other night.

There certainly hadn't been a sign of the night's activities when I had walked home from the station after leaving Dave to catch the last train back into town. Not a hint of what had gone on before.

The street was as dull and unassuming as usual, the sinister events from earlier hidden in the shadows of the night, behind the peeling front doors and the twitching drawn curtains. There were no flashing lights, no distorted voices rumbling from police car radios. The pavements were empty, no tiny groups of housewives huddled together, arms crossed beneath their breasts, twittering like hungry birds in each other's ears. There was nothing but the same cars, dotted along the road, parked in the same places. And the puddles left by the passing rain, shining as smooth as glass, motionless upon the slick black street, everything like a still from a film.

But the look upon her face, as she sat there, expectant and fraught with anticipation for my return, at the tiny kitchen table, still in her uniform, teapot in front of her, told me that she already knew. And she never sat down, never did a thing, didn't even make the tea, until she had shed the skin of work, peeled off the nurse's uniform, had always said that she couldn't stand to traipse the smell of the hospital around the house.

'John love! There you are… You okay? How's Dave?'

'Alright.' I shrugged, didn't know what else to say, what could I say? I stood by the sink, staring out the window into the night and saw nothing but my own sad-looking reflection staring back at me from the glass. I seemed to have aged since the morning, but maybe it was just the shadows playing tricks, shading in the contours of my face, the rings around my eyes. I shook my head, tried to dislodge the image from my mind, and pulled the yellow flowered curtains. Mum turned round, I could sense her staring at me, waiting for me to continue. But I didn't feel like talking, I was tired, drained, and my head ached from the beer. I knew she wouldn't push, that she was only concerned, that she must have been going spare with worry, so I poured myself a cup of tea and pulled up a chair. 'You know, Dave,' I said. 'Doesn't show his feelings either way… he's cut up, but he's all right… I mean, it's not like they were that close or anything.'

Mum frowned into her teacup. I had thought she was going to say something, but she obviously thought better of it, and I was glad, because I realised how cruel it must have sounded, unfair. I mean, it had never been what you could call a normal mother and son relationship, couldn't possibly be with a mum like Dave's. It was more of a role reversal, with Dave looking after her. For she had seemed to find everything simply exhausting, even the little things in life had appeared monumental to her. Sometimes she hadn't even got out of bed. And when I would knock for Dave on the way to school, it would wake him, and then we would be later than late. Because, on those days, he wouldn't leave until he had taken her a cup of tea and maybe a bit of toast, if she was up to it, always had to make sure that she was okay, that she hadn't sunk too low. So it had always been obvious to me that he had cared, that they both had, that the love was there, if only in glimpses, like blackened gold. But when life's that messed up, tipped on its head, back to front, the simplest things, like love and affection, aren't always easy to find; they're buried, like treasure, somewhere beneath the surface instead of bobbing along merrily, upon the waves of every day.

I could hear the faint sound of scratching coming from out the back, followed by a kind of cackling noise, almost like a firework fizzling out. I pulled open the curtains, ignoring the jaded face staring back at me, and cupped my hands against the window. I thought I could just make out the shape of something moving across the roof of the coal shed. I rattled my fingers against the glass and a pair of green eyes pierced the night, followed by more cackling and a kind of demented meowing. I unlocked the back door, pulled it open a fraction, just enough, and the chilly dampness chased the cat through the slim crack.

She made straight for Mum, brushing herself back and forth against her legs, but Mum didn't say a word, as if she hadn't even noticed. She would usually berate her light-heartedly, shoo her away, moan a little about the cat hairs left around the hem of her skirt or the foot of her trousers, like tidemarks around the bath. But Mum loved the cat, never settled if she wasn't in by the time she went to bed. She didn't even mention the trail of muddy paw prints left across the kitchen floor. Her mind was elsewhere, full of thoughts of Dave and his mum... his poor, sick, tragic mum.

And the more I thought about it, the more I thought it was just so typical of the woman. An accidental overdose, I could just see her, could just imagine it, shuffling around the house, stumbling upon a half empty bottle of pills, ones that she had forgotten to finish, or picking up the prescription, forgotten what they were even for, and taking two or three for good measure, to catch up on the time that she had missed taking them. And then she would be in her chair, a glass or two of gin perhaps, just to see her through the daunting prospect of the morning. Then there would be the pills that she *did* remember, and she'd let the gin chase them down too, just to take away the taste mind. But maybe she *hadn't* forgotten to take them, only thought she had. So she washed down a couple more, just to be on the safe side. And so on. After all, they were all there to help her, in one way or another. Even if she couldn't remember what was what, where was the harm?

Turns out one of the neighbours had found her in the end. Well, had *seen* her, and then called the police. After knocking for nearly an hour on the front door and finally, in frustration, against the front window, and apparently there she had been, the shape of her lifeless body, through the camouflage of the net curtains, moulded into her armchair. I could picture it so clearly, had played out the scene countless times myself before. And Elvis had been playing of course, voice rumbling like thunder inside, permeating through the walls, driving the neighbours mad.

And of course Mum had known. She told me, as we sat in the kitchen, the cold night air still swirling around our feet, bouncing off the linoleum floor, freezing the metal legs of the table, touching us like an invisible mist. She told me that she had been fully aware that the day would one day come when the body of someone she knew would come her way, that it was inevitable, part of the job. But she saw dead people every day, had had patients die in her arms before, seen them slip away from her as they had tried desperately to hold on, had held the hands of old ladies as they had taken their final breath. And yet, she had somehow managed to leave it all behind, within the sterilised wards and behind the swing doors of the hospital. It hadn't been easy, at first it used to cling to the soles of her shoes like chewing gum, hang on to the tail of her coat, weighing her down. Like so many things in life I could find a comparison with football, likened it to doing sprints at training. Pulled back by the old car tyres tied on a length of rope around our waists. But Mum had learnt to avoid it all now, built up a kind of immunity, never quite cured, but able to deal with it. But then Dave's mum had arrived, and she couldn't get over the shock of her lying on the stretcher, being lifted from the ambulance, her face as still and cold as ice. And the thing that had surprised her so much, that had stuck with her was how she had looked. Dead people, she said, hold a certain kind of peacefulness about them, strange but she couldn't explain it. But the face of Dave's mum had kept that pained, confused expression, as if the trials of her life still haunted her, and had followed her into death.

I couldn't sleep that night, I lay in my bed staring around the room for nearly three hours before I finally gave up, there was nothing there in the pictures and pin-ups, nothing to pull me into a story or to lead me into sleep. From Banks, Shilton, Corrigan, and Clemence, dreams of playing for England to fantasies of Debbie Harry and the sister in *The Dukes of Hazard* and all the things that we could do together, and in my stories being an innocent teenager was never a problem, never mattered. But it was no use, nothing took me to where I wanted to be, into the warm, cosy place that rocked me gently, slowly into the waters of sleep. I couldn't stay with anything for long enough, kept losing the thread of things, and found myself, inevitably, returning to the night's events, and back to Dave.

A pint and a half had passed between us before Dave had even broached the subject of his mum. It had been slow in the Crown and Sceptre, a typical mid-week night, and apart from a couple of local punks playing pool and drinking cider, there had been no one anywhere near our age. The rest of the punters were old enough to be our grandparents. Retired folk, regulars, sat playing dominoes or throwing darts. The landlord had looked twice at us when we had ordered our first pint. He knew us, knew our age, had a son in the year below us. At first I had thought he was going to refuse to serve us, tell us that we were taking the piss, coming in on a weekday when it was so quiet and all and we couldn't be overlooked. But he had just smiled and said that he hadn't seen the pair of us in a while. Dave had seen the apprehension that the landlord had seemed to show, and when we had sat down had smiled at me and whispered, 'Big time footballers… can open any doors.'

'Nah,' I said. 'Probably thought Bowie himself had walked in.'

And then we had just flipped empty small talk, like tiddly winks, across the table at one another. Hollow pieces of conversation marked "football, music, mates" and so on, barely scratching the surface of each before we flicked up another, chinks of our life, broken down into fragments; killing time until he was ready. We had supped our pints in between, the silence almost tangible. I had looked around; the bar seemed bigger than I remembered. Bare walls reaching up to a ceiling that seemed to go on forever, faded orange wallpaper, the colour of a peach, with darker patches betraying the original colour, dotted around where a few pictures and a mirror had once hung, before they had all been broken, smashed in fights. And then there was the bar; dark and defiant, curving round to the far wall. At the weekends it would be transformed, crammed toe to toe with youngsters, punks mostly. They would come from all over the borough. It had a good reputation, the Crown. Then finally Dave had said, as he folded another cigarette butt into the ashtray like a veteran, the way the old boys disposed of their roll ups,

'I couldn't have stayed Johnny.' And he had stared blankly into the mound of crushed filters before him, piled together like so many broken bodies in a mass grave, and had shook his head and exhaled a final stream of smoke. 'Not with him still there.'

'I know,' I'd replied. And it had sounded so pathetic, so lame. But it was true. I *did* know... knew that Dave would leave the minute that he could. Just hadn't realised that it would happen so soon, what with the music paper job coming out of the blue and all.

I had just felt so utterly useless; throughout our childhood we had always turned to Dave, the prudent one, who always saw things clearly, when the likes of me, Billy and Ketch simply couldn't, blinded by our immaturity. And he would come up with the answers, practical solutions that as kids we could make sense of.

And there was Dave, in need of support, and all that I could find to say had been 'I know'. I had searched desperately for something else to offer him. Some kind of assurance, to tell him that he mustn't blame himself, toss in a few pearls of wisdom of my own, instead of those empty topics of conversation that we had been juggling around. Tell him that he couldn't have been expected to watch over her twenty- four hours a day.

'I should have popped round... you know... seen if she was all right... that kind of thing.' I had wanted to absorb some of the guilt for him, wash it away, prevent any infection from settling in before it could take a hold, fester away and destroy his conscience.

Dave had smiled tentatively into the bottom of his glass. 'She wouldn't have even bothered to open the door, Johnny...you know that.'

'S'pose,' I'd muttered.

He'd leaned across the table on his elbows, head tucked into his shoulders, and almost whispered as if there had been someone who could overhear. 'I'm okay, Johnny... honest... I'll be all right.' And it was ridiculous that once again there was Dave looking out for me, pandering, to me, almost amused by my startling lack of comprehension. 'Why don't you go and get us a couple more beers while I put the jukebox on... and no Bowie... I promise.' And from anyone else it would have sounded belittling.

I had sighed, as if I were exhaling my own inadequacy. 'Do you think he'll mind,' I'd asked, motioning towards the landlord. He had been leaning across the bar, face buried in his hands, idly watching the two old boys playing darts. 'I mean, I don't wanna push it... him to think I'm taking the piss or something.'

'Don't worry about it,' smiled Dave, 'I got his son a couple of tickets for Siouxse and the Banshees the other week.'

But as we had trudged back through town and up to the train station he had touched on it again, trying to find traces of justification for what he had seemed to think was his own culpability. He had turned to me and asked, 'Do you remember what he did to me the day we did the *Aladdin Sane* cover?' And I could see how the question had sprung up, could follow the thread of his thoughts, for we had reached the church by then. And it had been the place where he had escaped to, had found solace in after his dad had chased him from the house, still swinging.

And he had pulled up in front of the uneven stone steps, leading to the uneven stone path, and had looked up at the matching grey church, followed its direction as it tapered away into the night, like a dagger to the sky. The whole place had always left me slightly cold, even the giant arched doors seemed sinister, and in the night time they were darker than ever, like the open mouth of some kind of furious, hungry animal. In the shadows of the night the whole place looked frightening, forbidding. The branches of the giant oak trees rustled like whispered voices, laughing, taunting us.

Even in the light of the day, to me, the church had always been clouded in a kind of mysterious aura, menacing almost. Despite the playful voices of children coming and going to school, resounding through the trees, bouncing off the great stone walls, or the rumbling from the constant stream of traffic that flowed in and out of town. In the midst of the everyday familiar sights and sounds, it still contained the ability to unnerve me, to seem out of place. And yet it had been there all the time, long before the oppressive concrete maze that wrapped itself around it now.

'Suppose the funeral will have to be here,' Dave had said morosely. 'I'll have to sort all that out... tomorrow I guess... maybe the day after.'

'I've never set foot in the place since that day,' I'd said, gazing up at the stained windows winking in the light from a street lamp. 'Dunno, just something about it,' I added with an involuntary shiver. Whether it had been from the cold or the thought of the church, I hadn't known. Dave had turned and almost seemed surprised to see me standing there, as if he'd been talking to himself, forgotten that I was there.

'I reckon he would have killed me if you hadn't stopped him,' he'd said, turning back to the church.

'I hardly stopped him,' I'd added neutrally.

'Well, you know... broken his *rhythm* then... still, I bet he nearly had a heart attack when he saw me,' Dave had smiled. And we had had a laugh about that, what his old man must have made of it all, coming home to find his son decorated in his wife's make-up, like some kind of bizarre clown.

'Best go.' He nodded in the direction of the clock, set just beneath the steeple, its face as black as coal, slightly raised off the ancient brickwork as if somewhere inside a giant finger had popped it out. 'Or I'll miss the last train… and the house is the last place I wanna spend the night.' Poor Dave, I'd thought. He couldn't even call it home.

That day kept coming back; I hadn't thought about it in such a long time and now it wouldn't leave the space in my mind, the empty chamber that I kept for all my "going to sleep" stories to flow into. I kept hearing the voice of Dave's dad, as deep and angry as thunder, resonating through my head, chasing away my dreams.

It had happened after school one afternoon, back in '73, the year that the album had been released, Bowie's *Aladdin Sane*. Dave and I had walked home together as usual, killing time and kicking empty coke cans down the road, our bags slung over our shoulders. And as Dave had swung back the gate to his house I had told him that I would be round in a bit, after dinner.

When he had answered the door I had actually stepped back in alarm, nearly falling off the step. I hadn't expected him to open the door so quick, had thought that I would have had to wait for a song break and then knock quickly again. For I could hear the ghostly sound of Bowie's voice meandering down the stairs from Dave's room, '*Oooh… We love Aladdin Sane…* ' But instead the door had been flung open, and there stood Dave, stripped to the waist, hair swept back, as though he had been standing in a wind tunnel. But it had been the make-up that had sent me reeling. A thick bolt of red lightning slashed across his face, a little smudged and crudely applied, but there had been no doubting the affect he had been after. It ran from the centre of his forehead, zigzagging across his right eye and the bridge of his nose and ended somewhere at the bottom of his cheek. I had stood there agog, mouth open, not knowing what to say.

'Come on!' he'd smiled, leaning out and pulling me in by the scruff of my collar.

'Good innit?' And he had opened his arms as if accepting applause. It had only been then that I'd noticed the attention to detail that he had shown, how he even had the black line separating the streak of lightning from its thin blue border. He had even tried to paint the little pool of water lying in the collarbone.

'Did you do that yourself?' I'd asked, still bewildered.

'Yup,' and he had run up the stairs into his bedroom, and before I had even thought of following him he had returned with a camera in his hand. 'I want you to take a picture... in here, the light's better,' and I'd followed him into the empty front room. I remember how strange the armchair had looked without his mum in the middle of it, sad almost.

'Where's your mum?'

'Must be out of fags, I suppose.' For she didn't leave the house very often, unless she had to, for something important, like running out of cigarettes. 'So we best hurry up... not that she'd be bothered I suppose... she never wears the stuff anyway.' He'd pushed the camera into my hands. 'With your back to the window.' He'd motioned for me to stand by the window. 'You need the light over your shoulder... I'll stand here... then we'll have the white background,' and he'd stood against the wall beside the armchair and closed his eyes, mimicking Bowie's pose from the cover of *Aladdin Sane*. I hadn't even bothered to ask how he knew things like that, needing your back to the light, it was just the kind of thing that Dave knew, grown-up stuff. I'd fumbled with the camera for a bit and then finally taken the picture. 'Take a couple, Johnny... knowing you I'll have one of mum's chair... make sure it isn't in it by the way.' Then the moment I had finished the front door had opened, and we had both known that it wasn't his mum returning. The sound of his boots, stamping on the mat, as if he were kicking off the dirt, the heavy-handed slam of the door and the noise of the keys rattling as he dropped them into the glass ashtray next to the phone told us that it was his dad. And there had been nowhere for us to go, to run to, we had just stared at each other, resigned to the situation.

'DAVID!' His voice had boomed like a cannon up the stairs 'TURN THAT BLEEDIN' ROW OFF!' And of course there had been no response, and then he was in the doorway, had seemed to fill it, head scraping the frame. 'What the fu... ' astonishment turning to anger, the lines upon his face twisting like snakes, cutting deeper as they changed their course across his skin. He had looked at the camera in my hands then over at Dave, bare-chested, back against the wall, his mum's lipstick smeared across his face. 'What the fuck's goin' on? Where's your mother?'

'Nothing... we're just... ' he'd jumped on Dave's words.

'Oh Christ...You ain't gonna turn out to be a poof!'

'What!... no, no I'm just....' He'd cut him short again.

'It's him innit?' He'd spat, jabbing a thumb at the ceiling. Bowie's voice still flooded the whole house... "Panic in Detroit"... apt.

'Fuckin' freak show.' He had turned to me, and it seemed as if the whole of his eyes were black, couldn't see a trace of white, just two black stones shining like onyx. 'Go and turn this *shit* off,' he'd growled. And I had shot up the stairs two at a time, glad of the opportunity to dispose of the camera, throwing it in the bottom of Dave's wardrobe. And I hadn't messed about, hadn't bothered to carefully remove the needle, slip the record back into its protective sleeve whilst at pains to avoid touching the playing surface, like Dave would always do, had simply turned the power off and watched as the spinning orange label became a kind of musical whirlpool, dragging down the music, sucking it back into its core.

And then I had heard the banging and crashing of furniture, the old man's voice rumbling up through the floorboards. And I had quickly discovered that taking the stairs two at a time was easier going up than down. I was all over the place by the time I had reached the bottom, misjudged them completely and careered headfirst, past the front room on my left, and into the tiny coffee table, sending the phone and ashtray full of keys flying. I'd looked up, from where I knelt, and had seen Dave's dad bearing down on him.

'Make a laughing stock out of me, would you? Been too easy on you, that's what it bleedin' is.' And Dave had attempted to duck beneath him, but his dad had been too big, there had simply been too much of him, and he had fallen upon Dave like a giant cloak. For a moment they had stayed there, Dave scrabbling, like a trapped animal, arms and legs protruding, flailing beneath this dark mass trying to pin him down.

And I had thought to myself, this must be what it's like to have a father, to be part of a whole family, a family with no pieces missing. The only thing that I really knew about fatherhood was through the experiences of my close friends, from what I had seen of the man in front of me, trying to nail my best mate to the floor, and of Billy's dad. Or was this the norm? A parent's prerogative like scolding the dog or kicking the cat, were we really that bad? Vile children who turned decent folk into hostile monsters, like turning milk sour.

But I hadn't pondered it for long, hadn't had time, for the old man had jumped up then, back onto his hands and knees, shaking his hand as if he had been stung.

'You little bleeder!' he'd cried. 'You *bit* me!... Why I'll bleedin'... '

And as Dave had peeled himself off the floor and begun to struggle gingerly to his feet, his dad had hit him, had drawn his arm back across his chest and smashed the back of his giant hand up into Dave's face. It had sounded like a huge slap, amplified in the emptiness since the music had been washed away. Dave had been lifted off his feet, stumbled and ended up where he had started, pressed up against the wall with his dad bearing down on him.

And then he had closed in on him again, like a fog, cutting off his escape. And I had just launched myself at him, without thinking, only knew that I couldn't stand to see that again, for it might have only been a backhander, but he had certainly caught Dave with his knuckles, really connected, for I could already make out the lump forming above Dave's left eye. I often wondered if he had actually meant to hit him so hard. I had been aware that it wasn't unusual for him to give Dave a slap now and then, but nothing like that, not with the force that he had hit him that day. That had been in Billy's dad's league. But whether he had meant it or not, it seemed to get him in the mood, really get his blood up.

'Come 'ere...' he'd sneered as he moved menacingly forward.

'What the bleedin!'... ' he'd exclaimed as I hung round the back of his neck like a cape, legs flapping. I could almost taste the cigarettes and beer stale upon his breath, smell the unwashed hair, could feel the grease clammy against my cheek. And he hadn't even faltered slightly under my surprise attack, simply shrugged his giant shoulders as if he were shaking off a troublesome fly. And I had shot across the room and landed backwards upon the upturned armchair, as he had calmly smoothed the back of his head, reshaping his DA with the palms of his dirty great hands. And before he'd turned his attentions back to Dave he had glanced down at me, his eyes nothing but dark empty holes. But before he could take a step closer there had been a noise at the front door, the scratching sound of a key in the lock, the exhausted sigh as she struggled to push it open, the muffled sound of slippers skimming lightly across the matt, the faintest whiff of cigarette smoke. And that was all the chance that Dave had needed, that sliver of opportunity that had crept through the open door. And as his old man had turned in distraction, he had ducked through his shadow, swift as a bird, grabbing me by the shoulder on the way, and we had flown past the rake-like figure of his mum and out the front door.

It hadn't been until we had stopped running, until we had reached the end of our street by the main road, that I had even noticed that Dave still had no top on. When I'd caught my breath I took off my jumper and threw it across his shoulder. 'Cheers,' he'd panted.

'Park?' I said, nodding across the road towards our gap in the railings.

'Nuh,' and he'd turned towards town. 'Come on,' he'd said over his shoulder, and I had fallen in line beside him.

We had walked along in silence, Dave with his head to the floor, following his feet. I had assumed that we were heading for Lui's but couldn't imagine what he would make of the sight of Dave in his present state. But as I had made to cross over to the tiny parade of shops he had placed a hand upon my shoulder. 'Not like this,' he had said, waving a hand at his face, and he'd turned and walked through the gate and up the steps of the old church.

Dave pulled at the gnarled iron knocker and to my surprise the great oak door had opened without a sound. It had been deathly silent inside, perfectly still, like stepping into night. I had stuck close to Dave's side, my eyes adjusting slowly to the darkness, as we had crept along the nearside wall and slipped into a pew near the front of the church. The only light had been the weak daylight filtering through the stained glass windows, absorbing its strength, so that only watery droplets of light spilt upon the faded wooden floors. I had glanced over my shoulder; the church was empty, no one but me and Dave. I had felt a shiver run up through me, the length of my spine. I had hoped that someone else would be there, the sight of an old lady praying perhaps, something comforting, easy on the eye. For the place unnerved me.

The swelling over Dave's left eye had grown, risen like a loaf of bread. A long lick of his bouffant-styled hair had collapsed, fallen across his forehead and it would have just about finished him off if I had told him that it reminded me of his old man, of that pathetic-looking kiss curl that he would pull down from his greased back hair. 'Ugh! You've gotta get that looked at, it's getting bigger.' It had turned my stomach to look at it. I had whispered the words even though we were alone, as if we had been at school, hushed voices at the back of the classroom. It had been so quiet that it seemed to almost hum, and I had been afraid that the sound of my voice would crack the silence like glass. It hadn't seemed possible that beyond the heavy stone wall, less than a hundred yards away, cars, lorries and buses flowed in and out of town, that passers by pounded up and down the pavements, the thick knot of suburbia choking the life out of the day. It had all seemed another world away.

My senses had seemed heightened by the unfamiliar change in surroundings. I was suddenly aware of the scent rising from the lines of wooden pews, it seemed to be coming from somewhere deep down in the grain, as if the wood itself were breathing, could smell the musty odour of the well-worn prayer books. Dave gingerly touched the lump above his eye. ' Nuh... bit of ice will sort it out.' He must have felt the lock of hair brushing against his head, and had felt blindly above the swelling and tried to replace it, but it had fallen limply back upon his forehead. 'Oh well,' he'd smiled 'Did you get one? A picture?' he'd asked.

'What... oh yeah, just the one though, threw the camera in your wardrobe.'

'Better come out.' He'd smiled again 'Don't wanna have to go through that again.' And I had been struck by his unshakeable optimism, he was trying to make light of it all. I had still been in a kind of dumb shock. It had all happened so quickly, I'd been transported to a place that I had never been before and was now surrounded by the eerie peacefulness of the church, drowning in a sea of silence with my best mate beaten and painted like a picture cover. And yet, less than an hour before, I had been sitting in front of the telly, dinner on my lap watching Dougal hover through the endless field of coloured flowers like a demented mop while Dillon the rabbit had struggled to stay awake.

I had shaken my head, tried to blow away the silence that was threatening to pull me down. It had hung heavy like a rock in the pit of my stomach. I had searched desperately for something to say, anything to fill the void, to stop me from listening to the thumping resonating from deep in my chest. 'How'd you get your hair like that anyway?'

'Soap' Dave had answered, as he thumbed idly through a prayer book. 'And Mum's hairdryer,' he'd smiled. 'Suppose I better wash this lot off,' he'd sighed as he replaced the book.

I had looked around, taken in the kaleidoscope of arched stained glass windows, the green border with gold leaves that ran horizontally around the walls, like a Christmas bow. And, of course, Jesus, upon the cross that hung like a giant medallion from the ceiling. His head hanging to one side, crown of thorns perched upon his head, blood seeping through the palms of his hands and running from his feet. And I had thought of Miss Gregg, the religious education teacher. Saw her standing in front of her desk, never sitting, straight and erect as if she had a plank of wood slipped down her back. I could see the gold crucifix dangling beneath her throat, the chain always tucked beneath her cosy woollen polar necks, resting delicately above the valley of her breasts, swaying slightly from side to side as she walked, and for a brief moment I had felt that tingling feeling of innocence stir inside me. I could hear her voice, sharp and piercing as nails, passionate, as she read from the Bible, explaining to us of the life of Jesus Christ. I remembered how I would watch her, study her, wish I was older, and then dismiss it all, turn my mind off and simply blank it out. And as I had sat there in the church, feeling open and vulnerable, I wondered if I would do the same with the day's events, dismiss them all, allow my mind to malfunction as before. As a child I learnt to become selective, sift out the crap, the things that didn't sit well. I remember how the story of the crucifixion more than upset me. What had really disturbed me had been the cruelty, but more than that, what had seemed the casual acceptance of it all. That haunted me.

'Won't be a minute,' Dave had said, pulling himself to his feet.

'Wh… where you going?' I'd stammered, uncomfortable at the thought of sitting alone in the church.

'To wash this lot off.' He had caught the tension in my voice and smiled at me, motioning towards the crucifix. 'It's all right… he's not real.'

I had ignored him, as it suddenly occurred to me, 'Where?'

'There's a bog round the back, behind the organ.'

'How do you know… you been 'ere before?'

'Once or twice,' he'd replied, squeezing past my legs and out into the aisle. 'You know… ' He'd shrugged his shoulders as if it was no big deal, had resigned himself to the fact long ago, and muttered, 'Whenever he's at home basically.'

CHAPTER TEN

April 1978

The cat hopped onto the bed, cackling for attention, searching for a warm place to spend the night, just as sleep had begun to lap slowly over my senses like a creeping tide. I clicked my tongue against the roof of my mouth and scratched her roughly between the ears. She didn't have a name, was just the cat. Mum had come up with suggestion after suggestion, all of which had been just too sissy for a young boy to even contemplate. She would suddenly appear, like a magician whenever I was in the house, in front of the telly usually, or she'd poke her head round my bedroom door, and conjure up these ludicrously girlie names: *Holly, Daisy, Gemma, Bella...Whiskers.'* And I would wrinkle my nose in disgust and carry on with what I was doing. Finally she had had to have a name of some description, for the veterinary records, after she had cut her front paw open on an old tuna tin that she had carried in from the alley. So I had come up with Harvey. Mum had thought it odd for a girl cat, thought it was just me being awkward but she had quite liked it nonetheless. Said that it was "quaint". I never did tell her that it was after the Leeds United keeper David Harvey whose picture I had on my wall.

I looked up at the cat's namesake, wedged in between pictures of Gordon Banks and Ray Clemence. I didn't really support a team as such, just goalkeepers. I mean, I had this thing for Fulham, but it was the keepers that I was interested in. Whenever someone would talk of a team, of a football club, it was always their goalkeeper that sprung to mind, that represented them in my head. I had learnt my geography by them, had this map of the country in my head, with tiny green shirts dotted all over, like drawing pins. Birmingham – Latchford, Derby – Moseley, Leicester… that would be Wallington, and so on. And with the images back where they belonged, my thoughts found their way back to football and to the coming Saturday, and my next game, my debut in the reserves. I hadn't mentioned it to anyone yet, not even Mum. And how could I have even thought about telling Dave. 'Sorry about your mum, but guess what, good news, I'm playing for the "ressies" on Saturday!' It hardly seemed important.

There had been a chance, a window of opportunity, to tell him about the game, the biggest of my career. Outside the train station, at the end of the evening, with the rain still visible in the half-light, swirling effortlessly like sea-spray, not even heavy enough to fall. We had stood with our hands buried deep in our pockets, not really knowing how to say goodbye, just as if it were any other old day.

'What you doin' Saturday?' he'd asked.

A chink of light… but I hadn't stepped through it, hadn't answered straight away, just puffed out my cheeks as if the words were all stored there, not being able to find their way out.

'After football I mean,' said Dave, replying to his own question, assuming that I would have an ordinary match for the youth team. 'Come up… stay… for the weekend, we'll have a few beers… do those other Bowie picture covers, yeah!' He smiled at the thought. '*Young Americans,*' now that you know I smoke, *Stationtostation*… God knows how!…And *Low*…yeah, we gotta do *Low*… while I still look so thin and pasty.'

And I could see that this was how I could finally feel of some use to him, that doing the covers, with him posing like Bowie and me taking the pictures, just like when we were kids, when bad things like savage beatings and death had no part in our intrinsic little worlds, would help to get him through the weekend, take his mind of his mum lying in a steel drawer down at the morgue. Because when you removed all the baggage, stripped away all the clutter, the people, places, the pubs, even the music and the football; it was just us. Players and props might change, but we were both there, painted on the backdrop of every scene of our lives. He had always wanted to recreate all of Bowie's album covers, have his own portfolio, we'd never thought anything of it, just part of what made Dave Dave, his imagination always racing ahead of him, like trying to step on your shadow.

'We'll go down by the river near where I work,' he'd said, warming to the theme now, 'I'll show you around, and there's loads of waste ground about… empty warehouses, factories, docks, that kind of stuff… the sunsets are something else there, over the Thames… perfect for the *Low* cover.'

I could feel the alcohol ringing in my ears now, could hear the humming of my own voice, hollow in my head.

'All right,' I smiled. 'Great.'

'Made it then?' remarked Dave as I stepped into his flat and dropped my kitbag unceremoniously in the doorway. He had a way of making his words smile, slip from his mouth with the minimum of fuss, as smooth as silk, no edge or cynicism attached to them. You couldn't help but take to him, there was something in the air around him that just seemed to ease the atmosphere. He was different now, since *The Kick In*. There was no doubting it, but that calming exterior still lingered, admittedly not always as obvious as before, but there nonetheless.

'You try walking through London with that thing!' I exclaimed, pointing at my bag as if it were something offensive. It was a good deal heavier than it had been when I had left home that morning. My boots and gloves had been caked in mud, so much so that I couldn't even find my laces when I had attempted to take them off. So I had just kicked them off and thrown them in one of the washbasins to soak and left them to turn the water into a kind of sick-coloured soup. I had taken my gloves in the team bath with me, given them a good scrub, scraping the mud from all the little raised squares that covered the palms like a grid reference.

And then they had been wrapped in my towel, dripping wet, and by the time I had turned into Baker Street, it had felt as if I were carrying a cannon ball in the corner of my kitbag.

'How'd you get on?' he asked, shutting the door and leading the way down the narrow corridor and into the front room.

'Won… 2-0,' I said matter-of-factly

'Play well?'

'Yeah… all right s'pose… looks a bit different,' I said, trying to steer the conversation away from football.

The room had a more homely feeling than I remembered, it looked "lived in" now, there was evidence of the individuals. A pile of papers and magazines were stacked either side of one of the armchairs, on the other a thick glass ashtray balanced on the square arm rest, a well thumbed paperback next to it. The old sofa appeared as decrepit and uncomfortable as before, but the crumpled newspapers strewn across the pillows for some reason made it seem more inviting. The walls now boasted a few posters. Just one on each side, but they were big ones. The kind you find plastered across empty shop windows and bordered off building sites. Flyers promoting concerts, gigs, live bands: The Clash, Siouxse and the Banshees and Roxy Music. And the other one was advertising an album release, some hippie, head banging group. It all conspired to make the place seem smaller, certainly more cluttered, but it had character to it now, a warmth that hadn't been present on my only other visit. Or perhaps that was it. Simply the fact that I had been there before, somewhere safe, made it seem more appealing.

'Where did you get the posters?' I asked

'The lads get them from work… record companies, gig venues, that kind of thing.'

'Still… *Roxy Music!*' I remarked in mock disgust.

'The trouble with you is, you're musically blinkered,' Dave said, pretending to be all high and mighty. 'Don't listen to anything other than what the radio feeds you… unless of course, I educate you.' And he was only joking, imitating the teachers, all condescending and belittling, but, as he well knew, it was all true. Anything different, anything slightly less commercial that I listened to would have come from Dave. Hours spent lying in his bedroom listening to his records whilst thumbing idly through an old football annual. 'Who's this?' And after a while it would usually grow on me, I would find that it would be inexplicably playing in my head a few days later, as if the red "record" button in my mind had secretly taped it.

It had rained all night, but not at all that afternoon. I had thought I felt a few drops halfway through the second half, about the same time that I had saved the penalty, but it must have been in my mind. And it had turned out to be a warm evening, the promise of summer in the air. Feeble-looking daffodils stood almost apologetically around the foot of the ancient trees that stood like great leaders in the grounds of the tenement blocks. Tiny splashes of nature landing in the greyness of the city, like wayward raindrops.

London didn't sleep. The streets were still crowded with an eclectic mix of people. Groups of boys and girls, laughing, singing, arms wrapped around each other as they flitted from one bar to another. Foreigners, tourists, rucksacks huddled on their backs like small children. And then there were all the "weirdos", the homeless, the kind of people you would cross the road to avoid, but up here, in town, no one took any notice of anyone. Anything and anyone goes.

Dave took me to a tiny hideaway of a pub, no more than a

broom cupboard, down a side alley. The bar could house no more than three or four people at a time. A far cry from the huge goldfish bowls that we were used to back home, the open bar rooms with their high ceilings and long sweeping bars. A dozen people and the place would be crowded, and Dave seemed to know them all, at least enough to say hello or nod an acknowledgment to.

'Your local then...*Old man,*' I whispered, looking round at the clientele, which consisted solely of men; not one, I reckoned, seemed younger than fifty odd. They sat along the dark red walls, staring into space, lost in their own worlds, or huddled round the tiny circular tables, in twos or occasionally threes, conversation as light as drizzle.

'It's just good to come here every now and then... away from the crowds.' Dave shrugged. 'Funny thing is, I've found myself in here more and more lately,' he reflected, scratching the back of his orange hair. The roots were growing through now, betraying his natural brown.

'Thought you liked the hustle and bustle of it all up here?' I asked.

'Yeah I do, but I thought you might appreciate a quiet drink away from the screaming hordes now that you're a top footballer... With a reserve match under your belt!' I looked up from my pint in amazement. 'Well... you gonna tell me all about it or what?'

So I told him, about the match and about my penalty save. I mean, for a keeper it is the equivalent of scoring a goal.

Afterwards, back in the warmth of the changing rooms, amidst the rising steam from the bath, the whole team had congratulated me. I had just sat there, grinning like a fool, gazing at the orange glow from the older players' cigarettes, which lit up through the mist like ships lanterns, whenever they took a drag. 'Great save, Johnny.' The younger lads had slapped me on the back or given me a playful thump on the arm. While the older players, the ones

I didn't really know, had nodded their approval or ruffled my hair on the way past. In truth it hadn't been a particularly good penalty, probably looked a lot better than it actually was. I always favoured my left side, there was no scientific reason why, I just reasoned that unless I was going to wait and see where the kicker would put the ball and then try and save it, which I didn't fancy my chances of at all, I might as well stick to one side, figuring that I would guess correctly a good percentage of the time. And the lad had opted for that side, his right, my left, had sacrificed power for accuracy, enabling me to stretch out and tip it round the post for a corner.

'How the hell did you know?' I asked, unable to understand how he had found out. But, of course, Billy had told him, had called Dave up the day after I had gone down to The Falcon to find him, which of course had been the day directly after it had all happened, when I had found Dave standing outside his house with the policeman, the blue light flashing like a silent, high-pitched scream piercing the night.

My mind flashed back to that night, I hadn't even bothered to try Billy at home, up on the seventh floor of the yellow tower block. At the end of town stood three ugly blocks of flats, one with yellow squares beneath the tiny balconies, one with red, the other green. Designed, I suppose, to add colour to the grimmest part of town, the very soul of the high rise hell that was sixties suburbia. But from a distance it looked as if a rainbow had melted away in the rain and dripped down the face of each building.

Instead, I had made straight for The Falcon, the pub at the end of the high street, with the three tower blocks looming menacingly overhead. I had hurried past Lui's, had resisted the urge to look over in case Lui had caught my eye and I would feel obliged, duty bound, to pop in. And it was nothing against Lui, I knew that he would mean well, but I couldn't face the questions, the explaining, it was going to bad enough having to tell Billy.

But the fat landlord at The Falcon hadn't seen him yet, although he was sure that he would later on. He mentioned that some of the lads from the pub football team were actually talking of doing a bit of training over on the recreation ground now that the clocks had gone forward and all. 'Don't suppose that it will amount to more than a kick about,' he had scoffed, downing the remains of his pint in one long swallow. It had looked so small in his hand, fat fingers wrapped round it like raw sausages.

I had never liked The Falcon, even when it had been one of the only pubs where the landlord would let us in, not seeming to give a toss whether we were under age or not. There was a feeling of hostility that was almost palpable. A typical estate pub frequented by no one but regulars, locals from the high rises and the tenements that lurked in their shadows. Sinister-looking men had sat, hunched inside their donkey jackets, along the bar, greasy hair and scars, something close to wickedness hovering in their eyes. The whole place had been dimly lit in a kind of orange hue, as if the light bulbs were fading. In normal circumstances, I would never have dreamt of going in there without Billy. Everyone around knew Billy, either because of his own, flourishing reputation or because of his old man's.

The recreation ground was no more than a patch of bare ground lying behind the tower blocks, about half the size of a football pitch, with a goal at only one end. It looked as if it had been constructed from old scaffold poles screwed together. For the other end The Falcon pub team had improvised with a traffic cone and an upturned shopping trolley with no wheels.

Thankfully Billy had seen me coming, as I stepped over the trodden down fencing and across the long since functional playground. There seemed something terribly sad, macabre even, about a child's desecrated playground. As if life couldn't wait for the young to grow up, it seeped into their world, polluting it like oil across the sea.

Bricks, empty beer cans and the odd dried up glue bag, even an old shoe, littered the ground. Frames, without any swings hanging, stood starkly like the skeleton remains of an old shipwreck, all traces of the innocuous days of childhood washed away.

I could see the faces of two or three of Billy's team-mates; Falcon regulars all of them. Looking over at me, wondering who the hell I was, could feel the heat of their stares, incandescent across the wasteland.

'J!' Billy had called in surprise 'What the fuck you doin' ere?' Looking for a game? Southfields finally realised how shit you are!' He'd grinned.

But the look upon my face must have told him that something was up, that something was very bad, I couldn't disguise it, for how do you disguise death?

And as he had stood, one hand resting upon his hip, the other ruffling his spiky blonde mop, I had seen the smile slip from his face, imagined it, that stupid, infectious grin of his dropping like a stone, past his scuffed knees, bouncing off his rolled down socks and smashing into a thousand pieces upon the rugged ground, then coming to lie among the chipped stones and the twisted bottle tops.

'Did he come and watch you?' Dave asked of Billy as we both finished our second pints and decided to move on.

'Nuh... said he would try, but that he was working somewhere over Croydon way in the morning and didn't think he would get back in time. I told him not to break his neck getting back... he was dead chuffed though.'

In fact, it had surprised me just how pleased he had actually been for me, I mean I didn't for one minute expect him to be resentful or anything. It's just that the joy he had showed on my behalf took me back a bit, patting me on the back, virtually hugging me at one point. Not the kind of behaviour you would associate with Billy. And maybe it was something to do with the dreadful news that I had told him earlier or maybe it was the beer, although I had only stayed for two. But it had made me realise just how deep our roots were; it was easy to forget sometimes, take it for granted, buried as they were beneath the shifting landscapes of our lives.

Dave and I made our way along Baker Street and turned left onto Oxford Street. The day didn't seem to want to go, reluctant to let the night in, it still held onto the blue hours of daylight, heavier than before, with dark scudding clouds dipping below the skyline, popping in and out of view from between the passing buildings. It had been a bright, sunny day, a stiff breeze but I had only felt it when the sun had hid behind a cloud. If it hadn't poured down the night before the pitch would have been perfect, not so slippery and unpredictable. I had lain awake half the night, listening to the rain drumming, rat-tat-tat, upon the coal shed roof, praying, willing it to stop, worried sick that I would be robbed of my big day.

An odd sense of ambivalence tugged away at me as we made our way easily through the crowded streets. "Saturday Night" seemed to linger in the air, sweet like perfume, I could see it on the faces of everyone, it lit them up like the glow from a buttercup. A part of me could feel the stress of the day crumble and fall away. I didn't realise the pressure I had put myself under, what with the match and coming up to see Dave for the weekend. And that was it, the reason for my uncertainty. Half of me felt good, contented, the game all done and dusted; a success. And that easy, first beer feeling was loosening me up, I felt cosily light-headed and excited at the prospect of the night ahead of us; me and Dave, just like old times. But the reason that I was there nagged away, bubbling like gas in my guts. How could I take pleasure from the weekend, when the reason that I was there was to console Dave, at least that's how I saw it, to try to help him through the next day or so, take his mind off Tuesday and the funeral.

We slipped into a pub somewhere near Marble Arch for a quick one, a noisier more lively kind of pub. The kind where no one batted an eye when we walked in, where the wall of cigarette smoke stung the back of your throat and a hundred different conversations overlapped each other, and hummed through the air like a swarm of bees.

And then we were at the top of Hyde Park... Speakers Corner, where the big Park Lane hotels stand arrogantly in the distance, like fanning peacocks. Dave jumped onto an upturned crate, threw his arms out wide and shouted, 'Ladies and gentlemen, people of London...here me now! Today Southfields reserves, tomorrow... Leeds, Liverpool, Arsenal...Who knows, maybe even Fulham!... I bring you the future of English goalkeeping... Johnny Chalmers!' A sheet of newspaper fluttered past and moulded itself round Dave's shins as he bowed to the imaginary crowd. 'Good audience,' he smiled. 'Not one heckler.' I ran at him, grabbed him round his thighs and lifted him over my shoulder, fireman style, and ran until my legs gave way and we collapsed on the grass, laughing out loud, and out of breath from the beer.

'What we doing here anyway?' I asked, pulling myself to my feet and looking around at the huge expanse that was Hyde Park as it fell away into the rapidly descending darkness. Outside the gates the traffic rushed by, up and down Park Lane. I hadn't realised just how open everything had become. With the park stretching out like an ocean into the night and the giant wall of buildings set back from the roads, unlike home where everything was crammed together. I suddenly felt exposed, and urged the night to close in and envelop my sense of vulnerability. I wasn't used to such space around me, where council estates and row upon row of terraced houses didn't dominate the view, crowding in on the skyline. The only time I had been aware of being so exposed was when I played in goal in the parks of South London.

'Fancy the King's Road?' he said, running his hand through the curtains of his fading orange hair and tidying himself up.

So we made our way through the park, kicked our way over the deep sands of Rotten Row, crossed Knightsbridge and jumped on a bus heading down Sloane Street.

The sense of royalty grew thicker with every step that we took. There was a kind of decadence to everything, the whiff of superiority floated through the elegantly-named streets and clung to the grand buildings. Back home across the river, when I would sit on top of a bus I would gaze at the people below, a habit of mine. I'd watch them go about their lives, walking down the road, standing in bus stops, and wonder what it would be like to be someone else, just for a day. Try to sneak a look through the bedroom windows as the bus trundled by, a glimpse behind the doors of suburbia. But it was a sluggish monochromatic world, where everyone always seemed to wear the same vacant, washed-out expression, the same wavelength running through the streets, like a field of corn swaying as one in the wind.

While up in town there was lucidity to everything, life seemed to have an edge to it, a world away from the lethargy of suburbia. Here I couldn't imagine bored housewives in drab-coloured aprons with their hair in curlers returning the milk bottles to the front step as the old man trudged wearily through the door, home from the nightshift, with not a word passing between them, nothing but the chinking of empty milk bottles echoing through their empty lives.

CHAPTER ELEVEN

April 1978

I awoke, as usual after I've been drinking, lying in my own dribble. Only this time it hadn't soaked into a cushion or pillow but had formed a pool of saliva upon a map of central London. The blurred colours and lines gradually came into focus as I slowly lifted my head. I was lying fully clothed upon a bedroom floor that I didn't recognise. I caught the faintest whiff from a half empty can of lager by my head and nearly gagged. The sun shone through a sash window where no curtain hung. It lit up the hair of the girl lying beside me. There was so much of it, it fanned out across the floor, covering her whole head, I couldn't even make out which way she was facing. She was my age, I think, maybe a year older. Pretty, from what I could remember, green eyes, nice smile. But her name wasn't so clear. *Sally, Sarah… Sharon* maybe? I had it, it was there floating somewhere around my head like a butterfly, just couldn't quite catch it yet. Definitely begun with an S though.

I looked around at my surroundings, trying to gauge where I was, searching for a foothold of familiarity. But my head hurt like hell, as if my temples were in a vice, couldn't hold my focus on anything for more than a few seconds at a time before I had to blink away the searing pain that had built up behind my eyeballs.

There was another girl, prostrate on the bed. From my viewpoint she could have been S's sister, same hair, wild and untamed, a kind of mousy brown. Where the hell was Dave?

I looked around for the time, but there had been no room for a clock upon the walls. Instead they were covered with paintings and posters: Jimi Hendrix, Joan Baez, Joni Mitchell and a few people that I hadn't even heard of. "Hippie shit" as Billy would have said. The paintings were all scenic watercolours, of golden fields rising and rolling endlessly on, or of cliff-top views stretching far out to sea. They were amateurish, weak-coloured and simple. But when I looked again, forced myself against the flying arrows in my head to fill my eyes a little longer, I realised that they carried with them dimension, hidden deep over the horizon. To me they were visions of hope, sort of looking to the future, they had me wondering what was over the last wave or hill.

The flat belonged to the girl on the bed. Nicola... Nikki as she had told me curtly the first time I had used her name. 'Using my name in its correct and full context is merely falling into step with the regiment that society parades... Break rank and refuse to conform.'

'Okay.' It had seemed the easiest answer.

We had met the girls in a pub somewhere off the Kings Road, friends of Dave's.

'Why didn't you tell me?' I had asked when the girls had gone to the bar.

'You would have only got all flustered,' Dave had shrugged. 'Besides, we'd have ended up all maudlin,' he added.

My forehead creased. 'English please!'

Dave rolled his eyes, the way he would with Billy, when acting all exasperated. 'Pissed and talking about mum. And I don't want that Johnny... if I start down that road... ' he shook his head, dismissing the thought as if it were too unbearable to contemplate. 'Anyway, now I can get pissed and look at a pretty face instead of yours.' He smiled.

And it made me realise just how diverse his circle of friends had become, people from all different walks of life. Virtually everyone that I spent time with was connected with my football;

friends from school, team-mates, coaches… and of course there had been Debbie, the posh girl from the other side of town. *The Connaught Garden Set*. But these two were even further up the ladder, rich kid girls, born with a silver spoon and all that, dipping their toes into the waters of real life, playing at it, both art students over at St John's Wood. But you could see that there was no real passion behind it all. Talent? In a mysterious way, yes, from the evidence upon the walls, but it ran deeper than eye-catching art. But there was no sense of dependency, big deal if they failed, or decided to drop out, what would it matter? Everything funded by their parents. Like the flat in Brompton that we had found ourselves in.

I looked at S's wrist but couldn't see if she was wearing a watch or not. One hand was pinned against the floor by the weight of her body, and the other was covered by the sleeve of her blouse, which was flared and flouncy, revealing only the tips of her multi-coloured fingers. Each nail was painted a different colour. 'Makes me forever hopeful,' she had explained, trying to sound all worldly-wise, when I had noticed them wrapped around her pint of cider. 'A rainbow constantly at my fingertips!' She had said, waving her hand through the air like royalty, before placing a red index finger tenderly upon my lips. 'Always looking for my pot of gold.' She had been trying to smoulder, ooze sex appeal, but it had been ridiculous. As pretty as she was, a nice girl too, it just didn't suit her, narrow eyes and pursed lips. I had caught Dave out the corner of my eye, sitting opposite, Nikki draped over his arm. And through the cloud of pub smoke shifting like mist across the bar, had seen him wink at me whilst stifling laughter, as if he had too big a mouthful of food.

The bedroom door swung open and Dave breezed in. He was wearing the same clothes as the night before, plain white T-shirt beneath a denim jacket and black pegs, but somehow he managed to look all crisp and fresh. Hair all wet, scraped back over his head, roots shining like onyx, clean complexion, eyes clear, sparkling almost, untainted by the previous night's activities.

'All right?' he asked brightly, as he stood in the doorway. I didn't answer, barely managed to roll my eyes and groan. S stirred slowly, sat up and brushed the hair from her face with a great sweep of her hand.

'Beautiful day,' she said to no one in particular, as she smiled towards the window with what seemed to be still closed eyes.

'Kettle's on,' said Dave slipping into an armchair that seemed to be covered with some kind of shiny red blanket. 'Find us then?' he grinned, motioning down at the map that had served as my pillow. S had been trying to show me where we actually were. But it had been no good, by the time she had come up with the idea of the map and spread it out across the floor I could barely focus on anything properly. The map had been nothing more than a colourful blur, chunks of solid grey sliding into the blue snake of the Thames; the solid lines of Sloane Street and the King's and Cromwell Roads, orange and green arteries of London, split crazily in two, had danced before me. Even closing one eye had done no good, the whole of West London had simply melted into one and slipped from view, like a pizza slipping from the pan.

By the time the four of us had staggered back to Nikki's flat, through the labyrinth of streets and swathes of elegant court gardens, I had been completely lost, disorientated by drink and the unexpected attentions of a pretty girl.

And we had carried on drinking, slumped upon piles of garishly-coloured cushions that lay scattered across the floor like a spilt bag of sweets. The strong scent of incense spiralled in wisps of smoke from joss sticks smouldering on the shelves as we had swigged down expensive red wine, its impressive vintage completely wasted upon us.

'You have to let it breathe to fully appreciate the full-bodied oaky flavour,' Nikki had instructed us matter-of-factly, uncorking the bottle and placing it upon the floor between us.

'To the trained palette perhaps,' Dave had said, giving the impression that he actually knew what he was talking about. 'But Johnny and me… ' he'd continued, reaching for the bottle. 'We're just a couple of uncouth South London boys.' And as the wine had plopped unceremoniously into my glass, he'd smiled his lazy, infectious smile 'High in spirit, low in culture… Cheers.'

Out in the kitchen the kettle was boiling, whistling with impatience. Even from another room, with the muffled assistance from the walls, it sounded like a drill boring its way through my head, an operation without anaesthetic. Dave sprung to his feet. 'Four teas?'

I nodded, still not trusting myself to construct an audible word. 'Please,' said S, answering for her friend as well. She had begun to stir, Nikki, moaning and snuffling like some kind of animal awaking from hibernation. She lifted her head and peered around the room. 'Where's Dave?' she croaked.

'Making tea,' answered S. Nikki's head fell back on the pillow with a groan, as if the effort of it all had proved too much. Just S and me… that awkward morning after silence deafening me, drumming through my already thundering head. The Dutch courage had long since evaporated, drained away like dirty bath water during the night, leaving behind nothing but the clinging tidemark of a stinging hangover.

I sat there, trying to be all cool, nonchalant-looking and relaxed. I was desperate to stand up and stretch my legs, it seemed as if all the blood running through my body had rushed to my head and settled there, curdling like milk, choking my senses. I needed to move, bend my knees, swivel my arms, start it flowing again, lubricate my aching body.

But I didn't want to offend S in any way, didn't want her to think that I was trying to disentangle myself from the mess of the night before. But if I remained there, upon the floor beside her, would it look as if I were too keen? Crowding her.

I found the whole thing exhausting, reminded me of trying to remove my football kit as a kid, standing at the back door, with Mum telling me not to get her clean floor dirty. And it was the same really, tiptoeing around like an idiot, desperately trying not to mark the clean slate of a new relationship.

I wished that I could be more casual, a bit more confident around girls, but I floundered through the whole experience of dating and relationships, even if the girl didn't mean that much to me. Was it the curse of Debbie? I didn't think so anymore, although I couldn't help but compare her to every girl that I met. Although nothing had actually happened between me and S, nothing more than a fumbling embrace and a drunken kiss, before we had finally succumbed to the weight of the alcohol, passing out across the heart of London, like a giant eclipse.

Finally I couldn't stand it any longer, simply had to stretch my legs, shake off the restlessness building up inside. Sitting there, beside her, I couldn't stop myself from trying to decipher the code of her body language; a swish of the hair, a twitch of a leg, searching for hidden messages in the most innocent of movements, transmitting nothing more than a hangover.

I browsed along the bookshelf, feigning interest as I tilted my head to read the spines. But everything in view shifted alarmingly, as if I had stepped off a giant kerb stone. I had to close my eyes and concentrate to stop myself from being physically sick. I picked up the nearest object to me, a photograph frame, trying to steady the seasickness in my mind. It was a picture of the two of them, Nikki and S, as children. No more than eight or nine years old, cheeks pressed against each other, two beaming faces. They shone with the absolute freedom of youth. Behind them the sea touched the sky as if it had been drawn with a ruler, the sea breeze whipping up white caps of foam and lashing the girls' hair across their faces at crazy angles.

'That's Cornwall,' said S, appearing by my side. I could feel the faint touch of her shoulder on mine, became aware of the softness of her breath brushing past my ear. The goosebumps lifting instantly upon my skin. But it wasn't like the drunken flirting of the night before. She was concentrating on the picture in my hands, a hint of something lost in her eyes. 'We used to go there every year as kids... both families... spend the whole summer on a farm... a sort of hippie commune for the fading children of the sixties.'

'But you both look so happy,' I said, forgetting my awkwardness, surprised at the trace of bitterness in her voice.

'Yeah, we were,' she said, suddenly perking up, blinking away the memories. 'It's just that it wasn't... well, a normal childhood.'

'But your still a hip... I mean you still dress like... well you know, with your rainbow fingers and that,' I blurted out, tripping over my tongue.

'A hippie, you mean?' she said, unoffended, piecing my inarticulate rambling into plain English. 'Yeah... I suppose I am... I mean I love the music, the clothes... the freedom of expression.' She was beginning to sound like the night before again, talking with her hands, like a mime artist. 'But it's all that I know.' Her arms flopped down by her sides, deflated like an old balloon, as the realisation of her words sunk in. And the strangest thing, I could see traces of me, right there in her eyes. No matter how she portrayed herself, no matter how she dressed it up, disguised herself, beneath the colourful clothes and make-up, she couldn't hide the lost child in her soul. Not completely comfortable with what she had allowed life to make her; what people expected of her.

I forgot about the time and looking for a clock, for a moment time stood still, carried no meaning, as we held each other's gaze, as if really seeing each other for the first time.

Dave appeared in the doorway, inadvertently breaking the spell, like the clicking of fingers in hypnotherapy.

'Tea is served,' he announced, holding a tray out in front of him, tea towel draped neatly over his arm.

We stood on the banks of the Thames, the empty warehouses behind us, Battersea power station looming like a giant upturned table in the distance, the river sparkling in the morning sunshine, covering the murky waters with a kind of orangey film. Summer wasn't far away now, somewhere in the distance, holding its breath beyond the skulking clouds, hiding behind the jagged London skyline.

Dave pushed a shiny black camera in my hands. 'Be careful… she'll kill me if anything happens to it.' He pulled it from a drawstring bag that he had picked up at Nikki's flat, as if he were a magician pulling a rabbit from a hat. It looked very smart, professional-looking, much better than the old camera of his that we normally used for his Bowie covers.

We had missed what we had been after… the streaky orange sunrise. It was too golden now. Dave had wanted to capture the exact moment that the yellow began to dilute the sky, spreading across the morning like butter.

He produced a long black cardigan now, leaving the empty bag on the ground, like a deflated balloon. And I had to laugh, as he pulled the cardigan up around his neck. It had thick collars and a kind of hood, like some kind of Dracula cape. He positioned himself sideways, on the edge of the old dock, ran his fingers through his hair and stuck his face out into the morning sun, facing back towards the East End, as if he were trying to see the tips of the Houses of Parliament and beyond.

'Come on!' he called. 'Or we'll lose the light!' He glanced over at me. 'Don't laugh! Hurry up!' But he couldn't keep the smile from his face, he was trying hard to be all serious, to keep a straight face, but it was if he had a twitch in the corners of his mouth, a tick, creeping into his hollow cheeks, forcing them upwards.

It was like being told off at school, the harder I tried, the more difficult it became, my sniggering polluted the air like fumes. Dave tried not to look at me, he turned out toward the river. 'Right… when I turn round I expect you to be ready… okay?' I nodded my head as if he could see me, not trusting myself to speak without cracking up. 'Okay!'

'Yep!' I snapped.

'Right then,' he said smoothly, as if he were ironing the crinkles of laughter from the situation. 'Here goes.' It was an odd situation, capturing Dave, giggling like the child that he had never been, in the viewfinder. Whilst all the time the death of his mum lingered like a presence, out of sight, intangible; but nonetheless around, clinging like the cigarette smoke on my clothes from the night before.

Acting out those album covers, trying to replicate a desired image, was the only thing that ever gave Dave's age away, revealed a sliver of the child that was inside, like the glimpse of bone from a deep slice, playing at being his hero. Admittedly it wasn't much of a revelation, not like running around playing soldiers or football, but a form of playing nonetheless.

It seemed to me that our teenage years had always been a step behind the decade, always running to keep up. Thirteen in '74, fourteen in '75, fifteen in '76, and Bowie would release at least one album a year. And I would hold my breath when Dave, always the first to have bought the latest, after saving his pennies for months, would reveal the cover to me, would deliberately make a big deal out of it as if he were lifting a sheet off an eagerly awaited masterpiece.

There had been the simple head shots, *Space Oddity, Hunky Dory, Heroes* and now *Low,* the cover we were attempting on the dockside, and of course *Aladdin Sane* hadn't created much of a problem, unless, of course, you count a beating from your old man as a problem. And then there had been the guitar pose for *The*

Man Who Sold the World, tricky but not impossible, we had managed to overcome it. But in '74 came *Diamond Dogs*.

'How the bleedin' 'ell are we going to do that!' I'd screamed. 'He's half bloody dog!' But Dave had just smiled. Unwittingly I had said "We" pledging myself to the cause. And Dave had noticed it, of course, and there had been that easy smile, spreading across his face. I had tried to hold onto my shocked expression, but it had been no good, it had slipped away like a snowman in the sun. I had been caught out, like in one of those infuriating school games that would infect a classroom for a while like germs. No one ever wanted to face Dave in a staring match, they would always smile or blink first. He would never crack, it was as if he didn't even see you, he would look right through you. And he was irritatingly good at the trick games, like the question game where you couldn't use "yes" or "no" as an answer:

'Is your name John Chalmers?'

'Ye… I mean my name is John Chalmers.'

'Have we got maths next period?'

'Erm… I mean we *have* got maths next period.'

'Fulham were lucky on Saturday, weren't they?'

No!… I mean, oh Bollocks!'

But Dave would go on forever, long after the given minute… until you would get bored.

'Are you David Connelly?'

'I am,' he would answer straight back, not a moment of hesitation in his voice.

'Is it raining outside?'

'I believe it is.'

'Are Fulham shit?'

'That is a question that cannot accurately be answered, it is but a matter of opinion.'

'Are your trousers black?'

'They are.'

'Are you... Oh what's the point!'

And so I had resigned myself to helping him, capturing his dreams through a lens. And we had re-enacted most of them to date, still had a few to do, *Ziggy Stardust* for instance. God knows how, but Dave had discovered that the sleeve cover had been shot in some street in London. Heddon Street... some little turning off Regent Street. He had even been up there, checked it out, the sign that read K.WEST, the phone box and everything. Had said that all he needed to do now was get his hands on an electric blue jumpsuit and a pair of red high-heeled boots!

He already had the guitar, had picked it up from a jumble sale at the old church one summer. It only had two strings but that didn't matter since he couldn't play a note, and it had done the job for his high kicking *Man Who Sold the World* pose.

'We'll have to wait until I cut my hair,' he had claimed, when I quizzed him about it one day. It needed to be short again, blonde, not the sweeping orange waves that he wore at the time.

'Why not just get a wig?' I'd asked, but I knew that he wouldn't fall for it, my gentle digging. Because really he was saving it, was really looking forward to playing out that scene more than any other.

I had to admit that of all the album covers, *Ziggy* was the most enthralling. It captured the imagination, had me wondering, asking myself questions. What was Bowie doing there, all alone in the glow of the giant yellow lantern? What did the boxes contain piled and discarded on the pavement? What lay round the corner and what was going on in the houses behind? What would those tiny boxes of light high above reveal?

After the incident with his old man and the make-up, I was always more than sceptical about Dave's Bowie characters, wary of where we should create them. Certainly didn't want to act out anymore at his house. But it didn't dent Dave's enthusiasm at all, if anything he became more determined in his ambition to create his own portfolio.

And so I wondered, as he stood in front of me, as still as a shop mannequin, how far his dad was from his mind. The funeral was only two days away and far as I could tell Dave hadn't seen his old man, had had no communication at all, not since he had walked out before Christmas. Does he even know she's dead, I wondered.

Tuesday loomed like storm clouds on the horizon but I couldn't think about it. Every time that I tried to imagine what it would be like I couldn't get a clear picture in my head, it was like trying to dream through the bottom of an empty milk bottle.

I had never been to a funeral before, except my nan's, Mum's mum, but I had absolutely no recollection of it, had only been a toddler. I used to wish that I had been to my own dad's, so that I had a kind of finality to that part of my life. But the enigma that was my father, he hadn't even had the decency to die, had just slipped away like a thief in the night, stealing my childhood, and something much more from Mum. To me he was nothing but an old story never told, an invention, no more real than Dave's images of Bowie.

I shifted around to my right-hand side, the camera stuck to my face, Dave trapped within the tiny square of my viewfinder, waiting for a gap to appear, like a missing tooth, somewhere on the London skyline. Finally I took the picture, snapped off three or four from similar angles, even took a couple down on one knee in an attempt to lose the buildings in the background, to steal the last of the early morning.

'Getting into this, aren't we?' quipped Dave, without breaking his pose, holding himself perfectly still with all the grace and discipline of a portrait model.

'Yeah well,' I sighed, rubbing my temples between the thumb

and forefinger of my hand. I felt dizzy from the concentration. 'That will have to do… if I don't eat something soon I'm gonna pass out.' The thought of food first thing had nearly made me gag, had barely managed to keep down the cup of tea that Dave had brought me. But now I ached for food, could hear the rumbling resonating through my empty stomach, punishing me for my neglect.

Dave clicked his tongue in a show of mock disgust. 'Last night catching up with you, is it? Bet David Bailey never allowed a hangover to stand in the way of his work.' He stepped down off the dockside and was making his way over to me when he stopped short, drawing sharply on his breath as he pulled up. 'Or is it more than that? Drunk on love… the heady sensation of Cindy perhaps!'

I walked over to the dockside where he had been standing and casually dangled the camera over the rippling waters of the Thames. 'Oh!' I gasped. 'Those heady sensations!… I'm losing all my strength!… don't know if I can hold on! I'm just *soo* love-struck.'

'Poor handling,' he smiled. 'Now how would that look for England's future number one?'

CHAPTER TWELVE

April 1978

'Try and eat something, dear,' Mum said, as I sat pushing my cereals around the bowl. They had been in there so long that they had absorbed most of the milk and had congealed into a soggy mess. I just couldn't face food, had tried to get something inside of me, force it down, like I had had to do last Sunday with Dave, but just like then it seemed to stick like tiny pieces of cardboard to the roof of my mouth, to the back of my throat, forcing me to take gulps of the hot tea.

She was going to the funeral as well, had known Dave's mum as long as I had known Dave, all my life. Probably longer if I thought about it, didn't just meet the day that we were both born, but I just never seemed to think of life for Mum before I was around.

They weren't exactly on "pop in for a cup of tea" terms, but then again nobody was with Dave's mum, but she was closer than most.

Somewhere in the archives of my mind I had some grainy footage; a few of the mums meeting once a week or something, round each other's houses, taking it in turns to host little coffee mornings, a few digestives and a gossip. Could vaguely picture Dave's mum sitting there, in our poky little front room, perched on the end of the sofa, her knees and feet squeezed neatly together, elbows tucked in as if she were wedged between commuters on a train in rush hour; smiling awkwardly, cup and saucer held tightly in her hands, always on the edge of the conversation no matter how much Mum would try to ease her in, troubled by the pace of it, like a hesitant child watching the others on the roundabout, but scared to jump on and join in.

But the coffee morning brigade had disbanded. Children grew up, some of the mothers returned to work, others moved on, I think one or two fell out with each other until there were no more than three or four, numbers slowly petering out like the batteries in a clock until the whole thing finally ground to a halt.

I had naturally assumed that she would be going to the funeral, would have looked disrespectful if she hadn't. But the whole experience would be bad enough anyway without the added discomfort of Mum being there, knowing that she was there, sitting somewhere behind me, out of sight but the knowledge of her presence rubbing away like a label in a shirt collar.

Oh, it wasn't the idea of Mum! She could never do that to me. It's just that I knew she wouldn't be on her own. Derek would be with her. And God it would drive me crazy! But I felt as if I were being disloyal… despite the fact I had no one to be disloyal to!

Thankfully I wouldn't be with them, couldn't bare the idea of people thinking that the three of us were some kind of cosy family, unted in grief. Instead I had the perfect excuse in the fact that Dave had asked me to sit in the front pew beside him.

It really screwed me up the whole thing, whenever I gave it the time of day, would find myself constantly running away from reason.

Everything pointed to Derek being good for Mum. I didn't want her to be on her own, alone for the rest of her life. And he was good to her, treated her well, never tried to involve himself in my life. He never offered parental advice or weighed in with his opinion siding with Mum if he happened to be there when she would be doing her half-hearted strict bit.

But taking all that into account, there was a side of me that simply wouldn't see it, a completely stubborn, unreasonable side. There were no grounds for it, no reason to defend it by, just blind ignorance.

The thought of it had crawled across my mind as I lay awake but with my eyes shut, the morning of the funeral. The picture of the three of us, slowly piecing together as I awoke, like a jigsaw puzzle in my head.

I only ever asked Mum why I didn't have a dad once and she told me that it was because he was a sailor in the navy, as if that were enough. And to me he was a war hero, aboard the battleships, king of the high seas. I had this Action Man, had named him Tommy, he had a hand missing, but he had come to me like that, from a jumble sale at Mum's hospital. But I loved Tommy, with his shiny brown painted head. He couldn't hold a rifle very well, had to sort of lean it across his handless arm, but he looked great with dagger or a pistol.

Tommy was how I imagined my father to be, handsome, rugged and tough, a man of action... a real-life Action Man. Mum took me up to the Thames, to see H.M.S Belfast, the Royal Navy battleship, because I loved ships. I took Tommy, dressed in his navy uniform. I just *knew* we were going to see my father. Mum hadn't said anything, but I was convinced. As I lay, sleepless, in bed the night before, I could picture this serious, stoical man, standing tall and rigid aboard the deck of his ship, behind him giant grey guns aimed at the sky. He was saluting me, ready to welcome me aboard.

But the only uniforms I saw that day were those worn by the dummies dotted around below decks, to recreate life aboard the battleship. Pink, lifeless figures, tucked away in cabins or sitting at desks with old headphones clasped over their empty, hollow heads. And I hated that ship, hated everything about the damn navy from that day on. And I realised then that there was no one waiting to greet me, never had been and never would be. And even though I had never had my dad, it felt like I had actually lost him.

The cramped claustrophobic conditions closed in around me, and the sweat seeped through my clothes, but I was shook with cold. I tugged frantically on Mum's hand, pleading with her to take me back up out into the day and back home. As we stepped off the gang plank onto the banks of the Thames, I remember thinking how small it all looked, the heavy guns like frozen tentacles, the aging conning tower, with its array of radars and aerials poking up into the sky within the shadow of Tower Bridge looming above us, rising from the murky waters, staring down upon the streets of London.

I remembered Tommy in my hand, dressed smartly in his navy outfit, and suddenly I hated him, hated him for making me believe. But as he soared through the air, arms and legs splayed bizarrely, I regretted it. The split second he left my grasp, long before he had landed in the opacity of the Thames. I looked at Mum in desperation, wanting her to somehow bring Tommy back to me. In the distance Big Ben sounded; its chimes booming down, echoing over the river and along the embankments, a death toll for Tommy and for the ghost of a father I would never know.

And Mum, she had just smiled. That sad, knowing smile similar to Dave's, cheeks puffed a little, lips barely visible. That thin smile without humour telling me not to worry, that she understood.

My eyelids had flickered, their translucence fighting against the morning light, something that I had always done since childhood, when the day promised to be unpleasant; a maths test or a punishment that I knew was awaiting me at school. For if I didn't open my eyes, didn't let the day in, maybe I wouldn't have to deal with it.

I had thought of the church; of how cold and dark it had felt that day with Dave, could still remember it. Almost like a dampness in the air, but yet so peaceful, the stillness had seemed to hum. I had squirmed down beneath the covers, I knew that I had to get up soon, that there was no hiding from the day, that being seen out in the same place, in the same building, as Mum and Derek was something that I would just have to deal with. The least of my problems that I would have to face that day compared to putting Dave's mum in the ground.

If I am honest I was more worried about how I would deal with the sight of Dave breaking down, bursting into tears perhaps, and sobbing uncontrollably on my shoulder. To be honest I couldn't see it, not Dave, too collected, if he was going to grieve it would be in the solitude of his room or something, staring out across the rooftops of London. And Bowie, hovering in the air like specks of dust caught in the searchlight of the sun.

The muffled sound of the radio had filtered up through the floorboards, like bees in the distance. It had told me that Mum was up, busy making breakfast. One of those background noises that was as comforting as finding a fresh spot in the corner of the bed with your toe first thing in the morning. The thing was that Dave had always been the one who we could tell stuff to, sort of spill a problem out across the floor and let him pick out the important bits. It was unlikely, but I didn't know if I could handle seeing that stoicism crumble like a sandcastle in the tide.

I had decided to try and not even think about it, any of it; Mum, the funeral, Dave's possible collapse, and of course his old man. *Would he show or not?* Decided instead that I would simply deal with whatever the day threw at me there and then. No theory, no plan. Speculation seemed to drain me, robbed me of the strength to even lift the sheets.

I had tried to replace it all with thoughts of good things. I replayed Saturday's match over again in my mind, had gone over it at least ten times already. It was the strangest thing, that I could remember it all so clearly; every incident that I had been involved in, every save, cross and shot that had come my way... except the penalty.

I could see myself standing between the posts, crouched on my line, muscles taught, ready to pounce into action, could picture the taker, standing hands on his hips, looking lazily over at the ref waiting for his whistle as if he didn't have a care in the world… and then nothing. The picture had gone blank, shining white. As if the projector in my head had become disconnected, run out of film. I could almost hear the loose end of celluloid flapping, as the reel spun harmlessly on.

It was a nice day when the sun finally found a break in the clouds. Really quite warm, far too hot to be wearing a black jacket and tie, both of which seemed to attract the heat of the sun like a magnet. It hadn't even occurred to me, the thing about the tie, not until the night before when Mum had asked me what I was going to wear for the funeral. I had been washing up the plates, staring out across the strip of garden like I did, watching the cat trying to catch moths in the fading light.

'What do you mean?' I had asked, only half interested, when she had called from the front room.

'I mean,' she had moved into the kitchen now, 'that you don't have a black tie, do you love?' I didn't answer, the thought hadn't even crossed my mind. 'Wait a minute… ' and when she had reappeared from upstairs she had been holding a thin black nylon tie, the kind that they all wore in the sixties' films. 'Here we are,' she had said, laying it out upon the kitchen table as if it were some precious gold medallion.

I had assumed that it was Derek's, why else would she have a man's tie in her bedroom? And I searched awkwardly for an excuse.

'Looks a bit long, Mum.'

'Nonsense,' she had said. 'Here… try it on,' and she slipped it round my neck as I stood defenceless with soap suds up to my elbows. 'Let's have a look at you,' and I could see that she was getting into it, liking the idea. 'There we are… perfect,' she had smiled, adjusting the two ends and pretending to flatten out my collar, even though I wasn't wearing one. 'You've shot up so much in the past year or so, you're just about the same size as him now,' she had sighed, flattening the ends of the tie absently. I hadn't understood, my face wrinkling in confusion; Derek was well over six foot. 'He only wore it the once,' Mum had continued, miles away now, in a different world. 'For *his* mother's funeral… your Nan… although you never knew her.' And then it hit me. I had jumped back in alarm, scattering clean dishes back into the sink, as if Mum had draped a snake around my shoulders. I had stared at her in disbelief, I couldn't ever remember her mentioning *him* before, not so… so *openly*, so casually, as if she were talking about one of her patients or the man who read the news on the telly every night.

There was nothing of him in the house. No photos or souvenirs from holidays or happier times. No evidence to prove that he had ever existed, except, of course, me.

'I'm not wearing that!' I had spat the words out as if they were a bad taste in my mouth. And I had seen the hurt well in her eyes. It had seemed to spill down as if her skin had grown too heavy for her face. 'I mean… it's just that… ' I hadn't been able to find the words, gave up trying, searching for something that I would never find. Simply hadn't been able to express feelings that I had never experienced.

'No, you're right… ' she had said, waving her hand as if she were shooing a fly. 'Sorry, silly of me.' She whipped the tie from my shoulders, the mustiness floating away. 'It's just that I knew you didn't have one,' she had continued, neatly rolling it up and placing it on the kitchen table like some giant liquorice sweet. 'And knowing my son as I do, probably hadn't even thought about it.' That "typical boy" look on her face drawing the sting from the moment. 'I could ask Derek… '

'No, no!' I had interrupted, a little more sharply than I intended. 'It's okay really... this will be fine... honest Mum... thanks.' I had smiled, picking the black coil back off the table and slipping it into my pocket. She had looked unconvinced, but I thought I saw a glint in her eyes, or maybe the faint twitch of a smile, gone before it could materialise. Anyhow, I had climbed the stairs feeling, for some reason, that I had done the right thing.

I walked past the park and the row of old cottages that looked so out of place. They drifted by out of the corner of my eye, like scenery from a slow-moving train. Funny, but I would always cross over and walk into town on that side of the road, even if I wasn't going to the station or Lui's, habit I supposed. And I did the same again that lunchtime, even though the old church was on "my" side. The bushes and the hedgerow were badly overgrown and neglected, spilling through the rusted railings and hanging over the pavement like the grabbing arms of some green monster. Probably the last thing on the council's long list, I thought. They had to be nagged to even cut the pitches on the park. The path that led from our tiny gap in the railings was barely visible, swallowed up by the invading years. I couldn't remember the last time that I had trodden through it, and it had evidently never been used or even discovered by anyone else. What were the kids of the time up to, I wondered, couldn't understand their lack of adventure. But for some reason I found myself smiling knowingly, pleased that no one else had found it. There was no doubt about it, it still appeared mysterious and inviting if you knew where to look. Hypnotic even, but its intrigue was lost on me, for I had passed through it more times than I could ever possibly remember. And as I gazed over I found myself thinking of the paintings that I had seen on the walls of Nikki and Cindy's flat, that sense of something waiting to be discovered, the faint echo of enticement rustling gently in the bushes.

My mind stayed on Cindy. I had found her pervading my thoughts a surprising amount since the weekend. I hadn't been aware of it at first, certainly not in the pub the night that we had first met. I had found her attractive of course, but there hadn't been much clarity attached to it, the edges of the evening had been blurred by drink. If anything I had found her to be a little dizzy, a bit childish even, performing her outdated free spirit bit, like an actor miscast in a play.

I fingered the tie as it flapped unfamiliarly against my chest, curling around the tips of my finger as I walked along. I could see the old church looming up ahead. Skulking between the giant oak trees like a haunted house. It felt strange... more than strange... incomprehensible! That I was actually wearing an item of clothing that he had once worn. I couldn't even use the words "dad" or "father", not even in my head. For whenever I thought to myself it was always in my own voice and those words didn't belong in my life, words that belonged to other people. But it was the stupidest thing, so stupid that it drove me mad, but ever since I had tied the damn the thing in a knot around my neck I had felt quite comfortable; soothed, like rubbing cream on a sting, easing some of the irritation that I felt over Mum and Derek.

'I didn't mean to upset you, dear!' she had said as I stood by the front door.

'It's okay, honest, Mum.'

'I have this box you see,' she had continued as if she hadn't heard me. 'No bigger than a shoe box really... ' She had begun to adjust the knot in my tie, as if she were looking for something to do with her hands. I had known what was coming and I hadn't wanted to hear it, had wanted to tell her to stop, that I didn't care! That I didn't want to know! But the incongruity of it all had frozen me into a kind of stunned silence. I could hear my voice screaming out loud in my head, rattling the bones in their sockets, but I hadn't been able to mutter a word, not a sound. For years now, since I had been a kid, the thought of him hadn't existed, just a figment, a story, as old as a nursery rhyme. And now there were actual pieces of him, tangible clues to scrutinise; a reality, here… in the house.

'A toothbrush, an old cufflink, a couple of books… silly really.' She had shaken her head, swallowing as if she had a piece of food stuck in her throat. She had tried to laugh at the silliness of it all but it came out as a kind of strangled cough.

'There we are!' She had smiled awkwardly, smoothing the tie down and straightening my collar as if it were my first day at school. '*Very* smart!' But I could see the dimples sunken in her chin, the glaze in her eyes like rain on glass, and then it was gone. Disappeared beneath the layers of fortitude and painted-on smiles.

I never thought I would find the sights and sounds of town so appealing, the smell of exhaust pipes and the trace of distant fumes carried over from the factories; breathe it all in, suck it down as if it were fresh mountain air.

I had stepped out from the yawning doors of the old church and let my gaze fall over the ancient graveyard, with its weather-beaten and illegible headstones that jutted haphazardly from the ground like rows of decaying teeth. I had wanted to immerse myself in the whole picture, try and wash away the funny tingling feeling that the church had covered me with like sea spray. I turned to watch the steady flow of traffic that rumbled in and out of town, welcomed the sound of the revved-up engines, the honking of car horns and the grinding of brakes; noises that shot through my head, as they ricocheted of the grey buildings and tower blocks around, like one of the older kids' air guns that they would fire in the underpasses.

Billy appeared at my side, he took one last, deep drag of his cigarette, before grinding the butt, beneath the sole of his DM boot, into the gravel, as if he was exterminating a nest of ants. He must have been smoking inside the church to have finished it so quick. I gazed down at the tiny ridges of small stones where his imprint had been, then back up at him, but he didn't seem to see the problem so I decided not to say anything. What would have been the point? What did it matter? Wouldn't change anything; wouldn't change Billy, or alter the fact that he had polluted the clean, cool atmosphere of the church. And Dave's mum would still be dead. Nothing was going to change the fact that Dave and the vicar were slowly making their way over to the cemetery, high on the other side of town, overlooking the factories and warehouses like a permanent black cloud.

He hadn't wanted anyone there, had requested that it just be him and the vicar present when they lowered her into the ground. And no one had protested, for there wasn't anyone there to care enough, no other family other than Dave. And some thought that maybe he had been hoping that the old man would show up, sobbing and racked with grief, but I doubted it. And if, like I thought, he had seen what I had seen, that was the last thing he would have wanted.

I rubbed my finger through the heavy condensation, producing a tiny window within a window, and peered like a half blind man into the early evening. The church was empty now, as if nothing had happened, looking as peaceful as a postcard, like nothing bad could ever happen there. The last lingering mourners, just a few neighbours and old acquaintances, from when she could still just about fit into the puzzle of society, had all sloped off, and it looked just like it always did, just another part of town, something that you just took for granted, something that was always there, a part of your life that never really affected you, as distant as the viaducts.

I turned my gaze from the old church and back to Billy. We were sitting in Lui's and waiting for Dave to return from the cemetery. Billy had finished his tea long ago and was playing idly with the sugar bowl. Lifting up a heaped spoonful before slowly pouring it back into the bowl, as if he were trying to tip a grain at a time off his spoon. And then his patience would run out and he would plunge the remains back into the mountain of sugar as if he were trying to inflict damage upon it.

'Want another cup of tea?' I asked.

'Naah,' he sighed, staring into the sugar bowl as if it were a crystal ball.

But Lui appeared anyway from behind his counter, three cups of tea in his hand, saucers overlapping, so that they all seemed to balance on each other. I really didn't know how he did it. He pulled up a chair and sank down with a huge great sigh as if someone had deflated him. If it had been another time, if the circumstances hadn't been so dire, I might well have laughed. The sight of Lui and Billy sitting next to each other, taking tea together, refined and comfortable like a pair of old friends. Instead not a word passed between them; no communication other than Lui nudging Billy's elbow, and Billy tutting loudly, short and exaggerated, rolling his eyes in his head. But understanding the gesture and placing the spoon back in the bowl. But making sure he spilt just enough to test Lui's patience. We sat and finished our tea in silence as the afternoon slowly ebbed away and the sun gradually passed overhead, settling somewhere in another world, beyond the rooftops. Every now and then it would catch the windscreen of a passing car and explode like the blinding flash of a camera.

It was hours until Dave finally caught up with us at the Crown and Sceptre; so long that already the funeral seemed like something that had happened almost another lifetime ago, just a bad memory tucked away in the corner of the mind, like a crumpled shirt screwed up at the bottom of the wardrobe, one that you had always hated.

All talk of the funeral had ceased long ago, we had exhausted all the clichés about what a "shit day" it had been and how it didn't seem right that the sun should have shone and the barefaced gall and sheer nerve of neighbours and so called friends, people who hadn't shown any concern for no one knew how long, crying crocodile tears, but careful not to shed enough as to smear their make-up.

Even the novelty of Lui's company had lost its appeal for Billy and me. At first it really had been quite bizarre, I mean sitting with us in the confines of his own café had been one thing but to look at him in the pub, again next to Billy, chubby dark fingers curled round the handle of his pint jug, was quite another. I half expected him to get up and start cleaning the place; wiping down tables, carrying stacks of empties in one hand with his circus-like sense of balance, whilst wiping out the ashtrays with the other, except he didn't have his customary dish-towel slung over his shoulder.

And so the conversation had flitted about like confetti, until it had landed safely upon the shoulders of football. We talked idly of Liverpool's marvellous achievement in retaining the European Cup at Wembley back in May. I recalled Dave telling me of the hordes of drunken scousers traipsing up and down Oxford Street on three and four day benders. We spoke of the disbelief we had each felt when Don Revie had resigned the year before. And it was funny because Lui seemed more upset about it than either Billy or me, horrified that a national manager could turn his back on his country. "Treason" he had called it. And inevitably the conversation found its way round to me.

'How-ah is it going?' he had asked. 'How you finding it, Johnny… big goalie now, eh?'

I had been able to hear the drink in his voice, not slurring drunk, but as if the words were heavy in his mouth, slowing down his speech. I hadn't mentioned my debut in the reserves. Not a word of the penalty save and the clean sheet; the congratulations, the backslapping. It just hadn't seemed right. And besides, I had just asked for a day off on account of the funeral, and God knows how they would look upon that.

Lui had said that he 'must come and watch me soon.'

'Ha,' Billy had laughed into his pint. 'Wouldn't bother… he's still shit!' he had said to Lui, nodding and winking in my direction. ''E's like those Scottish keepers… couldn't catch a fuckin' cold!'

And I was glad Billy was there, don't know if I could have handled waiting for Dave on my own, would have driven myself mad, didn't want to dwell on the day that much.

The reference to Scottish goalies steered the conversation away thankfully, from me to Scotland's chances in the coming World Cup in Argentina, and of course the fact that there was no England again, the whole decade, our whole youth, without our country performing on the world stage.

'I think they do okay,' Lui had reflected.

''Ope they get fuckin' hammered!' replied Billy, burping into his beer. And it had been like stepping back in time, couldn't believe four years had passed since Billy had expressed similar sentiments to me, Dave and Ketchup in Lui's café, back in the summer of '74. Funny how the silliest things stick, embed themselves, like splinters, in the memory. Could see in my mind's eye Lui appearing from behind his counter, trusty tea towel over his shoulder, telling Billy to watch his language. And now there we were, sitting in a pub sharing a beer together. I had found myself wondering what it must be like, suddenly being on the same level as children you had witnessed grow up. I had tried to imagine what he must have thought of us, tried to look at us through someone else's eyes. Did other people see me like I saw myself? Just an average kid, nothing special… but hopefully enough of a lad so as not to be gimpy. I couldn't imagine anyone could see Billy for anything other than what he was, raw and aggressive. But, as I've said before, you had to know him. He was what he was. Only now he burped into his glass of beer instead of his glass of Coke.

But I think he must have realised that there was something there, something that each of us had, running through us like veins in marble, or we wouldn't have all been so close.

But of course Dave was his favourite. His easy, mature manner seemed to simply intoxicate grown-ups. What did Lui, like so many others, see there, I wondered. This walking contradiction, a kind of human paradox, boy by name and numbers only; statistics, a date and a birth certificate, in my eyes he had never grown up… had never needed to, had simply always been that mature, that wise. Maybe I was *too* close, I had worn him like a child wears a security blanket, couldn't even see the physical changes, apart from the hair of course, like watching grass grow, you just don't see it from day to day. It was the same with *The Kick in*. For if you put your face too close to the page and the words melt before your eyes.

By the time Dave had finally appeared even the topic of football had been exhausted, cracks running through our conversation like a split river bed in a drought. Billy had given up even trying. Instead he stood leaning over the jukebox in the corner, his black tie dangling from his neck, brushing against the slanting glass top, nodding his head to the music that split the silence, pleased with himself, approving of his own choice as he tapped the toe of his scuffed up DM boot; every inch the Clash City Rocker that Strummer had ranted on about at the drop of Billy's coin.

In truth I had been mildly surprised to see Dave again that night. I had had visions of him standing alone upon the exposed hillside of the cemetery, staring blankly into the deep rectangle in the ground. Could see this lone figure, unflinching, shrouded in black, orange hair exploding in the dying embers of the fading sunlight as a couple of old gravediggers slowly scattered back the dried earth, quietly respectful but too experienced to care. And the sick irony of it all would be that he would look more like the Bowie we had tried to recreate up at the old docks than he could ever have imagined. The perfect picture for his personal portfolio; face as still as a statue, an emptiness, seemingly emotionless. But the truth of it was that the tears would be flowing inside, running like rivers through every fibre of his body as if he had been turned inside out.

'Alright,' said Dave as the door swept shut with a whoosh, the way pub doors do. He smiled, but there was no humour in it, he didn't even seem surprised to see Lui sitting there. I had seen him coming, that unmistakeable orange blob gliding past the frosted glass window, and had already been on my feet when he came in. We stood for a minute facing each other. And what could I say?

'Yeah, fine,' I said. 'And you?' It sounded so pathetic. Meaningless words that fell hopelessly short. He looked around at the surroundings that he found himself in, as if noticing them for the first time, looking like a builder might look on surveying the remains of a derelict house. And for the first time since we had walked in hours earlier I was aware of the gloom that stuck to the place like mud on the walls. Just a few regulars sat dotted around in their usual seats. On seeing us Billy shuffled over, tired from drink. He raised his eyebrows at Dave, not knowing what to say either. 'Wanna beer, boy?'

Lui looked up at the three of us standing round the table; we seemed to make the place look untidy, which was hard to believe. He could see that it was a delicate time, that we needed to be alone together, and took the opportunity to leave. As he slid his chair back under the table he looked into Dave's eyes with genuine concern.

'Look after yourself, my boy.' He smiled faintly, placing a hand on Dave's arm as if to hold it steady while he gave it a gentle pat.

'Thanks for coming, Lui,' Dave told him. Lui waved a hand in the air and was gone.

The three of us stood for a moment, if you'd have just walked in it would have been impossible to tell if we were coming or going. It was a strange moment, lost in transition; the world seemed to melt away, nothing around but the three of us, crystal clear against a distorted background; like the 3D cards you find in cereal packets.

'Let's get out of here,' said Dave.

'You know if a star were to fall from the sky and land on us it would actually be larger than the Earth itself.'

Billy propped himself up on one elbow, took a long swig from his can of beer, looked at Dave and said, 'How the fuck do you know shit like that?'

Dave didn't answer, didn't seem to hear him, just continued to stare vacantly up at the sky from where he lay flat on his back, watching the night dilute the day like drops from a paintbrush into a jar of water.

'Of course, it's hypothetical anyway... impossible... seeing as most of the stars that you actually see no longer exist... perished God knows how many years ago... so what you're actually looking at is something that isn't there.'

Billy shook his head and went to take a mouthful of beer before he realised that it was empty. He stared at the can vehemently as if it had done something to offend him.

'That's what I hate about drinking from cans... you can never see how much you've got left.'

We were in the park, just hanging around, drinking and letting the evening close in on us. We had left the pub with no plans other than to stay together. It wouldn't have mattered what we did or where we did it, as long as we stuck together. Neither of us had mentioned it, hadn't needed saying I suppose, but when Dave had slipped into the "Offy" and emerged with an armful of takeaways, we had just sort of drifted there, as if the cans had been carrying a label or something: *To be consumed in the park only*.

In a goalmouth over by the entrance some kids were still kicking a ball about, despite the fast approaching evening, playing on until the daylight took its final breath. I couldn't see them properly from where we lay, the night falling fast, just ghosts in the gloom, but the high pitched sounds of voices and their boundless enthusiasm told me that they were only young; ten or eleven maybe. And were they just like we had been a few years ago, I wondered. From broken homes, broken families with broken hearts, from places where discipline and guidance no longer flowed, where communication had shut down like the electricity in the power cuts that we had experienced a few years back. Forced to grow up quicker than the rest; finding a kind of solace in football, pulling them together like the neck of a duffel bag. I couldn't work out whether I envied them or not, feelings of ambivalence curdling with the beer. There was the sweet innocence of youth of course, but I pitied them if they had an experience like *The Kick In* awaiting, a kind of rites of passage ordeal that boys had to go through; you would carry it around like a dead carcass on your back until you finally had the strength of mind to shrug it off.

I sighed and turned back to face Dave and Billy; shadows in the night now, faces pale like blue marble in the moonlight, their cigarette ends glowing like ships in the night.

Funny how Billy's smoking had surprised me more than Dave's. It had never sat well with me watching him jam a smoke between his lips. With Dave it almost seemed obvious, the next step, part of the Bowie thing; cool, languid... mysterious even. And it just seemed to suit him, like an artist with a brush. And you would think it would have suited Billy as well, young punk, acting tough, boiling over with malcontent. But the thing was that Billy didn't need to "act" tough, he simply was. And I could never forget how much Billy had hated it when we had experimented as kids under the viaducts that year.

It was hard to believe, I thought to myself, as I watched their tiny orange dots jump through the gloom as they moved from hand to mouth, that I hadn't been dragged into it all, but I had my football I supposed. Forever my safety net, preventing me from falling to God knows where. And I could just imagine being thrown out, caught puffing in the boot room or something. It would have been bad enough if they could see me now, I thought; hanging around at night, drinking beer, pissed for the second time in four days. But the truth was that I knew that the day would end like that, the three of us drinking, tired and weary, looking older than our years, huddled together somewhere, swimming in a sea of alcohol like survivors of a shipwreck.

But then again, what could they expect? After all, my best mate had just put his mother in the ground, and practically alone as well, just himself, the vicar and his old leather bible. Dave said that it had felt as if he were the only living person on Earth; that even the vicar didn't seem real to him, just a sculpture, like the winged headstones that stood either side of the cemetery gates. Had said that even when he had said a prayer, his words just blew lightly away, like confetti in the wind.

But if anyone could have seen him then they would never have believed it, no one would. His demeanour, laid-back, easy-going, drinking in the summer evening and the beer in equal measure. But to me the insouciance was like the still, ripple-free waters that glided above the depths, couldn't believe that there weren't a sea of questions rolling around inside of him; like "Why?" or "Could I have done anything, seen the signs maybe?" But even when the sight of his old man had risen like a ghost, he had managed to keep the waters of his emotions steady. And even I had had to look twice. But by then he had gone, like a piece of driftwood rising in the trough of a giant swell, and when it sank and rose again I had simply disappeared, lost beneath the waves, as if it had never been there.

I had been standing gratefully outside the church, savouring the sights and sounds of town as opposed to the dank, biting gloom of the inner sanctum of the church. The gravel path had scrunched beneath my feet, as I drank in the air like a released prisoner, and then there he was. Standing across the street, in the doorway of the bookies next door to Lui's, no more than a speck in my eye line, a smudge on the page, but for a brief moment it was all that I could see. Billy had appeared by my side, the air filling with the smell of his tobacco, I had turned to face him, for no more than a split second, but when I had turned back, the vision had gone, the doorway was empty. Where it had gone I didn't know, back in the bookies, down the road? I didn't care, just as long as Billy hadn't seen him, for whether it was the day of Dave's mum's funeral or not, Billy would have gone after him, the red mist descending, and you would have needed a tank to stop him. And if it had been any other day I don't think I would have wanted to. It would have been interesting, that's for sure, the clash of two animals in the jungle, the old hand against the young pretender.

Had Dave seen him, I wondered. Must have, surely, couldn't see how he could have missed him. Or had he appeared after Dave had left with the vicar?... perhaps. And, of course, he hadn't said, gave nothing away as I watched him pull another can from the pack and hand it over.

'Cheers,' I said, pulling the ring-pull back and letting the pressure fizz out into the evening.

'Just what your coach ordered.' He smiled and somehow reassured me, just like it always had, even when I didn't know why I needed reassuring?

The scar on his forehead showed clearer with the dim glow of twilight upon us, like a cast shadow. It seemed more prominent now, at first when it had started to heal it had begun to fade as if it were simply going to melt back into his skin like ice in water, but now for some reason it was quite distinctive, as if he wore a permanent frown across his forehead. And for a moment I wondered if it really bothered him. He always said that it didn't, not with any kind of arrogance, just that he didn't really think about it. But every time Dave looked in the mirror it must have done exactly what it had been intended to, serving its purpose with a clinical efficiency, a constant reminder, opening up his mind to that dreadful day, evoking feelings of intimidation and utter powerlessness.

I caught his eye squinting at me through the blue plumes of cigarette smoke, and I knew he knew what I was thinking, as clear as if I'd been talking out loud. And there was that smile again… disarming my thoughts and fears with its elusive charm, telling me that "it's okay", that he was okay… just like always.

It had just gone midnight, the night slipping into tomorrow, by the time Dave and I dropped Billy home. We had to virtually carry him there, an arm each slung around our shoulders, feet dragging behind like a corpse, as he mumbled incoherently from one story or another from our past. And just when the pull of him threatened to drag us down altogether, as if the side that bore his dead weight had melted like wax, he would suddenly spring back to his feet, as if he had been jump-started back to life, and would break into some Clash or Pistols song at the top of his voice.

It was the nearest I had ever seen him come to showing any real affection, when we stood in the doorway of his flats. Despite the time of night there were still a few kids to be found, lurking in the shadows, sitting around on the front steps, smoking and seeing which one could spit the furthest.

'We gotta see more of each other, boys!' he slurred after booting the entrance door open. 'I fuckin' mean it… J!' He slapped a hand upon my shoulder. 'I mean what with your football… and you with your music… writing and stuff.' He waved a hand tiredly in Dave's direction, as if it had taken all the strength that he could muster. He had drunk himself to the point of oblivion, downed two and sometimes three cans to each of Dave and mine's.

'What the fuck happened to us, eh?' He was mumbling now, head bowed, swallowing his hiccups, beaten by drink. 'I thought we'd be kids for fuckin' ever.' He smiled stupidly at Dave. *'Boys, boys, it's a sweet thing,'* quoting Bowie from his *Diamond Dogs* album. His shoulders looked impossibly low, like a giant invisible weight had been heaped upon them, even his mop of blonde hair seemed duller, as if the colour had been drained away. '… And now look at us. You two proper grown-ups, pro footballer in the makin' and a bleedin' writer!'

And it was strange, because I had never looked at us as kids at all, even when we actually *had* been. Had always thought of it a bit like descending a towering ladder, instead of taking tentative steps, feeling with our feet for the next rung, instead we had had to fly down, clamp our feet and hands on the outside and simply hang on for dear life. But now that we were actually living in the adult world for the first time, just like Billy had said, meeting and working with grown-ups, coaches - the staff, the seasoned pros, even people like Cindy - I had felt more vulnerable and out of my depth than ever before. I hadn't really thought about it too much until then, only knew that everything had been moving too fast for me, even the giant leap into the reserves, despite the fact that I had seemed to take it all in my stride.

For a moment we stood in silence, each of us lost in our own thoughts, the faint glow from the one light in the doorway that hadn't been smashed turning our complexions a sickly yellow. The stale smell of piss wafting from the stairwells behind Billy seemed to grow stronger, smelled worse than the telephone boxes in town. And I found myself wondering how Dave and I must have seemed to Billy now. And then, as if to break the awkward silence, Billy glared down at the kids sitting on the kerb.

'Oi, you lot,' he growled, wobbling from side to side. 'Fuck off 'ome now. What the fuck you doin' out this late anyway?' And they didn't so much as look up or give Billy a second thought, simply did as they were told, obedient pupils listening to their master.

And I realised that he was right. I mean to Billy the pair of us must have seemed bold and adventurous, taking our chances in life, creating opportunities, just like all the other kids, the kids that we had never been. I certainly looked at Dave like that, everyone did I suppose, but I didn't think of myself in the same way because it had been football, my constant companion, that had taken me there. And, as if to prove my naivety, it had taken a pissed, out of his head Billy to make me see it.

Dave had missed the last train back into town long ago and was left with no other option than to stay at mine. Although it wouldn't be like the old days, with him zipped up in the old green sleeping bag, the pair of us whispering football games to each other. 'Name six players from Manchester City's '69 cup winning side' and such until we had fallen asleep.

In fact we didn't even head straight for home, even though I felt absolutely knackered. It seemed as if every bone in my body ached from the beer, the alcohol seeping into the marrow. But my mind just wouldn't slow down, whenever there was a lull in our conversation I could still hear voices resonating in my head. We wandered aimlessly through the streets, the place like a ghost town, past empty shops and blacked out pubs, every window a black hole. Our footsteps seemed to multiply in sound, thundering up the alleyways and side streets. We found ourselves up by the posh end of town. Where all the houses seemed to have room to breathe and elegant-looking trees lined the roads. There were gentle sweeping crescents looping off the bigger roads like the handles of a tea cup, they carried rural sounding names such as Orchard Drive and Foxes Crescent, and of course, Connaught Gardens… Debbie's road.

We stood beneath the canopy of the giant sycamore trees that lined the grass verges outside her front gate. I hadn't meant to end up there, certainly had no intention of knocking on the door or trying somehow to see her, could just imagine myself shimmying up the drainpipe in my state. Probably slip and hang myself from the tie that Mum had given me.

Dave looked from me to the house and then back at me. But I didn't say anything, just shrugged my shoulders and sighed ruefully. Maybe I had meant to come here after all, only my brain had decided not to tell me, I didn't know what the reason was, only knew that it annoyed the hell out of me.

The thing was, she had been on my mind of late, ever since I had met Cindy. Whenever I found myself thinking of Cindy, along would come Debbie, floating over the picture like a ghost, adjusting things, as if elements of the two had somehow fused together. Cindy, smiling at me, but with that slightly nonplussed look creeping onto her face, the one that Debbie would always give me whenever she had heard about something stupid that I had done, like she was in the company of some delinquent or something. Or the image would play across my mind of Cindy in the café where the four of us had met for breakfast the morning after we had met, after me and Dave had been playing at Bowie on the banks of the Thames. I loved the warm thought of that morning, how we kept catching each other's eye across the mountains of tea and toast, seeing each other in a different light, ever since we had noticed something familiar in each other's past, threading it's way through one another's childhood's like the delicate strands of a stitch. And just as I would begin to warm to the memory it would suddenly start to distort, Cindy with traits of Debbie again; the way that she would sip her tea, pout at the cup as if she were against the very idea of it actually touching her lips, placing it back in its saucer with pinpoint precision, in that meticulous way that only Debbie could, with that slight tilt of her head.

A faint breeze gently stirred the branches of the sycamores, but in the dead of night it blew through my head like the winds of a storm, dispersing the fuddled clouds of a hangover that were beginning to close in around me. I felt a sharp pang in the pit of my stomach, and of course it could have been the lack food, I hadn't eaten since God knows when, and I *was* hungry, starving in fact, but the pain didn't gnaw like hunger. It felt more volatile than that, like something angry ripping away at my guts. And as the wind picked up it brought with it all my childish insecurities; the itch along the inside of my arm, the prickly heat creeping up my legs, silly idiosyncrasies that took control whenever I found something uncomfortable or disturbing.

I knew what it was that was bothering me, it was just that I didn't want to accept it. All week long it had been creeping up, following me, no matter how hard I tried to shake it off, to twist and turn away from my own thoughts, it would follow me like a shadow; this pointless, irrational sense of disloyalty, the same way that I would feel about Derek being around the house. I hated it, absolutely hated it, the absurdity of it all! That sense of betrayal, but to whom or what?

Dave gazed along the silent street and sighed. He kicked a stone casually along the pavement, back in the direction of town, and nodded as if we should follow it.

'Come on,' he whispered, hands buried deep in his pockets. 'Let's get some kip... After all, you've got training tomorrow, haven't you?'

And he was right, of course, I did have training, would have to be up early to catch the bus. I vaguely wondered if it was even worth going to bed, it would probably only make me feel worse. By the time we arrived back home I wouldn't be able to grab more than a couple of hours anyway. And only then if I managed to find the "off" switch in my head, shut the door on the crowd gathering outside my conscience.

As it turned out we arrived home quicker than I could ever have imagined, courtesy of a milk float, of all things. We had just emerged from the mouth of one of the "hellholes" as we called them, one of the sinister-looking underpasses that led, like rat runs, from the edge of the estates and into town. Usually a pretty stupid thing to do but at that time of night, or day, with the dawn only a heartbeat away they were more or less safe; the druggies and the drunks long since passed out.

And then we had heard the soft trundling of the milk float smoothly up beside us.

'Hello boys! On your way home?' It had been Jack, our local milky, we had known Jack for as long as I could remember. And the name suited him as well, right down to the ground... a right "lad", always smiling, charming the housewives forever whistling a chirpy tune. He must have been about Mum's age too, I reckoned. I often thought that I wouldn't have minded if she had taken up with someone like Jack. Someone average, common almost, like the rest of us, someone who didn't carry the lofty title of a doctor. But, of course, if it had ever happened, I would no doubt have developed the same unreasonable animosity towards him. And besides, I could just imagine the gossip, all the old clichés about the milkman delivering an extra pint and so on. Don't know if I could have handled that.

Jack hadn't questioned our being out, walking the streets at such a peculiar time, had taken in our clothes, black suits and ties, and had been well aware of what the day before had been. The whole neighbourhood had known, and most of them from the likes of people like Jack, the power of gossip. But he was all right Jack, always seemed to have time for people, young or old, had always asked about my football, whenever I saw him, even as a kid. 'How you coming along, young Johnny? Still keeping 'em out, are you?'

But he hadn't asked about my football that morning, had

simply told us to hop on the back of his float, to squeeze between the piles of blue crates and help ourselves to a pint if we liked. And it had felt good, the two of us there, a sort of homecoming, like we were back from a dreadful war or something. And as we had popped down the shiny aluminium tops with our thumbs we had felt strangely alive, gulping it down, sharp and thick, like an electric shock to the system as the icy cold hit the empty pits of our stomachs. And just then the birds had begun their morning chorus, high above the rattling of the crates, somewhere up in the crisp nakedness of the dawn.

CHAPTER THIRTEEN

July 1978

When I think back it all seemed to start with *The Kick In*... the beginning of the end. That summer's day when our childhoods unravelled spectacularly, like a ball of string hurtling down a hill. But then there was also the Peru match. In fact the more I think of it, football never seemed so innocent again either, and that had a big effect on my general outlook. I couldn't help it, a habit of mine, judging everything in life by football, trying to find comparisons. And then of course there was this Peruvian goalie; Quiroga, diving to his right, parrying Don Masson's poorly-struck penalty away to safety, well off his line, and possibly moving before the ball had been kicked, but that hardly seemed to matter, as if the outcome had never been in doubt.

The whole pub seemed to roll as one, 'Oooohh!', as if we were perched upon a giant wave. And it certainly wasn't the end of the world, I mean it wasn't England or anything but of course we weren't even there again! But it *was* the World Cup after all, and Scotland's opening group four match, one they had been widely expected to win, or draw maybe, possibly, but to lose... unthinkable!

And there was the odd ripple of laughter, a few cheers, but nothing much, none as loud or as malicious as Billy's, there he was shrieking with laughter, spilling his beer as he leapt joyfully to his feet. There was a lifetime of hate ingrained in him towards Scotland, towards any of the other home nations, courtesy of his dad.

And there were three of them, the Scots brickies sitting round a table over to our right by the cigarette machine. And their faces were as dark as the replica navy blue shirts that they each wore.

'Sit down you little shite!' snarled the biggest of the trio through gritted teeth. Kenny was his name. In general they accepted the jeers and cheers that echoed around the pub, the ambivalence shown towards their national team. After all, they were on foreign soil so to speak, like so many of their compatriots who had crossed the border in search of employment.

But there was something about the sheer delight in Billy's celebration that riled them. Billy's clenched fist, the obvious hatred towards the builders' homeland spilling over, like a neglected bath. But in general I think most people wanted them to win, even if they didn't outwardly admit it.

'Fuck off!' Billy sneered back at the three Scots, waving two fingers at them and completely unperturbed by the fact that they were twice the size of us, and a good few years older as well.

And the biggest one was on his feet now, the one who had told Billy to sit down, like an animal on its hind legs ready to pounce. And the sheer size of him would have sent most people cowering back in their seats, but of course, not Billy. They just stood staring daggers at each other across the floor; Billy, small and compact, dangerous and ready in his DMs, faded jeans and Pistols T-shirt. "Big Ken", the flame-haired Scot, a brickie with hands the size of small shovels.

Suddenly a gravely voice boomed out from behind the bar, 'Oi! Sit down the pair of you, or you'll both be out the door!'

'Aye. sit down, Kenny man... watch the game,' pleaded one of his mates, placing a hand on Big Ken's shoulder.

'You should know better, Jock,' the landlord continued, and then turned to Billy. 'And you,' he gave Billy one of those knowing looks. 'Calm yourself, Billy son!'

Billy just shrugged his shoulders as if he had heard it all

before, and of course he had, but he sat back down anyway and turned back to watch the game.

But when the big man slowly returned to his seat I saw his giant hand tremble slightly as he reached for his pint, as if he was struggling to contain the anger boiling away inside of him. I should have known then, been a bit more wary, but of course, I wasn't. And to me that's where it all began, the beginning of the end if you like. Everything seemed to fall in on us from that moment on, like standing inside a giant sandcastle, we just couldn't seem to stop it, were unable to avoid it, any of it.

The last twenty minutes or so passed by almost unwatched, looking without really seeing. Dave hadn't seemed that interested from the kick-off, sipping his beer, one eye on the TV at the back of the Falcon, the other on the music paper on his lap.

'That's them fucked,' smiled Billy, downing the last drops of his pint. 'Beat Iran… get stuffed by Holland. What do you reckon?'

'Think you're right, young William,' sighed Dave, as he lifted his head from his paper and stretched out from his chair like a cat after a nap. 'For once,' he grinned.

'Fuck off!' Billy smiled back.

By last orders the pub was still more or less full. These were hardened drinkers, six or seven night a week men, not just in for the match. A few had left in dribs and drabs at the end of the game of course, and some had even moved on to other pubs, but the majority were still hanging around, propping up the bar or crowded round the tiny circular tables like the three of us. And I had stayed of course, felt predictably pissed by then, certainly more than I had intended to be. But it always seemed to work out that way. Had told myself that I wouldn't drink too much, maybe use one of my old tricks, leave a bit in each glass or something, or leave after the game even, but I didn't seem to be as good, as disciplined as I used to be. And the season had finished of course, but hanging round pubs and getting drunk weren't exactly the pastimes an apprentice footballer, especially one who was being tipped to break into the reserves, should be pursuing. And I knew that there was so much there for me to lose. I almost wished that there wasn't. It had been playing on my mind lately, not consciously, in dreams and stuff, that my ultimate dream, to be a professional footballer, was so close now that I didn't think that I could handle it, and I was on some road to self-destruction. And although I could see it, like some kid stepping off the kerb ahead, I couldn't seem to avoid it; bloodshed in the distance.

And also we had needed each other just then, didn't say it of course, but then again it didn't need saying, not between the three of us. The change that Dave's mum's death had had on us. It was almost as if we had found each other again, like an old record that you haven't played since you can't remember when. And then as soon as you put it on, hear those first, familiar chords, you can't for the life of you work out why you haven't been playing the thing every day.

But, in truth, we had always been there, watching over one another without ever really realising it. It was just that each of our lives had taken such different paths and, at times, days had turned into weeks as we became wrapped up in the changes.

But when you really thought about it, peered beneath the surface, the problems that we faced in the adult world were similar to those that we had encountered in childhood, at least for me, the need to belong, for instance. And the more that I established myself in my new, wonderful life, the more I seemed to turn and cling to the things that I knew so well, things... or people who I knew I couldn't let down: Dave and Billy. The kind of loyalty only found within deep-seated friendships.

It had remained a sultry summer evening despite midnight being less than an hour away. The day had simply refused to die, great chunks of sky still hung onto that clear, swimming-pool blue, with the sinister darkness of the deep end rising up in gentle waves, from somewhere behind the high rise rooftops and the cold grey skyline. We had been sitting in The Falcon since God knows when, and what I had needed was clean, fresh air but the humidity of the night had seemed only to thicken my senses further. When I had walked out the pub I had eagerly anticipated the cool breeze, the welcome change of atmosphere, but it had seemed as if the air itself had been struggling for air.

And after that the whole picture in my head changes, takes on a dreamlike quality, fuzzy images of me and Dave shuffling along the street, after we had, once again, walked Billy home, heads lolling, scuffing our feet, finally beaten by the drink.

When all of a sudden the air was filled with the angry cry of voices, thick Scottish accents full of hate, punctuating the night. And somewhere beneath them, like a deadly undercurrent, the sound of Billy's voice spitting obscenities.

And it was only a short distance back to where we had left him, his tower block looming overhead as if the very darkness itself had been caused by the giant finger of its shadow, but it seemed to take forever to get back there. I could feel the pavement pounding up through the soles of my shoes, could hear the ruckus grow ever louder, but it seemed like I was treading water, trying just to stay afloat on the sea of beer that swilled in my guts. But finally we turned the corner and there was Billy. On his back, kicking out, bucking like an insect struggling to right itself.

And, in the half-light from the street lamp and odd window above, I could make out the shapes of three figures surrounding him, jumping about, hopping from foot to foot as if they were performing some kind of bizarre pagan ritual, but the violence in the air was palpable.

'Not so fuckin' mouthy now, are ye?'

The small group of youngsters that Billy had scolded for being out late the time before, sat on their push bikes, utterly transfixed, just a few yards away in the shadows of the dimly-lit doorway of the flats. Each face a mask of horror as the kicks and blows reigned down on Billy's body.

And then the oldest of the tiny group, from somewhere, found the courage to act. Whether he caught sight of Dave and me steaming around the corner or whether he all of a sudden realised that it was Billy, a legend among the high rises, that he was watching being attacked, kicked and stamped upon from all sides I don't know.

And as the whirlwind of bodies spun wildly across the paved square before the entrance, the boy pedalled headlong into the eye of the storm.

'Ugh! Why you little… ' screamed Big Ken as the bike rammed into the back of his legs. And it had only been a minor disruption, had lasted no more than a few seconds, must have been the equivalent of being dive-bombed by an angry wasp to the great Scot. But it had been enough, time for Billy to scramble to his feet. Just as Ken had shoved the young cyclist away by planting the enormous sole of his boot in the boy's chest, sending him flying across the tarmac, limbs tangled beneath the frame of his bike, back wheel spinning horizontally in midair, trapping the boy's fingers as he yelped in pain like a puppy who had had its tail trodden on. But the boy would be a hero, street "cred" at an all time high. What were a few cuts and bruises to worry about when respect would be measured in scars and stitches.

And then it was three against three. Although they had the age advantage by… it must have been five years. Dave and I stood facing the three Scots like gunslingers in the street. For a moment it was totally quiet, just the sound of the boy's wheel, spinning slowly to a halt. Over to the right Billy emerged from the gloom, blood pouring from a deep red patch just above his forehead. The front of his spiky blonde hair looked as if it had been dyed red. And he wasted no time, didn't even look to acknowledge the pair of us, the look in his eyes was wilder than I had ever seen before, bordering on insane. He launched himself at the trio, screaming as if he were in the throes of some kind of demented fit. And it was certainly Big Ken that he was after, but it didn't stop him from lashing out at the other two for good measure on his way, connecting with one square on the jaw, sending him stumbling right in front of Dave.

And Dave was upon him in a shot, picking his punches, working his way round the Scot's body, using his reach to full effect, utilising every moment of surprise, jabbing away at his face with an almost nonchalant ease. The tables had turned now, without warning. They hadn't expected any of this, the builders, the young boy on his bike, Dave and I returning, and least of all the sheer bloody-minded resistance of Billy's defence, his refusal to accept defeat. They had probably assumed that he would simply cower beneath their barrage, roll himself into a ball and try and protect himself as best he could, wait for it all to be over.

But that simply wasn't Billy, he would fight like a wild cat, you would have to literally stop him from moving to actually beat him. And now the ambush had lost its edge, the Scots' element of surprise vanished, and Dave and now Billy were the ones taking the initiative, Billy upon Big Ken, in close now, not allowing the great man to use his height and weight advantage. They were in Billy's world now, fighting by his rules and the only rule that Billy abided by was that there were no rules. It must have been a terrible feeling; no matter how big you were, having Billy beneath you half crazy with rage, on your toes virtually, close enough to smell his breath, to taste his hate, fists pummelling into you, arms working like pistons. And as absurd as it seemed, for a moment I actually felt a twinge of sympathy for the big man. Despite his size and the fact that he had obviously planned the attack, must have sat brooding in the pub after his altercation with Billy. "Malice aforethought" a judge would have called it.

And then Big Ken actually screamed! His voice so pained and

high-pitched that unless you were there could have been forgiven for thinking that it had been the cry of a woman. The big Scot had been trying to back away, put some distance between himself and Billy so that he could trade with him, enable him to land a decent punch, but each time that he took a step back Billy moved with him, like a shadow, so much so that the Ken's punches fell harmlessly upon the back of Billy's head and shoulders, as effective as hitting a crash helmet. And then Billy had bitten him. He had actually taken a great chunk of his chest in his mouth. And there were punches and kicks landing all over Big Ken's body now, fists and elbows smashing relentlessly into his face, ribs, guts; knees and feet setting upon anything that they could make contact with, hell bent on damage. And this wasn't unheard of with Billy, not the first time that I had seen him take a bite of someone in a fight, every part of him a potential weapon.

And whilst all this was going on, Dave and Billy both engaged in one on ones, like tiny street plays unfolding around me, I was in a scene of my own. Only I wasn't the lead character in mine. We were weighing each other up, at least he was, peering malevolently through his long scruffy hair. Circling me, like a boxer in a ring, and he was on his toes while I remained flat-footed, rooted to the spot; stepping in, jabbing at my head, my face, then stepping back out again. I felt useless, could taste my blood like liquid metal filling up in my mouth, could feel the thickness from too many blows cloud in my head. I hated this kind of controlled fighting, would never have made a boxer, too much time to think about it. Better just to get on with it, like ruthless, methodical Dave, or frenzied Billy.

But instead I was taking a real thumping, absorbing far too much punishment than I should have been, allowing the lad all the freedom in the world to pick his punches, something that I would never usually have done, whether I was winning or losing.

It wasn't that I was scared, it was just that I couldn't seem to find the will from anywhere to fight back, to even defend myself. It was as if everything had drained out of me: anger, aggression, the instinct of survival even. I couldn't quite believe the situation that I had found myself in. Everything leading up to it, hearing the commotion, running blindly back to Billy, events leading up to the fight had felt like they had happened to someone else. Dave and Billy had acted instinctively, stepping into the fray, grabbing their moments, but I had just stood there, a human punch bag.

Maybe I had been dulled by the drink, slow to react, like getting down to a low shot when you haven't fully recovered from an injury of some sort.

What a fool I was! They would never forgive me!

And that was it, they wouldn't forgive me, not any of it... the getting pissed, the fighting... especially the fighting! Abusing the glorious opportunity that I had been handed.

I wanted to fight back, but whenever I looked at the lad in front of me, pummelling me, it wasn't the face of a stranger that I saw; I didn't see the long scruffy hair falling across his determined face as he threw his fist, time after time, at me. Instead I saw the features of someone familiar, images of the people that I would be letting down if I messed the whole thing up. I tried to shake the feeling off, blink away my conscience, but the face would only change, not go away, switch to another person. Mum, my coaches at the club, the boss, team mates... Debbie. Why the hell should she be there! But she was... tutting, shaking her head at me in disgust.

I couldn't seem to focus properly, everything blurred over like trying to see through a rain-washed window. Another punch landed firmly, this time on the side of my head, exploding in my ear. I felt my balance slip away, as if the ground had suddenly begun to tilt. I dropped quickly on one knee, more to stop myself from falling over than to avoid more damage. Despite the ringing in my ear I was aware of the noises around me, but they were distorted, volume turned down and then all of a sudden the voices rushed over me like an incoming tide.

There was Dave's man, gasping for breath, fighting for air as Dave punched it out of him with his barrage of body shots, the sound of Dave dancing around, still picking his punches as easy as apples from a tree. It would have been much better if he had faced long scruffy hair, they would have been more evenly matched, masters of the ring, Queensberry rules and all that. Except long scruffy hair had abandoned any principles that he might once have had, etiquette blown away in a storm of kicks and wild punches as he realised that there was nothing to be afraid of, nothing coming back at him. And I could hear Billy's voice, louder than ever, effing and blinding over to my left somewhere, hidden in the shadows, roaring like some crazed animal. And of all the times, to start daydreaming, for I suddenly had this cartoon-like picture jump in my head of the air surrounding him actually turning black and blue, little puffs of clouds visibly bruised from his verbal battering. I actually almost laughed at the craziness of it all; this bizarre image popping inconveniently into my head, whilst all the time I knelt, defenceless and dumbstruck, beneath a barrage of hate.

But they seemed to be coming with less frequency now, the kicks and punches, I could no longer feel the sting or the pain, mind and body numb from punishment. Long scruffy hair had definitely slowed, either tiring or simply growing bored. The tarmac around me began to light up, tiny patches blinking in the night as people above finally decided to see what the disturbance was all about.

'Oi!' a voice boomed out.

'What the 'ell's goin' on!' came another.

'I've called the police you know!'

The kids all of a sudden scattered, disappeared into the flats and melted into the shadows, running like rats this way and that at the very mention of the police.

And there was still Billy's voice, quieter now but still as determined and repetitive. 'Bastard, Bastard, Bastard!' like a scratched record, as the sirens wailed somewhere in the distance.

Dave finally sprang to my rescue, swapping punches with long scruffy hair that they were both too good to be caught by.

'Johnny! *Johnny*! Stop him, for fuck's sake!'

I couldn't hear him at first, couldn't pick Dave's words out of the night, he was too distant, like a voice in a dream. They were quite a way from me now, Dave and long scruffy hair, they had glided, like dancers across an empty floor, had waltzed out into the middle of the road, the street lamp funnelling down upon them like a spot light. But even from a distance Dave had been aware of what was going on. He could see Billy smashing Big Ken's head on the pavement, while I remained, motionless like a statue on my knees; useless, unseeing, unhearing, engulfed by this strange sense of vacancy.

'Johnny! He'll kill him!' Dave was screaming at me now. Not like Dave, not like Dave at all. He couldn't shake off the attentions of Scruffy, who seemed completely oblivious to his friend's predicament, intent only on trying to land a decent punch on Dave; like trying to catch a butterfly in the wind.

Oh No! I've ripped his T-shirt! His favourite, the one of Johnny Rotten! I couldn't stop thinking about it, as if it were the most important thing in the world, as I clawed at Billy, desperately trying to drag him off the big Scot. He had been sitting across his chest, alternating between smashing him in the face and smashing his head into the pavement. It was as if I didn't have the capacity to grasp the seriousness of the situation, I was running away from it all in my mind. Ever since Dave and I had first heard the commotion ringing out in the night, I had fallen into some kind of trance as we had retraced our steps back to Billy's flats, not

166

wanting to believe in what I knew we would find on our return; echoes of *The Kick In* growing louder in my head.

And the sirens were louder now, so loud in fact that I could barely hear Dave, although now he was standing beside me.

I read his lips, 'Come on!', and he grabbed me by the arm. It seemed as if the sound of the sirens would pierce my eardrums, drown out everything, would run down the alleyways and up the stairwells, filling every crack in the pavement. I caught a glimpse of Dave's face in a pool of light as he bent down to pull Billy to his feet. And he was back in control now, calm and collected. And I tried to take some strength from that; spit the blood from my mouth and clear my head, as I groggily followed the pair of them behind the flats and into the darkness.

CHAPTER FOURTEEN

July 1978

'Walked into a door you say,' said Albert, the club physio, his forehead knitted in a deep frown.

'Yeah,' I sighed, rolling my eyes and trying hard to sound believable and exasperated with my own clumsiness.

'Hmm.' There was more than a trace of doubt in his voice as he ran his fingers gingerly across the mask of bumps and bruises that covered my face, as if he were trying to decipher Braille, but he didn't press the matter.

I actually didn't look half as bad as I would have thought, I had expected a lot worse when I had finally found the courage to face myself in the mirror. I had a paper thin cut, as if I had been sliced, about an inch long that ran above my left eye to the bridge of my nose. It was what made me opt for the door story, had figured that the injury was comparable with walking into the edge of a door. It was the rest of the evidence that conspired against me, the slight bruising on the other cheek, faint but detectable, and the swelling on my top lip; it didn't seem plausible that all of this could have been the result of simply being caught in the face by a swinging door.

'Does this hurt?' Albert asked, as he gently felt about the bridge of my nose.

'Nah,' I lied.

'Should have had a couple of stitches in that cut,' he mumbled to himself. 'Still... ' He sighed, straightening himself back up 'Nothing to be done about it now, no other injuries then?'

'Nope.' I tried to sound innocent, deliberately not looking at him, pretending to be interested in a chart of the human body that hung upon the wall. I had gone along to Albert to cover myself, as it were. Once he had checked me over, accepted my story and given me the all clear, I would be able to present his words as a kind of reference in my defence against any doubters. So the last thing that I wanted was for him to start poking and prodding about on my bruised and battered body. He would read the boot scuff marks and bruises as clearly as if I had written a signed confession.

'Well at least, being a keeper, you won't be doing any heading practice, will you?'

'Nah… it's only light training anyway,' I said, hopping off the treatment table a little too eagerly and having to fight the urge to bolt for the door. 'Thanks then, Albert,' I said casually over my shoulder.

'Oh by the way, Johnny… '

I was halfway out the room, could hear the muffled voices of people in another room somewhere, the sound of someone's footsteps echoing along the corridor. For a moment I thought about ignoring him, pretending that I simply hadn't heard. But I knew that there was no escape. I slowly put my head back around the door, resigning myself to the truth, should have known better than to think that I could get one past old Albert.

'Yes, Alb?'

'What did you think of Scotland then?' he said with a shake of his head. 'Bloody awful, weren't they?'

I couldn't have slept for more than two or three hours each night for the next week or so, not until I had heard the welcome news that Big Ken was out of hospital and that the three of them had thankfully moved on to their next job, somewhere down the M4, Swindon way had been the general consensus from the Falcon but I didn't care where, as long as it was far away.

I still didn't quite understand how the hell we had managed to escape the police that night. Like soldiers behind enemy lines the three of us had made it back to the safety of my house, had taken the most unlikely route, up and down alleyways, treading down new paths behind the lines of garages, always keeping to the shadows. We had moved swiftly in silence, with a kind of dogged determination that the three of us probably hadn't shown together since our days of being part of the same football team. I had never in all my life taken such a bizarre route from Billy's to mine and I couldn't imagine they ever had either. But the three of us seemed to know where to go; seemed to know instinctively where every hole in the fence or gap in a set of railings lurked, as easily as if they were signposted, comfortable in our surroundings, like animals prowling through the jungle.

We had sat round the kitchen table in a kind of stunned silence, nothing but the sound of heavy breathing between us. Mum hadn't been home, as I had known she wouldn't, hardly was any more, whether or not she worked the night shift. Ever since I had turned seventeen and signed up at Southfields she had begun to spend more and more time over at Derek's place, something that she had very rarely done in all the time that I could remember them being together.

At first I had been over the moon, such a relief not to feel awkward in my own home as I had whenever he had been there. But just lately, much to my surprise, I had slowly begun to hate it, the coming home to an empty house, that hollow feeling of loneliness. At the beginning I had welcomed the solitude, the place to myself, played my records as loud as I wanted, watched whatever I liked on telly. But knowing that Mum wouldn't be coming home at all, whatever time it might have been, somehow took the edge off it all. I hadn't realised what a great sense of security I had always felt whenever I had heard her key jangling in the lock, even if she had woken me from coming home from a late shift. And now I found myself listening out for the clicking of her key, which used to annoy the hell out of me; or the sound of her footsteps on the path outside, that little bubbling feeling whenever I heard the squeaking of a front gate, although in my heart of hearts I knew that it was next door's, even though they were no more than a few feet apart; distinction finely tuned by the years.

I couldn't wait to get away from Southfields the next day. After my visit to Albert's I had spent the entire day on tenterhooks, waiting to be found out, every time someone called my name I had thought my heart were about to explode. I could never understand people when they would say that their heart "missed a beat". For whenever I faced anxious or nerve-racking times, mine would feel as if it were literally about to pound straight through my chest.

I didn't go home, instead I headed into town to see Cindy as we had arranged. What with Mum being away, most of the time now I looked forward to the nights, once or twice a week, that I would stay over at her place. It was hard to believe that I was quite content with all that was going on in our relationship, the maturity of it all, like… well like grown-ups.

Our relationship had moved onto the next stage, the end of my innocence. I had never lied about stuff like that, could never see the point. There had been opportunities for me in the past, I suppose, to go the whole way with a bird, chances that had come my way, but the idea of it all always seemed more seductive than the real thing. Daydreams and fantasies were never filled with those dreadful awkward silences, or drunken fumbles in the dark. And of course when I had hit that certain age, when it just feels right to take that next step, when that great window of opportunity opens up for teenagers of a certain age, I had been with Debbie, and I had felt so woefully inadequate; physically and emotionally, nothing like the older boys that she seemed to admire and attract.

But thankfully Cindy and I were past all those cumbersome first-time hurdles, comfortable enough to undress and touch each other in the light.

'Does he actually go out looking for trouble that boy?' Cindy asked incredulously, as we sat in the kitchen of her and Nikki's apartment. I had never seen her quite so agitated before, as if that gentle, calm outlook that covered her personality like flowery wallpaper couldn't comprehend the idea of people fighting.

She had met and knew Billy, had heard so much about him that when I had finally introduced them in a pub not far from Dave's, just off Baker Street, she had totally disarmed him with the warmth and enthusiasm of her greeting, hugging and kissing him on the cheek as if he had been an old friend.

'Christ, J!' he had said, dumbstruck, as we had made our way to the bar. 'What the fuck did you tell 'bout me?'

'Nothing,' I'd shrugged.

'She thinks I'm a bloody saint!'

'Hardly... Now get the beers in... it's your round.'

Cindy slid back her chair and started to busy herself with making tea, more for something to do, I reckoned, than anything else. She had been squirming in her chair, like a child who needed the toilet, as I had explained the reason for the state of me, as honestly and openly as I could, as if I were flipping the pages of a picture book before her eyes. I hadn't lied or kept anything back; didn't invent a few extra Scots to make us sound tougher. Didn't need to with Cindy, I never felt I had to be someone or something that I wasn't. It was the silly things like that that made me feel good about us, we were compatible, like two jigsaw pieces fitting together.

And she was pouring me a cup of tea now, even though she hadn't actually asked if I wanted one. I groaned inwardly, I had tried one at lunch up at the club, one of the lads had poured me a cup from the giant enamel urn that seemed to be constantly full of piping hot tea. But as soon as I had put the thin plastic rim to my lips I had nearly jumped through the ceiling, as the heat and the steam stung the gash inside my mouth like vinegar on an open cut. But I just smiled and mumbled a 'thank you' as she placed it on the table in front of me, dragging one of the Cornwall placemats beneath it; funny, but I didn't feel so upright about the truth now.

'It's not so much that he looks for trouble,' I told her as she put the milk back in the fridge, still busying herself. You would never have known that there was even a fridge there, it had been covered from top to bottom with a kind of montage of wine labels peeled off the front of empty bottles, the way a traveller would cover their rucksack with badges from places they had been. The whole flat had these odd touches, the place screamed of money, all mod cons - the fridge, TV, stereo system, plush settee - but the girls had tried to take the polish off, hide the decadence beneath their "hippie" lifestyle. A tie-dyed sheet draped over the sofa, bright flowers painted on the front of cupboards and the side of the TV; playing at being poor, as if they were ashamed of the money that Nikki's parents had inherited, although they didn't seem to resent their place in St. John's Wood Art College. It was cynical really, but I found it all quite amusing.

'It's just that… well… ' I struggled for the words to explain it all as she pulled up a chair beside me, waiting for my explanation. As if I could explain it all!

Although Cindy had taken to Billy, had liked him even before she had met him, purely because he was… well, part of me really, when it came down to it, they were just stories, a part of my past, back when we were boys, amusing, but she had been unaffected by them. But this was different, this was now, and if it involved me it involved her, at least Cindy seemed to think so. And I could tell that she wasn't comfortable with it, not comfortable at all, not the kind of behaviour that she was used to from a boyfriend.

I fiddled with her art folder on the table in front of me, grateful for something to look at, to avoid the disappointment etched upon her face. It was full of black and white pencil sketches of a lady with a dog on a lead. There were four drawings in all, each of the same subject, the lady and the dog, but each from a different perspective: one of the dog, a scruffy-looking terrier thing, sitting stubbornly on the ground, his tongue hanging out, an almost wistful look upon its face. And then there was one of the lady, Cindy had hidden her face beneath a curtain of shadows, but her body language spoke of her cold and impatience. Hunched shoulders, free hand buried deep in the pocket of her long, thick overcoat. And the other two sketches were of the whole scene but from different angles, of the lady leaning, trying unsuccessfully to coax the uncertain creature into life.

Suddenly I felt unbelievably tired, my whole body beginning to throb with aches and pains. This wasn't supposed to have happened, this feeling of awkwardness. And how I was I supposed to explain all the disruption that had touched Billy's life? To offer an explanation for the violence that seemed to hold him together like glue, and my part in it all?

Of course there were his parents... his dad, the obvious answer. But it sounded so lame, I could hear myself trotting it out, the stereotypical bad father... the root of the problem, and I couldn't bring myself to say it. Instead I said nothing, carried on pretending to be interested in her folder. Until Cindy snapped it shut and pushed it across the table like a parent demanding the attention of an ignorant child.

I continued to stare at the table where the folder had been, let out a deep sigh and felt the cut in my mouth with the tip of my tongue, wincing from the sharp stab as if I were trying to jolt myself from the depths of a bad dream.

But it was no good, I had kidded myself that I could tell Cindy everything, tell her absolutely anything about my life and the world that I had grown up in, that we were one of a kind, me and Cindy, soul-mates who had just been waiting to find each other. The complete opposite to what Debbie and I had once been, we didn't have to cross that yawning class divide that loomed between us. I had tried so hard to break the hold that Debbie had on me, poured so much into this "me and Cindy" thing, that I had completely smothered anything "real" that had been there.

And who was I kidding? I wasn't on her level, not even if I had looked up. She had sailed through the choppy waters of her adolescence with all the stealth of an impressive cruise ship, and there was me... a tiny rowing boat floundering in her slipstream by comparison.

All of a sudden I felt like the bullied dog in her drawings.

'It's not that he looks for trouble exactly,' I mumbled at the table, not wanting to see the look on her face, afraid of what I might see. Oh God! I didn't think I could handle that look of disappointment, the pursed lips, the one that Debbie used to wear. Was it a built-in female reaction to the ineptitude of their male counterparts, I wondered.

'It's just that... well... it kind of always seems to find him,' I shrugged. But it didn't sound convincing, not even to me, certainly wouldn't cut any ice with the girl sitting beside me; this stony-faced young woman who had suddenly replaced the Cindy I thought I knew. It had just been something to say, something to fill the ever-increasing chasm suddenly opening up between us. But it simply floated and disappeared in the air, like a whisper floating through a canyon.

CHAPTER FIFTEEN

August 1978

It felt good to be sitting in the park again, swaying lazily on the swings waiting for Billy, and despite the drop in temperature with the setting of the sun, I felt that warm daytime drowsiness washing over me, like when you're awake, aware of the world around you, but only the daylight seems to penetrate the thin shutters of your eyelids.

Everything there was just so familiar, could have been sitting in my own back garden. There was the strained creaking of the swing as I rocked gently to and fro, as if my weight was too much for the old frame, but it had been like that for as long as I could remember. And the muffled sound of the traffic beyond the thick wall of hedgerow and trees, like it had been smothered by a giant pillow, even watching the sunset itself, sinking deep red beyond the line of viaducts, seemed like saying goodnight to an old friend.

To those who didn't know us it might have appeared strange to meet Billy at the park when he would have had to actually walk past the train station if he were to come directly from his flat, but neither of us had questioned it, hadn't even given it a second thought. For it had always been the meeting place, there or Lui's, and besides, Billy always seemed to be coming from somewhere else these days.

I gazed out over what had been the backdrop to so much of my childhood; across the lines of football pitches to the old pavilion, still standing alone and defiant, like a fort in the desert.

There was something comforting about being surrounded by so much of my childhood, drifting across a sea of memories. Even the bad things seemed to lose their potency when they had been safely bedded down beneath the layers of the years. All except *that* one of course, it still lingered, silently like a deadly gas.

Billy suddenly appeared from out of a weed-invested alley over on the dodgy east estate side. It was a Friday evening and we were going up town to meet Dave. Watching Billy stride purposely out into the park, he reminded me of some kind of dangerous animal, a lion or a tiger or something, prowling menacingly across the plane, body language screaming truculence.

'Alright, J,' he nodded. He must have seen the faintest hint of distaste on my face for when I looked up he wore that devilishly satisfied grin, like a cartoon cat that had cornered a mouse. It still grated after all these years, him calling me J. I don't know why, it just made me sound like I thought I was something special, I couldn't really explain it, other than it annoyed the hell out of me. But if I was stupid enough to let Billy see that I was annoyed then I supposed I deserved it somehow.

'Heard anything?' I asked, as he plonked himself down on the swing beside me.

'Nah,' he shrugged and dribbled a huge frothy gob into an empty crisp bag that lay between his feet.

'SHOTTT!' he exclaimed, raising a clenched fist as if he had scored the winning goal in the cup final. 'Anyway, I won't hear nothin' now,' he said, kicking the bag away and sending his spit in an arc across the tarmac.

'What do you mean... *now*?'

'They've fucked off 'avn't they? Finished their job and moved on... or so they say.' He craned his neck and attempted to hit the crisp bag with a fresh gob.

'Who says?' I asked, as the exasperation crept into my veins.

'Malcom... the landlord of the Falcon... YEEES! Bullseye!'

he grinned, all pleased with himself as the saliva slipped thick and smooth off the shiny crisp packet like a tiny bubbling river of lava.

For weeks now I had been going around with this kind of pressure gradually building up inside my head, ever since we had had the fight with the Scots, but now I could feel it instantly start to slip away, slowly, like fizz escaping from a bottle.

'And that Ken bloke...?' I asked, trying to sound all casual; just because Billy hadn't mentioned that he was okay didn't mean to say that he was.

'What about 'im?' He was becoming irritated now, I could almost hear it crackling like the beginning of a fire. He scuffed the toe of his Doc Marten boot across the tarmac, tutting as he tried to wipe away a stray globule of spit.

'I dunno... I s'pose he's all right.' My concern annoyed him I knew, he just couldn't see what all the fuss was about, why I should even care? Despite the fact that the police had badgered and hounded him ever since. It had bordered on harassment really, but they had known that Billy had been involved, even though Big Ken hadn't admitted to anything. Ashamed of being done by some kid half his size and age we reckoned. Although taking a hiding from Billy was nothing to be ashamed of, but he wouldn't have known that. In fact none of the Scots had been prepared to place any of us in the picture. And the rumours had blown around town like germs in the wind, you would have had to hibernate to avoid them; a fractured skull, a coma, paralysed even!

But it turned out that although he had spent a week or ten days in hospital, Big Ken had suffered nothing worse than concussion and a good kick in.

But despite all the attention from the police, and one copper in particular, a local bobby by the name of Collins who had known Billy ever since he was a kid, it turned out that Billy had been more concerned with the part I had played in the fight. Or rather how I could have allowed myself to take so much punishment without offering any resistance.

'And what the fuck's the matter with *you*?' he'd spat, face twisted in disgust as we had sat breathless in my kitchen at the end of the night. And I hadn't even bothered to answer, hadn't offered any kind of explanation at all, had just shrugged my shoulders and gone to help Dave with the tea. And as I had handed him the cups he had winked at me.

'Think you better feed her,' he had said, motioning down at the cat as she rubbed herself against my calf. 'Or you'll have another fight on your hands,' he had smiled. That Dave smile.

The sights and sounds of the West End seemed to be careering by at twice the normal speed as Billy and I weaved our way down Oxford Street. Cars, buses, swarms of black taxis and the crowds of people marching up and down the pavements, all looking as if they had somewhere important to be, the whole atmosphere seemed more intense. The soundtrack of London crackling with energy, touched by that Friday madness, the dusk of the day... the dawn of the weekend.

Dave was waiting just where he had said he would be, standing patiently, head resting against a bright yellow poster advertising some rock 'n' roll revival concert that same night. He stood a few doors down from the small crowds of punks milling around outside the entrance of The 100 Club. He even looked exactly as I had imagined, leaning casually against a wall, hands buried deep in his pockets, cigarette hanging from his mouth. You could pick him out a mile away, that shock of swept back orange hair with the black roots coming through. It seemed as if he stood out, his image sharp and in focus while everything else around blurred into a kind of mass of moving shapes and colours, like one of those 3-D images of footballers or wildlife animals that you find at the bottom of a box of cereals.

And Billy and I wouldn't have even made it as far as the door without him, would have been intercepted by the ridiculous-sized bouncers standing like pillars either side of the entrance. But one of them just nodded his scarred, shaven head when Dave indicated that we were with him. It was only a little nod, a slight tilt of the head, but it spoke volumes. Dave was known, recognised and, more importantly, accepted.

'Alright, Bowie boy,' mumbled the second bouncer, through a mouthful of gum.

And as we passed through the door I was instantly aware of the atmosphere bubbling like a cauldron below. The pressure growing, rushing up too meet us with every downward step that we took, the layers of voices, the clinking of glasses, the smell of beer, fags and bodies swirling up and around us. Down there even what little air there was seemed to sweat, it hung so heavy that it seemed as if we had to actually wade through it to the bar.

Billy was buzzing; a frenzied ball of energy, bubbling with excitement.

'This is goin' to be fuckin' brilliant!' He grinned like a madman. His eyes seemed to glow like cat's eyes in the dark. He had had a few already, before I had even met him, had probably popped into the Falcon on the way. I doubted whether he had ever walked past the place since he was fifteen without being drawn in… the ultimate moth to a flame.

In fact if I hadn't have known him as well as I did, I would have sworn that he was on something. But I knew how much he hated drugs, would never have touched them, probably the only thing I knew that really scared him. Ever since he had witnessed a dreadful moment at his flats.

'Jesus, J! The fuckin' mess he made!' He had shaken his head ruefully when he had told me about the time a boy who had lived on the floor above him, out of his head on something heavy, had dropped from the balcony, straight past Billy's front door, convinced that he could fly. And I remember one day seeing the stains on the tarmac. It had taken nearly a year for them to finally fade, and even then you could still make out the traces of dark blood etched into the tiny cracks in the concrete, like grain in wood.

I had felt utterly exhausted by the time we climbed back out onto the pavement. The chill in the fresh air, the promise of winter, stung the back of my throat as it hit. Everything seemed muted, drowned out by the constant ringing in my ears. The buses, cars and taxis still rushed continuously by, like a never-ending merry-go-round, only they sounded as if they were behind some giant sheet of glass.

I caught a glimpse of myself in a shop window and quickly turned away in disgust, a strong sense of self-loathing rose, like bile, inside of me. What a state to be in, I thought to myself. I kept thinking of my team-mates, had this absurd picture in my head of all of them tucked up in bed with a cup of cocoa on their bedsides.

It wasn't just because of the drink that I felt so wretched, I felt physically drained as well; my whole body ached from the mayhem of the concert. It had taken all my effort just to stay on my feet. As soon as the first note had burst from the tiny stage, tearing through the muggy air like wind through sails, the floor had begun to move and it had been like trying to stand up in a hammock or something. In fact the only thing that had prevented me from toppling over and being trampled alive, on more than one occasion, was the fact that I had been wedged between the throng of pogo-ing bodies, and had been literally lifted of the ground as they jumped manically up and down, as if the floor were a sea of sharks snapping savagely away at their feet.

Billy was still on fire, stamina to burn that boy, singing out loud, jumping up on my shoulders and then running up and down the road like a demented dog let off its leash.

We were heading towards Baker Street, back to Dave's, and no doubt round upon round of hot tea and toast, when we were suddenly caught up in a steady throng of bodies. Waves and waves of punks had started to flow in our direction; a sea of spiky hair and crazy-coloured Mohicans bobbing up and down like exotic birds, zips, safety pins and chains twinkling in the street lights. I could sense the violence in the air, could smell it. And I knew where we were going, just didn't want to believe it; the fifties rock 'n' roll revival. I glanced over my shoulder and back across the street, there were more punks than ever now, it didn't seem possible that they could have all spilled from the depths of The 100 Club. And the pace had begun to quicken, the anticipation of trouble revving up the hordes. A chorus of The Clash's "White Riot" rang out, booming down Oxford Street like a blast of cold air, and I could have sworn that Billy had been the instigator.

I looked over at Dave, desperate for some reassurance, a knowing nod or a half smile or something, anything that told me that we were going straight back to his flat, that it was merely a coincidence that it happened to be in the same direction as the rock 'n' roll venue. But I couldn't catch his eye, couldn't even see his face, just the fine edge of his profile. His stride was so long that I struggled to keep up, always a pace or two behind him. He looked for all the world as if he could have been ambling through the park on a Sunday morning; fag dangling lazily from his mouth, collar of his denim jacket turned up against the elements, his hands buried deep in the pockets of his baggy black pegs.

I wanted to call out, 'We *are* going back to yours, right? Not looking for trouble, are we?' But I didn't think I could control the tremor in my voice enough to stop myself sounding pathetic. And besides, I knew I had no choice, that there would be no way that I could let Billy and Dave go without me. I felt as if I were about to cry, could actually see the watery haze swell in front of me, like rain on a window. It wasn't that I was scared, not actually of fighting, although I certainly didn't get the same buzz that the likes of Billy experienced, adrenalin rushing to their heads in waves. In fact it was quite the opposite, I would feel nothing; my whole body vacant, heavy with that kind of dead unrelenting numbness that you would wake to find in a hand or an arm after you had slept heavily on it.

It was just that I could see it, sense it all slipping away from me, everything that I had worked so hard for. I caught my reflection again in a shop window among the sway of bodies, only this time I looked sick, not tired. I closed my eyes and saw this image of myself hanging over the edge of some bottomless pit, desperately clutching at somebody's hands. But when I looked up the pair of hands belonged to me! But I couldn't hold on much longer, neither version of me could! I was losing a grip on myself. As if something inside wanted to self- destruct, to tear me away from everything that was safe.

If I kept walking straight on, past Marble Arch and skipped through the gardens, I thought, instead of turning off with the rest of the crowd, I could be outside Cindy's door in half an hour. Twenty minutes even. Maybe we could find a way to retrace our steps back to when we had both thought that we had stumbled upon something special, when we were both on the same wavelength; no adjustment necessary. Suddenly the idea of sitting beside her, sinking into the artist's palette of coloured cushions that she had scattered across her floor, with the smell of the burning joss sticks floating through the room – even the sickly smelling ones, the ones that would linger in my head for days after, like the words of a song – and all the while her moody, meandering hippie music gently playing, seemed almost impossible to resist. I had to fight the urge to break away from the pack and drift off into the night, had to swallow it down like rising bile.

I don't know what the hell I had expected to find, a bunch of tired old teddy boys in faded old clothes, I supposed, filling the night with the clickety-clack of their walking sticks like a field of chirping crickets. But the majority of them where youngsters, older than the likes of me, Dave and Billy but in their twenties or thirties, with everything just a little exaggerated: enormous bobbing quaffs, ridiculously tight drainpipe trousers and garishly-coloured outfits.

And it seemed as if it were the women, the "girls" hanging on the arms of their men, who saw us first. Suddenly pointing frantically, tugging at sleeves, screaming out, sending their ponytails bobbing up and down in a frenzy. And all of a sudden there was a change of direction, like a herd of startled sheep they turned as one, suddenly aware of the danger.

A mighty roar broke out as wave after wave, a mass of bodies, girls and all, swept past me. It must have been a terrifying sight. But there were a cluster of good old-fashioned teddy boy's up for a good old-fashioned scrap, and there were more than a few rockers who stood their ground as well. They were dressed mostly in grubby leather jackets and dirty looking jeans, not the modern Showaddywaddy brigade.

But they didn't stand a chance, engulfed like trees in a forest fire. The whole scene reminded me of a Saturday night western, the wailing Indians descending upon the tiny ring of wagons, cutting the white men down, women and children and all as they fled for safety. All that was missing was the taking of scalps. And even the girls were joining in, it could have been almost comical if it weren't so horrific, struggling in their skin-tight leather miniskirts, unable to obtain any significant power and keep their balance as they kicked out at the lifeless bodies strewn up and down the street.

I mentioned it to Dave as we stood taking it all in from a safe distance, Dave with his pen and notepad in his hand.

'Nah,' he said in that tired, laconic voice of his, the one he would lapse into when he found everything around him tiresome or boring. He was leaning against a wall, arms and legs crossed as he were waiting for a bus or something.

'What do you mean... *Nah?*' There was an edge to my voice, I had almost snapped at him in a manner that neither of us was used to and he turned to look at me, that all knowing, all seeing look etched into his face.

'There's nothing you can do about it,' he shrugged. 'They're just... ' He paused for a moment, surveying the scene in front of us as nonchalantly as if he gazing out to sea. There were still a few fights going on, dotted about the place like sideshows, but the main parade had moved on, a running battle through the streets. A crowd had gathered now across the road but no one looked as if they fancied jumping in to try and break any of it up.

'They're just following the rules really,' he continued. 'Everyone's a product of their own environment... it's what's expected of them, almost tribal really,' he concluded sagely.

I shook my head in irritation.

'What do you mean... *Naaah?*' I asked again, over emphasising his word, dragging it out as if I had trouble speaking. A slight frown wrinkled his forehead and the corner of his mouth sunk into his cheek as if he were partly amused, partly baffled by my struggle to contain my petulance.

The thing was I knew what he had meant up to a point, that there was a kind of truth in what he said, an answer to my question. I just had to untangle it. And usually I would find comfort in listening to his observations, a sense of relief almost, he had a way of putting into words what we, as kids, felt.

But I wasn't in the mood, I was struggling with his indifference to it all.

'All I meant *waaas*,' he dragged the words out, as if he were giving himself time to think, 'Well, you reckoned it reminded you of some sort of bad western, but to me,' he shrugged, 'it's like watching one of those wildlife documentaries you see on BBC 2.'

I frowned, lost.

'Look,' he sighed, as if it were all plainly obvious. 'You know the tiger or the lion stalks the petrified deer or whatever, pouncing on it, ripping it to shreds, right?' he said, even bothering to remove a hand from his pocket to help him explain. It was as if he were explaining something on the telly, that we were separate from the mayhem that was taking place before us. That it was no more than a scene from a film or a play, not really there.

'Well I've always thought to myself, why can't they stop it? You know... the cameramen or the man introducing the programme, go and save the poor thing from being torn apart. But it's like I said,' he shrugged, turning back to the fighting and slipping his hand back in his pocket, 'nature, isn't it?'

And as usual he had managed to stop me dead in my tracks, only this time I wasn't sure. In the past a Dave theory like that would have diffused any tension I had felt about a situation, as easily as pulling a plug from its socket. But I still felt the small sparks of something more unsettling. But then the police arrived.

Three meatwagons, their sirens drowning out the sounds of the night, policemen in helmets with visors and armed with long batons, pouring from the back doors. Pouncing upon people, punks mostly, dragging them away, filling the vans with bodies, and they didn't half put up a fight, the punks, kicking and screaming like rabid dogs.

And then Billy appeared from out of nowhere, popped up behind us and shoved the pair of us in the back.

'Alright, wankers!' He was grinning but he had that mad look in his eyes, the one that he always had when he had been fighting. They shone like sheets of glass in the light, wild and staring, as if he couldn't blink; I could almost hear the adrenalin pumping round his body. His T-shirt was covered in blood, all over his chest as if a tin of red paint had exploded in his hands. It obviously didn't belong to him. Apart from appearing slightly out of breath he seemed fine. He only seemed to notice the blood when Dave and I stared at it.

'Oh fuckin' 'ell!' he cried. 'I've only just bought this one!' It was another Sex Pistols one to replace the one that I had ripped in the row that we had had with Big Ken and his mates.

All of a sudden three policemen charged past us chasing a youth with a spiky green Mohican, he was struggling to get away, hampered by the bondage strapped between his tartan trousers. One of the coppers dived, rather dramatically, and hooked his truncheon through the straps of loose material, sending the young punk headlong into the road. And then the other two were upon him, and all you could see were the soles of his boots as he disappeared beneath a hail of uniformed bodies and flailing batons.

Dave, all of a sudden, pushed Billy into the darkness of a back street and I instinctively followed.

'They see you in that state and you're nicked,' he said, as we plunged further into the night. The shadowy figures of two policemen suddenly appeared in the light of the entrance, their silhouettes magnified against the wall opposite, like a pair of giant aliens. They leaned, as one, cautiously to one side, trying to peer through the gloom, truncheons raised at the ready.

We pressed ourselves into the crevice of a doorway, trying desperately to melt into the night. I could hear their footsteps grow nearer... louder, drowning out the noise and commotion coming from the streets. I could hear the blood pounding in my head. *I haven't even done anything!* I said to myself, guilty of nothing but not having the strength of mind to walk away, to not follow the crowd. I hated myself. This was it! Southfields would never tolerate my being nicked at the scene of a riot. I had already sailed pretty close to the wind, what with the flimsy excuse that I had given concerning the state of my face "walked into a door", I still cringed at the lameness of it. I knew that they had suspected that I had been fighting, but they had chosen to say nothing. I had taken it as an unofficial warning and just prayed that no one at the club would hear about it. There had been a small piece about Big Ken being in hospital in the local paper. But thankfully it had all blown over in time. Even P.C. Collins had seemed to lose interest, hardly bothered Billy at all now, not that Billy cared one way or another.

And then, with my heart somewhere up in my throat, just I had been preparing to shout 'Leg it!', a sudden roar erupted from out in the streets, the punks regrouping, charging, taking on the police. The screams and shouts grew louder, flowed down the roads and backstreets like running water.

'Come on, Len better get back,' said one of the policemen, and we heard the sound of their boots retreating up the alley, melting back into the night, and with that my body crumpled like a deflated balloon. And I hadn't even been aware that I had been holding my breath.

CHAPTER SIXTEEN

August 1978

The pain in my head was beginning to make me feel sick. A dull, monotonous throbbing deep in my skull that didn't seem to want to get any worse or any better, and now the sound of my team mates' studs rat-tat-tatting upon the changing room floor had begun to sound like nearby machine-gun fire, forcing me to screw up my eyes. It was usually the little things like that, the chattering of boots on tiles, the heavy odour of liniment invading my senses, that would get me going, start the adrenalin pumping, set me in the right frame of mind. But just then it had the reverse effect, instead it ran through me like a thousand fingernails being raked across a blackboard.

'Alright, son?' asked a team mate sitting beside me. Johnny Hatch, a seasoned pro, a towering centre-half who had been around for what seemed like forever. He had played for four or five Division One clubs during his career, none of the big ones, not your Manchesters or Liverpools but the dependable, mid-table clubs, the ones that never seemed in any danger of going down or winning anything.

He handed me a piece of gum and gave me a friendly slap on the back, which felt as if it rattled every rib in my body; his hands, like every other part of him, seemed to me like a giant's, like he didn't know his own strength. But he had a real delicate touch on the ball, could caress and stroke it across a pitch beautifully, seemed to make it glide, it could be really lovely to watch.

I popped the gum in my mouth and closed my eyes again, pretending to be wrapped up in my thoughts, gathering my concentration, but really I was just trying to escape into myself for as long as I could, had this stupid thing in my head that if I blocked as many openings into my body as possible it would somehow shut out all the commotion around me, of players stretching and warming up, geeing themselves and each other up, but, of course, it didn't. Instead it upset my sense of balance so much so that for a moment I actually thought that I was about to topple off the bench and land flat upon my face.

It wasn't a hangover, had nothing to do with the alcohol... well, hardly anything to do with it anyway. It was just that so much had happened since I had taken my last drink, that being in The 100 Club seemed to belong to another time, disconnected from the rest of evening's events. For one thing I had hardly slept; a couple of hours if I had been lucky. I had drifted into sleep roughly between four and six in the morning. But even that had been splintered with a kind of restlessness that prevented me from even lying still at times. The rest of the night I had spent wide awake, clock-watching or gazing absently out the window across the jagged silhouettes of London rooftops, like a scene from *Mary Poppins*.

I kept replaying it over and over again in my head, and each time never quite believing what had actually happened, until it would finally become too much for me to comprehend, as if my mind were being worked to its limit, and the whole thing would run like a speeded-up film, the way the educational films used to when some joker at the back of the class would speed up the projector.

I straightened up from tying my laces for the umpteenth time, checking and double-checking them. But it hadn't been a good idea, I felt even more nauseous than ever bending over. I closed my eyes again, took a deep breath and tried to regain my composure.

'Not bothering you is it son?' Johnny Hatch had asked, nodding at the purple bruise around the top of my left eye that had deepened overnight.

'Nah… it's fine,' I said, trying to sound confident, as I ran my fingers tenderly across the bump that had popped up the night before, almost from the moment that Billy had struck me.

'Boss alright, was he?' He spoke through a huge mouthful of gum, his jaw working away furiously. Even the way he chewed seemed to carry an edge of menace; typical centre-back, must have had four sticks in his mouth all at once.

'Yeah,' I answered vaguely. 'I think.' The manager's words came back to me.

'You're a good young keeper, Johnny,' he had told me earlier that morning, leaning back in his swivel chair. He was a great big bull of a man, had a real forbidding presence about him even though he must have been well into his fifties, had that look of controlled menace about him, and I never saw him in anything other than a shirt and tie.

'One of the best I've seen for a many a year,' he had continued, nodding his head ever so slightly like a wise old owl. 'A natural… you've a bright future ahead of you,' and then he had picked up his pen and returned to the paperwork that had been spread across his desk, indicating the end of the meeting. *Is that it?* I had thought to myself but of course the moment I had put one foot out of the door he had looked up as if something had just occurred to him.

'Oh by the way… something you might like to think about.' All the while he had been saving his most poignant remark till last, the way Columbo would do on the telly. Pretend that his most telling question had been nothing but an afterthought, clicking his fingers above his head: 'Oh, I nearly forgot,' he would say, wafting his half-smoked cigar through the air like a magic wand.

'Every Sunday morning the parks and playing fields of London are overflowing with… ' he had paused for a moment, to create the full effect, 'with *natural talent*. And it had been as if the words had hung there, in the space above our heads, like a cartoon bubble before drifting slowly out through the gap in the door.

As I stepped off the train and shuffled down the steps from the platform, idly kicking out at old crisp wrappers and scuffing cigarette butts beneath the soles of my shoes, like a bored school kid, it suddenly hit me how utterly alone I felt. I mean it had been exactly what I had been waiting for all day, at times like after the match, when everyone had bathed and could afford to relax, enjoy the prospect of the Saturday night ahead with all the adrenalin washed away with the sweat and mud in the bath.

'So come on, what really happened to you then?' or the jokes *'Nice shiner Rocky... couldn't stop that one, could you?'* I had almost ached from the desire to be on my own, to hide away from all the questions, the inquisitive looks, but now that I had finally found my way home, a sense of isolation suddenly swept over me.

It seemed as if I were swimming alone against the tide, while the rest of the world headed in the opposite direction, into the crazy seas of a Saturday night in town or up the West End. When I had stepped off the train I had seen dozens of people congregated on the opposite platform, excited, tiny clusters of friends dressed as bright and shiny as Christmas baubles. A group of girls had shrieked and laughed in amazement as one of them paraded her new hairstyle as if she were on a cat walk, all crinkly, as if it had been pressed between one of those new sandwich toasters. While nearby a gang of boys had loitered near the edge of the platform, trying to look cool and impress, thumbs tucked into the front pockets of their jeans, pretending not to be cold in their open-necked shirts and cap-sleeved T-shirts.

Something that Dave had said the night before as we had sat in a kind of daydream in his flat kept playing over and over again in my head.

The streets seemed less restless than once before, the young people around filled with more sense of hope than I could ever remember. England's "no future" that the Pistols had promised us seemed that it might now belong to yesterday, that we were finally leaving behind the grim wastelands of the '70s, a time when dads were reduced to a three-day-week and the country had been dominated with strikes, political unrest and power cuts.

But now that the decade was drawing to a close, ever since the Pistols had split and Sid had been found, obliterated by drugs, in a New York hotel room, the whole thing didn't seem to carry as much weight, seemed less threatening... simply wasn't as raw.

At first punk had been all so new, fresh and exciting, finally an alternative to the bell-bottomed freakishness, the multi-coloured tank-tops and ridiculous footwear. The uproar that the Pistols had created when they had sworn on Bill Grundy's *Today* programme at the end of '76 had sparked a cultural phenomenon. But now it seemed to be fizzing out like a spent firework.

'Bollocks!' Billy had snapped defensively, suddenly coming to life like a jack-in-the-box. Up until then he had been slouching across the tiny table next to Dave, chin resting upon the backs of his hands, gazing sullenly into space.

I had planted myself deep within the cushions of the old sofa, sipping black coffee and trying to make some kind of sense from the whole evening, and trying desperately not to think about tomorrow's game.

'What do you mean... *dead*?' Billy had demanded, his face lined in confusion.

'Like I said,' Dave had shrugged, continuing to write in his notepad, 'Died with the Pistols.' He dropped his pen onto the table with a sigh and leaned back in his chair, stretching his arms above his head. He had been writing down the evening's events, about the gig at The 100 Club and all about the fight, the punks marching down Oxford Street and descending upon the poor bastards who had been leaving the rock 'n' roll revival. On the spot journalism, I suppose. 'Perhaps they'll use it along with the gig review, who knows... can but try,' he had shrugged. And as soon as we had walked through his front door he had begun scribbling away in earnest. 'While it's all still fresh,' he had explained, leaving me and Billy to make the coffee and endless rounds of toast together. Trying to avoid eye contact, fumbling about in a kind of bewildered fog, deliberately being a little cumbersome, using the drink as an excuse, welcoming the clinking and clattering of open cupboards and cups and saucers; noise, anything to fill the silence.

'What about The Clash and Siouxsie? What about tonight!' Billy had exclaimed, desperate to defend, to cling to the one thing that he had probably ever really believed in. Without punk, Billy's life consisted of pubs and building sites, at least with the music and the bands, the concerts that he would go to, he had a kind of incentive, a goal if you like. I mean he even read the music papers sometimes!

'Yeah,' Dave had nodded, conceding that Billy had a point. 'But the Pistols, well, they *were* punk,' he had added, sitting up straight as if to emphasise his point. 'Everything else... ' He had shrugged, sinking back again into his chair. 'Well it's all just an aftershock.'

'Bit like that stuff you were going on about, the stars and that, down the park that time,' I had mumbled, more to myself than anything, as I had flicked robotically through the mass of music papers and fanzines that lay strewn across the coffee table.

'What!' Billy had exclaimed, shaking his head. I had seen the irritation building up in his face, as he realised that the conversation was about to digress, as it often did when Dave was involved, completely losing him along the way. And I had wished that I had kept my mouth shut now, had felt bad enough as it was, for Billy used to hate it when me and Dave would get into some long drawn-out conversation about something or another, he would kick his heels, or rip up a beer mat or something. *'Borring,'* he would finally moan, before tutting loudly and going to play the fruity or stick some money in the jukebox.

'That's right!' Dave had beamed with the kind of satisfaction that a teacher shows when he realises that something that he has been harping on about for God knows how long has finally sunk in.

And I had given a kind of half smile, raising my eyebrows sheepishly, a little embarrassed even, for what was there to smile about? I didn't know where Dave found his resources, I really didn't, to continually bounce back, come up smiling from the depths that his old man seemed to always plunge him into.

The house was eerily quiet when I arrived home. Cold and dark, just the pale yellow light from the alleyway shining weakly down through the kitchen window, lying on the linoleum like spilt butter. My footsteps seemed to bounce back at me off the walls, ricocheting off the emptiness, and the sound of my kitbag as I threw it carelessly in the cupboard under the stairs cracked through the house like thunder.

I made myself some beans on toast, more for something to do than to satisfy any hunger. I tore through the bread, all soggy with bean juice, with my knife, and shovelled it robotically into my mouth. *'Cut your food, Johnny, don't pull it apart!'* Even the memory of Mum's voice sounded distant in my head, almost out of tune, as if it belonged to someone that I hadn't seen or spoken to in a long, long time and I was having trouble placing it.

It certainly wasn't my usual Saturday night, that's for sure, wallowing in the solitude of an empty house. I don't think I had made a conscious decision to actually come home, just knew that I had to be on my own somewhere, and I had just seemed to take myself there, had needed somewhere to sort out the jumbled mess that was racing around in my head, like a fly trapped in a jar.

So much had happened in the past twenty-four hours, I

simply hadn't had a moment to stop and think about it, to take stock. It was all a series of images overlapping in my head, like a box of loose photographs all mixed together, with no dates, names or places, just captured memories with no reference. And I needed to categorise it all, sift through and piece it together, try and work out why and when things happened.

I shuffled into the front room, switched on the TV set and plopped myself in front of it, staring mindlessly at the screen. I had never felt so tired. Not sleepy, can't keep your eyes open tired, but more drained tired, mentally exhausted, so that even the sound from the television seemed to reverberate through my head, hum through my empty shell of a body, like wind whistling through a pipe.

The next thing I knew *Match of the Day* had started. That familiar theme tune triggering something off inside, wrenching me up from the depths of my thoughts. I couldn't believe that it was so late, I must have been sitting there gazing blankly at the wall, the curtains, the telly and whatever for hours; seeing without seeing. Saturday night prime time TV passed unnoticed before my eyes, it might just as well have been some political or religious discussion programme, the kind that you would find on a Sunday morning, for all the notice that I took.

And for all I knew it could have been. Time meant nothing, had been suspended the moment that I had closed the front door behind me, shut out all the madness that seemed to be hovering around me, swirling before my eyes, distorting everything like walking in fog.

The next couple of days passed in a kind of slow motion, they possessed a dream like quality, as if I were looking down, watching myself from up above. I gave up going to bed at night, would either simply flop on top listening to records or slouch, like a zombie, in the armchair, didn't even bother to put the telly on, would just find something to look at and spend hours just staring at it. I saw things in the house that I had never seen before, they had always been there, it was just that I had never really taken any notice of them. The picture hanging above the sofa, for example, the one of the little boy drinking from the stream as the horse and cart pass by. Was he with the people on board, I wondered. His parents perhaps, or was he a poor orphan boy? Half-starved and dying of thirst, thanking his lucky stars that he had stumbled upon the pool of water. I would make up stories of what had happened to him, where he was from, of what lay around the next corner, letting my imagination run wild. And there was this little sugar spoon that Mum had brought back from Swanage one year, how many times had I seen that without even once thinking of the times that Mum had taken me there? And they had been wonderful trips. I had loved them, used to get so excited days before. And every hour that dragged by seemed to stupefy me more than the last until the day would finally break and pour through the house, washing away the last traces of sleep.

Mum didn't come home at all the whole weekend. She had never done that before, stayed away for two whole days and nights. Did it seem like home now, I wondered, resentfully at first, Derek's swish Bayswater apartment, arriving there after another busy shift at the hospital. Eating, sleeping, waking there; did she sit in her dressing gown, the one with the faded orange flowers and hole in the elbow, and sip tea at the kitchen table? *Was* there even a kitchen table? Or some kind of American style breakfast bar. Did she listen to the radio first thing in the morning there? Sink into the cushioning sounds of Radio 2 with a cup of tea before she would even contemplate doing anything?

And then all of a sudden I found that I had grown quite comfortable within the solitude of my own company, welcomed it even. For without realising it, I had become used to not expecting to see Mum dotted around the house in familiar "Mum like" places. Like standing in front of the kitchen sink, hands immersed in soapy water, or sitting at the table, sipping tea and staring into space. And I had grown accustomed to walking into a cold bathroom, not all stifling and steamed up from one of her marathon soaking sessions in the bath (I knew she used to fall asleep in there but she would always deny it). And oddly enough I realised I especially liked the tranquillity of the night times, for some reason I felt a kind of peacefulness that the daylight hours wouldn't let me find. And I found that I couldn't really remember what it had been like *with* Mum there! It seemed ridiculous, but there it was.

I couldn't concentrate on *Match of the Day,* couldn't find the enthusiasm. There seemed a dreary inevitability about it all; Forest and Liverpool still winning... untouchable. But as much as my aching body actually craved the warmth of my bed, my mind wouldn't switch off, continued to wonder at recent events. I lay there with the pale light from outside cast across the far end of my bedroom wall. I closed my eyes and tried to unpick at the knot in my head, fix my attention on one incident at a time, but it was no use. And when I opened them again, the silhouettes from the football posters on my wall began to move, little figures dancing crazily on the paper, like a hazy distorted cine film, until finally I gave up and went to sit and stare out of my window instead.

And I vaguely remember thinking to myself, wondering how many times I must have sat there gazing out of my bedroom window, wasting the endless time of childhood, staring down upon the old coal shed, across the tiny patch of worn out grass, over the sinister-looking alleyway that ran like a trench between our street, and the street behinds back fences, and finally out beyond the regiments of South London rooftops.

Once again I tried to settle on just one event at a time. It should have been the easiest thing in the world to think about football, but it was as if the weekend, or the last twenty-four hours at least, had run into one long story with no chapters or paragraphs to break it down, without even a coma or a full stop to pause for a moment and take a breath.

I pressed my head against the coolness of the glass, closed my eyes and forced myself back into the match that I had played earlier that afternoon. I tried to unlock the atmosphere, tried hard to remember what it had been like to get an early feel of the ball, its polished leather squeaking as I rubbed my hands over its skin and across the shallow paths of its stitching; tried to dredge up the smell of the turf, of the white horse oils and muscle liniments, to remember the squelching of my boots as I warmed up in the goalmouth.

I really shouldn't have had to try so hard, it should have flowed as smooth as silk across my mind. Especially the good things about the game, things like the thought of another victory… and of course *another* penalty save. My second in as many games, as everyone kept reminding me, as if I could forget. Not a bad start to my promotion to the reserves.

But I couldn't sustain the picture. It kept fading in and out of focus, superimposed with other less favourable images; Billy's face for instance, all twisted and screwed up at the end of my arm. Lines and contours winding their way round his eyes and mouth, adding years that he hadn't yet reached.

It had been a face haunted by confusion, a mixture of hurt and bewilderment as my hand had clasped around his throat and pinned him up against the steel shutters of the doorway. The picture in my head grew clearer, overshadowing the image of the match, as I recalled the look of suppressed anger that had been boiling inside of him, a fury that I had witnessed more times than I could remember. But it had lacked a certain something… It hadn't held a trace of malevolence, had lacked that one vital ingredient that gave it its kick… *hate*.

And I had regretted it instantly of course. Is it possible to feel sorry for someone that you know is just about to thump you in the face with all the speed of a cobra?

And that was what I couldn't get out of my head, that "lost boy" look that had been there, hiding behind Billy's eyes, a place where most people wouldn't think to look... wouldn't *dare* to look!

Because he hadn't *wanted* to hit me, we both knew that. But what else could he have done? I had simply left him no choice, and we both knew that as well. And it had been just like I had expected... quick, sharp and accurate, almost like being stung by a bee, just above my left eye. But it had been no more than a jab to Billy, a warning shot borne out of necessity more than anything, brutal enough to make the stars dance before my eyes but controlled enough to keep me on my feet.

How could two people who knew each other inside out, who were fully-fledged blood brothers, a ritual performed by me, Dave, Ketchup and Billy, with a little help from Billy's rusty old penknife, beneath the viaducts, find themselves in such a mess, face to face, with violence crackling between them like an electrical undercurrent?

I still couldn't believe that I had done it, actually lashed out and grabbed Billy, *my* Billy, by the throat! In all the years, throughout all of our childhood, we had taken pleasure in riling each other, at times we would even go out of our way to wind one another up. And sometimes even to the point where his blood would literally boil or I would be irritated enough for my skin to actually crawl. But in all that time, during every up and down, across the landscape of every scene, no matter how rugged, I had never once felt, or even thought, that we would come to blows... not ever. The bond that we had always shared with Dave and Ketch had always been too strong. Fighting was simply something that you did with other kids.

Recalling the whole episode, reliving it, sent a shiver through me. I imagined the sensation creeping through me as I sat there staring blankly into the velvety black of the alleyway, like an ice cube bobbing over the discs of my spine, travelling up my neck and finally settling into my brain. A bit like the night trains that I would hear as I lay in bed on sleepless nights, rumbling along the tracks in the distance, keeping me awake until their resonating sound would fade away, slowly melting into the contours of my head.

I squirmed at the thought of it all, and rubbed my forehead harder against the window as if the cold from the glass would erase the memory. But it was no good, it wouldn't budge, couldn't turn it off like the TV. The likelihood was that we would be okay, for we were afterwards, except of course for the discomfort we had both felt back at Dave's. The whole scene would surely fade with time, like a picture left in the sun, but it could never be undone, a bit like scoring an own goal or giving one away, you could always atone for a mistake, score one up the other end or save a penalty. But you could never remove it.

Why had I done it? I asked myself for maybe the hundredth time already that evening, as I fumbled through the few albums that I had stacked on my sideboard, going by memory more than looking at them, not wanting to turn the light on, as if the brightness would expose the darkness of my mood like a piece of coal in the snow. The idea strummed on my vulnerability, I preferred instead to immerse myself in the gloom, find my way about in the half-light filtering in from the window.

There were a number of reasons that I could think of, but none of them seemed to make any sense now. All tiny little things, but they had all added up, jangled around my head like coins thrown into an old tin.

There was the sheer casualness that Billy had shown towards all the violence for one thing, also the narrow escape that we had had from the police. And then his laughter at it all, breaking out into fits of giggles like a child being tickled, especially when he had told us of this one man that he had seen, on his hands and knees, scrabbling blindly along the pavement, trying to find his glasses. And just as he had stumbled upon them, this peroxide blonde had appeared and pinned his hand to floor with the heel of her knee-high black plastic boot. 'And then right,' he had grinned, relishing every word, 'he squints up at her like a fuckin' mole and she gobs on his head and kicks his front fuckin' teeth out!' And he had doubled over, dribbling with laughter, eyes still wild from the excitement, walking backwards up the alleyway to face us, jig-jogging on the spot, unable to settle.

'What's so fuckin' funny about *that*!' I had snapped. And I could tell without looking that I had surprised the pair of them by the venom trapped in my words, could feel their eyes upon me, picturing the open-mouthed expressions of shock, at the anger that had weighed heavy in my voice.

'It's pathetic, is what it is!' I had continued, still avoiding their gaze. But the thing was, even though it was true, all of it, I hadn't really expected anything different. And had certainly witnessed Billy behave the same, if not worse, many times before. And there had been this niggling feeling inside, scrabbling away at the door of my conscience like a mouse at a tin of food, telling me that I was being unreasonable, that Billy was just being Billy, not even trying to annoy me.

I had looked down the alley, past Billy and into the night, and then back over my shoulder as if I was expecting to see someone step from beyond the shadows, anywhere rather than their faces. The truth had rubbed me raw inside, like worn skin. The thing was that I hadn't really been annoyed with Billy, not really. My anger had been misdirected. It should have been aimed at Dave! I couldn't explain it, not even to myself. The perplexity that I felt had kept gnawing away; his flippancy, the weary manner in which he had explained his philosophy to me. I had found it all so uncomfortable, couldn't shake it off. It had felt like walking through a cobweb, its silky threads brushing creepily across my face like invisible feathers.

But the thing was that I simply didn't know *how* to be annoyed with Dave. The idea seemed preposterous... perverse even, as logical as blackening my own eye. So I had simply turned to Billy instead.

'What the fuck's the matter with you?' he had exclaimed, after what seemed an eternity.

'Nothing,' I'd mumbled. I just wanted to forget it, get back to Dave's and then get my head down as soon as possible. Close my eyes and shut it all away, try and get some rest before the match, which was now later on that day. The thought of Dave's old settee seemed more appealing than anything that I could imagine.

But Billy had been gathering himself, stepping out from the shock like a vision through fog.

'Touchy aren't we?' he'd smirked.

'Fuck off!' I'd spat the words out, as if they were leaving a bad taste in my mouth.

Dave stepped forward. 'Heeey,' he'd sighed, 'calm down.'

I could see the frown spread like ripples on a pond, the scar on his forehead sink beneath the lines creasing his forehead. I hadn't wanted to be there, had wished I could be anywhere other than in that gloomy alleyway, where the nightlife of London rumbled in the distance, muffled, on the outside as if we were trapped inside some kind of giant test tube. I hadn't known what was happening to me, I was like one of those wild animals that could sense danger, only they're not quite sure from which direction it's coming from.

And then it had struck me. Exploded like a firework in my head, so brightly that I could almost see the blinding flashes before my eyes, so much so that I actually had to squint as if I had stepped out from the cinema into the daylight. I had thought that I was annoyed with Dave and his ebullience. I had taken it out on Billy, lashed out at the most obvious of scapegoats, when in fact, all along it was actually *myself* that I couldn't bare to be near: I was disgusted with myself. But, like trying to out-run your own shadow, there had been simply no escape.

'You know your trouble, J?' Billy had said, his cocky self again, swaggering towards me, sending an empty beer can clattering against some steel shutters with an absent swing from his boot. He had piss-take plastered all over his face, had been closing in for the wind up. Fair enough, I supposed, it had been the least I deserved.

'You're always so fuckin' serious,' he had said. 'What?... You worried your big football buddies will find out that you're... ' And then it had happened. I don't even remember actually doing it, the moment that my brain had instructed my hand to grab Billy round the throat and, without even telling me, shove him up against the steel shutter. Everything had seemed unnaturally still, as if all the life had somehow been sucked out from the atmosphere. It had felt as if my body wanted to float away, had taken all my efforts to keep my feet planted on the ground, even the rumbling of the shutters, as they rippled like a sheet drying in the wind, seemed far away, as distant as the Oxford Street traffic.

'Oi! You two! Cut it out!' I had heard Dave's voice, exasperated, disbelieving, sounding somewhere outside the ringing in my ears; the result of Billy's swift response.

'He started it!' Billy had cried, his defences springing into action. The angry schoolteacher in Dave's voice had instinctively triggered some kind of defence mechanism in his subconscious, left over from Billy's school days, when trouble would linger round him like a scent.

'Billy, I...' I hadn't been able to find the words, I had known I never would; I hadn't seemed to have the energy to even look for them. "Sorry" seemed so pointless, so absurdly lame... so pathetic that I didn't want to insult him by uttering it. But without something, without even offering an explanation of some kind, it seemed... oh I didn't know what the hell it seemed like! There was no neat and tidy conclusion to a landslide like this.

But Billy had seemed not to notice me anyway, as I had stood, struggling to comprehend what had just happened, staring stupidly at my hand as if I didn't know how it had got there, seeing it for the first time. Or at least he hadn't seemed to care. He had seemed more upset by the fact that Dave had shared the blame between us, berated him as well as me, when it had been obvious that Billy thought that I was the instigator.

'Behaving like a couple of little brats,' Dave had said, clicking his tongue and glaring at the two of us, unsettling us, forcing me and Billy to look away, hang our heads in shame.

There had been reason enough for me to avoid his withering look, my face had been covered with shame by my actions. But the fact that Dave's unexpected outburst had pacified Billy with the shock of it all revealed just how high mine and Billy's respect for him stretched.

Billy's guilt had betrayed itself in the confusion, gathering like clouds around his eyes. The way his head had tilted ever so slightly to one side, the way his shoulders sagged, it rose like bare wood through a coat of paint.

Dave had switched his gaze from one to the other, eyes still burning.

'If anyone should be pissed off or losing their temper tonight it should be me,' he had continued. And Billy and I had looked up simultaneously, unable to think of a more unlikely candidate to act as petulantly as Billy and I had done. We had stood there, the three of us, in stony silence, staring from one to the other, and for a moment time had seemed to stand still, the world had paused in suspense: cars, buses, the people on the streets, as motionless as statues. It had affected even the intangible: exhaust fumes, the curling smoke from cigarettes, even the breeze blowing down the alley, everything frozen like a picture, waiting expectantly for Dave to elaborate.

And there had been something about the way he looked at

Billy and me, a darkness in his eyes that had told me it was going to be something important that he was about to entrust us with. He had seemed older, the scar on his forehead had looked denser, like deep water.

Finally Billy had broken the spell. 'Well come on then!' he had demanded, confidence fully restored. 'What the fuck are you on about?'

And in the blink of an eye Dave had been back to his old, easy-going self. 'Oh well,' he'd shrugged, as if the sound of Billy's voice, the impatience that it carried, had suddenly blown away the darkness that had converged, like rain clouds around the sun, upon him.

'After all… ' a smile slithered across his face, like a split ball,. 'After all, *I'm* the one who's just seen his old man kick the shit out of some spotty punk kid who couldn't have been older than sixteen.' And with that he had turned and made his way off in the direction of Baker Street, wandering down the alleyway towards home.

'Well come on then!' he had shouted over his shoulder, 'We've got a serious amount of tea and toast to get through.'

CHAPTER SEVENTEEN

August 1978

On the Tuesday morning, by the time I had closed the front door behind me and stepped back into the real world, felt the morning awaken my senses, stinging my nostrils and watering my eyes like flowers, I knew that it was over.

In fact I had almost grown accustomed to the idea, so much so that I had vaguely begun to wonder what I would do after the final nail had been hammered into my footballing coffin. The only thing was that I didn't know *how* or *when* it would die on me. But I was quite calm about it all as I made my way down our street towards the bus stop, past Dave's old house, through a lifetime of childhood memories, a terraced tunnel of my youth. In fact I didn't seem to feel anything anymore, except for the crisp morning air; had anaesthetised myself to the point where even the sound of my feet carrying me along the pavement reverberated through my body like echoes through a cave.

I didn't know *how* I knew. It wasn't as if I had spent the Sunday and Monday analysing my performances, locked away in my room slowly picking my game apart, before settling on the conclusion that I simply wasn't good enough, that I didn't quite have what it took to make that final, yet daunting step into the ranks of professionalism.

Instead it had just sort of come to me. After one of my, what could only be described as, lightning spells of sleep. The night times had been like living through a collection of short stories. I would drop off, sometimes deliberately, forcing myself, squeezing my eyes shut, willing myself to sleep. And at other times I would find that I had simply drifted there, without any effort at all, whilst reading a book or just lying there, staring at the walls or the ceiling, too tired to move, as if I had eaten too much, bloated on emptiness. But they would never last for more than five or maybe ten minutes, these bouts of sleep. And they always produced some kind of dream, ones that would spring instantly to mind as soon as I awoke. They were mostly the usual kind of thing, discovering that I couldn't run away from whom or whatever had managed to worm its way into my head when my defences were down. Or my usual nightmare: finding myself rushing to get changed for a match with the rest of the team already out on the pitch, waiting impatiently for me to appear from the changing room, and me not being able to tie my laces up, my fingers not having the strength, as limp as spaghetti.

I didn't delve too deeply into these imaginings, didn't try to untangle some mysterious hidden meaning behind them, although at times I would awaken with such a start, feel so disorientated that for a split second I was sure that I was still inside my head, living in the dream itself. And I couldn't believe how brief they could be, ones that seemed to unfold over such long passages of time were, in reality, over within a matter of minutes. I could drift off with my music playing gently beside me, just audible enough to soothe me through the night, and then the next thing that I knew I would be wide awake, eyes popping out of my head like ping-pong balls, and not only would the record still be quietly spinning, but I would find that the needle had barely moved, merely spun it's way only as far as the next track on the album.

But on this one particular occasion there had been nothing. Just a blank screen in my head, no blinding white light pouring down the corridors of my mind, no glaring images or message written in ten-foot red letters penetrating my dreams. Just this feeling that felt so real, so definite and pure, that I hadn't for one second doubted it. It sliced through me as clean as a surgeon's scalpel. Even though I couldn't see what lay behind it, I knew without doubt what it meant. It was like dreaming with my mind's eye shut.

I gazed idly out from the top of the bus, watching the world pass slowly by. Landmarks unravelling before me like a scroll of the town, as the bus bobbed and bumped its way through the morning traffic. There was the park, the back garden to my world, and then there was the line of immaculately-kept cottages, so out of place, which proudly put the rest of the town to shame. Under the railway bridge now, and I slipped into that childhood fantasy, couldn't help it, that silly notion that we had just travelled through time. The cottages representing a post-war England, all green and pleasant land. And then, as we emerged from beneath the bridge, we were back in the grim brick city of the '70s, concrete closing in all around as the town centre loomed into view.

The bus juddered to a halt beside the little parade of shops opposite the old church. From my seat on the top deck I could see straight into the betting shop, peer down from above its covered windows to where the old men studied papers tacked on walls. And next door I could see Lui. Leaning over, wiping a table top clean with that exaggerated sweeping motion of his, as if he were levelling off wet cement. He looked reassuringly the same, old Lui. The years had treated him well, except for the covering of grey hair, which seemed to suit him anyway, made him seem sort of distinguished. I remember when it had first began to show signs of changing colour, flecks of white caressing the tips of his hair as if he had just stepped in from a snowstorm. And then all of a sudden it was completely the opposite, within a matter of weeks, the next time that I saw him he had turned into a photo negative of himself, just his dark roots showing now, hidden beneath a thick white mop.

I had a sudden urge to jump off the bus and go and see him. To sit in my old chair and write my name in the condensation misting up the shop window. To just tell him everything, unburden myself, hands cupped round something nice and warm, let it all pour out over the worn table tops like spilt tea. And I could picture us sitting there, Lui and I, me trying to explain the unexplainable and him listening thoughtfully, taking it all in, never judging, just listening. And I would feel better, I knew that I would: purged, lighter, cleansed... as if he had wiped it all away with a majestic sweep from his trusty dishcloth. But still, I knew that I wouldn't.

I suddenly realised, sitting up there, gazing down upon the people and the cracked pavements, just how vulnerable I felt. Locked away at home it had been okay, I could deal with it all. The sanctuary of its four walls draped around me like a child's security blanket. Where everything I touched had felt like touching the past, had a reassuring feel about it, where every room reeked with the unique fragrance of my childhood. I had managed to somehow detach myself from the certain realisation that football would no longer be a part of my life. I hadn't doubted it, this... prophecy if you like, which had invaded my senses, it was just that the air at home, the familiarity, had somehow tranquillised me. And I had been so reluctant to let the numbness wear off, to start feeling anything at all, that I had phoned the club on Monday morning and feigned illness. Had spent the day drifting like fog through the house, cocooned in my own thoughts, as if by traipsing through the house I was walking through the avenues of my own mind, living within the landscape of my own memories.

I had dug Mum's old records out from the back of the cupboard in the front room. There was some Elvis, obviously, some rock 'n' roll compilations, and the rest was the likes of Matt Monro and Shirley Bassey, the cream of "Easy Listening". There were melodies there that would reveal a few memories if I looked hard enough. Images of Mum at the kitchen sink or flicking through a copy of *Woman's Own* with her feet up on the sofa, singing softly to herself, in that high-pitched, airy voice of hers that only seemed to reveal itself when she was singing, as light as a feather as if she were slightly merry from drink.

I had wanted to dislodge as many memories as possible from beneath the surface of my mind, immerse myself ever deeper into the safety of the past.

I left the bus two or three stops before the ground. It actually stopped directly outside but it was something that I would often do, preferring the surroundings of the bustling South London streets to the muggy atmosphere of the bus. I drew a kind of reassurance from the people, always upbeat and chirpy. There always seemed to be a whistling postman or housewives brushing down their front step, replacing the milk with yesterday's empties. Their camaraderie lifted my spirits, I found the steady hum of their lives therapeutic.

There seemed to me to be something special about life within the shadow of a town's football club, an intimacy you didn't find anywhere else. A patchwork of people: friends, neighbours, kids, work colleagues... the person who lives at the end the street whose name you have never known but who you have said 'hello' to every morning, all woven together. Spread across the community like a giant blanket, everyone of the same mind, swaying as one like a field of corn in the summer; Southfields in their blood.

I had just begun to feel a bit better about things, step a little lighter, the blood that had seemed to freeze like ice in my veins over the past few days slowly melting. A warm began to radiate through me as if I was surrounded with a red glow like the boy in the Ready Brek commercials, when all of a sudden, from out of nowhere, P.C. Collins appeared.

'Hello, Johnny!' he chirped, as if I was the last person in the world he had expected to see. 'How are you?' he asked, almost as if he meant it.

What the hell is he doing here? Southfields was miles off his beat. I felt my breath wedge in my throat, it was as if he had sprung from out of the pavement in a puff of smoke or something. Caution fluttered inside me, I could feel its wings beating at my ribcage.

'Been fighting with that little punk mate of yours, have you?' he said, nodding at my eye. He tried to fake a smile but it came out like a sneer.

My blood froze again. *How the hell does he know?* I thought to myself, placing a hand on the side of my head as if I were trying, too late, to hide it. And then I realised what he meant, fighting *with* Billy, not fighting *against* him.

'Nah,' I shrugged, gathering myself quickly. 'Football, innit.' I tried to sound unconcerned, cocky even, what he expected me to be. But then he was there, in my face, his voice hissing through gritted teeth, like air escaping from a tyre.

'Well I warn you, Chalmers, I'm gonna have that little shit of yours... Billy the fuckin' punk rocker!' The words fell like drops of acid from his mouth. 'And that cocky little bastard Connelly... thinks he's so clever that one ... we'll see.' He was so close that I could see the flecks of green camouflaged in the darkness of his eyes, see the pitted holes of his skin. He must have had bad acne as a kid, I reckoned; funny the things that run through your mind at the most inopportune of times. The heavy odour of his uniform wafted up into my face. Its smell unnerved me, it smelled of long polished corridors and lacquered courtrooms. As if every time that he had stepped down from a witness box, where he would enthuse a little too eagerly over some young tearaway's misdemeanours, he had taken part of it with him, and it had seeped into the fabric of his uniform like smoke from a bonfire.

P.C. Collins, P.C. Collins… the name kept rolling round and round in my head like a marble in a tin box. He completely took over my thoughts for the day, the look in his eyes burnt into my brain.

At the training ground I kept thinking that every speck in the distance, every spectator standing on the boundaries, anything that appeared in the background of my eye level was P.C. Collins. Watching me, spying, waiting for me to do something stupid, step outside the boundaries of the law, or reveal some piece of vital evidence, although I had no idea why or even what about.

'Oh… Johnny! Stop thinking 'bout your penalty save and start thinking 'bout what your doin,' yelled the coach as we jogged around one of the training pitches. 'Now go!' he bellowed at me. I was at the end of the line and when he called out the man at the back had to run to the front, you didn't have to break your neck or anything, just open your legs a bit, stride out past the rest of the lads and take the lead. But I had been miles away, mind locked so tightly into thoughts of Collins that the coach's voice had barely registered. I nodded rather meekly in way of an apology and set off on my way, injecting a burst of speed, trying to redeem myself.

'Wow! Look at him go!' said one of the lads in mock admiration.

'Wish you were that quick off your line, Johnny!' joked another, and laughter rang out, resounding across the pitches like the distant echoes of a school playground.

'All right, all right you lot!' the coach's voice boomed across the training ground. 'Stop there by the corner flag and we'll do our stretches. Find yourself a space.'

But what the hell had Collins been doing outside the ground? The question kept nagging away at me all the time, even when the boss had asked if I had given anymore thought about moving to the borough, into digs near the ground. 'Where we can keep an eye on you,' he had said when he first suggested it. He had gone on to say that they didn't usually encourage it with the youngsters, liked them to be in a stable family environment, but given my "circumstances", as he had put it, he thought it worth considering. 'Talk it over with your mother,' he had told me, 'see what she thinks… my door's always open.' They had a few places dotted around the ground. Every one run by kindly old ladies who looked after their boys like one of their own, all clean clothes and home-cooked food. The kind of little old lady that Collins had nodded a neighbourly "good morning" to as he had ambled off hands clasped behind his back, whistling merrily as if he were the local bobby, everybody's friend. And me standing there, dumbstruck, as if he had just dumped a ticking bomb in my lap.

And why me? Why not simply confront Billy himself? Or Dave, for that matter, seeing as how he obviously had him high on his list as well now.

It wasn't until I was on the bus home later on that it really hit me. Despite it being the end of the day, I had only really just begun to feel a part of it. Everything around seemed to be tinted with that end of day yellowness. Hollow and empty as if all the goodness had been drawn out of it. But I felt completely the opposite now, as if I had started the day back to front. Travelling with the lads to the training ground, the stories and banter floating through the club minibus like confetti. Tales of who did what on Saturday night, the birds they pulled and so on, talk of the match, lots of leg-pulling and, of course, my penalty-save, and then there was the training itself, it had all served to re-invigorate me, the lethargy that had clung to me earlier in the day washed away liked a hosed-down car. Was I really prepared to accept that this was all over? I wanted to be happy and enjoy the trappings of my life but there always seemed to be so much mess squirming around in the back of my mind. I looked around at the other passengers, tired faces surrounded me and I could begin to feel the weight of the day dropping upon me like raindrops on a petal, so I turned and gazed out at the pavement beneath me.

But my confrontation with Collins wouldn't leave me, kept throbbing away like an infected cut. *P.C. Collins, P.C. Collins…* and of course it was so obvious! I felt my guts tighten, as if they were clamouring to squeeze out of my body. P.C. Collins! Why had I not seen it? For he was after *me* as well!

It had been a warm day, summer still hanging on, but the sun had begun to set as I approached town, fading from yellow to pink as it slipped behind the viaducts. Lui's was shut now, all darkened windows and chairs stacked upside down on tables. But he was still there, could just make out his barrel-like figure pottering about in the thin strip of light behind the counter. And he would have let me in if I had knocked on the door, made me cup of tea and a bite to eat, despite having washed and cleared up. Somehow just knowing that helped to make me feel a little better.

The house was still empty. I may well have grown accustomed to spending my time there alone but I could somehow never get used to the silence that confronted me whenever I first opened the front door. The stillness that hung there brought to mind the time Dave and I had taken refuge in the old church to escape his old man, with Dave still covered in his mum's make-up. And it was as though I was afraid to step inside for fear of what might happen, worried that the atmosphere might very well crack like a mirror, or even crumble like sand all around me.

I hovered from room to room, unable to settle. Not even the sweet melodies from Mum's old records could ease the restlessness that clung to me like the sticky weeds that we used to find wrapped around our legs after scrabbling through the bushes behind the park. It had worked over the weekend, I had wiped away hours that way, lying on my bed and allowing them to invade my senses. But they did nothing for me now. I had drained the well of magic dry, so I went to the kitchen and turned the radio on instead. I opened and shut cupboards, looking for something to eat, but it all seemed like too much trouble and I couldn't face beans on toast again. *'I'm wishing on a star, to follow where you are…'* sentimental slush poured out of the radio. It was no use pretending, I needed to see Billy. Telling him about Collins and what had happened, were, I knew, just excuses to go and see him, to see if *we* were still all right.

I found him in The Falcon, didn't even bother to look anywhere else. I walked there, had had enough of buses for one day. I wanted to feel the pavement beneath my feet, there seemed to be something reassuring in the solidity of it all; the familiar sound of my shoes scraping against the concrete. I wanted to be a part of the streets, melt into the atmosphere instead of looking down upon it all from some stuffy, mobile window.

He was sitting on a stool in the public bar. He didn't see me when I walked in, had his head turned towards the far wall, telling some bloke standing over the jukebox to 'put something fuckin' decent on, not more of that disco shit!' The man lifted his head a fraction, looking at Billy through the curtain of his neatly-combed centre-parting, he wore those new kind of jeans, the ones with the white piping running down the sides, the kind that all the disco people seemed to wear these days, and then quickly he turned back to the jukebox, as if he were trying not to be seen. Maybe he knew Billy, who knows.

'Billy,' I said, pulling up a stool. It wobbled and creaked beneath my weight, and I had to hold onto the bar for moment for fear of it collapsing beneath me. He turned and grinned without batting an eyelid. His face was filthy, sweat and grime smeared across his forehead, and his hair was covered with what looked like red brick dust, as if embers from a fire had floated and settled on his head.

'Ha! The rickety stool.' And I had never been so pleased to see that annoying little smirk in all my life.

I ordered a pint for the pair of us. 'I'll get 'em.' He clicked his tongue as he saw me fish deep in my pocket for some change. He never seemed to be short of cash these days. I knew that the labouring paid pretty well and that the builders that he worked for were all friends of friends, cash in hand, no questions asked; jobs passed around by word of mouth, deals done in the public bars of South London, pubs like The Falcon, at the end of a working day. But I was pretty sure that he had acquired an extra income from somewhere, from something dodgy… something illegal. Dave had asked him one time why it was that he always seemed to have so much money. And he had just winked mischievously. 'Just lucky on the horses ain't I?'

I took a long pull on my beer, feeling it slip down my throat, cold and sharp.

'Billy… ' I began hesitantly.

'Don't bother,' he cut in sharply, stopping me dead in my tracks. He sighed deeply and stared down at his pint. I could sense the struggle that he was having finding the words to explain his reaction, it meandered across his brow like the contours on a map. It wasn't what Billy was used to, finding answers for his behaviour. He fidgeted on his stool, shuffling from side to side as if he were sitting on something uncomfortable. Seeing him like that was enough to know that he cared. And this wasn't supposed to happen, the idea had been for *me* to offer some kind of explanation for what had happened between us. To say sorry, brush away any cobwebs of doubt that may have been spun between us. I should have just kept my mouth shut. He had already shown me, from his initial response, that he was okay with everything… that *we* were okay.

'What I mean is,' he said, without looking up from the bar. 'Is that it don't matter, J… I ain't annoyed or nothin'… let's just forget it, eh?' And with that he lifted his glass to his lips and poured the remains of his pint down his throat in one go.

We had a few more, four or five maybe. I felt pissed, but it was a nice sort of drunk. Not "falling off my stool" hammered, but instead that kind of relaxed drunk, a state reached by slow, easygoing drinking, so that the edges of life seemed to be blunted, like dozing in front of a glowing fire.

'I'll have to borrow a fiver,' I had told him earlier.

'Don't worry,' he had shrugged. 'How many times 'ave you seen me through the night?' And it was true, we'd always looked out for one another, the three of us, didn't matter who paid, whoever had money at the time, money was simply a means to an end. But still, I had to ask, even though I had known what he would say.

And it felt good the two of us just hanging out, sinking a few. We weren't touched by that Friday night restlessness, there was no air of expectancy hovering in the early evening, the kind that made you think that you should be drinking up, as fast as you could, and moving on to the next pub, constantly haunted by the feeling that you're always one step behind all the action, that you're missing out on something special. Even Billy was taking it nice and steady, staying with me pint for pint, not downing them quickly and racing two or three ahead the way he usually did.

We chatted easily about stuff - football, birds, music… the usual - conversation flowing as easyily as the beer, the corners smoothed off a rough day. I urged him to tell me more about his chance encounter with Jenny Hargreaves. They had bumped into one another near Oxford Street the other week. And they had ended up going for a drink, and not even in a pub! She had apparently aroused enough of something inside of Billy to persuade him to join her in one of those fancy coffee shops. That's why I knew that there was more to it all than Billy was prepared to admit… even to himself. Although he had confessed that they had arranged to meet again, he had stopped short of calling it a date, but you could tell that that was what it was.

He had started to tell me about it on the train on Friday night, just as we had crossed over the river and begun to slow into the station. I remember looking back at the reflections of the South Bank simmering on the Thames, like underwater lights, when he had first mentioned her name, unlocking a corridor full of memories. But then the subject had gradually tailed off as we had bustled our way along Oxford Street, through all the Friday night mayhem to meet Dave outside The 100 Club. And I had planned to press him further about it but of course any thoughts of Jenny Hargreaves and wherever that trail of conversation might lead had been totally lost, blown away in the storm that was about to erupt.

'Nothin' to tell really,' he shrugged as we sat drinking at the bar. 'We went for a cup of coffee, chatted 'bout things... didn't tell me what she was doin' and I didn't ask.' He screwed his face up as if the effort of recalling even this much information was beginning to irritate him. He lit a cigarette, tilted his head back and exhaled a thick plume of smoke into the air. And all of a sudden his eyes narrowed mischievously. 'Oh yeah... ' he smirked, as a fragment from their meeting that obviously amused him slipped into place. I could imagine him piecing it slowly together, like a jigsaw puzzle in his mind. 'She still ain't forgiven me for puking on her mum's flowers.'

Billy was just about to order two more when, without warning, the door swung open with a crash and from nowhere his old man suddenly appeared.

He was flanked on either side by two men, both towering over his short, sturdy frame. All three of them wore thick black donkey jackets, despite the warmth of the day, the kind with the black plastic coating across the back of the shoulders. They had burst in like a trio of storm troopers, rattling the stained glass in its frame and thundering on about something or another, so wrapped up in their ranting that they didn't even bother to look up at their surroundings, just pulled up automatically at the bar as if their feet had been programmed.

'It's fuckin' Callaghan!' moaned one of the men.

'He'll ruin the whole bleedin' country, just you wait and see… ' agreed another.

I asked Billy what he wanted to do. His dad had ignored him completely, taken no notice of us whatsoever. I couldn't believe he hadn't seen us, for there were only a handful of people in the place.

'Don't mind,' he shrugged, he didn't seem at all bothered about being in the presence of his old man, or about the fact that he seemed totally oblivious to our even being there!

And it suddenly occurred to me that this behaviour was probably quite normal. After all, they must have both frequented the place regularly, it being their local and all. I found myself wondering how they did it. Perhaps they had made some sort of pact, an agreement of some kind to keep out of each other's way… or a rota system even! Only this time one or both of them had misjudged their hours. For I knew from all the years that they couldn't be trusted in the same room together, not since Billy had reached the age where he could stick up for himself (a frightfully early one). On the rare occasions when they were both home, Billy would always decide to go out. Hang round the streets and on the old piece of wasteland long after all the other kids had gone home. Waiting for his old man to go to bed or allowing sufficient time enough for him to have passed out on their dirty old sofa. He had even turned up on our doorstep once or twice. And Mum would always throw something together on a plate for him, something hot, pretend that we had only just eaten ourselves, no matter what time of night it might have been, and that it would only "go to waste", as she put it, as she had cooked too much. She could be good at that, Mum, turn things around, so that it looked like *he* was doing *her* a favour. All part of being a mum, I suppose.

But the thing was I still needed to tell Billy about my run-in with Collins. Hadn't known how to broach the subject up till then. For it had been such a calm, relaxed evening, just what I had needed and certainly not what I had expected, that it seemed such a shame, criminal almost, to spoil it.

For a moment I wondered if I should keep it to myself for a while longer, tell him another time. Why, I thought, throw stones into the still waters of the evening? But it was no good, I was just trying to kid myself. He needed to know, to be made aware of just how serious Collins had been. If only Billy could have seen the hate burning in his eyes, been there to sense it hum through his body like electricity coursing through a pylon.

And it was sure to antagonise when I told him, send anger boiling to the surface like clouds of stirred-up silt. And so I thought it would be best if we were outside somewhere, somewhere out in the open, someplace less… restricted. I don't know why, it just seemed safer that way.

'Mmm,' Billy mused through a mouthful of fat, greasy chips. He had taken the news about P.C. Collins better than I could ever have imagined, so much so that I wondered if he had actually been listening properly. There had been no effing and blinding, not even a grimace touching his face. Instead he had sunk into kind of a cloud of thoughtfulness, had been pensive almost, although it was hard to describe Billy as someone who had the patience to grow pensive.

But there he was, staring down at the tiny cluster of chips that lay scattered on the ground in front of him. He had been throwing every other one that he lifted out from the crumpled sheets of greaseproof paper in his hand, aiming it down at the empty beer can on the pavement. Stuff one in his mouth then throw one at the beer can until he had nearly half a portion lying there, like tiny curled up animals beneath him.

We were sitting on the wall outside the fish 'n' chip shop on the edge of the town centre. It was growing darker now as I watched Billy throwing his chips in silence, looking for some sort of clue as to what he was thinking. The last dregs of the summer's day were evaporating fast, caught in the brief spell between light and dark when the birds wind down their evening song and everything seems to mist around the edges and you try and re-focus, blink it away like tears floating in your eyes.

And then all of a sudden he looked up as if he had just shaken off the cobwebs of a dream. 'You're up at Birmingham this week, ain't you?'

'What!' I stammered in confusion. I knew that he was talking about the match coming up on Saturday, the one against Birmingham City reserves at St. Andrews. But him bringing it up now had completely thrown me. One minute he's sitting there chewing on the thought of Collins and greasy chips, and the next he's asking me about my football as if we had just been discussing nothing more important than the weather!

And of course it was true that I had mentioned it to him and Dave, had told them about the game some time ago. In the vain hope that maybe one or even both of them could manage to come with me. Had thought it would be a laugh seeing as I would be up against big old Kenny Dennis, the giant African kid we used to play against: the kid with rockets in his boots.

'Why, you gonna come then?' I asked, trying to sound casual but still bemused with this mild manner that Billy seemed to be approaching everything with. Earlier I had welcomed it, had slipped cosily into the groove of the evening. But now, back out on the streets, it was beginning to unnerve me. Maybe I should have been a little more appreciative, honoured, even. For when I thought back, he had been like it from the moment that I had walked in. For there he had been, one minute growling abuse in the direction of the bloke at the jukebox, the malcontent rumbling, as usual, beneath the surface, and the next he was all smiles and laughter...from the second he had laid eyes upon me.

'Naaah... gotta work, ain't I?' he said wearily, sounding as if the thought of it bored him rigid. He hopped off the wall and set about scuffing his discarded chips across the tarmac, smearing them back and forth beneath the sole of his boot like run-down birds on the roadside.

'Still... ' he smiled at me wickedly. 'Would have been funny though, watching that big black bastard smacking 'em past you.'

'Naaah,' I sighed, doing my best to mimic him, 'I'll be all right now... without Dave in front of me to get in the way.' And we smiled as the memory of Dave spinning like a top as Kenny Dennis' shot sent him spiralling into the baked earth of the park popped up in our minds. And the beer made it easy for the smiles to transform into laughter, bubbling and rising in our throats until we couldn't keep it in any longer. Mates, as close as can be, on the same, stupid wavelength, knowing instinctively what pushes each other's buttons. And I don't know what made me do it, bring up the subject of Collins and his malevolent threats again, something to do with Billy's apparent insouciance to it all I suppose, but it was like sticking a pin in a balloon, the laughter escaping with the air from his body. And all of a sudden I could see the lines deepen on his face, burrowing across his brow, the darkness clouding in on his eyes, and in the fading half-light he looked as dangerous and as desperate a boy as I had ever seen.

His words, when they came, were a deep rumble, like distant thunder, I had to strain to catch them.

'Don't worry 'bout him, J.' His voice seemed to resonate in his chest, rattling through his rib cage. 'He'll get what's comin' to 'im.'

And as we began to make our way back towards the high street, beneath the shadow of Billy's high rise, as it loomed above us like some gigantic headstone, merging with the pallid night sky, I found myself scratching furiously away at my arm, the itching seemed unbearable, and when I peered through the gloom to inspect it, I realised that I had actually drawn blood. Not a good sign, I thought wearily to myself. Not a good sign at all.

The streets were all but deserted by the time we reached the spot where our old entrance to the park used to lie, just a few drunks stumbling home from chucking out time. Billy had decided to walk all the way back with me, we had stood in front of his tower block and I had watched as he looked up at the tiny square of yellow light that represented his home, with this kind of glazed look in his eyes.

'Might as well walk back with you,' he sighed.

'Sure you don't wanna come in for a cuppa?' I asked.

'Naaah, you're alright,' he mumbled. He forced a smile out but it sort of died halfway across his face. 'S'pose I better get off 'ome… get some kip,' he said, looking back in the direction of town. He looked tired, as if he had resigned himself to something.

'Can kip at mine if you want?' I said, trying not to sound desperate or needy. The truth was that I didn't fancy being on my own in the house tonight. But I sensed that there was something nagging away at him, something that he wanted to tell me. He was never one to hold anything back, Billy, no airs and graces about him, would always speak his mind irrespective of whether his words were liable to cause offence or not. But he couldn't seem to unburden himself from whatever it was that was praying on his mind, kept filling any silence that fell between us with constant chattering. Another time or another place I might have enjoyed watching Billy flounder, relished the discomfort that he was in, but what with everything that was swimming around inside of me, this constant sense of insecurity that seemed to be lurking like a stalker somewhere deep in my chest, never more than a heartbeat away, I just wanted him to be his natural, cocky little self. I pretended not to notice, joined in enthusiastically as he rambled almost incessantly on about how great it was to finally have that "tosser" Travolta off the number one spot. And even though the Rats were good, they weren't punk. Never had been in fact, according to Billy, even their early stuff, good but still only New Wave in its earliest form.

The hit film of the summer had been *Grease,* a romantic musical of American life in a '50s high school, and as a result the charts had been littered with songs from the film, with "Summer Nights" the latest and, for us, the final straw.

And The Boomtown Rats and their rites of passage anthem "Rat Trap" had climbed to the top and dislodged them. And we had pissed ourselves watching *Top of the Pops* when Bob Geldof had ripped up a pin-up of Travolta that he had been hiding behind as Johnnie Fingers had mimed his piano-playing intro.

'Fuckin' hell, you sound like Dave,' I smiled and rolled my eyes the way that Billy and I would always do to each other, whenever we found ourselves caught up in one of Dave's musical lectures that he would spin around us like a web.

'Yeah well… the thing is…' he mumbled tentatively, realising perhaps that he had been twittering on a bit and that I could see that there was something playing on his mind, something that he was trying to share with me.

But before he could go any further a bus pulled up beside us and two girls jumped off. They were deep in conversation, chatting as rapidly as machine-gun fire about two boys who had apparently just chatted them up at the pictures. And then they saw us; Billy and me in front of them, standing there like a pair of lemons as if we had been caught in the middle of some mischievous act. And they looked at one another knowingly and then proceeded to collapse on each other's shoulders in fits of giggles before linking arms, the way girls do, and tottering off down the road as if their ankles were tied together by a short piece of string. And as they faded into the night we could hear them singing and laughing, mimicking Geldof's lyrics. *'Hey, Billy, take a walk, take a walk, take a walk… Billy take a walk, take a walk, take a walk, Hey Billy… take a walk with me!'*

'Ere, weren't that Clive thingybob's younger sister?' Billy asked. 'You know… the kid who used to play left-back at school.'

I shook my head. 'That was Danny's sister.'

'What, Danny Beavis' sister!' he exclaimed. 'Never!' He stared disbelievingly at the spot where they had stood, as if by doing so he could conjure up some sort of recognition. 'She used to fancy me as a kid, used to drive me fuckin' mad.' And then a wicked smile crept across his face. 'Wouldn't mind now though.'

'Come on, Billy.' I motioned in the direction of home. *'Take a walk with me…* ' And he smiled at the irony, could see the humour in it, with him yammering on about the Rats and all.

'Cheeky little tarts,' he muttered, and I pissed myself at the sight of his indignation. And we headed for home laughing out loud, trading dead-arms like trump cards, the weekend that had just passed, nothing but an old memory.

The trouble was that by the time we reached my road the moment had well and truly gone. That chink of vulnerability that I had momentarily seen was buried once again beneath his shell-like exterior. And the suspense was beginning to drive me mad, I didn't know how much more of it my fragile state could take. I don't know what I imagined it was that he had been about to tell me but the notion of it had imbedded itself under my skin like a stubborn thorn and no matter how hard I tried I couldn't dislodge it. And I could see that it had reared its head inside Billy again. He hadn't been able to drink or idly talk it away the whole night. And I knew what that restless feeling felt like, as if you're harbouring a guilty secret, how it nagged away inside. You want to hold on to it, but its like trying to shelter a naked flame between cupped hands, sooner or later you have to let go, the sheer ferocity of it burning away your defences.

It was too much. 'What's on your mind, Billy?' I finally asked.

He stood there for a moment, devoid of expression, and then something close to relief fanned like sunlight across his face. And then he spoke to me, his voice as neutral as a newsreaders.

'I'm gonna fuck off, J.'

His words didn't seem to make any sense, I had heard them clear enough but their intention wouldn't register with me, as if my head wouldn't let them in. At first I thought that maybe he had ignored me, decided against opening himself up and that he was simply telling me that he was off home.

But he didn't turn to leave, didn't move at all in fact, just stood there staring blankly as if looking right through me. Or maybe I had misheard him and he was actually telling *me* to eff off. Not with any hostility, just letting me know in that unmistakable way of his that he just didn't have the enthusiasm for this kind of heart to heart, that he would much rather talk about something else, like the maturing of Danny's sister, for instance, from spotty little girl to curvy blonde.

But I was only kidding myself, trying to shy away from the truth, and it didn't take long for my brain to unscramble his logic. And it was then that I wished that he *had* told me to mind my own business or that he was buggering off home, anything rather than face the sombreness of his intentions.

I could feel panic beginning to swim inside me.

'What do you mean?' I spluttered.

He looked almost disappointed by my show of naivety and swept an arm out at his surroundings.

'Oh come on, J,' he said. 'What the fuck's left for me round 'ere, eh?'

I exhaled out of puffed cheeks and glanced around me, in search of some sort of an answer, something to offer him. I tried to look at it all from a different perspective; down the road that gradually grew narrower, building by building, shop by shop, into the centre of town. I peered into the night until the streetlights tapered off and fused together into one bright yellow blob in the distance. I couldn't find anything to say. I took in the cramped houses packed together like rows of stacked matchboxes… nothing. High in the distance the black shapes of Billy's and the other tower blocks cracked the night sky above, even the viaducts bordering the park behind me offered nothing inspiring, it was all so familiar, all the same, like staring at my own reflection in the mirror.

'You're a footballer now,' he continued with not a trace of humour in his voice. Usually when he talked of my football it was always with a large dose of sarcasm, 'Look out 'ere comes Banksy!' that kind of thing, never nasty, just typical Billy, taking the piss.

'Be turning full pro soon and all.' He nodded. I shrugged my shoulders as if I had never even given the matter a second thought.

He smirked at my attempt at modesty and motioned in the direction of the river, 'And Dave's already gone… what with his writing and stuff.'

And I just stood there, couldn't think of a single thing to say, it was as if my grasp of the English language had simply slid from my brain, like an egg off a plate.

The wide-open space of the park shimmered like an ocean in the moonlight, I wanted to dive in, submerse myself in its tranquillity; it felt as if I had a million questions buzzing like trapped bees inside my head but I started with the obvious one.

'Well, where will you go?'

'Dunno,' Billy shrugged. 'Thought maybe I'd try Blackpool or some place by the sea.' He smiled as if the whole thing were a big joke. 'You know, be like David Cassidy in *That'll be the Day*.'

'Essex,' I told him flatly. I don't know why I felt the need to correct him at that moment, probably habit, as that sort of stuff would always wind him up.

'What… like Margate or some place you mean?' And he

appeared to give the idea some thought. 'Maybe.' He shrugged.

'No,' I explained, 'it's Essex, David Essex in *That'll be the Day*... David Cassidy's in *The Partridge Family*.' I didn't have the energy to tell him that Margate was in Kent as well.

'Oh yeah... right.' He nodded as the penny dropped, and then a frown set upon his face. 'What's the fuckin' difference, anyhow?' he grumbled. 'They're both poofs anyway, you picky bastard.'

'So what you gonna do then?' I asked. 'Stack deckchairs all your life?'

'No!' he looked perplexed, hadn't expected me to be quite so persistent. 'Get a job on the funfairs or somethin' s'pose.' He shrugged.

'What about in the winter? What then?' It was all coming back to me; lucidity seemed to wash over me, invigorated my senses like a cold shower. I could hear echoes of Mum in my speech, envisaging only the practical problems facing him, as my words spilled out like hurdles at his feet. And it took Billy quite by surprise, the concerned parent was something that he had never had to deal with before, had never had to have a back-up plan, memorise carefully thought out answers to questions that a parent might well throw at you.

'Where you gonna live?' I pressed on. 'What if you can't get no work? What if... '

'For fuck's sake, J!' cried Billy. 'Give it a rest!'

We stood there for a moment in an awkward silence, both feeling rebuked and more than a little embarrassed by all the fuss.

'Let's face it, J,' he sighed finally. 'Sooner or later I'm gonna pull you down with me.'

I turned back to face him in astonishment, I had been staring back out over the calm waters of the park, watching the silhouettes of the birds skim across the surface as if fishing for prey. I wanted to protest, to tell him not to be so daft, but the thing was, we both knew that he was right. It was true, if I carried on staying out late, visiting pubs, going to punk concerts, getting pissed, it would sooner or later catch up with me. That it wouldn't take long for someone at the club to find out about it. And that would be that, no more chances... but wasn't that what I wanted?

But how could I tell him that it didn't matter anyway? That I was haunted by this undeniable feeling, that sooner rather than later it was all about to come crumbling down around my ears. It was all so crazy, I mean there was no denying that I walked a fine line most of the time by being with Billy. But as for "bringing me down", it sounded so ridiculous! As if I were above him or something... when the truth was, where the hell would I be without him?

A moment passed in silence between us, like so many before when we didn't need to lean on words, both knew what the other was thinking as clearly as if we had passed each other handwritten notes. When you grow up sharing the same grubby little patch of earth you get to know every twist in each other's bark.

There was nothing that I could say that would make him change his mind and stay. The three of us together had always instilled a kind of strength within me, there was a resilience about us, a buoyancy that made us unsinkable almost, not even *The Kick In* had truly pulled us down, it was as though we were tied together like the logs of a raft. And now the currents of life were tearing us apart. First there had been Ketchup following his dad up to Scotland and then Dave of course, riding the crest of a wave up in London. And without him to navigate, Billy and I would surely be lost, drift hopelessly into treacherous waters.

But then of course I had my football to anchor me down, with all its promise of a glittering and illustrious career to steer towards, gleaming like a lighthouse on the horizon. But then how could I abandon Billy?

He looked round, as if he were scanning scenery, surveying the arena of our childhood, taking in the chimney pots and the TV aerials silhouetted against the summer night sky. The buildings and high rises of town jutting up and down in the distance like the broken teeth of a comb. He shook his head slowly and said with a sigh, 'I'll end up in fuckin' prison if I stay round 'ere much longer.'

I didn't bother to question him. It was a statement more than a remark.

Boys on motorbikes had entered the park, driving down the footpaths leading from the grim Northside estate, and were practising wheelies and skids across the open space of the playing fields. The high-pitched revving of their tiny 50cc engines whistled through the night, rising up from behind the bushes like a swarm of angry wasps. A night bus, empty of passengers, carrying nothing but blocks of yellow light, passed by us so fast that it was as if it had whipped up every speck of dust and dirt from the streets, lifting it, in the driver's rushed frenzy to end his shift, out of the doorways and gutters of town like the winds of a storm.

But Billy didn't even seem to notice, didn't move a muscle, barely even squinted as it gusted on by. The sound of whooping and laughter from the park finally broke the spell cast over his thoughts. He looked in the direction of the park and frowned. 'Little bastards,' he growled. For someone who, as a child, had been anything but an angel, he had developed a curiously short temper when it came to other young tearaways.

I used to think that we had always been different to other kids, had never really been children, me, Billy and Dave. Not in the real sense of the word, our circumstances had never allowed it. We never had the pull or the strength of parental guidance, there had never been anyone with the time or the inclination to take us to the park and kick a ball about with us, teach us to swim maybe, or to ride a bike up and down the street with us, to share that beaming moment when it's just you and two wheels.

In many ways we had been left to fend for ourselves, a childhood without stabilisers.

And as I stood there staring at Billy in the mist of the summer evening, I felt as if I had taken a step further inside. Peering cautiously into the darkness of our insecurities, I could feel their grip tighten around me, touched by the inevitability that everything was about to come crashing down.

And maybe it was the glow from the streetlamps or a trick of the moonlight but he looked frighteningly older than his years: pale, washed out... wraith-like.

Images of the young boy I had grown up with flashed across my mind; tousled haired and fresh-faced, the most fearless in the playground, climbing higher and spinning faster than anybody else, a bubbling barrel of exuberance, tearing round the football pitch...what was it that Dave used to call him?... the Tasmanian Devil, that was it, the manic little monster from the Bugs Bunny cartoons.

He sighed and lifted his eyebrows in the direction of town. 'S'pose I better be of,' he muttered reluctantly. 'He's probably passed out by now anyhow.'

And I couldn't seem to find a trace of that boy in the young man who stood in front of me now. Seventeen years old and contemplating the prospect of prison as if there really weren't any other option, just another step along life's rutted road, as if it were expected of him almost.

And all of a sudden it was as if a shadow had been cast across his face, as dark as death, a fearsome intensity burning in his eyes. 'Tell you what though... ' And I knew that whatever it was that he was about to tell me, I didn't want to hear it. I could feel the anxiety crawling up the inside of my arm, knew that his words would form into threats and that they were very seldom idle, that trouble was never far behind.

'I'll settle a few old scores before I go.'

CHAPTER EIGHTEEN

August 1978

The journey up to Birmingham that following Saturday was about as tedious as travelling to away games could get. The thing was, usually I would find the whole experience pretty exciting, it would remind me of the times as a kid when Mum would take me on a coach trip down to Swanage for a couple of days, the nearest thing that we ever had to a holiday.

But I couldn't seem to find that sense of comfort, that excitement that would usually bubble away as I watched the world from the security of a coach seat. No matter how hard I tried, I couldn't fire up my imagination enough to explore the towns and the oceans of countryside that passed my window, to see it all through different eyes, instead just watched it roll wearily by, like the credits at the end of a film.

A few of the older lads had busied themselves with a game of cards while the younger lads lounged about chatting about birds and stuff, taking the piss mostly. And a few of them had even managed to grab some sleep, feet up across the seats, heads pressed against the window as their bodies swayed unconsciously along with the rhythm of the coach; floating in the motions of car sleep. I tried to focus my thoughts on the match and the thrill of playing at Birmingham's famous St. Andrews ground.

Reserve team football can be a peculiar experience, the team can seem constantly in limbo with some players on the up, and others, usually first team squad members, on their way down. It was very rare, well at Southfields at least, that a regular first team player would find himself running out with the reserves. His presence would usually be the result of an injury or suspension.

As an apprentice or semi-pro in the "stiffs" you always found yourself hoping that your opposition would be fielding one or two full-time ones. Well known names, familiar faces instantly recognisable from the back pages of newspapers and sticker albums. And who knows, if you were really lucky the odd international among them. Some of the lads had started to discuss the idea, the thought of facing the likes of Tony Towers, Tony Want, Jimmy Calderwood, Joe Gallacher and, of course, Francis. It was beginning to pump them up already, could sense the enthusiasm rise in their voices, and we were only just on the outskirts of Birmingham, leaving the countryside behind as the buildings and housing estates of the suburbs grew denser, like slipping through the depths of a forest.

But I couldn't seem to concentrate on any of it, couldn't sustain my train of thought long enough to get excited. Instead my mind kept leaping back to Billy and all the people who could easily be marked down for retribution.

His words had stuck with me ever since, all the way home that night they had jabbed away like needles in my head. Each time I had passed beneath the glow of a streetlight and found myself gazing down at the elongated figure of my shadow, I had imagined these giant needles sticking portentously into my brain, like pins embedded in a voodoo doll.

There was certainly no shortage of candidates to fill Billy's hit list. I never imagined that I would ever think it but it seemed that Mr Brown, our old P.E. teacher, had been right, had summed it up one time when we had all been sitting rather despondently in the changing rooms of some school over Croydon way. We had just drawn a match that we had never considered we wouldn't win. But Billy had been sent off along with their right-back for fighting and it had disrupted the whole game and somehow we had allowed them back in it enough for them to grab a last minute equaliser. Old Browny had looked down at Billy as he sat wiping the blood from his split lip across the sleeve of his shirt, and the whole room had held its breath, expecting him to blow his top, but instead he simply shook his head sagely and said, 'If you choose to walk through life with violence as your companion you will always come across those who wish to test the strength of that bond.'

His words didn't seem to make much sense, had been unexpected due to the circumstances but not entirely surprising. He would often quote famous writers or poets if their words seemed to fit the circumstances, seeing as he taught English Literature as well as P.E.

And I hadn't thought too much about their meaning, too busy stifling laughter as Dave had leant over and whispered into my ear, 'That little pearl of wisdom is all his own work I can tell you.'

But I *did* follow the thread of Browny's words. The thing was that Billy hadn't *started* it. The problem was that his name had preceded him. They had also had a boy with a reputation of his own to live up to, a brute of a lad. And this kid had made his intentions pretty clear from almost the very first whistle, constantly straying out of position if there was a chance to hit Billy with a hefty challenge or leave a foot in somewhere, all very sly. Mr Brown had been yelling at him, telling him to ignore it and just play his normal game. But that *was* Billy's normal game! All game Billy had been on the receiving end of things, caught from behind time after time, well after the ball had gone but always seemingly out of sight of the referee. And then with about fifteen minutes left, Billy had seen his chance. He had charged after the boy, and his intentions had been clear for all to see, there was no way he was going to pull up and simply close him down, instead he was going to career straight through the great lump, like a wrecking ball through a derelict building. And with nowhere to run and the match apparently lost, the bully had finally lost his cool. During seventy-five minutes of what added up to little less than assault he had failed to stop Billy playing, there he had still been, bearing down on him, larger than life and spitting revenge. And so as Billy had closed in the kid had simply turned sideways on and stuck his elbow out straight into Billy's face.

I don't think the kid had ever imagined Billy would actually get back up; the look of utter horror on his face as Billy had dragged himself to his feet and begun slamming his fists into his head had been an absolute picture.

But now as I sat there trawling through all the memories of all the confrontations and all the fights that Billy had been involved in, sometimes recalling incidents that I had totally forgotten, would probably never have remembered if I hadn't been looking in their direction; it suddenly dawned on me that all the names and faces that sprung to mind, the ones that I could imagine Billy really unleashing his brand of revenge upon, all belonged to the kind of person who had, at one time or another, had something to prove to him, who had tried to yield some sort of power over him.

Not the likes of the big kid from the school in Croydon. He had tried but, like many before and after him, he had failed. No, the ones who kept coming back, floating to the surface of my mind, as ugly and unwelcome as dead fish floating on a pond, were the faces of people who had actually succeeded in hurting him in way or another, either physically or by getting inside his head.

His old man appeared to be an obvious choice, but it had always seemed to me that Billy didn't look at their relationship like others did. And he had begun to even things up of late. Returning his father's windmill-sized slaps and backhanders with more than a little interest. No, his twisted relationship with his dad didn't worry me or start the smooth strip of skin along my scar crawling with irritation. Billy and his old man... well, it was "in-house", to me the whole thing had always seemed to be cloaked beneath a macabre sense of pride. I couldn't really explain it other than... well, spilt blood or not, it was a match, the same type running through both of their veins. Like he could call his old man all the names under the sun but God help anyone else who insulted him.

And then there was Dave's father. For a start they certainly disliked each other with a passion. It had always been there, for as long as I could remember. The thing was, Billy had never been intimidated by him, not like the other kids were, and that irked old man Connelly something rotten. His presence could dissolve you, whenever he walked into a room or turned up down the park looking for Dave, not like an ordinary parent might, to tell him that dinner was on the table or that it was getting late, but usually to accuse him of stealing fags or some money that he had been too drunk to remember he had already lost or spent, you would find yourself wishing that you were invisible. But Billy would never shrink, I could still see him standing there glaring back, almost as if he was willing old Connelly to scold him as well. And as the years had passed Billy had probably seen more of him than Dave had, what with the pair of them in and out of the pubs in town all the time. And I knew for a fact that they had often had the odd word or two, replaced "crossed swords" with pool cues or the like, arguing over a touching ball or something, the pair of them overreacting.

The thing was, Billy could not stand bullies, and that was what he classed Dave's dad as. Although Billy could be a right bastard he never regarded himself as a tyrant, the sort of person who singled out victims. The simple fact was that he didn't pick or prey on the weak, he would stand up to anyone, big or small, young or old, it didn't matter who they were if they had the misfortune to antagonise him, in Billy's eyes they were fair game.

And this wasn't some gimpy kid in class that Billy saw being constantly harassed, it was Dave... *our* Dave, and that meant trouble.

But despite all this there were two other individuals whose images kept jumping to the front of my mind, who, disturbingly, I knew would be Billy's main targets. I kept seeing their faces everywhere that I looked, in the features of my team-mates sitting around me, replacing the expressions of the manager as he marched up and down the aisle telling us to start "focusing our minds" now that we had arrived at St. Andrews, as we pulled up somewhere beneath the lattice pattern of a floodlight stanchion.

But how could I even begin to "focus" or "visualise" when I couldn't escape from the dark, malignant images that were burned into my brain... the ones of P.C. Collins and of the tattooed skinhead who had led *The Kick In*.

I seemed to have no problem in visualising *their* faces, close up and in detail. The texture of their skin; I could clearly see the grainy look in the eyes of Collins, his pock-marked cheeks ruddy and irritable from the heat of his uniform. Could picture the crazed, glassy-eyed stare of the tattoo boy, could plainly see that mess on his forehead, the bodged, crooked attempt of a crucifix that had been scored into his skin by the point of a compass and then filled with school ink. As Dave's had so nearly ended up like.

And I knew that sooner rather than later I would have to look into those dreadful faces again, so full of anger and ill will, that we would *all* collide: Collins, Billy, the tattoo boy, Dave and I. The whole damn lot of us; explode like so many trains all hurtling into the same station from different directions.

And what could possibly be salvaged from so many lives on a crash course to destruction? Who could drag themselves clear from such a wreckage? The chances were that it would be none of us.

Funny, the things I missed when they were no longer there. Used to do it with home as well, would always miss it when I was some place else. Not just the roof over my head but the whole scene: London, the suburbs, the people. I always used to think how great it would be to go somewhere else, to get away for a while, but my imagination didn't have the capacity to stretch that far. Daydreams most likely ignited from the sparks left by the glorious tales of trips and holidays told by all the other kids. It wouldn't have mattered to me where I went - the country, the seaside, even another town or city - it would have just been enough to see life through other people's eyes for a while.

But the thing was, whenever I *did* find myself somewhere unfamiliar, like in Birmingham that Saturday after the match, it wouldn't take long before I started wishing that I was back home again.

I would begin by comparing things, shops, people, judging them by the clothes that they wore. Would try and gauge how good the atmosphere in the pubs would be. Nothing ever seemed quite... *as good,* somehow. I would even catch myself comparing the state of the buildings and streets, almost looking down my nose snootily at the architecture or at the grime etched into walls and brickwork. It was as if the intimidating high rises of London, with their stinking stairwells and forbidden underpasses, were better than any other soulless '60s development. My hometown might have been wretched, desolate even, but it was still *my* hometown. I thought of it almost as a possession, as if I owned every street, knew every alleyway and crack in the pavement like the back of my hand. What it boiled down to, I suppose, was a feeling of security. Even after *The Kick In,* I still kind of felt safe back in town, like I belonged there.

The thing was, our coach had broken down. Well, hadn't even started would be more accurate, the thing hadn't stirred whenever the driver had tried the ignition, it had just sat there hopelessly like some giant stranded whale dying in silence, nothing but the faint clicking of the key turning in its slot. We had just slumped down in our seats, preparing ourselves for the monotonous drive back down the A1, loosening our club ties and fidgeting for comfort as if the pressure from being so polite needed to escape from beneath our collars. We had shaken hands and said our formal goodbyes to the players and representatives of Birmingham City, conducting ourselves, over a couple of halves and the neatly cut sandwiches provided, in the appropriate manner deemed fit for members of Southfields Football Club.

People hovered around outside, heads bobbing up and down, appearing and then suddenly vanishing beneath the line of my vision as they each peered in at the engine to offer an opinion. The majority of them seemed to settle on the idea of something called the starter motor, but they might as well have been talking in Japanese for all it meant to me. Anyhow, they had us trooping back off the bus and lined up in two groups either side, rocking the great thing too and fro in a bid to jump-start it back into action or something I suppose.

'Fuckin' 'ell,' smirked the young lad who had been our sub, a boy from Streatham who I vaguely knew from old school matches. 'This is just like my old punk days,' he said, as if he were some ancient relic. 'Roamin' round the streets lookin' for fights, smashin' shop windows and overturnin' motors,' and with one hand resting lazily on the bus he laughed, 'never fort I'd be *asked* do it.'

'Ay!' growled old Johnny Hatch, his giant hands spread across the side of the bus. 'And you'll be back on the bleedin' streets if you don't help us push this heap of bleedin' junk,' he said as his face turned a deep shade of red, the muscles tightening from the effort and the beer. The senior players were always allowed a couple more than us apprentices... a lot more, a sort of unspoken law.

But it was all to no avail, the bus didn't make a sound, didn't make the slightest purr of life, just sat there, it was as if someone had removed its insides, like a stuffed animal, leaving nothing but a shell.

Staff and officials of Birmingham rushed back and forth, huffing and puffing, all trying to find a solution. They all seemed desperately embarrassed, as if the predicament we found ourselves in was their personal fault.

But there didn't seem to be any solution, nobody could manage to find any alternative transport. The first team had yet to return from their away fixture, apparently stuck in traffic somewhere further north, which we all reckoned suited them just fine. 'So they don't have to lend their nice luxury first team coach to second class shite like us,' Johnny Hatch had muttered under his breath.

So there I was, sitting in some dingy-looking pub somewhere in the heart of Birmingham sharing a beer with Kenny Dennis, and wishing for all the world that I was back in London, covered in the dreary familiarity of home.

Not that it wasn't good to see old Kenny again, because it was, to spend some "proper" time away from the stiff restrictions of a football club, where we could be ourselves and not... well, footballers I suppose.

I don't know, it was just that seeing Kenny like that, so at ease with everything, relaxed, taking this role of apprentice professional maturely in his stride, sort of unsettled me. Don't know why it should have, I mean all the time that I knew him he had been a laid-back sort of boy, to the point where it seemed that he glided through life almost in slow motion. But there was this kind of aura of self-belief about him now, I could sense it even stronger than before. If I had just met him for the first time I would have mistaken it for a kind of arrogance, you could see that he knew, with an absolute certainty, that he was going to make it. So I guess in way it was a form of arrogance, but not the distasteful kind.

But I couldn't help it, the whole thing began to weigh me down, Kenny's confidence, the air of contentment that hung around him, which seemed to hang heavy, like a rain cloud, on my shoulders, so it felt as if my stool were about to collapse beneath me at any moment.

It wasn't that I begrudged Kenny even one drop of the success that was destined to flood over him, it was just that knowing that none of it would even so much as drizzle upon me made it harder to take than I had ever imagined.

And it was everything about him, the way that he held himself, not just on the pitch but out in the "real" world as well. He had that way about him, Kenny, a bit like Dave. The pair of them could swagger down a street without ever seeming to be haughty or over-bearing. He had obviously slotted into the way and pace of life up there, just the same as in a match, in tune with the rhythm of his surroundings from the outset.

When we were kids playing against him in our schooldays he was always the heartbeat of the opposition, in complete control of proceedings. Just like that afternoon, everything that Birmingham had created had come from Kenny. He had had that touch of class about him that Saturday. Everyone could see it, seemed as if he were head and shoulders above all the others, but the funny thing was, when there had been a corner down the other end and I had actually compared his size to that of the other players around him, he was really no taller than most of them, it just seemed that way. In fact he probably hadn't grown at all since we were kids, had probably reached his full height when the rest of us were still outgrowing our school shoes. Not for the first time I had found myself wondering just how old he really was.

The interior of the pub that we were in was so dim, the walls covered in dark stained wooden panels like a courtroom, and so poorly lit that for a moment, as Kenny sauntered back from the bar with our drinks, his long black fingers wrapped round our pints like spiders' legs, his head and shoulders actually melted into the background, indistinguishable from the surrounding gloom.

'Cheers,' I nodded. He raised his glass slowly in acknowledgment and when he lowered it, shook his head and smiled languidly at me.

'Man… I thought you had that one for a minute.'

'Yeah,' I sighed. 'So did I.' My words tailed off as if they had run out of puff so all that I could manage was a shrug of my shoulders. I couldn't seem to raise the enthusiasm to talk about football or even think about it for some reason. The very idea seemed so exhausting, too much like hard work, like the feeling I used to get when I would try and concentrate on some passage from a history book or something, only to find a page or two had passed without a single fact or figure lodging in my head.

Kenny had been remarking on his penalty against me earlier that day. Which of course he had thundered home, but not before I had managed to send the ball up into the angle of my right-hand post and crossbar before it fizzed like a pinball in a machine back down into the net. Three penalties in three games! It really did defy belief, and I had so nearly saved all three, what a start that would have been. But in truth I had never expected to save Kenny's, had been happy just to get a hand to it really. But I couldn't seem to muster up the will to discuss it, any of it, must have appeared so rude, but talking to Kenny about football and stuff like that just seemed to sink me lower. I had wanted to discuss our good fortune together, would have loved to revel in his plans for the future and share mine with him, but it was all just daydreams, fantasy; would never happen, at least not for me, and seeing it all so close, like a mirror to my life, which I never experienced at home, having no one to compare myself with, made me feel so impossibly sad.

I took a long swig from my beer, downing nearly half a pint in one. The boss would love that. The narrow strip of daylight that ran across the top of the blind-covered windows seemed to be fading by the minute, as if the pub was submerging into deep seas, becoming more sinister-looking than ever with the light barely trickling from beneath the lampshades.

'Is this where you go then?' I asked, trying hard not to let my disdain for the place show.

But I could see the mischief creep into his eyes, glinting like onyx.

'A bit too cosmopolitan for you, eh, Johnny?' And I remember that I had never heard the word before but knew exactly what he meant. He blinked amusement through narrowing eyes. He had always worn that expression, I thought, ever since I could remember, sort of lazy-looking, as if he were struggling to stay awake all the time. But he was all right, big Kenny, knew how to take the piss out of himself, never seeming to take things too seriously. I remember Dave's words one time after we had seen him hassled one Saturday by a gang of young punks in town. And they had all been a year or two younger and half the size of Kenny but had found courage in their numbers. And it had been the usual stuff, name-calling, monkey chants, the odd Nazi salute even though they didn't have a clue what it actually meant, just mimicking their older heroes like kids playing football in the playground.

'Shall we have a word?' I had asked Dave.

'Why bother?' he had shrugged. 'He couldn't care less anyway.' He had nodded in the direction of Kenny as he had ambled past the bench that his aggressors were congregated upon, completely unruffled, offering nothing more than a curious sideways glance. The thing was, if he had so much as turned and raised his voice at them, they would have scattered like a pack of frenzied sheep. He could have taken the lot of the spotty little bastards on with one hand tied behind his back. But he hadn't, hadn't done or said anything, had just kept on walking, almost as if the whole episode had amused him, kids being kids and all that.

'If you've seen what he's seen,' Dave had shrugged, 'don't suppose anything seems that important anymore.'

'Guess not,' I'd said, somewhat vacantly, sort of understanding but, as usual, left a little uncertain by Dave's uncanny wisdom, a bit like trying to work out Mum's pools lines on a Saturday. But I never did have the ability to see things in the same light as Dave.

'No, no,' I insisted a little too eagerly. 'It's nothing like that... it's just... ' I searched for the right words. For, although he wasn't the kind to take offence, I didn't want him to think my discomfort was because the place, since we had been sitting there, had gradually grown busier, bodies popping up here and there at the bar and around the pool table, slipping through the doors in ones and twos, slowly filling the place up like a cup beneath a dripping tap. Because the thing was, every face was black, and of course I felt as if every set of eyes was upon me, I felt conspicuous, as if I had just let a soft shot trickle under my body and the entire ground was staring, disbelieving.

But the truth was, I didn't feel threatened at all, had received the odd second glance but nothing that betrayed even a hint of malice, and besides, Kenny seemed to know virtually everyone anyway, nodding "alrights" and lazily slapping open palms as people passed by.

'No,' I said airily, a little more composed now, gazing casually around at my surroundings, pretending to be taking in the drab décor and furnishings, deliberately avoiding eye contact. 'It's just that... ' I wrinkled my nose in a show of distaste, 'Well it's a bit dark in here innit?' Then, 'Shit!' The horror of my words hit me like a giant fist in my chest, knocking the wind out of me. 'I didn't mean!... ' But by this time Kenny wasn't listening to me. Instead his shoulders were heaving up and down like giant pistons, the whole frame of his body rocking to and fro until he collapsed from his stool onto his knees as the tears streamed down his cheeks amidst deep rumbling bursts of laughter.

And of course after that, the tension between us simply crumbled away, disintegrated like a dried-out elastic band. Although I don't think it had ever existed for Kenny, just something I had conjured up in my head, the idea that there was a strain between us, two lads who were both on the verge of a massive turning point in their lives; one with the world at the end of his giant size twelves and the other just about to let it slip spectacularly through his hands.

Even the mood in the pub seemed to lighten, it appeared less gloomy than before, had lost that sense of oppression, the way a graveyard loses its ability to send shivers up your spine in the daylight.

And Kenny had obviously mentioned my blunder to a number of people in the bar, judging from the amount of visible amusement that my return from the toilets seemed to produce, nods of the head and knowing smiles everywhere that I looked, and then from out of the jukebox exploded a familiar sound, a slice of music from my youth. It was strange because I had just assumed that the thing had contained nothing more than a variety of different reggae artists, for that's what had been playing ever since we had walked in: Bob Marley and Peter Tosh anthems over and over again. But it had been silent as I had made my way back to my seat from the toilets, and then just as I had sat down Strummer's voice had burst from the speakers. 'One, two, three, four... ' And then the whole pub had erupted with laughter, deep and chesty like a hundred Kennys, as the sound of The Clash's "White man in Hammersmith Palais" filled the bar.

And then there was a world of grinning faces all looking in my direction, taking the piss out of me, out of their selves.

'Sorry, Johnny,' Kenny grinned, 'I couldn't help it... But man, you should have seen your face,' he said, still shaking his head with laughter.

I smiled thinly. 'Just glad there's some decent music on that thing.' I nodded in the direction of the jukebox, trying to act all cool.

'Yeah right,' smiled Kenny knowingly. 'Perhaps I should have put 10cc on.'

My forehead creased in confusion, he'd lost me. What is it with the kids I've grown up with, I thought, they seem to leave me standing with their world-weary wisdom and insights.

'"Dreadlock Holiday",' he continued. It had been number one earlier in the year. 'You know… ' he rolled his eyes. *Don't you show some respect…* ' he sang mimicking a West Indian accent. *'I don't like reggae-ah… I love it-ah…'*

'Jesus!' I exclaimed. 'I can do a better bloody black man impression than you!'

And from then on the beer really started to slip down, even smoother than before, so much so that I reminded myself of Billy, the way he would keep putting down and picking up his pint before it had even settled in the glass.

'S'pose I better start getting back.' Time had flown. I gazed wistfully at the clock on the wall behind the bar, as if I were almost willing it to slow down, to stretch each minute out like pastry. Funny what the beer and seeing an old mate can do, I had felt awkward and uncomfortable a couple of hours earlier, and now I didn't want to go. Kenny turned to the clock and nodded. 'I'll come with you,' he said.

'It's alright, I'll be fine,' I insisted, swallowing back a mouthful of gas. 'Be able to find my way okay.'

'Not too pissed then?'

'Nuh,' I shrugged, cocky from the beer, puffing out my chest, playing at being a lad. 'Us London boys… ' I finished my pint and rose reluctantly to my feet. 'Can look after ourselves, can't we?'

The thing was, now I really didn't want to go back to London and my empty house. Nowhere would be open by the time we arrived home. But here, I gazed around again at my surroundings as if I were seeing it through different eyes, I felt… *accepted*, I suppose, didn't have to be anything other than Kenny's mate.

The beer helped of course, it felt soothing as it crept, like hot water through a radiator, into my bloodstream. And then there was also my newly-found status to consider, as if I had passed some kind of initiation test or something. For, although I had never really felt any ill will towards me, I had nevertheless been more than just a stranger to them, an outsider, an oddity even, like a supporter cheering a goal against Chelsea in the Shed, or a blue and white scarf swaying along in the Kop or something. I vaguely remember wondering if this sort of thing could ever happen back in London. You could almost call it a kind of racial harmony, I suppose, but then the thought of the NF marches and the Anti-Nazi League protests and the riots that followed floated like a rain cloud across my mind, and the idea suddenly seemed preposterous.

I hadn't been completely ignorant to it though, I mean it had always been there, hovering just beneath the surface, white boy in a black man's pub sort of thing, but it had sparkled with light-hearted innuendo, the sting drawn out of it, like a terminally ill patient taking the piss out of his condition.

But then of course Kenny had been the real reason behind it all. A bridge that joined different lands, I mean I wouldn't have even been there if hadn't been for him. So in truth I had really been accepted from the start just because I was with him, like being signed in as a member's guest at some exclusive club.

We had chatted so free and easily ever since I had put my foot in my mouth and broken the ice that had frozen up all my words. Earlier on, when we had been back in the players' lounge as St. Andrews, talk had been more hesitant, stilted pieces of conversation interspersed with pockets of awkward silences that we had filled with hastily-formed opinions about the match, 'Didn't think so-and-so was offside then… did you?', that sort of thing.

It was odd because although Kenny was an old mate, a friend from my youth, he wasn't a Dave or a Billy, well who was? But he wasn't even a Ketchup. And it had been a while since I had last seen him, couldn't remember the moment exactly when time had made us almost like strangers.

But now we were swapping and exchanging stories about our lives as semi-pros, like school kids trading swaps in the playground. Discussing the variation in training routines, fascinated to compare each other's ground rules, the little idiosyncrasies that each club held dear, what time they expected you to be in bed or what sort of diet they had you on. And we had laughed as we came to the conclusion that beer certainly wouldn't be on either club's agenda. But most of all we had talked about being kids, about school, football and kids we had once known, of girls we had once fancied, of the excitement of power cuts and the bad fights that we had seen, of a time when growing up seemed something that other people would eventually do, but certainly not us. And I remember thinking how funny it was, how very ironic, that he had wanted the same thing from our time together as me. To reminisce, to let the tide of our childhood creep back to the front of our minds, at least for a while. To remember a time before our careers and late teenage years had made us so reflective, of a time when every day didn't seem so, so… vital.

Like a housemaid shooing away mice in the old cartoons, we had chased each other's memories out into the open from the cellars of our minds, and had been fascinated at what we had found hiding beneath the cobwebs. For, although we were supposedly the same age and had grown up in the same South London town, we had gone to different schools; same rats, but different grammar school runs. So certain stories that we had told had been seen from different perspectives. But what had really captured my imagination had been when Kenny had reeled off his memories of some scrape or another, of some adventure that I couldn't for the life of me remember. I had sat there transfixed, in a kind of bewildered amazement, desperately trying to fit the memory together like a jigsaw in my mind. And sometimes I would have the satisfaction of finding the missing piece and wondering how the hell I had ever managed to misplace such an integral part of my childhood's puzzle.

Such had been the case with one of Kenny's favourite stories, one that must have somehow been lost within the archives of so many other memories filed in my head.

It had been during one of those endless summer holidays, the ones when time lasted forever, one day indistinguishable from the next, blending into one another like waves lapping on a shore. And a gang of us had apparently ended up hanging around beneath the viaducts behind the park, something that we would often do. There had been no particular reason that we had gone there, the winds of boredom simply blowing us in that direction, across the park and through the railings, gathering up stray kids during the day like a tumbleweed.

And while the rest of us had gathered beneath a towering arch, Billy had popped up from an exploration of his own, beaming from ear to ear and wielding an old car tyre, which he then preceded to set alight. And as the flames had slowly begun to take hold, spewing out great plumes of choking black smoke, he had started jumping in and out of the tyre trying to instigate a game of Dare. But somehow he had managed to get his foot trapped. At first we had thought that he was joking, but his cries for help had grown more frantic by the second as the fire had started to lick its way up his jeans. Kenny had said that we had barely been able to see him by the time we had actually dragged him out through the clouds of coal black fumes, had said all he could remember seeing was these arms flailing about like a ghost. And then it had come back to me, as if someone had suddenly turned a light on in my head. But it had been the smell that I had remembered the most. The sickly stench of burning rubber that wouldn't leave me, I could taste it in everything that I ate for days after. And then of course the sight of Billy had begun to come through clearer, as if the smoke were clearing from that particular memory: Billy lying on the ground, eyes red and watering, half choking through his laughter, scorch marks all along the length of his jeans, blackened and still smoking like a spent firework. And of course he had had to run all the way home with only one trainer on, for P.C. Collins had shown up, this tiny black figure beneath us marching determinedly up the bank, the colour of his uniform and the distinctive shape of his helmet; the sight of him in the distance had reminded me of a pawn from a chessboard. How the hell had I forgotten that?

When our coach pulled back into the Southfields car park, late that night, most of the lads didn't even realise; crumpled across the seats in alcohol-fuelled slumbers like tramps on park benches. In fact they only began to stir when the driver switched off the ignition and the steady hum and motion of the engine exposed the frailty of their sleep; without a rhythm to soothe them they awoke, like restless babies in cots.

The boss hadn't minded in the end though. I mean what else could he have expected under the circumstances? And besides, you could tell that he had had a few as well. We all had. Whilst he had undoubtedly enjoyed the hospitality offered by the staff and officials of Birmingham City, I reckoned he had been in the players' lounge secretly waiting for their first team to arrive back, hoping to meet the boss Jim Smith, glean a little managerial advice perhaps and maybe snatch a word with Trevor Francis, their centre-forward, who had been banging in goals left, right and centre, and maybe plant a Southfields seed or two in his head. I mean if what the papers had been saying was true, a few of the big names, the likes of Francis and Joe Gallacher, were growing pretty restless and sniffing about for a transfer.

A shame it hadn't been a few months earlier, back when Sir Alf Ramsay had been in charge. I vaguely wondered if he would have said anything to the great man.

But as I watched him walk down the aisle of the coach, waking the lads in that submissive way of his, gently shaking a shoulder or tapping sticking out feet, I concluded that he probably wouldn't have said anything, not if what Kenny had told me was true. For Kenny had been there when Ramsay was still manager… or director of football, managing consultant, whatever they liked to call it. And apparently the sheer talk of the man's presence could starts nerves jangling. Kenny had said that whether at the club or the training ground, you always knew when he was about to make an appearance. Everyone's senses heightened, the atmosphere crackling with anticipation, word filtering through the ranks like the sudden sight of a headmaster marching down the corridor. And it came as no surprise to hear that virtually all the reserves were completely in awe of the man, and if what Kenny had suspected were true, a fair few of the first team squad felt intimidated as well. For how could you possibly follow in the footsteps of all the great players who had passed through his hands over the years? The Moores, Charltons, Hursts and Greaveses of the world. God knows how I would have felt knowing that I might be compared to Gordon Banks! How could you live up to his expectations? To the man who had led England to their only World Cup victory?

Everything had seemed to be heading down hill since those exciting days of Ramsay's appointment. And now the likes of Francis wanted out.

'I reckon he's worth a million,' Kenny had said.

'Bollocks!' I had scoffed. 'No one will be worth that much…
not in the '70s.'

But we certainly hadn't heard much talk of football that
evening. A few people had asked Kenny how he had got on that
afternoon, inquired if had played well, if they had won, or even
scored. But to me it had just seemed as if it were people being
polite, offering courteous comments to a face they know, someone
they might see three or four times in a week but whose second
name they don't even know, like acknowledging your bus driver
on the way to work every morning.

It had seemed to me that the main topics of conversation
taking place had surprisingly consisted of work and politics! From
what I had been able to tell, most of the pub seemed to be
employed at the giant Leyland car plant on the outskirts of the city
and this, more than anything else, was at the heart of virtually
every discussion. Callaghan's *Winter of Discontent* was brewing up
nicely; firemen, bakers, heating engineers and, above all, the
transport workers were all out for higher pay; car plants lay idle all
over the country with the threat of worse to come. Shop floor
politics had filled the air, just like in any working-class pub back in
London, talk had become more intense with every beer that had
been sunk.

The bitter strikes and feuding of a few years back still hung
like a forbidding, elongated tower block shadow across the
workshops and factory floors. What Kenny had seen and heard
had made him wonder if the city would ever fully recover.

'Strikes and bombs, man… ' He had shaken his head, sounding
older than his supposed years, sounding like Dave. 'Some people
talk about it all as if it were only yesterday… you know sometimes
I wonder if this place will ever stop trembling from the aftershock.'
He had become hunched, as if he were trying to shield his very
words behind the frame of his giant body, eyes wide and alert now,
like olives rocking in a bowl. Of course it could have been the

drink but it had seemed more than that. He had outlined the shape of a box on the table with the sweat from his finger, as if it would help explain his thoughts clearer. 'We're all pigeon-holed,' he had explained. 'Do you see?' I wasn't sure that I did. His cool façade and his accent had slipped, it was still very South London but with a heavy African slant, his words could have been lifted from a Bob Marley song sheet. Or perhaps it was the voice of the *real* Kenny: the philosophical, slightly mad Kenny, the boy older than his years, an African version of Dave, the boy who had seen too much to ever take things seriously. But maybe that was really it, he had seen so many unspeakable things that he could no longer see the hope in anything.

CHAPTER NINETEEN

August 1978

I thought about old Kenny quite a bit over the next few days or so. About lots of different aspects of our relationship and what I knew, or had thought that I knew, about him; of how maybe I had misread him and how I simply had to go and visit his mum in the laundrette where she worked and relay Kenny's messages. And of course I had thought about the match.

I had begun to try and analyse my performances of late, replaying each game over in my head. It helped to pass the time on the bus journeys to the ground more than it helped to improve my game in any way; helped to steer my mind away from the demons that I knew were gathering in the dark corners of my mind. Sometimes it seemed as if I could almost hear them, shuffling around in the back of my head, behind the heavy curtains where I tried to cram all the unwanted baggage from my past: thoughts of a father, Debbie, Cindy… and *The Kick In*.

The thing was, as professional as I might have tried to be, visualising plucking crosses out of the air or repositioning myself for attacks that I had faced, my mind would inevitably drift off the subject and back to people watching.

My concentration was no more substantial than a paper lid caught in a breeze, the world passing by below somehow always pulled me in. I found a sense of comfort in daydreaming that I could never really fathom. Even if I were to catch my reflection in the light of the bus window, grinning stupidly back at me at the memory of some save or another, I could never seem to stay on the path for long. More often than not I would catch sight of someone in the corner of my eye and before I knew it I would find myself wondering where they were going or where they had been, idly sauntering through the possibilities of strangers' lives. *Why did he look so happy? Why does she look so sad? Are they happy?* I mean *really* happy or did they sort of limp, uncomfortably through life, weighed down but not by anything serious, a bit like staying on the pitch after receiving a dead leg.

There was something about people watching that made me feel less alone. It was crazy really because it could make me feel that way even if I were in a crowd, I would shroud myself in the anonymity. Like sometimes when I would find myself in a busy pub or some party with the lads from football or whoever, and all of a sudden I would feel this utter sense of emptiness, as if I had been hollowed out or something, like I'd never been so lonely in my whole life. That the people around me, the friends I was with, would never understand a word that I said, that my voice wouldn't have even come out if I had wanted it to. And I would suddenly feel this panic welling up inside of me, flooding through the emptiness until I would think it was going to drown me and that I was about to scream out at the top of voice! And then, as quickly as it came, it would subside, like a ride slowing down at the fairground.

Nearly a week had passed by the time I eventually called in at the laundrette. Despite telling myself every day that I would pop in on the way to the ground, and then after I'd let the stop pass me by again without making any effort whatsoever to leave the bus and making some vague, half-hearted promise to myself that I would go on the way back, I knew it wouldn't be before Friday until I actually went. Friday was late night opening. And I knew in the back of mind that I could shoot in on the way to meet Billy. He had set me up on a blind date with one of Jenny Hargreaves' friends and the four of us were going into town, and maybe with a little luck we would catch up with Dave. It spoke volumes for my state of mind that I didn't even feel a sense of guilt anymore about going out on the town the night before a game. That would come later, when I had time to myself to think about it, usually in the shape of a Monday morning. I would wearily climb the stairs of the bus and it was as if it were there, waiting for me in the shape of some giant cloudy blob that no one apart from me could see, waiting patiently for me to take my seat beside it, where it could engulf me, hover over me all day like the early morning fog across the park.

I don't know how I let Billy talk me into a blind date of all things! But the truth was, I didn't care one way or the other, just wanted to get out of the house. Forget myself for a while. There was a time when the very thought of meeting up with a bird, any girl, let alone one who I hadn't even met, would have nagged away at me all week, tormented me the whole time like a face with a forgotten name.

The laundrette looked strangely exciting, the only shop with the lights on and condensation clinging to the windows, shrouding the interior with a kind of mystery that made me feel as if I were about to step into the heart of a cloud. I could feel the steam as soon as I opened the door, drying the back of my throat with its heat. The place was empty apart from Kenny's mum, who was busy scooping great handfuls of clean washing from behind one of the many circular glass doors that lined the wall like the portholes of a ship.

She was a forbidding sight, as tall as her son but more than twice the size with her bell-shaped hips and great wobbly arms. For me she had always been the lady of the house in the Tom and Jerry cartoons, would have looked exactly the same if you had ever been allowed to see more than stockings, slippers and the hem of an apron.

She stood, hands on hips, facing me, the buttons of her apron straining to stay fastened across the huge expanse of her chest, and then all of a sudden, as my face clicked into place and it dawned upon her who I was, the knot in her brow loosened and confusion gave way to a bright beaming smile and she flung her bouncing arms in the air and let them fall heavily upon my shoulders.

'Kenny's football friend… Johnny!' she nodded as if she were confirming to herself our acquaintance. 'How are you? How are you?' She shook her head in disbelief, as if I had been away at sea or something. 'My, oh my how all you boys have grown!' And there was such an affection there in her voice, etched in her face, that for a moment it left me quite stunned, could feel myself instantly drawn to her by something that was almost mother-like. I was aware of the comfort in her grip, as if she were worried that if she let go I might topple over. Had it really been so long since I had shared anything with my own mum? Other than pieces of fragmented conversation about what I might find in the fridge as she busily flitted from room to room, scooping up clean clothes and bottles of perfume and make-up, all her essentials for another night over at Derek's place.

We chatted for a while over a cup of tea, which she insisted on making and how could I possibly refuse? Even though I knew it would make me late and risk the wrath of Billy for having to find the charm and make the effort to entertain *two* girls. One would be hard enough, the whole reason for his enthusiasm for our double date. That and the fact that he knew I had an empty house.

I passed on Kenny's messages and expressed to her his greetings as best that I could, even going as far as to plant a kiss on her cheek and give her a big hug, which Kenny had urged me to do.

'Aww go on man!' he'd begged when I had baulked at the idea. 'She'll love it!'

And he had been right, she *did*, squealed with delight as I embraced her, squeezing me so tight I had almost felt claustrophobic. And I surprised myself to be honest, but she was so kind that I couldn't help but warm to her, this big, slightly eccentric lady... well, eccentric compared to all the mothers that I had known. I can still see her at that school cup final back in '74, bouncing up and down on the touchline, screaming out in that unmistakable African lilt, deep but yet high-pitched at the same time, every time the ball came anywhere near Kenny.

I told her what she wanted to hear. Not so much about the football but the sort of stuff that I reckoned a mother would find important. That Kenny had settled in nicely, and that his landlady was a diamond and kept him well-fed with a hot home cooked dinner each night. And she gasped out loud and clasped her hands together in delight when I told her that he would be down to visit in a fortnight's time, when they were due to play Fulham reserves at Craven Cottage.

So there we were the two of us, sitting in The Falcon across an old worn table from each other and neither knowing quite how to start the conversation, Jenny Hargreaves and me. Her friend, and Billy of all people, had failed to turn up! A blind date within a blind date, and for all the years that we had known each other, grown together like the baby trees planted on the slopes of the viaducts, we just didn't have a clue what to say, or even where to look. I could have killed Billy.

'Friday!... was it Friday?... Fuck, I thought it was Saturday,' he had gasped from his end of the phone as I stood in the corner of The Falcon with a handful of 2ps on the bar in front of me.

'Well it's fuckin' not!' I hissed into the mouthpiece, desperately trying to conceal my obvious anger from Jenny. I could feel her eyes on me, burning like lasers into my back. Silently pleading for me to have traced him down and return to the table with a simple explanation for his absence, that he was running late or something, had just stopped off at the Crown after work with a couple of the lads and time had just run away, and that he'd be here soon. Annoying, inconsiderate, but typical Billy! The kind of thing that made him, well… *him*.

But Billy wasn't going to show. And I didn't for one moment buy his excuse about getting the wrong day. Although I wished that I could, it would have been so easy to believe as well. Just the sort of empty-headed thing that he would have done, organise something, get everyone together and then bloody well forget it himself!

But I could tell from the tone of his voice, trying to sound all blameless and surprised, and how could he pretend to be the picture of innocence when he hardly ever was! It was a good job that I had only spoken to him on the phone, his face would have been laughable… to me anyhow, but heaven knows what Jenny would have thought.

And that was it… Jenny. She was the reason. If I'm honest I had known it even before I had made my educated guess and phoned the Crown, it had all suddenly become so clear as the two of us had sat there, clumsily trying to fill in the gaps of our last few years. When Jen had told me that she was training to be a police officer. He had found out.

We had been sitting there, beside The Falcon's frosted window, sipping our drinks between uncomfortable, stilted bouts of conversation, as the splintered light from the streetlight outside cascaded over us like stinging shards of humiliation, when Jen had told me what she was doing now.

'Oh, right… Great!' I had stammered. And it had sounded so empty, like I really didn't mean it. And I could see her thinking that now I must be feeling even more awkward, spending my time with a trainee copper of all things!

But that wasn't it, wasn't it at all. It was just that I knew in a flash why Billy hadn't turned up. That and the fact that I couldn't believe that I had been so ignorant as to not even ask, especially as she had enquired about my football.

It wasn't that being with Jenny was so bad, and I was pretty sure she felt the same about being in my company. I mean we had always got on well, Jenny and I, and she had never been like the rest of her mates, never looked down her nose at you, the way Debbie and her cluster of little friends had, as if they could always detect something that others' couldn't see, something disappointing. It was just that we both felt so skin-crawlingly embarrassed for one another.

'Fancy another?' I had asked, motioning towards her empty glass.

'Thanks, Johnny, but... ' she paused, her nose wrinkling as if a bad smell had wafted beneath it.

'Not to worry.'

No, no! It's not that!' She leant across the table and grabbed me by the wrist 'It's just... ' She looked around her sheepishly as she shrank back on her stool 'Well, do you think we can go some place else?'

I smiled knowingly. The Falcon, with it's dingy depressing décor and rough and ready clientele was no place for a nice girl like Jenny, a girl who came from the top end of town, with all it's fruit trees and perfectly pruned rose bushes, up there where even the air smelled sweeter.

It felt unseasonably cold as we floated aimlessly like discarded sweet wrappers through the streets of town looking for somewhere to go, somewhere more appropriate, more neutral where both of us might feel at ease. We didn't talk much at first, even though we had left the heavy clouds of awkwardness back in the gloom of The Falcon traces of it still clung, disintegrating slowly, like melting ice, with every step that we took through the night.

But when we found ourselves back out on the pavement again, shaking with laughter from being thrown out of a wine bar for being under age, we felt completely and utterly unburdened. The whole night had been so excruciating that there really was nothing else for it but to give in to it all.

And then it was simply as if we both suddenly tuned into the same wavelength, comfortable and compatible, chatting away and laughing like good friends... became like boy and girlfriends. Passers-by looked twice at us as we weaved along the pavement like drunks. And it must have looked that way, because that moment in the wine bar had simply eroded the last of the shackles that had held us into a pile of dust and we were now different people.

'Should have flashed your badge, or card or whatever you have,' I joked.

'What, pretend I'm working under cover?' she laughed incredulously. 'Can just see them buying that one!'

Her eyes flashed at me in the glare of the streetlight, bubbling with fun and watery from the chilly night air. She had really made an effort on her appearance tonight I reckoned. Her hair looked so smooth, reminded me of silk the way she had scraped one side back and clipped it behind her ear. I thought how nice she looked, really nice, the kind of girl any boy would be proud to have hanging from his arm, prettier than I ever remembered her.

I hadn't really noticed any of this earlier back at The Falcon, embarrassment, I supposed, had blurred the edges of everything so much that I hadn't been able to see or think straight. That and the fact that it had taken all my effort and concentration to suppress my anger at Billy.

'Yeah, why not?' I went on. 'You look old enough.'

She didn't answer, just glanced up bashfully trying to avoid eye contact. And I was aware of the moment as well, the way everything else seemed to suddenly slip into the background, the sounds of the street, the traffic whooshing by, the tinny music and the Friday night voices coming from behind the doors of the pubs. On the face of things it appeared just a harmless comment, nothing more than a weak, but well-meant compliment, but it carried with it the undertones of something more.

Was I flirting with her? Furtively leading up to something

more suggestive? No surely not. After all, this was Jen! *Billy's* Jen. If this had been back in the days of school I would be contemplating stepping into forbidden territory, highlighted even more by the obvious fact that I was who I was. You couldn't say that I was just Billy's *mate*, no more than you could call me and Dave just mates and the same applied to Dave and Billy. We, the three of us, were simply so much more, closer than brothers even, because we weren't connected by any sibling rivalry or we weren't touched by those irrational moments that only siblings seem to have when the tiniest thing the other does sends them into a blood boiling rage.

We walked on, and for a while the uncertainty of my words trapped us into another awkward silence, our breath forming faint white clouds in front of us. Jenny somehow seemed smaller than before as she walked beside me. I didn't know if she had shrunk from embarrassment or if she were simply shielding herself from the night inside the warmth of her coat. Personally I couldn't feel the weather, it could have been raining pins and needles and I doubted whether I would have felt a thing. Couldn't believe what I had said... or hadn't said even. But as much as I tried to tell myself that there had been nothing in it, just a throwaway comment, designed to fill an empty pocket of the evening, I couldn't run away from the truth: I fancied her.

It wasn't just since I had realised how good she looked, although I couldn't believe that I hadn't noticed before. It was everything about her, the way we connected, how I didn't feel cumbersome around her, the way I would whenever I went out with some bird, like my fingers wouldn't even hold onto a glass without dropping it or the way words seemed to back up in my throat and then all fall out at once, as if I were inflicted by a speech impediment or something.

The stupid thing was I knew Billy didn't give a toss, had told me as much on the phone back in the pub. 'If it's just the two of you... ' he had said, his voice slurring with smut and beer, 'You've got an empty 'ouse, 'avn't you?'

Jen would have loved that, being passed on like we were swapping football stickers. For she was a young woman now, a career woman, confident, pretty... classy, but not unapproachable. Back at school she must have missed out on countless potential boyfriends, all scared off by the knowledge of her earlier dalliance with Billy.

We found ourselves, for no particular reason, nearer my home rather than hers. It seemed to dawn on us at the same time, just as we emerged from beneath the train bridge by Lui's. We stopped outside a dimly-lit footpath that divided the park and row of picture-postcard cottages. She looked around her as if only noticing the visible differences from one side of the bridge from the other for the first time. And it probably was, I reckoned, for how often would someone like Jen have been this far down town?

The change hadn't even registered with me. I didn't like to think that I had grown immune to it all, or that I took for granted those timeless few hundred yards of town that belonged to another world: the old church, stoical and proud behind the oak trees that stood like bodyguards in front of it, or those quaint thatched cottages untouched by time, and, of course, the greenery of the park with it's birdsong soundtrack constantly playing. But then again, maybe I had.

The thought didn't sit well, upset me more than I realised, and I didn't want Jenny to think me so ignorant that I couldn't see it for what it was, despite the fact that I obviously passed through it every day, like a farmer admiring his fields. I wanted her to know that I was aware of it all, sort of grateful... stupid really.

I followed her gaze across to the old church, staring up as it hung as still as stage scenery in the night.

'Remember the funeral for Dave's mum in there?' I said matter-of-factly.

Jen nodded. 'Yes.'

It was a stupid comment... pointless. I mean where else would it have been?

I suppose I could have told her about the time Dave, covered in his mum's make-up, and I had fled there for sanctuary from his old man. But the memory of the two of us sitting all alone on the front row pew, hunched over and buried beneath the impenetrable layers of silence, felt too depressing to relate. It had seemed to make perfect sense at the time, but I didn't think that I would be able to articulate exactly how we had felt that day... kind of insignificant, like grains of sand on a beach. How was a seventeen year old boy meant to explain all that?

The truth of the matter was that we could both see the moment for what it was, hesitancy crackled like firewood around us. It was a pivotal time in the evening and neither of us could pretend otherwise, and our small talk only fuelled the flames.

For if Jen decided to follow the alleyway that ran along the side of the park she would come out slap bang on the route of the number 67 bus, and if she waited by the stop directly in front of the alleyway, it would eventually take her almost to her front door.

I had made the exact same journey many times myself, in what seemed like another lifetime now. It was the quickest and simplest way to Debbie's. Cut through the alley into the heart of the east side and, if you timed it right, hop on the 67 and let it transport you through the slate-grey maze of the estate, past the overflowing skips, boarded-up ground floors and patches of litter-strewn wasteland, and up to the loftier heights of the outskirts of town. It was like a suburb within a suburb, but accessible only for the middle classes, geographically it was part of the same borough but the social divide might just as well have spanned a million miles. Up there everything had room to breathe; the horseshoe cul-de-sacs and delicate arced crescents belonged to another world. At first I used to make the journey every time that I had arranged to meet Debbie, just for the hell of it. Even if it was easier to meet someplace in town. Just sit and watch as the landscape gradually opened up where light and space dominated, and the rows of terraced houses and defiant blocks of flats gave way to driveways and flower-riddled gardens.

And it didn't occur to me at first, nervous enthusiasm clouding my naivety I guess, but she had always been ready and waiting... too ready. Standing tentatively beside the net curtains or by the front door... and then the front gate and then eventually it dawned on me, when she started to meet me half way along the avenue between her house and the bus stop.

The sound of Jenny's sigh dragged me back, clouds of hot air hid her face as she exhaled. 'Cold, isn't it?' She hugged her rib cage as if to drive home her point. She sounded exasperated with my dithering uncertainty, I didn't blame her, it annoyed me too. But I couldn't ask her if she would like to come back to mine, I just couldn't do it. I didn't have that sort of confidence... a sure sign that I liked her.

I peered into the gloom of the alley and felt my heart sink, it looked pretty uninviting, a patchwork of sinister-looking shadows and overhanging branches.

'I'll walk you to the stop,' I said, sounding more disappointed than I had meant to, didn't want to sound so... desperate, so expectant. It was just that I sensed that she wanted to stay as much as I wanted her to, that she didn't want to go but that she could hardly invite herself... and... and... well what the hell was my problem!

I thought desperately for something to say, for something for us to do, any excuse for her to stay but there was nothing down my end of town, no pubs or cafés only Lui's, and even he had gone home I'd noticed when we had passed the parade of shops.

If only I could find the courage to ask her back, while we stood, like half-remembered friends who had met in the street, acknowledging each other but each afraid to take it any further for fear of having nothing to say. I was conjuring up these images of the house with Jenny in it, tried to imagine her sitting at the tiny kitchen table blowing gently on the mug of tea cupped between her hands. Or in the front room, lounging cosily, feet up on the sofa listening to Mum's old records, the house full of life again, the smell of her invading every dusty corner, wafting like air freshener from room to room. Every picture that I saw in my mind's eye was basked in sunlight and resonated with the sound of happiness. And then I could see her in my bedroom... and in my bed... the feel of her smooth skin against mine.

The number 67 swung round the corner just as we stepped out beneath the streetlights. It made you feel exposed and vulnerable standing in the glare of the notorious east side estate after being shrouded in the half-light of the alleyway.

'Right then.' I shrugged, hands buried deep in my pockets against the cold. I had no more than thirty seconds, I reckoned, before the bus pulled over, to suggest seeing one another again, or who knows when it might be before we next bumped into each other? We hardly moved in the same social circles. But what I would in fact be asking for was a date and the very idea of the two of us going out together seemed ludicrous, me and Jen! What would Billy say? Or Debbie even? But I already knew the answer to that... nothing. Probably wouldn't even question or see anything bizarre in it. But I knew that that wasn't the reason that I wanted to see her, to spite anyone, that it was a genuine desire to be with her, but I would have to figure all that out later, right now I was running out of time.

But just as the bus signalled to pull over she spun us round, thrusting her arm through mine.

'Come on,' she said

'What! Where too?' I asked, baffled. But I thought, *hoped* I already knew the answer.

'Back to yours,' she said, staring determinedly ahead. 'You can make me a nice cup of tea.' And as we made our way back down the footpath I was thankful for the sound of our footsteps rattling upon the tarmac, for it covered up the furious beating of my heart.

CHAPTER TWENTY

December 1978

Jenny came to dinner on Christmas day, who would have thought it? Though it wasn't until very late in the day, long after the pubs had turned out and the husbands had tottered home to carve the turkey and fall into a fitful sleep in front of the Queen's speech, paper hats sliding off their heads and glasses of sherry slipping from their hands.

Although I didn't imagine for one moment that Jen's Christmas had been anything like that, not up in "happy family land", where I imagined it to be all log fires and perfectly wrapped presents... hell, it probably even snowed up there at the top of town!

But for me the real surprise had been Mum. For she made a real effort with everything, would have thought that she was cooking dinner for the Queen herself the way she went to town with all her preparations, you really would have. And there was me thinking that she probably wouldn't even be around, had taken it for granted that she would be spending the day over at Derek's swanky flat. It said a lot for where we were, me and Mum, that I had basically assumed even before I had asked Jen over that I would be spending the day alone at home, slumped in front of the telly with a plate of beans on toast on my lap, and I wouldn't even have held it against her.

But when I had mentioned to Mum that I had invited a friend over for Christmas, a "girl" friend, she had started flapping around like I couldn't believe, clasping her hands with joy and telling me how she "couldn't wait to meet her", acting as if the very thought that she could possibly be any other place than at home for Christmas was absolutely absurd.

'You don't have to make such a fuss,' I had told her as she had busied herself in the kitchen, hovering over various pots and pans boiling on the tiny stove. I couldn't remember the last time that the kitchen had seen so much activity.

She hadn't bothered to answer, either too busy to reply or simply choosing to ignore me. So I had chosen a different tact.

'She will have eaten already… ' I had added, leaning against the frame of door, almost drowning in the fragrance that I was wearing, half afraid to step inside in case I was suddenly burdened with some chore or another but at the same time wanting Mum to catch a whiff of the Christmas present that she had bought me. *The great smell of Brut* as Keegan and Cooper had absurdly told us on the telly. I had never possessed my own set of toiletries before, and as I had torn away the wrapping paper to reveal a neat little green zip-up bag containing deodorant, soap and talcum powder, I had supposed that I had reached another one of those landmarks on the path to manhood. A wave of affection towards Mum had suddenly crashed over me, the kind of longing that I hadn't felt for I didn't know how long. Not because I no longer looked upon her as my mum or anything like that, it was just because, well, there hadn't really been anyone around all that much for me to feel much about.

But as I had sat there on my bedroom floor surrounded by the football annuals, new pair of goalkeeping gloves and new pairs of socks and pants that I found in my stocking every year, that one present had made me realise that she was still aware of me. That the lack of her presence hadn't affected her mother's intuition, that she had noticed the creeping transition from grown boy to young man, had probably been more conscious of it than I had myself.

And it was as if she had read my thoughts, had known that I had been fighting this inner battle with the boy that was still inside me to overcome my sense of embarrassment to go and buy my own.

She had still ignored me. Choosing to cast me an interrogative look from over her shoulder instead, which I in turn had tried hard not to notice. She had been trying to act all casual, as if spending hours preparing food in our tiny and under-equipped kitchen was a normal occurrence, something that you would find her doing every Sunday or something. But the flustered way in which she had huffed and flicked away at a stray strand of hair that had fallen across her face had told me otherwise.

'You've made enough for… ' I had puffed my cheeks in exasperation, I knew what I had meant, had intended to say "enough for a whole family", a mummy, a daddy and the kids, but it wouldn't have sounded right somehow, the word "family" simply didn't belong in the house, about as welcome as those weirdos who knock on the door every once in a while and try and sell you a membership for God's club.

"Family", it represented domesticity, a unit, it was simply a part of suburbia that we didn't belong too.

'Well,' Mum had smiled serenely as Boney M's Christmas number one, "Mary's Boy Child" played softly from the radio on the sideboard. She had regained her composure now, straightening the front of her apron with her hand as if she were readjusting herself, a little embarrassed after chasing a fly around or something. 'It's a good job that I've invited Derek over as well, isn't it?'

The last few weeks had passed by so quickly that I hadn't really had time to digest it all properly, it had been like scoffing down your food and moving straight on to the next course without allowing your taste buds to fully appreciate what they have just experienced.

The whole of the country was slowly grinding to a halt around me, the *Winter of Discontent* just a gust of wind away, everywhere you turned it seemed as though industry was on the verge of self-destruction. You could blame who you wanted: Callaghan, the unionists, the service industry, even the dying breed of punk rockers if you wanted! But through the uneducated, or to put it more accurately, uninterested, eyes of a teenager who lacked the ammunition to be prejudice, the wounds that were about to be directed into the flesh of the country in the shape of firemen, bakers, transport workers, dustmen, gravediggers, they all seemed self-inflicted. As bad as mutilating yourself with a compass and bottle of Indian ink, like the "tattoo skins" that had led us to our very own *Summer of Discontent*.

Jen and I had seen a lot of each other since that memorable night. "The night of the blind-dates" Jenny had named it, as if it were some infamous occasion, something unforgettable that in the years to come would be celebrated and remembered, marked down like an anniversary in a calendar.

It was as if I had drifted into a kind of light-headed daze the day after the "blind dates", and it had only been the last few days, as Christmas had slowly crept closer, since December had climbed into the twenties, that my head and my feet started to reconnect with the rest of me. I couldn't help but feel a little glum about that, hoped that that wouldn't be it, the end of the buzz of a new relationship, like sobering up from one giant piss-up.

So there we sat, the four of us crowded round the tiny kitchen table, knees rubbing and trying hard not to step on one another's toes. I vaguely recall wondering whether or not the table legs, hollow tubes of aluminium that gave the impression that could buckle at any moment, would be able to withstand the sheer weight of the food. There were dishes of roasted potatoes and parsnips, Yorkshire puddings and balls of stuffing, clustered together like tumbleweed, heaps of vegetables, runner beans, carrots and cauliflower, which would have taken up even more room had they not been served up in one giant dish that was divided into four different segments. I didn't recall having seen anything as grand as that before in our house, why on earth would Mum and I ever need something that big? And then it hit me… it must have been Derek's. And then of course there was the turkey, and add to that our plates, cutlery and crackers and there was hardly a glimpse of the red tablecloth, which I had also never seen before, visible.

'John,' Derek said expectantly as he handed me the carving knife and fork. For a moment he lost me, took me by surprise. But then I noticed the look on his face, if I hadn't have known him like I did, I would have sworn that there was a touch of desperation in it. He certainly didn't seem his usual, confident self; that controlled air that seemed to hover intangibly around his shoulders had deserted him. It was as if he were almost… humble, somebody whose company I might actually feel comfortable in.

And it was then that I realised the importance of his gesture. For he had been acutely aware, even if Mum hadn't as she finally pulled up her chair to join us and absent-mindedly placed the knife and fork beside his plate, what it would mean, what the practice of standing up and actually carving the bloody thing would represent. Maybe it wouldn't seem so obvious to Jen or even Mum, for in Christmases past the meat was always prepared, neatly sliced and already stacked on my served plate, the carving of the bird had never held any great festive tradition for us. But why then had she handed the responsibility over to Derek?

And he was fully aware of the connotations, a silent act that screeched like fingernails raked down an imaginary blackboard between the pair of us, with the title "Man of the House" scrawled in capital letters, upon it.

But he didn't look ready to step that far into my world, I didn't know if it was like some sort of territorial thing, as if it would mean that he were wrestling away my status, my newly-founded manhood, or was he simply respecting my place in Mum's life. All I knew was that I couldn't have appreciated it more if I had stood up and carved the words Thank You across the table.

And I actually began to enjoy the day after the act with the turkey had been played out, even made a fair job of it too, and of course it helped that the best slices, the first ones, were served to Jen and Mum, tender and thick, just the sight and smell of them enough to start your taste buds tingling as I flopped them carefully down upon the plates.

And I couldn't see why I had been working myself up about it all, started to feel a bit foolish about it actually. And that was it I suppose, the reason I had been stewing myself up lately, because it meant so much to me, even if I didn't have the sense to see it. The past few days I had felt as if I had had an egg boiling and bubbling away inside of me, with the walls of my guts as the saucepan, slowly coming to the boil as the day had grown nearer. I had known that I would be nervous about Mum meeting Jen. But all of a sudden I had found myself fretting about the prospect of Jen meeting Mum! I mean I knew it was the same thing whichever way you looked at it but somehow I couldn't seem to convince myself of the fact. It was like an optical illusion in my head, whenever I said the line to myself, 'Mum meeting Jen' or 'Jen meeting Mum', the whole thing took on a different angle, couldn't for the life of me work out who I was more desperate to impress... or not to let down. And of course there was this whole other dimension to the picture... there was Derek.

I had certainly looked forward to impressing him with Jen, the thought of him sitting there wide-eyed and lost for words had made me almost squirm with delight, I'd show him that dim-witted, uneducated Johnny Chalmers was capable of meeting a decent, clever girl.

But was I being fair to Jenny? Hell, was I even being fair on Derek! I mean did he really hold me in such low esteem? It would appear not after his care not to offend me at the dinner table. And if I was really honest with myself, looked beyond all the disorder that swirled around like tea leaves in my head, muddling my judgement where Derek was always concerned, he had never actually given me any indication that he thought so little of me. It was just the way that *I* felt in *his* presence. Like I should be intensely grateful for any effort that he was prepared to make for me. Oh I don't know… probably just me, all in my head, like when you think everybody's looking and laughing at you after you've had a crap haircut, when really no one takes a blind bit of notice seeing as they don't know you anyway.

And Jen looked a picture, her hair twinkling in the light, outshining the decorations on the tree, all shiny and smooth, curling up at the ends. And for some silly reason it reminded me of the slide in the park, each time that I looked at her I would imagine tiny little people sliding down it, whooping with delight as they flew off the ends. Crazy thoughts every time I watched her eat, flicking it casually from her face with every dainty mouthful, her whole persona easy and unhurried as she chatted with Mum and Derek, fielding their questions about the force and asking a few relevant ones of her own, completely comfortable, seemingly fascinated by Derek's work.

I felt this strange inflating feeling fill my chest, as if I'd taken a giant deep breath that was almost too big for my body to hold. Was this pride, I wondered, or just the awakening of a pleasure that I'd not yet experienced with a girl? Not Debbie, not Cindy, not anyone, a gratifying sense that could only be gained from a relationship where we on the same level, where I didn't feel patronised or less than equal.

And it was turning out to be a really nice day, couldn't think of anywhere I'd really rather be, or of anyone I'd rather be with.

In fact it had been pretty good from the very beginning, from the moment that I had opened my eyes and felt that warm, cosy Christmas feeling greet me. Staring bleary eyed at the translucence of the curtains as the grey light of the morning seeped like strained tea through the thin material. It had appeared just like any other winter's day but of course it wasn't, it was Christmas, and all those boyhood feelings and memories had suddenly sprung to life from out of nowhere, as though they'd been hidden away like the old tree from one year to the next. And when I had come down and saw the eggs that Mum had boiled for me as a treat, just the way she always did, I had known that it was going to be a really good day, the kind of day where nothing in the world matters other than those who matter. And I could tell that Mum felt the same way as I had smiled and sat down, that she knew how much I appreciated it, not just the breakfast but the fact that she was there... alone, just the two of us on Christmas morning, the way it had always been. My smile, I knew, would convey how I felt more than any words that I would be able to find.

If only Dave could have been there, well I wouldn't have been able to ask for more if Father Christmas himself had slid down the chimney. I had invited him of course, pleaded would be a more accurate description when I realised that he was going to decline. My mistake was to mention that Derek would be there.

'And where would I sit exactly?' he had asked. 'On your lap?' Typical Dave, the thought hadn't even entered my head and there he was visualising the scene, working out the seating arrangements for five people around our tiny kitchen table the moment that I had mentioned it.

'No... I'll tell you what,' he had concluded whilst browsing through the rows of Bowie albums on offer as we stood in a little known record shop the size of a telephone box hidden somewhere behind Oxford Street. The walls were plastered with billboard posters advertising concerts, all overlapping one another, so it felt as if you were standing in the middle of some kind of weird kaleidoscope, a whirlwind of flyers and posters. If I had spun round quickly I don't think I could have found the door.

'I'll see both of you down the Crown later,' he had said.

'The Crown?' I had exclaimed. 'It's Christmas night, it'll be closed.'

'Officially, yeah,' he had told me as he flipped over a copy of *Aladdin Sane* as if he were expecting to see something he hadn't seen before. 'But he has a do for his regulars at Christmas, you know the kind of thing,' he had gone on, 'all taps on the window and drawn curtains.'

'Oh right,' I had muttered, trying to sound more enthusiastic than I felt. He had finished his record sleeve inspection and turned to me knowingly.

'What's the matter?' he had grinned. 'Don't tell me,' he had carried on before I had a chance to even think of an answer, 'you'd rather snuggle up and watch *The Morecambe and Wise Show* instead.'

I had sighed heavily, trying my best to sound frustrated; he didn't know how close he was to the truth. But then again, knowing Dave, he almost certainly did.

'Why do you bother?' I had asked, nodding at the record sleeves that he had been poring over, protected and pristine in their transparent covers. He had gazed down almost wistfully at them again and, sensing that I had successfully thrown him off track, a trick that he himself had taught me, I pressed on, 'You've got them all anyway.' And it was true, he even had spare copies of his real favourites in case they were to develop a scratch or carry the faintest crackle: *Hunky Dory, Ziggy* and the more recent stuff that he really seemed to relate to, *Low* and *Station to Station*. I had seen them all lined up like books in order of their release high up on a separate shelf to the rest of his record collection, their slender spines presented proudly, each one protected in plastic folders like the rows of covers in the shop.

He had pulled out a copy of *Ziggy Stardust* and gazed, just like he must have done a million times before, at the saint-like image of Bowie standing in the damp London night like some kind of rock 'n' roll spaceman in that luminous blue jumpsuit and his guitar resting across his thigh.

'I mean I'm always on the lookout for imports...' he had said almost apologetically as if this were the only explanation he could offer but it was more than that, something that maybe not even he could explain or find the right words for. I didn't find it patronising that he saw the concept as beyond me. I understood enough to realise that you had to be more than just a mild fan, someone like me who might have bought the odd album or single here and there over the years that might have taken their fancy, that you had to be someone like Dave, if there was anyone else in the world like him, someone who seemed to be on the same wavelength as Bowie.

He had waved the sleeve at me. 'Imagine seeing *this* for the first time,' he had said. I looked at the cover flapping about in his hand, not really knowing what to say. He had sighed deeply, knowing that he wasn't getting through. 'You know... brand new, discovering that thrill of discovery, imagine having all that waiting ahead of you.'

'Discovering that thrill of discovery,' I had grinned. 'Sounds like some of his lyrics,' I had added, nodding at the album cover in his hand. But he hadn't seemed to hear me, lost now in his own thoughts. He had run his fingers delicately down the list of songs on the back as if they were petals on a flower.

'Listening to it in the solitude of your own room, lying on your bed and letting the words fill your room, playing it over and over again, as much as you like until every line has soaked into your head like a sponge.' We had stood for a moment in silence. I'd got it. And then he had sighed, another of those long, comfortable sighs of his, the ones that don't offend or carry any disdain, but instead make you somehow feel that you've unwittingly pleased him, helped in some way to satiate a need that you don't quite understand.

'As I say... ' He had shrugged, replacing the sleeve exactly where he found it. 'I dunno really.'

The mood in the Crown took me by surprise. It was much livelier than I would have ever imagined. Ever since Dave had suggested meeting there I had had this rather depressing picture in my head, a black and white image looming like a storm cloud across my mind, like when I tried too visualize stories from Mum's past, for some inexplicable reason they always formed like one of those old films, as if colour hadn't been invented when she was growing up. Just a handful of people, pensioners mostly, scattered wearily throughout the pub. Old men playing chequers in silence, sipping their Double Diamonds through toothless mouths while their old ladies sat huddled together, a mass of hair-nets and dangling ash, muttering sullenly across a sea of stout about the price of washing powder and fish.

But it was nothing like that; there was a warmth there that engulfed us the moment the landlord locked the door behind us.

'Hello, son.' He had grinned as his giant head had appeared from behind the slightly open door, ready to slam it shut if faced by unwelcome visitors trying their luck for a Christmas drink. 'Still keeping them out are you?'

I smiled amiably. 'Trying,' I replied. It was ungracious, but I couldn't help thinking if I had kept a clean sheet for every time someone had asked me that, I'd already be pushing for an England cap.

'They're over there,' he said, motioning towards Dave and Billy, who sat huddled around one of the sturdy circular tables drinking and chatting with some people I vaguely recognised from around town: two girls and a boy of roughly the same age as us, maybe a year or two older, they certainly hadn't been in our year at school, had probably left the year before.

The bar seemed to throb with life, there was a blend of young and old, a mixture of both ends of the scale dotted all over the pub. But they all had one thing in common, something which was fundamental to the mood of the whole evening, something that meant more than anything else that night: togetherness.

Bonds, no matter how thin or threadbare, that weaved their way through the pub, connecting everyone to someone else. Neighbours from the same street or workers from the same factories, there were also whole families, cousins, aunts and uncles, knitted together, the typical South London community.

The air hung heavy with smoke and the steady hum of voices, layer upon layer of conversation and laughter all droning into one. I loved that feeling, of entering a bar when there were a million and one different words being spoken at once, like so many radios all playing at once but all on different wavelengths, it made me feel secure with all those people around but it also allowed me the solitude I sometimes craved, it meant that I could people watch without being seen, like those old slap stick films when they all pile upon one body and the culprit ends ups crawling out from beneath the bundle of flailing bodies, too close to ever be seen.

It was all quite a contrast to the eerie Christmas day outside. The sound of our footsteps had echoed through the empty streets resonating off the houses and buildings, distant drumming that always made me feel as if the very walls themselves were watching you. Not one car had passed us on our journey there, we hadn't heard any trains rumble over the viaducts or bridge overhead or any buses whoosh through town, nothing but the sporadic dull rumble of a car somewhere far off in the distance as families were no doubt travelling back and forth visiting relatives.

Billy was on great form, laughing and drinking like a mad man, regaling us all with stories from our past: football matches, school summer holidays, legendary classroom antics. He explained them all so clearly, painstakingly painting the picture for every scene that you would have been forgiven for forgetting that we had actually been there in most of them, Dave, Jenny and I, like actors dotted around the stage in his play.

The others were totally absorbed, lapping it all up hanging on his every word. And the thing was, he wasn't even exaggerating, it was all absolutely true. It was just that Billy's enthusiasm was so infectious, the way that he expressed himself, laughing along as the memories poured out of him, as if the notion of actually hearing it out loud, amplified outside of his head, made it all the funnier. He had the two girls in stitches, gasping dramatically, raising their hands to their mouths in typical girly fashion in an act to hide their astonishment.

He could have his pick tonight, I thought to myself, he had hooked the pair of them whether it had been his intention or not. I'm not even sure if he was aware that he had, but if he was I don't think he was that bothered, he was just enjoying the evening, relaxing with people that he didn't have to be on his guard with, not that Billy was ever anyone else other than Billy, but in the sort of circles that Billy moved in it always paid to watch your words. But with us, me, Jen and Dave, well it was like old times, reliving the insouciance of childhood whilst playing at being grown-ups. And I must say I loved it, I wallowed in the warmth of the moment. I mean what else could I ask for? I don't think I actually realised just how happy I was at times like that, a contentment that was almost uncomfortable for the reason that it was unfamiliar. Of course I had moved the goalposts a little at first, altered things by way of me and Jen. But Billy was fine about that, after all, he had been the one who'd instigated it! Besides, she was as much a part of my childhood as the others, in the same way as when I thought back to times I'd spent with Dave, inevitably I saw Billy and Ketchup there too. And it was the same thing whenever Debbie sprung to mind, Jen was always there as well.

Billy was deep into a story from our schooldays, the two girls transfixed like disciples waiting for the pearls of wisdom to fall. It was a classic, I had to admit, but not one that I thought really fitted the mood, but he could have chosen worse, I supposed.

I had heard the story a million times before, so it was easy to switch off and lose myself in the mood of the evening, to hide behind a vacant stare and people watch as the cheer of Christmas played itself out around me, like a Sunday afternoon film. I recognised virtually every face, like landmarks in town. I must be as ordinary to them as they are too me, I thought. It felt good being part of this community, deep down in the heart of town, where everything is just as you see it, where a spade's a spade and folk tell you it straight. But it was the little things that made me realise that I did "belong". The manner in which the landlord had welcomed us at the door, the way people nodded or smiled a hello, wordless acknowledgements that told you that you fitted in, so much so that I had begun to feel guilty for not having been there in so long. When was it, I thought to myself as Billy's story reached its conclusion, much to the disgust of the girls and the amusement of Billy and Dave, that I had actually last been in here for a drink? A couple of months perhaps? Maybe even longer. Everything, including time, seemed to be moving so fast around me these days.

'So what did you two love birds get for each other then?' Dave asked, stirring me out from my daydreams. Jenny had been waiting for this moment all night but was much too polite to have prompted such a question. But now she was gleefully showing off the earrings that I had bought for her. The look on his face told me that he had known all along. I had had a hell of a job picking them as well; jewellery, it seemed such a serious present to give someone, so very... grown-up. But then I supposed it was about time that I faced up to the inevitable, I mean the evidence was all around, confronting me every day in new and different circumstances. Ever since the day I had walked out the school gates for the last time. There was no denying the pubs, the concerts at places like the Marquee and The 100 Club, my job, the contract, and of course, my feelings, pubescent crushes that had gradually developed into an unfamiliar longing. Desire was too strong a word for it but I couldn't deny to myself, and nor did I want to, the urges that I felt for Jenny. It was only that I didn't know how to deal with them, when to suppress them and when to let them out.

It all boiled down to, I guessed, the father figure thing, and of course my previous experiences with Debbie and Cindy hadn't exactly helped either. I just wasn't comfortable and didn't trust myself to expose such vulnerability, it was like there was this last remaining set of heavy wooden doors protecting the deepest part of me and I just didn't have the courage, the belief to fling them open. Instead I chose to peek through a crack barely wide enough for a sliver of light to escape. For what if someone, anyone, passed beyond them? What then? What else would I have left to protect myself with?

'Oh, very nice,' Dave nodded, and then the girls were there.

'Oh aren't they lovely!' they cooed in unison.

'It'll be a ring next,' Billy grinned, flashing me the wanker sign whilst Jen's head was turned. I was just about to return the gesture when the blonde-haired one asked me what Jen had bought for me. I hated those questions, always had, those 'what did you get for Christmas?' moments in the playground that always felt like contests and interrogations. It was probably just because Mum had never had much money, child support and a nurse's pay cheque didn't stretch as far as most of the other parents' incomes.

They didn't let up there, the girls. 'Oh, what album?' exclaimed the dark-haired one when I'd casually mentioned that Jen had bought me a record as well as some goalkeeper's gloves… my *second* pair.

'What?' The pain was almost physical. 'Oh… Blondie,' I mumbled *'Parallel Lines.'*

'Cor! Debbie Harry,' sneered Billy. 'I'd give her… ' And then he remembered himself, or rather he remembered Jen and the girls, and it was so unlike Billy that for a moment there was a stunned silence as we all stared disbelievingly at him. 'What?' he cried, trying unsuccessfully to look hurt.

'Blimey,' shrugged Dave, 'it must be Christmas.'

Conversation floated gently about like so many butterflies flitting around our heads, it was all very pleasant and the sound of laughter echoed heartily around the pub. A group of the regulars sitting at the bar sang drunkenly along with the jukebox, "Darlin" by Frankie Miller, a real grown-up's song that had reached the top ten back in October. I didn't particularly care for it, in fact it was one of the few songs of the year that really got under my skin, due to the fact that all the older players and staff at the club all seemed to love it. But that Christmas night I had to admit, right there and then it seemed to complement the mood perfectly, fitted like the old wooden benches with the frosted glass above them; belonged as much as the clouds of cigarette smoke drifting above our heads, like a Christmas decoration, as fitting as the paper chains and the pop-up bell that hung from the ceiling.

I stifled a heavy sigh so as not to catch the attentions of the others as they were all deep in the mood of the evening. Why was it, I wondered, that I always ended up liking things that I wasn't comfortable liking? It wasn't just the stupid songs like "Darlin" or Renaissance's "Northern Lights", another easy listening song that was as gentle as an armchair which had been in the charts that summer. It was all the other stuff that would send my arm into an itching frenzy or leave me struggling to hold my own stare in the bathroom mirror.

As the evening tumbled playfully on, I sat back a little and let my mind take me off to places that would have been better left for another time. The laughter and talk from the others seemed to be coming from behind a glass window as I mentally stepped out from the bar and just my shell remained.

He wasn't a *bad* man Derek, I could see that now. He had made a real effort tonight, in his own clunking "this is all beneath me" sort of way, I thought, just as Billy's laugh nearly shattered the glasses on the table. His jokes were turning dirty again, I could almost see the air blend into blue around him.

I don't know, it was as if he gave with one hand, Derek, and took away with the other. I so much *wanted* to like him for all the right reasons, because he was a decent man, a caring man obviously, being a doctor and all, and because he showed an interest in me, which at times I could have sworn was genuine, and of course because of Mum, but... Oh I didn't know!

And then there was Jen. I really shouldn't like Jen as much as I clearly did, I couldn't kid myself any longer. How far would I have fallen by the time it was all over? For, as good as it was and as close as we were growing, I couldn't shake off that impending sense that it would all some day end. It was the same feeling that seemed to hang over everything that my life touched. It was like living under a rainbow that had no colours.

It wasn't as if I felt permanently depressed or awoke each morning full of dread for what might happen. In fact it was just the opposite. I found comfort in knowing the outcome, a conclusion that was out of my hands no matter what I did, like reading the last page of a book before you're even halfway through. The only time it really got to me was when my guard was down, when I was asleep and the dreams that floated through my mind all had the same predicable outcome, that of hopelessness.

The drink flowed freely, fuzzing the edges of everything a little. Dave sat chatting amiably with the two girls, answering their questions about his job and what working for a music paper actually entailed. He was still his usual laid-back laconic self but you could see the glint in his eye, the enthusiasm hidden beneath the surface, smouldering away with every word, discussing the only thing that seemed to light any kind of fire inside of him these days. And you could see that he took genuine pleasure from the interest on the girls' faces, almost blushing at one point when the dark haired one let out a gasp of disbelief when Dave confessed to having met Jilted John earlier in the year at some backstage party up in town. She seemed to know what she was talking about as well, asking Dave some really knowledgeable questions about music and journalism in general and she gave the impression of being absolutely fascinated with how he had managed to land himself such a plum job without any further education to back him up.

I thought she was going to fall off her stool with excitement when Dave also admitted that he had met, on more than one occasion, in fact was on nodding terms with, the hip music journalists Julie Burchill and Tony Parsons.

'Oh my God!' she cried, flapping her hands in front of her face as if she were fanning herself down. 'What are they like? They both seem so… ' She rolled her eyes in frustration searching for the right word.

'Cutting… ' Dave ventured.

'Yes!' she nodded vigorously. '*Cutting*… that's right.' She looked at him with growing admiration. 'Scathing,' she added, desperately wanting too show him that she was up there with him.

'So, Dave,' she purred, there was no one else in the pub as far as she was concerned now, I'd seen that look too many times before, 'Why's Bowie your favourite artist?' And at that moment I knew that she had hooked him; checkmate. Well played, I smiled to myself, you had to hand it to her, for he was right there now, in her face, just where she had wanted him to be, close enough to feel his breath, close enough to kiss. Dave about as open as Dave ever gets, inviting her to join him in his eyes as he lost himself in the world of Bowie that spun constantly in his head.

'Right then,' said Billy, jumping to his feet. 'Same again?' he asked, even though everyone else's glass was nearly half full. 'Oh no!' he groaned, draining the last dregs from his glass. 'Not fuckin' Boney M again!' We all laughed as "Mary's Boy Child" started up from the jukebox for about the tenth time that evening. 'Anyone got any change?' he asked.

'Come on,' smiled Jen, 'I'll give you a hand with the drinks… I've got some 10ps in my purse I think.' It was just another chance for her to bend his ear about P.C. Collins again, but she would be wasting her breath, just like she had been the other week when we had all gone up the West End to meet Dave. 'You want to watch yourself, Billy,' Jen had warned as we'd sat in a quiet little pub in Baker Street. We had stood out like sore thumbs, four teenagers surrounded by beer-soaked middle-aged men in dreary suits, all slackened ties and crumpled newspapers, who would rather spend their time propping up the bar and complaining about their work than at home with their families.

Billy had just rolled his eyes and lifted his pint as if he'd heard it all before, which of course he had, but this had only made Jenny more insistent. I had learnt the hard way myself to not take her seriously when she was being exactly that. The thing was, to Billy it was all just a game, the lot of it: Collins, the stealing off sites, selling the tools, the foremen… them knowing but not knowing enough to prove anything. It wasn't just the money with Billy, it was the damn thrill of it. I knew it, Dave knew it but as close as Jen was, it was something that she would never be able to comprehend.

'I mean it, Billy!' He had set her off now, she was determined to be heard. 'P.C. Collins is after you, he knows about the tools and the sort of people that buy them from you.' She hadn't been able to hide the annoyance in her voice. 'He talks about it all the time! How he's just waiting for the right time, he's got his little spies out everywhere, you'd be surprised, he's got no scruples that one, they're all a little scared of him at the station.' She let her breath escape through pursed lips the way only women can do and crossed her arms with a "humph".

For a moment I had wondered if Billy was going to tell her what she could do, for he had glared at her resentfully over the rim of his pint. But there had been no real malevolence there, though Jen's rebuke had stung just as she knew it would, but then that had been her plan, the value of deep-seated friendship buried like playing cards in a game of Snap beneath layer upon layer of life. For Jen was fully aware that nothing got to Billy like being scolded like a child, and of course Billy *knew* that she knew that... and there lay the respect, that's how important it was, that's how much Jen cared.

He had placed his glass deliberately back down on the table and looked from me to Dave, searching our faces for any clues that we might have put Jen up to it, but he had found none. I had already tried some weeks before to warn him of the danger that we could all see coming, but I had known even as I could hear the words coming out of my mouth that they might as well have been bubbles floating silently up to the sky.

He had sucked in sharply over his teeth and gazed discontentedly around at the narrow little pub with all its brow-beaten commuters drowning in pools of cigarette smoke and large scotches. Just how did Dave find these places, I had wondered, but the barmaid had seemed to know him, greeting him with a wink. 'Allo love,' she had said, smiling flirtatiously, the way barmaids do.

'Are we goin' someplace else,' Billy had sniffed finally, treating Jen's words with the contempt that he obviously thought they deserved. 'Or are we stayin' in this shit hole all night?'

But Jen was nothing if not determined, although I did wonder if Christmas night, of all nights, was really the right time to persist. I looked over my shoulder at the pair of them standing at the bar just in time to catch Billy roll his eyes in an expression of tiredness and quickly turned myself back round again, not wanting to know. I'll have a quiet word with her when she sits back down, I thought to myself, tell her that as well as she means, tonight's not the night.

But that moment would never come, for, little did we know, the night was about to come to an abrupt end. And afterwards Jen would never have to bother with her warnings again.

For all of a sudden there was an almighty crash against the entrance door. It was so thunderous that the walls either side resonated from the force.

'What the fun – !' cried the landlord as he stormed over to see who or what was responsible for shattering the mood of the evening. My first thought, after the waves of shock had ebbed away, was that a car must have careered off the road and into the front of the pub, that somebody with a little too much of the Christmas spirit inside them had climbed foolishly behind the wheel. But I soon discarded that theory when a second bang followed soon after, and then a third, rattling the great door's narrow frosted glass. It was a small miracle that it hadn't shattered after the initial battering.

'All right, all right!' the landlord boomed, struggling to undo the slide bolts placed at the top and bottom of the door. He had turned into all fingers and thumbs, shaking with rage at this violent intrusion. His huge dome of a forehead glistened with sweat in the lights of the Christmas tree and his shirt stuck to his back, his giant spine visible through the polyester material.

The mood in the pub had changed dramatically, the sound of animated voices, gasps from the women and growls of disapproval from the men, had replaced the laughter and singing. Nobody knew who was out there yet but already a feeling of resignation had taken hold of me, sweeping through my veins like an anaesthetic.

'Oh no,' I groaned to nobody in particular as I slumped back against the seat.

'What's the problem?' Billy asked, the picture of innocence. 'If it's the Old Bill we ain't done nothing.' That streak of defiance rising within him, his eyes growing darker and meaner like the threatened animal that he was.

'He can't be found in here,' Dave sighed, seeing what was about to happen all too clearly.

'Why not?' asked the dark-haired girl.

'Because of his football… ' answered Jen before Dave had a chance to explain. 'If he's involved in any more scrapes… ' She squirmed restlessly in her seat, looking frantically over at the door and back again. 'They'll… they'll… oh I don't know what they'll do!'

'Southfields will terminate his contract,' Dave sighed. I just sat there like an idiot in silence, drawing outlines in my mind around the paisley shapes on the carpet whilst the rest of them talked about me as if I wasn't there, which in a way I no longer was. It was like when people hover above an invalid in a wheelchair discussing their ailments as if there's nothing more than a sack of spuds in front of them.

'And what about you an' all,' said Billy, pointing at Jen.

'He's right, Jen,' Dave nodded. 'We've got to get you two out of here.'

But just then the door finally crashed open with such ferocity that it sent the landlord staggering right back until the bar was the only thing that stopped him from toppling over. And all of a sudden we could feel the cold air against our cheeks as the December night drifted through the bar like smoke.

There were faces at the door, pairs of crazy eyes darting manically from side to side, seeing but not really there, eyes vacant from substance abuse. Their heads were barely visible behind the wall of protesting punters shouting and cursing, closing in like a pack of wolves upon the intruders, but I had recognised those faces the second they had spilt into the bar, like a nightmare bursting into life. The mood in the pub had completely changed now, the festivity and the warmth of the evening disappeared in a flash and it was hard to imagine that it had ever been there at all, swamped like writing in the sand, these were folk who could be as angry as they were happy, hardened like steel in a furnace by the streets of London.

Jen looked as if she could well be sick, she seemed to be trying to make herself invisible, and the reason for her actions soon became clear for the skinheads hadn't been in the pub two minutes before a handful of coppers rushed in after them.

Apparently the crazed-faced men had been trying in vain to get a drink, had seen the light through a chink in the curtain, obviously heard the ripples of music and laughter from the street and decided to try their luck. But what we didn't know at the time was that they were also trying to hide from the police. We were later to find out that they had been chasing them halfway around town for trying to break into an off licence two miles away.

There was a lot of commotion, people pushing, warnings and threats drowning out the songs on the jukebox, the sound of Christmas trampled to death beneath the stampede of growing hostility.

And then there was a hand on my shoulder and Dave's voice somewhere outside my head.

'Come on, you two.' His tone authoritative, dragging me from my gloom and to my feet while Billy grabbed Jen by the elbow and together the pair of them led us like naughty children across the pub floor.

'Under 'ere, Dave,' winked the barmaid and we followed him as he ducked below the bar and through a narrow, dimly-lit corridor, which seemed to house nothing but a phone on the wall, and out into the backyard.

'Where's Billy?' I called out. Somewhere along the line he had left us, slipped off and returned to the bar. 'Shit!' the sudden night blindness had sent me cursing and stumbling into a pile of empty beer crates.

'What now?' hissed Jen, I could hear the frustration in her voice. 'This is ridiculous!' Christmas night and there she was skulking around like a thief in the night.

'Over here!' Dave called under his breath. He was standing beside the far wall, a mysterious figure faintly illuminated by the pale light of the moon. He was motioning to the two of us from out of the shadows of the beer crates.

'Bring a couple of those over here, Johnny.'

'But where the fuck is Billy?' I protested.

'He's alright, they won't let him do anything stupid... now come on!' he hissed, aware that my career, and possibly Jen's as well, hung in the indecision of the moment. We stacked the crates three high, clambered over the wall and fell into the darkness below, swallowed up by the night just as what sounded like a thousand thundering footsteps poured into the yard from out of the back door, sending empty unseen beer crates crashing to the ground, the sound of braking glass chasing us like a wind down through the alley and out into the deserted back streets.

CHAPTER TWENTY - ONE

December 1978

I sat perched on the end of the tidy leather sofa at Jenny's house, afraid of I didn't know what, feeling unworthy of the comfort that it offered. I glanced over at Dave lounging in the matching armchair across the room from me; how was it that he never looked out of place anywhere? Just seemed to fit in whatever his surroundings.

'I can't believe we just left Billy there,' I was still moaning, shaking my head in disbelief at what felt to me like treachery.

'I told you,' sighed Dave, seemingly unbothered. He was spinning a cushion round and round in front of him like an empty record sleeve. It was as if we were just wiling away a lazy Sunday afternoon, the way he sat languidly back in his chair as if what had just happened was nothing out of the ordinary in the scheme of our lives… which I suppose, it wasn't.

'He'll be all right.'

I ran my fingers vigorously up and down my arm. 'How can you be so sure?' My words resounded with a contempt that made Dave look up at me with that "don't you understand?" look, as if my inability at times to grasp the situation baffled him.

I withered a little inside, sometimes his ability to stay cool when chaos reigned down all around could really make me crazy.

'Look,' he said reassuringly, as if he were pacifying a small child, 'I told him to come with us but he said "How the hell will it look if old Collins catches sight of me slipping off out the back as well?" He held out his hands and sank back into his chair. 'Would just have made the old bastard even more determined to have him, wouldn't it?' He shook his head slowly. 'No, better to stay and front it out… after all, what's the worst he could do to that lot? Send 'em all home with a slap on the wrist?' He averted his gaze from the cushion and to me, 'It's the likes of you and Jen who have something to lose, not that crowd.'

Before I had a chance to reply Jen came in from the kitchen carrying a tray containing a pot of freshly-brewed tea, cups and saucers, which was just as well because as usual I couldn't think of a single thing to say.

'Here we are,' she cooed like the miniature grown-up that she was, and placed the tray carefully down upon the glass coffee table between the sofa and Dave.

'Blimey!' smirked Dave playfully, 'Don't tell your mum you've risked her best china on a couple of tearaways like us.' It was the little things like that tray that could hang heavy in my heart.

They were around me all the time, inconsequential, nothing; things that I wouldn't notice because they were right in front of me. And then all of a sudden without warning they would jump out at as if they had turned into 3D images in my mind's eye, and it seemed as if their purpose was to never let me forget the great social chasm that yawned between us, the same void that I had stood across from Debbie. For theirs' was a world of matching, chip-free cups and saucers, where broken biscuits were never left to linger in biscuits barrels and all the magazines that lay seemingly casually on coffee tables were the latest editions.

Jenny set about pouring the tea, relieved, I could tell, to be busying herself rather than sitting there twiddling her thumbs, especially with me nothing but a twisted knot of anxiety beside her. Her parents were away for the night, down by the coast at her mum's sister's. Apparently they had agonised over whether to leave her there in the house on her own, even though she was

seventeen now, and on Christmas night of all nights. But Jen's
aunt hadn't been well lately and she had never married so Jen had
persuaded her mum that they should go, besides, they had spent
the whole morning together and Jen had convinced them that as
soon as she had seen them off she would be going to a friend's to
spend the night.

Dave smiled a thank you as Jen carefully handed him his tea.
He looked the same Dave, that easy air of ambivalence floating
around him as usual. But I could sense the darkness inside him,
he wore that look beneath the surface, broody, his eyes betrayed
him, as if the brown from his irises had leaked across the whites.
And of course there was the scar, redder than normal, a warning
light revealing his inner mood.

But he never let it show, would never rant or rave, he could
disguise his emotions better than anybody I knew. But then it
wasn't really a matter of "disguising" anything, I supposed, he just
dealt with things better, that sagacity that never failed to amaze.
Most people just thought that he was laid-back, the cool kid in
school, which of course he was. But it was more than that, I could
never put my finger on it or put it into words, but it had always
been there from the beginning… whenever that was… it went
deeper than simple maturity, it always seemed as if there wasn't a
problem I had that he didn't have the solution for.

We sat there for a minute or two in silence, sipping our tea and
gazing at the perfectly-decorated Christmas tree that twinkled and
sparkled in the corner of the room. It had all been so tastefully
arranged, shiny baubles of silver and gold hanging evenly about
the tree, every decoration had been planned and measured to
within the millimetre, like a department store showroom.

The minutes began to feel like hours, the silence growing
heavier, nothing but the gentle clinking of Jen's cup as she rested
it delicately back on the saucer that she held up around her chest.
Up and down, sip after sip, like Billy with his pint, I thought to

myself as I carefully set my own cup back down after two or three failed attempts, when I had succeeded in simply rocking it in its little tray. I wasn't used to such luxury at home, even when I did use a cup and saucer down at Lui's they were always big ugly things, not dainty little specimens like Jen's mum's; I couldn't even fit my fingers through the handle, had to pinch the thing between my fingers and hope to hell that it wouldn't snap off. They held so little liquid that Jen was already on her third cup whilst Dave's sat still untouched on the table in front of him, his gaze fixed upon the cushion that he had begun to spin again round and round in front of him. And me desperately trying to keep a lid on things, a conflict of emotions raging like a war through my head.

Eventually Dave broke the silence, 'Any records around?' he asked, nodding at the sophisticated-looking hi-fi equipment sitting over on the side.

'Nothing worth listening to,' Jen shrugged. 'I mean nothing that you'd like,' she added, a touch apologetically.

'Oh you'd be surprised… ' replied Dave, pulling himself to his feet before turning to the pair of us and deliberately looking down his nose in a frighteningly accurate impression of our old music teacher. 'You seem to forget what an eclectic taste I have.' His voice was plummy and upper crust, a relic, something that belonged back in the forties. It was just how the old boy used to talk, everyone was addressed by their surname, even the girls, but at least they had the respect of "miss".

'After all,' he continued as himself but still with a hint of mischief in his voice. 'Music *is* my business, you know!'

'Well in that case… ' said Jen, the mood a little lighter. 'You can listen too… ' She flicked determinedly through a stack of LPs stored in a cupboard beneath the stereo system until she found what she was after. 'Here we are… it's our favourite at the moment.' She smiled sheepishly. 'John bought it for my birthday.'

'Heatwave,' nodded Dave, inspecting the cover.

I groaned silently into my tea.

'No, no… that's cool,' insisted Dave, shaking his head as Jen began to blush, sensing that she had embarrassed me in some way. "Always and Forever"… I mean,' he continued with a shrug, 'it's as if it was written for you two.' And I could tell by the look on Jen's face that she didn't know if he was pulling her leg or not, that twinkle in his eye, stripping you down until your vulnerability showed… teasing you.

But when a cushion flew through the air and landed in his face her laughter filled the room. 'Bastard,' she grinned, picking up the cushion and belting him round the head with it.

I was in the middle of the weirdest dream when the distant ringing coming from across the landing from Jen's mum and dad's room eventually woke me from a disturbed sleep.

Dave and I had been on this ship, one of those old pirate ships, a galleon, and we were both perched on top of one of the masts. It was all so vivid, even in my sleep I could feel the wind trying to blast us off and out to sea, and when I looked over at Dave I could see him squinting into the glare of the sun, his hair whipped up crazily on his head. I could feel the motion of the sea swaying to and fro, could hear the thunder of the sails billowing beneath my feet. And as for the sight of the sea below! It was simply awesome, I mean it was just the ocean but it seemed to go on forever until it touched the sky, it was as if I could see for a million miles, until the world curved away. Down below silent waves swelled in caps of white before crashing back down to start again.

I looked frantically across to Dave for guidance of what we should do, but he seemed to be enjoying himself, smiling up at the sun, hair dancing about in the sky, madder than ever, as if it were being worked by a puppeteer's hand.

'DAVE!' I yelled. But my words were lost in the wind, I could hardly hear them myself and the louder I seemed to shout the stronger the wind seemed to blow.

But then he turned to face me, still smiling, not at me it seemed, but through me, as if I wasn't there. And then he was gone, in the blink of an eye, down towards the sea, twisting majestically like an acrobat in flight. I remember seeing the decking of the ship stretched out like strips of plasticine beneath him and just as he was about to crash down upon them, only a couple of seconds away from certain death, the sound of the phone forced me awake, leaving me staring blindly in the dark and wondering what the hell was going on.

A quick glance at Jen's clock told me that I had only been in bed for just over two hours, probably only asleep for about half that, I reckoned. She then came stumbling back in the room, eyes barely open and dressed in an absurd *Love is…* night shirt, the cartoon couple dressed in pyjamas and holding hands.

'It's your mum,' she mumbled, running her hands down her cheeks as if she were trying to rub the sleep away from her. 'Says she's been trying to get through for ages.' She switched on the light and the sudden brightness stung my eyes like needles as posters of Starsky and Hutch and John Travolta leapt off the walls at me. 'Your boss has been on the phone,' she went on, slumping down beside me, 'something about the match tomorrow.' She peered at the clock on her bedside table. 'Well… today actually… '

'Match?' I jumped out of bed. 'What match? I haven't got a match!' I fumbled, bleary-eyed, for my jeans. 'Only the first team has a ma… ' My words faded as the consequences of Mum's call began to sink in… surely not!

'That's what I thought,' Jen sighed, creeping back beneath the covers.

'Mum?' My nerves were still shredded from the dream, her voice, like my own words, jangled like broken glass in my head.

Ridiculously I wanted to tear downstairs and check that Dave was okay and where we had left him, lying on the sofa and listening to records.

'Oh, Johnny!' Mum's relief whooshed down the phone line like a rush of warm air. 'Where the hell have you been? I've been phoning for hours!'

I doubted that, playing on the mothers' prerogative of exaggeration, I thought, but I got the point. The downstairs phone in Jen's house sat on a petite half circle glass table by the front door and the music that we had been playing would easily have drowned it out. It was only due to Dave's consideration that it had been turned down when Jen and I had gone up to bed, we certainly hadn't asked.

'You okay, Mum?'

'Yes, Yes!' She sounded calmer than before, relief softening her words. 'It's your boss, Johnny… Mr Mackintosh.' I stood there in silence, phone to my ear, waiting for her to tell me what I already knew but still couldn't believe. This wasn't at all like I had imagined it, this was going to be another one of those "landmarks of life" moments that I had mapped out for myself and so the setting should have been more appropriate, surely I deserved at least that! Not half pissed and half asleep, standing like a fool in my underpants in my girlfriend's parents' bedroom.

I should have been slumped on a changing room bench covered in mud and dripping with sweat from after a lung-bursting training session or something, and the boss sidling up to me all casual like, placing a hand on my shoulder as he broke the news. I couldn't even get that right.

But the oddest thing was that I never got to hear Mum tell me, never could actually remember her say the words "You're in the first team", or whatever she truly said, for I was already there. Picturing the scene in my head, stepping out on the pitch with the rest of the team, most of them virtually household names, to face

Fulham, and fifteen maybe twenty thousand fans cheering and singing, on every side a wall of nameless faces all watching. But they would all know me, or at least they would by the end of the afternoon. *But why wouldn't they forget me? For good or bad?* My imagination began to run away from me, I started to envisage all kinds of dreadful outcomes - own goals, slips and fumbles - until I all of a sudden tuned back into the sound of Mum's voice. And the full reality of her words brought it all home with a crash, just how much of a boy I still was, trying to live in a man's world.

'... and I know it sounds silly, love, but you won't forget to brush your hair, will you?'

'Can't sleep?' I asked needlessly. I had wandered down the stairs following the gentle hum of music that drifted through the house like smoke to where Dave lay on his back cross-legged on the sofa, still listening to records. It wasn't that he was playing them loud or anything but at three in the morning even the slightest sound amplifies itself out of proportion.

'I didn't know Jen had any Bowie!' he said, his voice heavy with surprise. I shrugged indifferently as I realised that the faint sounds of guitar were cords from "Rebel Rebel".

'Oh yeah, she must have forgotten,' I said vaguely, my head wasn't clear yet, everything that I did or said still felt as if it belonged to someone else.

'Hmm, she's not so bad after all then,' he mumbled to himself pretending to be thoughtful, as I fell back into the armchair that I had vacated what seemed like an age ago, 'I mean after all...' he clicked his tongue 'Heatwave!' He turned idly to face me 'Problem?' he asked, already aware of the answer.

'No, not really a problem... ' I gazed about the room, as if seeing it for the first time. There must have been over a hundred Christmas cards in there, standing in rows on the sideboard, hanging over pieces of tinsel suspended from the ceiling, slotted neatly into some sort of wooden lattice contraption that was fixed to the wall and obviously designed for the exact purpose of holding greeting cards. How did people get to know so many people? We were lucky if we had twenty up at home, I thought to myself.

'What then?' Dave continued, he was up on one elbow now. 'Johnny?… ' He let his words tail away, inviting me to fill in the gaps. I could never hide anything from him, not that I wanted too, the opposite, in fact, but this was all part of his magic, the ability to make stuff that anyone else would have to gruesomely extract from you seem as easy as brushing your teeth.

I shook my head, still unable to get my head round it. 'You're never gonna believe this… ' And when I looked up there was that effortless, easy grin stretched across his face, eyes all soft and droopy at the corners, and when he spoke there was real pride in his voice as if he had been waiting for this moment all his life.

'Bet I do.'

CHAPTER TWENTY - TWO

December 1978

It rained on Boxing Day in 1978. White Christmases were only ever seen in films. It was the kind of steady, unspectacular rain that's neither a drizzle nor a downpour, so that in the end you don't even notice that's it's there, simply becomes a part of the day, as natural as the chill in the air.

There were some great goals scored that day up and down the country, the Boxing Day fixtures always threw up plenty of drama. No doubt there were some great saves made as well, they were probably all shown on *Match of the Day* later that night, but I didn't get to see any of them. I didn't remember anything other than sitting groggily in Jen's kitchen hunched over a bowl of Weetabix with Golden Nuggets sprinkled across the top and trying hard to keep it all down.

It was two days before my memory of the collision in the match came back to me. Two days of lying in a hospital bed staring vacantly at the ceiling wondering what the hell I was doing there and how I got there. Of course Mum, Jen and Dave all told me, different versions of the same story each embellished with their own personal touch but it didn't really matter, they all concluded with the same ending... with me waking up in a hospital bed.

'Well you've been moanin' that you should pop in and see your old girl sometime,' joked Billy on his one and only visit. It was the day after it happened, came straight round when he had heard but the place had given him the creeps more than anything

I had ever known. It was the institution of it all, the uniforms, the rules, the regimental lines of beds, the smell of disinfectant, like a school for the sick. I didn't really feel the same but I could sympathise, I knew how those sort of places restricted him, made him feel as if the world was closing in, squeezing the air from his lungs. So at the end of visiting time I assured him that he didn't have to come again, that I would be out in a day or two and that it was hardly worth it.

'You sure, J boy?' he asked, trying hard to hide his relief. 'I'll come back tomorrow… it don't bovva me.' And the fact that he would have if I'd asked him was enough. Watching him squirming in the chair beside me was almost as painful as my arm.

'If that had been a bleedin' Brazilian they'd still be raving on about it this time next year!' the old boy in the bed beside me crowed. He was referring to Bob Latchford's goal for Everton against Coventry as he read the back pages of the *Express*. Latchford was in line for the "Golden Boot" that season, ended up taking penalties in the end, which I thought was cheating a bit, but he deserved it for the season that he had had so I supposed it didn't matter.

'Young laddie here wouldn't have even got near it, would you?' he laughed good-naturedly in my direction. A few days before my name had been among those very pages. I had read them all, Jen had kept them for me, one particular paper had even carried a picture. You couldn't actually see me just a pair of legs sticking out from beneath a huddle of concerned-looking players. There had been a write-up as well, it told of the young teenage goalkeeper who had been making his first team debut for second division Southfields at home against Fulham. It went on to explain the unfortunate debutant had suffered a badly broken arm in a collision with Fulham's young protégé, who had also been making his debut. "Two stars of the future", it had called us, there was

"Southfields up and coming young keeper who had really been catching the eye as well as crosses in the reserves of late, who had built quite a reputation for his uncanny ability for saving penalties", who had been involved in a sickening clash with "Fulham's precocious young striker". It had happened just inside the home side's penalty box, a complete accident… "A freak accident", as one reporter had written.

… It was midway through the second-half when the young custodian raced from his line and dived bravely at the feet of his fellow debutant, who had been on the pitch for only a matter of minutes. But already in that short time he had impressed with one or two nice passes and touches but most of all by a snap turn and shot inside the box, which had seen Chalmers scurrying hopelessly across his line as the ball flashed narrowly past the post.

But on this occasion Chalmers beat his adversary to the ball, scooping it off the young substitute's toe just as he was preparing to pull the trigger. But disaster struck as the ball bobbed harmlessly away to safety, for as young Danny Beavis swiped at thin air his flailing boot connected with Chalmers' flapping limb, and the Southfields keeper's forearm took the full impact of the kick.

Some of the crowd were reported as saying that they heard the crack from the stands.

And in a twist of appalling irony there is a close connection between the two debutants. They were classmates a few years ago, had played in the same school team throughout their schooldays before both passing trials with their respective clubs…

I closed my eyes and searched for some sleep, since I had awoken in the hospital I seemed to be constantly tired. In fact it felt more like exhaustion than merely being sleepy but, whichever it was, I still found the whole business of actually going to sleep as frustrating as ever.

I tried to conjure up some heroes to ease my mind and send

me off, people, who, over the past twelve months had left some kind of mark on me. There was the inevitable list of goalkeepers that sprung to mind: Shilton of league champions Nottingham Forest, Clemence and Corrigan of course. I tried really hard to imagine what it must have been like to be the Liverpool keeper back on that sweet May evening when they had regained the European Cup, and at Wembley of all places.

But the thing was, none of it worked. My imagination, like my body, simply lacked the strength, couldn't seem to find the spark that would usually transport me into the heart of my daydreams, let me slip into the skin of my heroes. In fact if there was anyone who stood out from the past twelve months that had left an impression on me it came from the most unlikely source, you could hardly call him an idol but for some reason he had certainly left a mark on me. It was a character from the sitcom *Butterflies* that had begun in the summer. It was a show about the slightly kooky, slightly above middle-class housewife, Ria, who constantly fantasised about breaking free from the chains that tied her to the monotony of family life.

But it was neither of her layabout teenage sons, who, much to their father's disgust, were too busy enjoying being young to find a job that I admired. Almost inconceivably it was the old man himself that I found myself looking up to! A bloody father figure! It simply didn't make any sense, none whatsoever, and it annoyed the hell out of me. I mean where the hell did the affinity with a *dad* come from? Obviously not from me, Dave or Billy, that much was certain. But there he was nonetheless, standing above a mountain of footballers and punk rockers like some victorious mountaineer.

I loved watching *Butterflies*. The Parkinsons were my idea of a family heaven, their lives were how I envisaged all the "nice" families of England lived, what life up in the Connaught Garden Set and beyond must have been like; the two-parent, two-children households that stretched out across the countries leafier suburbs and rolling shires, which I had only ever seen on maps. All detached houses and neatly-kept gardens, not overly grand but three or four bedrooms and a tidy little garage attached at the side.

I loved Ria and her husband, Ben, and their open-plan kitchen and dining room. I felt the soft fabric of their sofa against my skin every time a scene was set in the front room, the bamboo patterns in beige and brown had a strangely reassuring effect that never failed to calm me, their whole house screamed of a sense of security that only being with Dave, and Jen of late, had ever really given me. They were parents who cared, parents who could afford to care, okay they employed a cleaner but she was there for comedy value as much as anything, but the overall picture that leapt out at me every Thursday evening when I tuned in was of a sanctuary that could never be breached… family life as it should be.

And these two boys, they just didn't see it, took it all for granted, and poor old Ben Parkinson would despair, simply couldn't understand why they didn't want to work, he couldn't understand their world at all. For his was one of old-fashioned standards and values which meant nothing or very little to them. *'It's 1978, Dad!'* the skinny one had exclaimed in the first episode. And it had said it all, set the tone for the whole series for me.

But yet I found myself sympathising with this man, if I had been one of his offspring I wouldn't have taken it all for granted, I would have appreciated what I had… I would have made my dad proud.

It was a comedy, an easy-watching gentle half hour of light entertainment, and I had laughed along with the canned laughter. But there were dark undertones that ran beneath the surface, and I had been aware of them from the beginning although it took a while for me to tune into their wavelength, and whether I read them right or not, they seemed to me to be uncomfortably close to my old enemy… hopelessness.

When the boss strode purposefully through the ward the next day, glancing from side to side at the rows of beds with a look close of disgust on his face, thankfully Jen was already there beside me. And of course Mum had popped in just before the beginning of her shift so it made it all the more difficult for him to put too much pressure on me. I know it sounds ungrateful but I was glad that Mum wasn't one of the nurses assigned to my ward. And although she never said, I think she was pretty relieved too. Besides, I don't think I could have stood it with Mum hovering around me all day, would probably have ended up discharging myself or something, could just imagine me skulking out in the dead of night with some old boy's raincoat over my pyjamas. I mean it was bad enough having to contend with Jen fretting at my bedside every evening, it was a dreadful thing to think and I felt about as awful as I could over it but nevertheless it was true. It really unnerved me to see her so concerned.

'Honest, boss, I'm fine just here,' I smiled at him in what I hoped was a show of contentment. I even gave old Matthews, who I knew would be eavesdropping from his bed beside me, a friendly nod in a bid to strengthen my case.

The boss still looked unconvinced. 'Hmmm.' He puffed out his cheeks. I'd seen that look on his face before, a few days before, on Boxing Day, just before he had announced his tactical changes at half-time.

'Boss, I'd like to introduce you to my friend Mr Matthews,' I extended my arm in the old boy's direction. 'He's been dying too meet you.' That took the old bugger by surprise, but he was really chuffed.

'Well not literally I 'ope,' he grinned, sitting himself up, 'still a few years left in me, I reckon.' He tapped his chest where he thought his heart should be and extended a hand. 'How do you do'.

'Pleased to meet you.' The boss nodded, reaching up with a groan and taking his hand.

'I remember you in your playing days,' said Matthews. 'Good little tackler he was,' he said to me and Jen as if the boss was some frail old man sitting vacantly in his chair and couldn't hold the thread of the conversation, all slowly and patronising, and I had to swallow back my laughter. And I swear that the boss blushed but it was so hard to tell for his cheeks were always so ruddy, tiny broken veins snaking across his weather-beaten skin, like cracks on the glaze of a porcelain cup. Years of sitting in dugouts in all kinds of weather, I supposed. Anyway it had done the trick, had succeeded in steering the topic of conversation away from me and a private room. I had really dreaded it, for if I had to be stuck in hospital I couldn't think of anything worse than being cooped up all alone in my own solitary hell. The luxuries of a TV or a radio to myself wouldn't have been able to stop me from mutilating my mind with thoughts that I simply couldn't control. Nothing could have prepared me for the week that I had just passed through. A Christmas Day spent playing "happy families" with Derek as "Daddy", followed by the mayhem of the evening spent in the Crown, where the night had been shattered by two nightmares from our past, rising up like ghosts to haunt us. And then of course there was my early morning call-up, one minute I had been trapped in the heart of yet another disturbing dream that had seemed to be screaming some sort of warning at me which I simply couldn't for the life of me decipher, and the next all the ones that I had tried to imagine ever since I could remember, the ones where the sun had always shone and I was the keeper that I had always wanted to be, had come true.

It was bad enough as it was, lying there at night staring at the walls or at the shadows of my companions sleeping soundly in their beds whilst my mind replayed over and over again the sight of Danny bearing down on me, and then, like some out of body experience, seeing myself diving at his feet. And I would hear my voice in my head questioning the decisions that I had made, again and again, questions that I had asked I didn't know how many times before: if my blood hadn't been swimming in so much alcohol would I have been sharper off my line? If I had had a decent night's sleep would I have read the situation earlier? If I hadn't have felt so hazy, a little sharper maybe, would I have gone to ground so soon? The answer to them all was probably. But I could never be sure. For I had had to make a split second decision, like a hundred times before, and besides, I *had* won the ball. But the doubt wouldn't leave me, wouldn't even fade slowly, instead it screamed at me from beneath my breath, how could it not? When the result was me laying there with my wreck of an arm stretched out and taunting me like a red rag in front of a bull.

'And how are we today, Johnny?' enquired the nurse, as she moved expertly around the bed tucking the sheets back in after another restless day had passed. I could never see how my bed became such a mess, it wasn't as if I could toss and turn about in it, not when you're hanging from the ceiling by your arm, but it was just that I never seemed to feel comfortable, especially at night, it was as if someone had tried to stick my legs to the sheets and I simply had to keep moving them.

The warmth in her smile always seemed to stir something inside of me, I couldn't put my finger on what it was, I mean I didn't know if it was sexual or something beyond that. Or maybe I did fancy her but just didn't want to admit it to myself, I mean she was certainly pretty. Not Debbie Harry or Olivia Newton John in the end of *Grease* sexy pretty, but more sort of unspectacular but comfortably pretty… like Ria in *Butterflies*.

Oh God, I thought, I hoped to hell that it wasn't a "mum"

thing, attracted by the sense of security, of being mothered. It was confusing because she wasn't old enough to be my mum but far enough away to be awed at and yet she was young enough, late twenties I reckoned, to understand and still remember the troubles that awaited you as you made your way through teenage land.

'Fine thanks,' I replied, a little too goofily, and was instantly aware of Jen's eyes upon me, her female instinct alerted. I pretended not to notice.

'Ooh,' she crowed, her voice dripping with sarcasm, as the nurse carried on with her rounds. 'Developed a little *crush*, have we?'

'*No,*' I sighed, reaching for the newspaper and trying my hardest to sound bored by her little snipe. But just then she returned pushing a trolley containing a bowl of soapy water, a sponge and a towel.

'Silly me,' she smiled with that gentle smile of hers, 'You're first down for a bath, Johnny.'

'Time I was off anyway,' said Jen. 'I'll see you tonight after my shift,' she added, rising from her chair.

'You don't have to bother, really,' I muttered not really paying attention, one eye on the nurse's tray. Jen stopped for a moment, halfway to the bed, about to kiss me goodbye. 'No... what I meant was... ' I said desperately trying to backtrack.

'It's okay,' smiled Jen knowingly.

'I just meant that you've been once today,' I tried to explain. 'You shouldn't have to worry... after work an' all.'

She kissed me on the cheek. 'See you tomorrow,' she smiled and, as she left, slipped back past the bed, turned and said, 'Enjoy your bath,' and was gone.

'Am I next, love?' smirked old Matthews, nodding at the bowl of soapy water. The kind nurse rolled her eyes in a show of light-hearted exasperation and told him to mind his own business. She must get that a lot, I reckoned, dirty old men who looked forward to their bed baths more than they looked forward to going home. And who knows, maybe I'd be like that one day, a young man trapped in an old man's body, the heart of a teenager beating behind the bars of frail bones. But right then it was just about the most embarrassing thing that I could have possibly imagined, what if her hand was to accidentally brush against me? A wave of dread swept through me, what if something were to happen to me down there? If I couldn't control the flow of blood rushing to the core of me, I'd have a heart attack right there and then.

On each occasion that it was bed bath time, which for some reason always seemed to fall on the kind nurse's shift, I would squeeze my eyes shut and force myself to think of football. Dredge up memories of certain saves that I was particularly proud of or even certain goals conceded that I was particularly ashamed of, ones that still nagged at me, the ones where I felt I'd let myself down. Even the gnawing irritation that replaying those moments left me with was better than focusing on what "might" happen beneath the sheets.

'Relax!' She smiled as she carefully lifted my pyjama shirt and placed the sponge on my stomach. She clicked her tongue as if exasperated by my lack of cooperation, but there was no frustration in her voice. 'Honestly,' she sighed, 'you're as stiff as a board.' And thank God the innuendo was lost on her, for as unintentional as it had been, I could feel the beads of sweat beginning to sting my forehead.

I had had enough of visitors. Ungrateful as it might sound, it seemed to me that I saw more people whilst lying in a hospital bed than I did when I wasn't. They had all been told what day I was to leave: Mum, the boss, Jen, even old Danny. He had been racked with guilt, was on crutches himself, nothing more than severe bruising but he would still be sidelined for three weeks at least, they reckoned. I couldn't handle seeing him, to be honest, I hated to admit it but the same went for Mum and Jen. The guilt or the fussing was just too much, I wasn't used to so much attention and I felt swamped, claustrophobic almost. It wasn't that I wasn't grateful… it was just that it unnerved me, in a way that I hadn't experienced since Lui had first started to pamper us down at the café.

Dave was the only one I felt comfortable with. So I had told them all not to worry, that he was going to meet me on the day that I was to be discharged. I'd really had to play the whole thing down, especially to Mum and Jen, insisting that it was no big deal, and besides, they'd both be at work. I had made sure of that.

So it came as quite a surprise when my kind nurse told me that I had a visitor enquiring after me at the front desk.

'I think it's one of your Jenny's colleagues,' she whispered reassuringly, seeing the mild surprise on my face. But the thing was I didn't *know* any of Jen's colleagues. It had always been a bit of a difficult subject to broach, a sort of wasteland that lay between us. Not a contentious issue but nevertheless avoided, the fact that she had decided to become a policewoman, to walk on one side of the law, if you like, when so many of the people I knew and had grown up with chose to live on the other. But they had a stigma attached to them, coppers, despised in certain social circles, such as amongst the punks, almost as much as Pakistanis, or Mods and Rockers. I mean there were so many songs that ranted about or taunted them: The Clash's "White Riot" and the Pistol's "Anarchy in the UK", for example.

It's funny but I still remember laughing at the memory of Billy a few years before, I mean it hadn't quite been punk, typically had been the usual… Bowie, but it had all amounted to the same thing, I suppose… to be seen as not conforming.

There had been me, Dave and Billy sitting around the old lido in the blistering summer sunshine of '76. We couldn't have entered the pool if we had wanted too, for there had been barely a drop of water visible, just a mass of bodies, red raw and pink with the occasional splash of colour from a bikini top jiggling around, all crammed into this giant hole in the ground. And there had been hundreds more like them, like the three of us, flaked out on towels upon the paving stones and the scorched grass. But then a man dressed in shirt and tie had appeared, sticking out like a sore thumb with his helmet upon his head despite the relentless heat. The fact that he wore no tunic just a white short sleeved shirt and tie had been completely lost because of that helmet.

There had been an air of arrogance about him, the way he swaggered through the sea of bodies littering the ground, hands clasped behind his back in classic copper style as if the grounds of a swimming pool were logically a part of his beat. And when he had been only yards away, leering down from beneath the dome on his head at the girls and sneering at all the skinny boys as if the very sight of them with their tops off disgusted him, Billy had pressed the PLAY button on Dave's tape recorder. He had been frantically searching through the cassette from the minute he had spotted him, rewinding and then stopping to find the exact line that he was after. And the sound of Bowie's voice, wailing with emotion, had suddenly exploded from the speakers, drowning out the chatter and laughter: *'Take a look at the lawman beating up the wrong guy...'* And old Collins had nearly had a heart attack, the look upon his face when he had spun around had been a picture, sending not just the three of us, but every kid around into fits of laughter.

And then it hit me. Collins! Shit! It was Collins waiting to see me! The realisation hit me like a giant fist in the chest, the wind forcing its way up and escaping in a kind of pathetic gasp that sounded almost like a whimper.

'You all right, Johnny?' the kind nurse asked, her face creasing in concern. 'Johnny?' For just a moment, despite everything, my pulse quickened. Just recently she had taken to calling me that;

"Johnny" instead of John and I couldn't deny that I loved it. For it was who I was to the people who cared for me, a sign of affection, a sign that in some small way, and who knows, maybe even in a big way, had crept behind the barricades, a sign that I was more than just another patient.

'Yeah, fine,' I replied, painting on a smile.

'I'll just go and fetch him then.' But as she turned to go we saw him already making his way in our direction, nodding and smiling his way along the ward, his hands clasped behind his back like the friendly copper he always pretended to be, and then with a friendly sigh he plonked himself down right beside me as if I had been expecting him to call all day.

'Whoa… it's cold out there!' He looked from me to my nurse and forced his smile even wider. The result was even more macabre than before. 'How are you then, John?'

He looked different with his helmet under his arm and not on his head, his neatly trimmed jet black hair plastered with perspiration to his skull and smoothed to one side by the sweep of his hand. He looked uncomfortable, hot and flustered by the rise of temperature that must have occurred from one minute being out in the cold December air and the next engulfed by the stifling radiator heat that lifted in invisible waves from the ward.

'Right then,' the kind nurse said, 'I'll leave you to it,' and she breezed off down the ward with that dainty little walk of hers that never failed to lift me whenever I heard her approaching, a sort of *skippity-skip* sound, as if the soles of her shoes were dancing across the floor.

Collins peered over his shoulder. 'Not bad,' he sneered. It was an attempt at a smile but his face wasn't designed for such an expression, he looked almost demonic, his mouth creeping up at the corners as if they were unsure where to go whilst his eyes narrowed into slits of malevolence. 'Bet you've been knocking one out over her, 'avn't you, Johnny boy?'

I didn't answer. He turned back round, his face a mask of disgust. 'You dirty little bastard.'

I had always felt intimidated in his presence, whether or not there had been a group of us taking the piss in town or something or at the times when he had managed to corner me on my own and threaten and harass me. But I always felt that I made a good job of disguising it pretty well, I had never given him any lip, well… not compared to the mouthfuls Billy would sometimes spit at him, and I certainly wasn't able to deliver some off-the-cuff comeback the way Dave would. But then nobody could. Mostly I would hide any fear or anxiety that I might have felt behind a show of indifference, but lying there in a hospital bed with my arm suspended there like a cracked branch hanging from a tree filled me with a vulnerability that I hadn't felt in what seemed the longest time.

After what seemed an age but couldn't have been more than a few seconds I found some composure.

'What do you want?' I asked neutrally.

His face changed in an instant, the manic smile vanished in a heartbeat, replaced by an anger that he had struggled to conceal. It was hate that burned away inside him, untainted by anything else, as pure as snow.

'What do *I* want?' he snarled between gritted teeth, his voice trembled from the effort of containing it. He took a step closer and glared down at me. 'I'll tell you what I *fucking* want, shall I?'

I could feel tiny beads of sweat popping to the surface and prickling my forehead, could feel the blood pounding in my ears, my heart trying to thump its way through my chest, but I stayed firm and held his stare as he closed in even further.

It was like a cloud across the sun, he glanced quickly around the ward, making sure that no one was within earshot, all the nurses seemed to be somewhere else and old Matthews was snoring soundly, a newspaper spread open across his chest. I braced myself, waiting for I didn't know what, a poisonous threat relating to Billy, no doubt. It would surely be about Christmas night and how once again Billy had somehow managed to evade Collins' hand on his collar. But drinking underage and after hours were hardly significant offences when there were a bunch of tattooed skinheads forcing their way into pubs and breaking into off licences in the same street.

And then, just when he looked like he was about to unleash his verbal assault, he stood up, ramrod straight, like a solider on guard duty. He fiddled needlessly with the knot in his tie, back in control now, chin jutting out defiantly as if to show his composure.

'Bad break, they said in the papers.' He nodded, looking down at the length of plaster hanging beneath him. I didn't answer, was too busy watching his hand as he carefully raked the tips of his fingers over mine. 'And even more serious than they first suspected,' he went on smiling without a trace of humour, 'considering that you've broken it before.' I couldn't take my eyes off his hand, dancing delicately across my fingers, the whole thing looked ridiculous, like some sort of game that lovers might play. 'And how did you do that then eh, Johnny?' He seized my index finger and squeezed it tight 'EH!' His teeth ground from the force, he was searching my face for signs of pain, his forehead knotted in confusion, his eyes growing darker as I stared blankly back into them. He squeezed even harder, not quite believing what was happening, for I couldn't feel a thing. I could see his knuckles whiten as he frantically moved from one finger to the next, his grimace deepening as each time he applied even more pressure but still he failed to get any kind of a reaction.

My fingers! Panic flowed through me. *I can't feel my fingers!* The thought that they might have been affected by the injury had never even occurred to me. My concern had always been for my forearm, if the screws that now pinned the smashed bones together would be strong enough or if the damage on top of the original break would prove to be too much.

Somewhere outside the chaos of my thoughts I was vaguely aware that Collins had given up and was simply standing there. But I took no notice; he had ceased to be of any importance, his threatening manner lost. In fact his whole presence was now inconsequential to me, just as the worry of my broken arm would be if the nerve damage that was affecting all feeling in my hand proved to be permanent. For what good would a fully healed arm be if my hand couldn't function properly? If I couldn't grip, hold or punch a ball. Gordon Banks had made a courageous recovery of sorts with only one eye but I doubted that even *he* could have managed with only one hand!

For a moment the world seemed to freeze as I struggled to take it all in, Collins and everything else in the ward stood as still as stage scenery. What was that line of Bowie's that Dave often used to sing? Something from the *Aladdin Sane* album… *'Time, suspended like a whore…'* that was it. It's funny how the fragments of songs spring to mind at the most inappropriate, yet exact of times.

But I couldn't ignore the ominous presence of Collins forever, he stood out so starkly in the pastel light of the ward, this dark man in his dark uniform, like some dangerous cavernous hole lying in a field of snow.

He had regained his menace and looked me up and down with that look of utter disgust that he always wore whenever we had the misfortune to come up against him.

Not five minutes before I had been lying there basking in the warm glow of my secret pleasure, finally coming to realise that all my butterflies and going to pieces around the kind nurse amounted to nothing more than a school boy crush. Nothing to feel guilty about, I had decided, it wasn't like I was going to do anything about it and the understanding of this felt as if a nest of snakes had been removed from my guts.

But all that contentment was short-lived. For Collins was

here now, glaring at me as it were an absolute liberty that I was lying in a hospital bed that some "decent" human being could be occupying. And then he was there again, his face in mine, so close that I could feel the heat of his breath against my skin, that I was swamped by his air of menace.

I wanted to scream, to yell back into his face, 'Leave me alone!' Demand 'What is your fucking problem?' But of course I knew what his problem was, what it had always been, ever since he had first chased us through the park as kids after Billy had set light to that old tire, under the viaducts and back out into the industrial estate. I remember Dave singing, '*Which way you going, Billy…* ' a song in the charts at the time by a bunch of hippies… The Poppy Family or something, goading him, for it was Billy he was really after, anyone else would simply have been a bonus. And the bastard wouldn't give up, even though we had had virtually the width of the park between us when he had decided to come after us. Funny but I hadn't even remembered, would probably never have remembered if old Kenny hadn't mentioned it that time up in Birmingham, but now the bloody-minded, dogged determination of Collins came flooding back. Every time we had looked over our shoulders there he had been, puffing and panting, the sweat glistening on his face, squeezing through the gap in the fence, scrabbling up the bank that led to the viaducts, cursing us out loud whenever he found the breath. He had never caught us, but he had never forgotten us either, had already known who we were, boys from broken homes, boys with a touch of something different, but to him we might as well have been the children of the damned. And since then we had been his problem, had unwittingly wormed our way into his consciousness, so deeply engrained that we had become an obsession, an obsession that wouldn't die until each of us, me, Billy and Dave, were crushed, broken beyond repair beneath the weight of his contempt.

I stared into the narrow slits of his eyes. 'You tell that piece of scum that he won't be so lucky next time… that next time I'll… '

'Yeah, yeah,' I butted in with a roll my eyes. 'That you'll "get" him next time, I know.'

For a moment I thought that he was going to explode, his cheeks on fire, eyes nearly popping out of his head. I had gone too far, I knew, overplayed my show of confidence, but I just hadn't been able to help myself. And besides, I had already seen my saviour. The appearance of my kind nurse making her way along the ward with her eyes burning into the back of Collins.

Collins must have caught the sound of her approaching for he straightened up sharply, or maybe it was a policemen's instinct that warned him, some kind of secret sixth sense that they implant in them whenever they become coppers.

'Everything all right here, Johnny?' she asked with a look of concern, her eyes flicked from me to Collins.

He had that air of defiance about him again, the one where his jaw jutted out as if it were chiselled from granite, where his fingers adjusted the already perfect knot of his tie.

'Fine thank you, Nurse,' he said. 'Nurse… ?' He made a show of searching her uniform for a name badge or some form of identification.

'It's Nurse Wallace,' she informed him, 'Elaine Wallace.' She leaned forward to meet his gaze as if she were swatting his eyes off her chest.

'*Elaine.*' He stood back up and smiled unnervingly from me to her, that meaningless, empty smile that reeked secretly of contempt.

'How very… ' he clasped his hands behind his back and stared thoughtfully at the ceiling for a moment, 'informal.' He smirked, all pleased with himself.

They stood for a moment at the end of my bed sizing each other up like boxers before the first bell, it was no longer about me, this was about respect; Collins expecting the sight of his uniform to answer any questions before anyone even had the temerity to ask, expecting it to speak for itself for his behaviour or his methods.

And Elaine determined not to be undermined, the hospital ward was *her* world, a place where she and the rest of the nurses were like angels floating from bed to bed, where each patient laid themselves bare, literally placing their lives in their hands.

Elaine… I had never known her name, not even her surname, Wallace, simply didn't have the maturity to ask. And there was Collins, the most contemptible man, the biggest bastard that I had ever known, and he had found it out in a heartbeat, the simplest, most natural, thing in the world to ask on meeting somebody: their name.

She seized the initiative and spoke first. 'You are aware, Constable,' she began firmly, 'that officially you are here outside of visiting hours and Johnny is still very much a patient here and therefore my responsibility.' She paused as if allowing the tone of her words to penetrate the armour of his uniform. 'So if there's a problem,' she continued 'perhaps you could speak to the Sister before you… '

Collins' eyes narrowed even further. 'That won't be necessary, Nurse Wallace.' His smile as thin as paper, his look more dangerous than ever. 'You look after Mr Chalmers here for me,' he said, patting my feet. 'We've got lots of catching up to do, haven't we… *Johnny*?' And as he made to leave he stopped for a moment and leant into her ear, 'I'd check his blood pressure if I were you, *Elaine,*' he said, exaggerating her name. 'I think it rises considerably whenever you're around.'

She watched in silence as he sauntered back along the ward, smiling insincerely at my fellow patients, bidding them farewell and wishing them all a happy new year, and then just before he left, a hand already upon the door, he turned suddenly on his heel and called out, 'And I don't think that's the only thing that rises for him whenever you're in the vicinity, Nurse Wallace!'

CHAPTER TWENTY - THREE

January 1979

When I returned to the ward from the physiotherapy department it was as if I had already left. My bed had been stripped down to the mattress and a nurse, not Elaine, was emptying the litter bin beside it. She looked up as I approached and smiled warmly at me.

'Expect you can't wait to get home, Johnny? Do you need a hand with your packing or anything?' she asked.

'No thanks, I'll be fine,' I answered, trying to smile, but for some reason I didn't much feel like smiling and it felt as if my cheeks were being stretched. 'My friend's coming in a minute… ' I told her. 'Dave… ' as if the name explained everything.

'Right then,' she smiled, 'I'll be off then… good luck if I don't see you again.' And she carried on emptying the bins into a black bin liner.

I couldn't explain how I felt, I knew I should be happy to be going home but for some reason I felt this sensation of unease, I couldn't explain it, whenever I attempted to figure it out, if I closed my eyes and tried to tell myself not to be so stupid, I would be overcome by this kind of dizziness, as if I were falling out of the sky or something, a bit like the dream I had experienced on Christmas night, that same giddy feeling of nausea that had touched me when I had watched, from inside my head, Dave plummeting to the deck below.

I was like a prisoner afraid of the outside world. What did they call it? Institutionalised.

I could hear the muffled melody of "Rat Trap" as it played on a portable radio somewhere down the ward. It seemed so long ago, was it really only a month or so? Laughing at the young girls from town as they teased Billy with their renditions, *'Hey, Billy, take a walk, take, take a walk, take a walk...* ' I found myself singing along in my head, picturing the image of Geldof's Billy drunk and traipsing down to the Italian café, I couldn't help but think of *our* Billy making his way to Lui's.

Life had come in waves since that song had been in the charts. There had always seemed to be something different, some new kind of experience washing over me. And what would I be doing this time next year, I wondered, where the hell would I be? I wouldn't be living at home with Mum, that was for sure.

For if 1979 was to be nothing else it would prove to be the year that Mum and I would finally let one another go, I knew that much, it would be the year that she gave up our terraced council house that had always been home and moved in permanently with Derek. And if it hadn't been for me she would have gone long ago, she only really came home to make sure that I was okay. She would pretend there were some clothes that she needed to pick up or something like that, knowing that I would have hated the fuss, but she wasn't able to hide the concern from her face, no more than I could ever hide mine from her.

But it was different now, now that I had a proper job, that I was earning a wage and a wage that was guaranteed to improve dramatically once I signed full pro, which everyone but me seemed to think was a certainty, especially now.

It had been inevitable that she would go, in fact I had expected it sooner but what had really made her mind up, I reckoned, was Boxing Day. I don't think she had been fully aware of the impact a debut in the first team would have on my life, my name in the papers, even a mention on *Match of the Day,* and to be honest neither had I. We simply hadn't had the time to think about it, one call late at night and then bang... I was playing. No time to even sleep on it!

"Rat Trap" had finished and Rod Stewart was asking the world if it found him sexy now. They must be playing the number ones from last year, I guessed. It was weird to think that the year had ended and a new one had begun whilst I had been there in hospital. It was ironic considering how hard I found it to sleep what with one thing or another, but at the time that '78 had become '79 I had been fast asleep, had celebrated with nothing stronger than a cup of weak tea before tiredness had finally caught up with me. Elaine hadn't even been on duty. Jen had wanted to come and spend the evening with me, said she'd bring a cake in and maybe sneak a bottle of champagne if I was lucky. But I couldn't have handled that, it was bad enough on a normal night, I no longer looked forward to visiting times, it had slowly become the most uncomfortable part of my day. That time in the early evening when she would bustle through the door with a smile painted on in the corridor outside, kiss me and sink down into the chair, almost out of breath, with a hearty sigh that said, 'Isn't this cosy?' I hated the fact that she was running around every night to come and see me. I would tell her not to worry about coming *every* night, that I was sure that I would survive one day without her, but of course it would come out all wrong.

'Don't you *want* me to come?' she asked, the hurt crumpling her face.

'Yes, of course I do!' I exclaimed. But I knew that it was already too late, knew how ungrateful it all sounded.

To my surprise I had managed to win the battle over the hospital room so there would be no way that the boss would let me get my way over living arrangements as well, the likelihood was that I would end up in digs, he would insist upon it, I was sure. I had to admit the whole thing left a bitter taste in my mouth, everyone else seemed to be getting what they wanted out of me, except me. The boss had wanted me nearer the club from day one, somewhere where he could keep me under his wing and Mum could move without having to pack her conscience in her luggage. In my darkest moments I felt as if I were being punished for... well, for not having a dad almost.

CHAPTER TWENTY - FOUR

January 1979

'I don't know how you can afford to live here,' I said, leaning against the kitchen worktop and eating bread straight from the bag.

'I can't,' Dave told me through a mouthful of crumbs. It was thickly sliced, as white as snow but hard work without spread, but we were beer hungry and needed filling.

I peered at him through the fog beginning to rise in my eyes, nose wrinkled in confusion, so he pulled out a chair from under the table and sat down to explain. 'I won my room rent free for a year in a bet.'

I choked as the bread dried in my mouth soaking up the saliva like a sponge. 'What do you mean, a *bet*?'

'With Ronnie and Stuart,' he explained. 'You know… my flat mates.'

I looked at him questioningly. 'Right?'

'We were having a few drinks one night,' he began, 'I'd only been in the job a couple of days,' he gazed down at the floor, 'just getting to know everyone really.' He was muttering to himself now, lost in his head for a moment, the way he often would, disappearing without ever going anywhere. And then he looked up as if he had suddenly remembered he wasn't on his own and gestured towards the bag of bread. I spun him another slice like a frisbie and he continued.

'We came back here after the pub and carried on.' He tore the bread into strips and dropped them into his mouth like a seal. 'Anyway,' he chewed thoughtfully, 'we started testing each other with music questions and that,' his face split into an easy smile, 'I think they thought I was just some stuck up little shit who'd come out of college with a stack of qualifications and no idea.'

And I could see how they might have mistaken Dave's manner as arrogant, supposed that his quiet, laid-back demeanour was nothing more than an air of superiority. In fact I had often wondered how someone with such an inward bearing could succeed in such an outward world. But then of course that was Dave... that exceptional ability to change a room simply by entering it, to excite you without ever breaking loose. I had seen it with so many others, not me, Billy or Ketch, of course, but kids who would try and hang round with him, the way he could open them up with nothing more than a handful of words and that easy smile, friendly but remote, like an echo.

'It started getting pretty stupid... you know, the more we drank,' he continued. 'Have to down a glass of wine if you can't name three songs by Gordon Lightfoot... that sort of thing.'

'Who?'

He rolled his eyes, telling me that it wasn't important. 'Anyway,' he took a deep breath and went on, 'they were quite amazed at how much I seemed to know... ' And then he stopped and gazed at the ceiling for a moment as if a thought had just struck him. 'Come to think of it,' he muttered through a smile, 'I sort of surprised myself.' He shook himself back to the story, 'Anyway they were getting more pissed off the more pissed they got.'

He leant back on two legs of his chair and reached for the ceiling. 'Fills you up doesn't it, the bread?'

'Well how did you feel?' I asked, ignoring him.

'What do you mean?' he said, swallowing down a burp.

He was annoying me now and knew it. 'Weren't *you* pissed?'

'Yeah,' he admitted, 'just not as pissed as them. You should have seen them, Johnny,' he went over and began to fill the kettle, 'every pint that they had in the pub had to have a chaser with it, scotch mostly, as if they were a pair of hard-nosed Fleet Street journos or something.' He shook his head at the memory, 'At first I thought that they were trying to impress me, though I couldn't think why, but then I reckoned that they were just trying to outdo each other.'

We stood across the kitchen from each other, leaning against the worktops with our arms folded, waiting for the kettle and letting the bread soak up the beer.

'We started betting,' he went on, 'nothing much, 50ps, the odd pound.' He stared at the floor through narrowed eyes. 'But they were getting really cocky... ' His words fell away as they often did with Dave before he picked them up again, as if you were expected to follow the trail of his thoughts through the silence.

'Anyway I saw a chance,' he sighed. 'It was getting light by then and I'd had enough, I remember the light shining through the gap in the curtains.' He pointed towards the window in the next room. 'So I told them I bet them a hundred quid that I could answer any three questions to do with the Top Ten from 1970 until now.'

'Hundred quid! Where did you get hundred quid from?' I asked incredulously.

But then there was that easy smile.

'I didn't. I put my hand in pocket... and they just *assumed* I suppose... told you they thought I was some rich kid.' And his face broke into a grin..

I shook my head in disbelief. 'I can't believe they didn't ask to see the money.'

'And of course they didn't have it,' Dave said. 'So they offered a room here for year.'

He switched the whistling kettle off and began making the tea.

'So what were the questions?' I asked.

'Oh they were easy,' he said over his shoulder. He went to pass me my tea and then noticed the loaf of bread cradled in the crook of my broken arm and my good hand buried inside it. He tutted and rolled his eyes in mock irritation, 'Cripple,' he smirked and placed the mug beside me.

'What, *easy* easy or "music gimp" easy?' I laughed, in an attempt to get my own back. He had his back to me again, busy tidying the worktop, and when he turned I could see the mischief dancing in his eyes.

'Hmm.' He stroked his chin and stared at the ceiling. 'On the surface they did indeed appear complex,' he mused playfully, 'but to anyone with a shred of musical knowledge they were… '

'I'm sorry I fuckin' asked now!' I interrupted with a groan and drained my teacup and plopped it in the bowl in the sink. How many seventeen year olds spoke like that? I knew he was messing about, but still! If I hadn't known him so well I would have assumed that it was the influence of his new work environment, but being that articulate was one of the reasons that he *had* such a job at such a young age. The boy who was curious enough to find out who wrote or sang a song that he didn't even like, the boy who could see punk for what it really was: a movement, a statement, not just the music, the boy who could wade through the lyrics of a Gilbert O'Sullivan song and see just how deep they were, whilst the rest of us would just think of him as a bushy-haired ponce, but in the same breath praise Marc Bolan's corkscrew curls.

'Just tell me the *last* question, I can't face them all,' I muttered. 'Then we can go to bed.'

At the mention of the third question he gazed almost wistfully into space.

'Ah,' he sighed, 'now that really *was* a great song.'

'What,' I said, throwing my head back, 'don't tell me they asked you something about Bowie!'

'Badfinger.' He nodded and swallowed the last of his tea. 'They asked me who wrote Nilsson's "Without You". He shrugged as if the last piece of information had been unnecessary.

'Right,' I said neutrally. 'Bed?' And with lightning speed he picked up a dirty old tea towel and threw it in my face.

'If you could be anything in the world, what would you be?' What a bloody stupid question!

I had eaten so much bread that it clung to the roof of my mouth and lay like wet cardboard in the pit of my stomach. The effects of the beer had long since faded but still sleep wouldn't come. I had felt utterly exhausted when I had first sunk into the old brown armchair but as usual I couldn't seem to switch off my mind, instead I had just lay there until the fuzzy, warm glow of the alcohol had drained away, leaving behind the scratchy debris of a hangover until it felt as if my veins were full of sand.

I levered myself on my elbows from out of the armchair, made my way into the kitchen and from a glass obviously lifted from a pub gulped down two pints of water.

A familiar but unwelcome sensation crept through me, the feeling that the whole world except me was asleep. Standing in the kitchen tucked away at the back of the flat I couldn't even hear the distant drone of life lifting like heat from Oxford Street. Somewhere out there, over the rooftops and beyond, I knew that it would be as busy as if it were day, people stumbling in and out of clubs, taxis and buses cruising through the streets, the wall of flashing neon lights stacked around Piccadilly Circus. But knowing it was all out there, beneath the same silhouetted skyline, couldn't even comfort me the way that it would back home when I would listen to the trains rattling over the viaduct. It was crazy because the thought of them trundling off in the distance, up into town, had always soothed me in some strange way, but now that I was actually there, in the heart of their destination, I felt even more alienated. Stuff like that drove me crazy.

I plonked myself back down in the armchair but what was the point? Each position that I tried was more uncomfortable than the last. Dave had insisted that I take his bed but that was before I explained that the armchair would be more convenient, allowing me to rest my plaster cast upon the arm. He had slid the chair over so that I could put my legs up on the old sofa but it had all been to no avail, sleep would only come in pieces, splintered by veins of restlessness, as shattered as my arm. So I returned to the kitchen and, as quietly as I could, made myself a pot of tea, sat at the table by the living room window and idly watched as the falling temperature crept across the windscreens of the parked cars below and sparkled in the moonlight like crushed glass upon the black bin bags piled high upon the deserted pavements.

Whilst I had spent the end of the year and most of January lying in a hospital bed, the troubles that had been crippling the country had rumbled on and on, like a snowball gathering pace and growing bigger and bigger each day. I didn't usually take much notice of the news and would hardly ever turn the paper over and read the front, but this so-called *Winter of Discontent* seemed to affect everybody. Everywhere you turned you couldn't help but be aware of the sense of unrest that was sweeping across the land.

I had certainly heard the nurses talk about it, even Elaine had shown concern. Although she hadn't become as animated as her colleagues, I had seen the doubt weaving through the contours of her forehead like a sinking stone rippling across a pond.

So I suppose it was that that led me to finally flip the paper over and see what the hell was going on outside of my world, after all, what else was there to do other than lie there?

But of course it was all beyond me, written lines about the government "in a state of near-paralysis" and the talk of meetings of "heads from the industrial nations" left me inwardly groaning and reaching for my football magazines. Union, Union, Union: to me the word seemed to appear on every other line, that and the name of Callaghan, the Prime Minister. And if what they were saying were true, he'd been on holiday during it all. One particular headline had stuck with me: *Crisis! What Crisis?*

One day when Dave had come to visit I had asked what he made of it all, the strikes: the car industry, dustmen, lorry drivers, gravediggers, even the nurses. I had hoped that he could sum it all up for me, do what he often did and simplify it into a language that I would understand.

'About money,' he had said neutrally, running his hand through the curtain of orange hair flopping down in his face. 'They all want more… and the government don't wanna give in.' He had tossed the paper back on the bed. 'Or they don't want to be *seen* to be giving in,' he'd concluded. He'd waved a hand in the air. 'It's all bollocks, why do you wanna know, anyway?'

'No reason,' I'd shrugged.

That knowing smile had crept across his face. 'Your little nurse, is it?'

'Piss off!'

'You going to take on the might of the Labour party for her, are you?'

I hadn't answered, just gestured two fingers at him.

'I can see it now,' he'd continued, holding up imaginary headlines between his hands. *'Young Superstar "Saves" Britain's nurses from life of poverty.'*

That time he got my pillow, between his raised arms and straight in the face.

I sipped my tea and smiled at the memory. Hanging around with Dave, like so often in the past, was about the only thing that pacified my insecurities.

I must have drifted off some time after for I had the dream.

Except it was more like going back in time, for dreams have that sense of fantasy about them, no matter how clear they may be. But my memories of the match, just as with visions of *The Kick In*, were recollected to the tiniest detail. And it wasn't just when I had found sleep that it would come back, it could happen anywhere. I could be in the treatment room at the ground or at the hospital having a check up on my arm, sitting at home or on a train, standing at a bus stop or walking along the street and all of a sudden, without warning, I would be back there, Boxing Day '78, my first team debut.

It would start from the moment we had stepped out of the tunnel and onto the pitch…

… The crowd… the noise… bouncing off the four sides of the stadium like an echo trapped inside a box, round and round, over and over; it took your breath away, like rushing into the cold sea. And it seemed as if every pair of eyes in the place was fixed on me, they might have been aware of the other twenty-one players on the pitch but their gaze never really left me.

The warm-up settled me down a little, a good feel of the ball always starts the blood pumping, loosens my shoulders and gets my fingers twitching. I got a feel for the pitch too, firm on top but sure to cut up underfoot… But the crowd… the noise…

… I was focused now, concentrating on nothing but the game in front of me. I had what every keeper dreams of: an early touch. I had come out and collected a cross, nothing spectacular but far enough off my line to warrant a respectable round of applause.

What was there to be nervous about? I had done all this a thousand times before, trying to anticipate the danger before it surfaced, work out which foot their centre-forward favoured, all part of the goalkeeper's job.

But it wasn't the same, the game moved at such a furious pace, like nothing that I had ever encountered before, it didn't look that quick when you watched it on telly, the ball pinging about the pitch, and with such accuracy, at a speed that I had never imagined, playing against names that I have grown up with, players that I had pretended to be, faces in my sticker albums, was it all going to prove too much?… and the crowd… the noise…

'If you could be anything in the world that you wanted, what would you be?'

I shook my head wearily; I didn't feel up to Dave's mind-bending philosophy, not after two hours of restless sleep and a head that stilled hummed with the noises from the night before; the clinking of glasses and background drone of voices seemed to fill my skull like a fog.

Whether or not I had woken him with my awkward attempts to be quiet or he had found sleep as elusive as me, Dave had wandered into the front room long before the crack of dawn in an old Bowie T-shirt, the *Aladdin Sane* album cover, and his pants, looking more alert than somebody who had only just, a minute or two before, opened his eyes.

He had found me sitting in the armchair, staring morosely at the plaster around my arm, like a child cradling a dead pet.

'Can't sleep again?' he said, flopping down beside me. I screwed up my face and gave a half-hearted shrug for an answer. We sat there for a minute or two in silence, the both of us exhausted from lack of sleep and too tired to move or even talk. It was that easy, comfortable silence that we could often share between us, the kind that we had shared countless times over the years; lounging in his bedroom, over a cup of tea down at Lui's or lying idly beneath a fading summers' day at the park, words not necessary, as if there were an invisible telly in front of us that only the pair of us could see, and me with half my mind somewhere else…

… Half-time came and went and I had done okay, a couple of saves, a couple of crosses, nothing spectacular but enough, at least no goals conceded.

I stepped back out onto the pitch with my back still stinging from the heat of the approving slaps, the words of encouragement still ringing in my ears, the last lingering effects of the beer blown away, back out into the cold, bracing air. The floodlights were on now, sparkling in the December afternoon, the hot air from thousands of cheering mouths exploded in tiny puffs of smoke like gunfire in the stands… and the crowd… the noise…

From the corner of my eye I'd seen Dave look across at me for a moment, taking in my mood in an instant, and then from out of the blue he'd asked his schoolboy question.

'What? I dunno,' I mumbled, not really understanding what he meant… but that was nothing new.

Undeterred, he carried on. 'Me,' he said, staring up at the ceiling, 'I'd be a songwriter or maybe a producer for Bowie.'

'Right.'

'Couldn't be singer,' he said with a shake of his head. 'Can't imagine me performing on stage, I'm not really cut out to be a pop star.'

I was only half listening, what was the point? He was off and away now anyway, lost in the backstreets of his mind, no chance of following him even if I'd wanted to, all you could do when he was like this, I knew, was wait until he decided to resurface.

'We'd be like Elton John and Bernie Taupin,' he considered. 'Each dependent on the other…'

I was exhausted, my body like a shell, I felt like I didn't even have the strength to lift a spoon and yet my mind wouldn't allow me any peace; a part of it trying to keep up with Dave and the rest wouldn't let me forget the match, kept running through every minute, every kick, every save, reel by reel in my head…

… And then after a goalless first-half; like buses through town, two in two minutes. The first for us, out of nothing, what with Fulham in possession, but then, after a tackle that we had no right to win, and within a heartbeat,

333

defence became attack. The commitment at that level is almost frightening, every player on the move every second, on the ball, off the ball, making angles, opening up and closing down spaces. In a strange way, it must be easier to play in, what with so many players offering so many options, every one of your team mates working their socks off to help.

And then there was a quick one-two in and around their box and within the blink of an eye the ball is resting in the corner of their net... one-nil, one- nil! They cheered... and the crowd... the noise...

'But wait a minute!' Dave's sudden gasp brought me back. 'What the hell am I talking about?' He was holding his chin like some pondering professor, but his roguish grin told me that it was all an act and that there was something more to come.

'What the hell *are* you talking about?' I said, impatient for him to reach his point.

'How could *I* help Bowie?' Although I knew it was all for my benefit, he looked crestfallen, his face crumpled in confusion. He had my attention now and of course, knew it.

'What do mean?' I tried to sound casual and not a little bored but curiosity seeped into my every word.

'What about Visconti or Eno?' He was staring at the ceiling as if I didn't exist, nothing more than a pattern on the wallpaper. He was scolding his own stupidity, his own ineptitude at not seeing whatever it was that was so obviously clear to him now. He slapped the sides of his head with open palms, berating himself 'How could I *possibly* help Bowie to write songs?' he moaned.

My head ached from the lack of sleep. 'I dunno.' My voice was nothing more than a croak, responding to his thinking out loud out of habit.

'He doesn't need any help!' he cried, jumping to his feet and scaring me half to death.

'Everything he does is brilliant!' His face wide-eyed in amazement, the actor in him rising to the surface. 'What could I give him, what could *I* add to his songs, his lyrics, his music that he hasn't already got?'

And then I saw what he was trying to do, the reason behind his little pantomime, and I couldn't help but smile to myself. For only Dave could make a point in such a way; a way that was so overly dramatic and drawn out but yet so oddly clear.

He slumped back down beside me wearing his mock resignation like a clown in his make-up. 'Guess I'll have to think of something else,' he sighed, resting his head on his knuckles, and then a moment later, after just enough time to allow the impact of his little play to really hit home, for he knew that I had got it, he performed his last lines: 'Just imagine… ' he said, rising to his feet and making for his bedroom, 'some bastards are so lucky that they're already living their dream, already have it, there… ' he held out his hand, 'in the palm of their hands.' And just as he was about to disappear into the darkness of his room, he turned, almost comical in his old T-shirt and pants, and stopped as if a thought had just occurred to him, and I could just make out that thin, easy smile in the gloom; the Thin White Duke himself. 'Bit like you really.'

… But then we go and commit the cardinal sin, we had let our concentration slip, and within a minute of scoring, they get a corner… and from our throw-in! And it had been an out-swinger, too far for me to go and catch. It sailed over everybody's head… all except one bugger… their centre-half who stole in right at the back… and the moment that he had headed it I knew that I'd been beaten, that it was a goal, that you could have told me where the ball was going before he had even made contact and I still wouldn't have reached it. He had caught it somewhere around his temple and the glancing blow had sent it spinning unstoppably round into the top right-hand side of my goal. And I had had full-backs guarding my posts like always, the fella at the back was even an ex-international, twenty-odd caps for Wales… but he was never going to reach it either, not even if the bugger had used his

hand. Down behind the other goal the Fulham fans were celebrating, cheering the equalizer, singing the praises of their big, burley centre-back. From where I was standing, no more than two feet off my goal-line, the other end of the pitch seemed miles away, their cheering detached, like distant thunder. Even though it was only a minute or so ago it seemed as if their joy was happier than ours; somehow better. And there was nowhere for me to hide… because that's all I'd wanted to do, I knew the stand behind me was still full but apart from the odd groan I couldn't hear a thing and nothing on earth was going to make me turn round and look at them, at those hundreds of blank faces I imagined all staring, accusing me… the crowd… the silence…

'Let me take you by the hands and lead you through the streets of London…' That song kept playing in my head. *'Have you seen the old man in the closed down market picking up the papers with his worn out shoes…'* The words rolling over and over again, continually spinning round on the turntable of my mind. *'In his eyes you see no pride, hands hanging loosely by his side…'*

There were plenty of songs that accompanied me on my more and more frequent trips up into town, I couldn't help but find Gerry Rafferty's "Baker Street" starting up every time I went to Dave's, for instance, but on that freezing cold January morning, before the dawn had even broken over the streetlights and frosted windscreens, that old folk anthem about an old tramp shuffling through the streets of London to fill the emptiness of his life seemed to suit me perfectly.

Not for the first time I had found myself in that ludicrous situation where my dreams had kept me awake again. Each time I awoke from another small pocket of sleep, the real nightmare had crept a little closer, the giant clock above the goal at the far end of the ground had ticked a little nearer that fatal, unavoidable moment.

I knew that I had to break the pattern, to drag my tormented, sleep-deprived body up and out the door and try and let the raw winter dawn numb the sleep channels of my mind... and numb the fear.

I pulled the collars of Dave's denim jacket up around my neck and buried the bottom half of my face beneath the neck of his old grey sweatshirt, breathing in his familiar smell. Wearing the jacket that he had always looked so cool in steadied my nerves a little. I knew it was stupid, and that there was hardly anybody around anyway, but I found myself imagining people looking, saying to themselves, *'Hey, that kid's wearing Dave's jacket! He must know him!'* I had picked them both off the rickety old coat stand by the front door, burying myself beneath the layers in an attempt to shield the rest of me from the cold. And then a thought had occurred to me... that without even lifting a finger or uttering a word he was doing what he always seemed to do... helping me.

On and on I walked, and with what seemed like every passing minute London grew busier; the traffic, even at that ungodly hour, grew steadier, buses multiplying like flies, buzzing up and down the roads, their yellow blocks of light already filling up, newspaper and delivery vans on their rounds and even the odd milk float rattling by, which for some reason looked as if it didn't belong in the hustle and the bustle of the city, something that I just naturally associated with the suburbs; like the distant sounds of the trains and Dave's Bowie albums.

I had no idea where I was going, simply followed my feet along the ice-covered pavements, but somewhere in the cycle my brain must have relayed a message to them, slipped it down the back alleys of my consciousness while my mind was still trying to shake off the suffocating web of the nightmare, for before I even had a chance to realise it, I was standing outside the passage way of Heddon Street.

I stood there for a moment sinking further beneath the collars of Dave's jacket, arms wrapped tightly around my chest even though I no longer felt the cold now that the blood was pumping back through my body. I gazed through the gloom of the archway at the phone box at the far end, half expecting to see Bowie or even Dave peering from behind it's tiny glass windows, and then, again on auto pilot, found myself staring vacantly up at the infamous K.WEST sign like some drugged up Ziggy freak.

What was I doing? This was Dave's world not mine!

Or maybe that was really it, the reason I had ended up there without even realising it, at a place where I felt a sense of comfort, a place that held only fond memories, no disappointment, no heartbreak… no sense of hopelessness.

Maybe *I* wanted to be Bowie as much as Dave… maybe I wanted to be Dave as much as the other kids. Maybe I just didn't want to be me.

I still couldn't get used to it, it just didn't look right, the K.WEST sign. It was the first thing that you saw the moment that you entered the side street, it leapt out, demanding your attention. I don't even think you had to particularly be a Bowie fan, just of a certain age, that album cover was that much a part of the early '70s; as much as Don Revie's Leeds, as much as Donny Osmond and *Top of the Pops*, as much as Radio 1 and breakfast shows with Tony Blackburn, as much as *Dad's Army* on a Saturday night and other people's dad's down the pub on a Sunday lunchtime, as much as wondering why you're not like any of them.

It was the colour of it. I still couldn't get used to it actually being white instead of the aluminous yellow portrayed on the *Ziggy* album cover, I'd seen it two or three times now and each time it took me by surprise, I couldn't help but feel a sense of disappointment, as if I'd been cheated out of something.

There was a stack of empty cardboard boxes beside the door though and they went some way to authenticating the mood. I dug out the biggest one I could find, kicked one side down, leant it against the wall and sat inside it. And the strangest thing happened... I fell asleep. Right there out in the freezing city dawn, surrounded by the debris of yesterday, curled up like a park tramp in the sanctuary of my cardboard box... *'Have you seen the old man who walks the streets of London...'*

My body was still numb from last night's beer and the lack of sleep and I felt strangely cosy. When I closed my eyes I could hear my blood pumping through my body, probably from the walk, I guessed. Up and down my arms and legs, through my body and throbbing in my head. The world outside my box sailed further away as I drifted deeper into the whirlpool of shadows clouding in on me, the early morning traffic: buses, taxis, milk floats and all faded like dying echoes. The smell of the dawn, the grime from the pavements, petrol and the pollution of the city became overpowered by the unmistakeable odour of damp cardboard, it enveloped me like a warm blanket...

... I was glad Danny was on, I thought to myself, two kids from the same school team making their debuts in the same match... against each other! Life... you just never know... and then him coming, baring down on me... he'd timed his run to split-second precision as usual and beaten the off-side trap... I felt a wave of pride for my old team-mate, couldn't help myself, even though he was about to try and wreck my debut... he was on the edge of the box, closing in fast, that hunched up bustling way of his with the ball at his feet... they had no chance of catching him, too quick... but as I came off my line to meet him I had an advantage, an ace up my sleeve... for I knew which way he was going to go... knew with all my heart that he would go to cut across me and favour his right foot... Of course Danny knew that I knew this and so just maybe he would attempt to stay on his left or shoot early even... but I didn't entertain the idea for more than a fleeting moment, I had never been more certain that Danny would stick to what he knew best, to follow a path of execution that had served him so well over the years... never been more certain of anything in my life... I had almost felt sorry for him... about to rob him of the moment that every debutant dreams

of, whilst fuelling the glory of my own... And then he was upon me, his frame blocking everything else from my vision... he had filled out, I thought to myself, they must have had him in the gym lifting weights... I had feigned to my left but in the blink of an eye had sprung to my right... and just as I had expected the ball was there to meet me... With the tips of my outstretched fingers I had scooped the ball off Danny's toe and away to safety... There was no time to admire my handiwork though, I had to get up on my feet and back in goal... But I couldn't seem to move, my whole body felt numb... I looked up at the sky, as dark and forbidding as a stormy sea... heads appeared around the edges of my vision, looking down at me, the faces of players... I heard their voices but couldn't make out what they were saying... there was a burning sensation somewhere at the end of my arm, it felt as if my hand was on fire... everything blurred over, I couldn't hear a thing... And then I was on my own, drifting in my own sea of blackness... no crowd... no noise...

CHAPTER TWENTY - FIVE

February 1979

The next few weeks passed by unspectacularly, everyday as monotonous and colourless as the last: leaving home in the morning, shutting the door with a sense of relief, shutting the door on the eerie, empty silence. It was only a little terraced house, identical to the rows of front doors on either side, but every time I turned the key and stepped into the silence, each room seemed to echo like footsteps in the old church.

I would make my way to the ground, burdened not with the weight of a kit bag but with the heavy knowledge that I couldn't train, the one thing that had always kept me from driving myself mad, without it I thought I would explode.

The spirit of being all in it together, the camaraderie of the lads, running until your lungs hurt, the jumping for endless crosses until my legs felt like jelly, scrabbling from one side of the goal to the other during shot-stopping drills, getting covered in mud, all of it never failed to leave me with a strange feeling of contentment. It was almost masochistic, I would be physically drained, knackered, yet totally relaxed. It was like a drug, I suppose, for a short time all the anxieties that I carried around with me would be purged by exercise, my body cleansed of all the hang-ups that clung to me, washed away in a sea of hard-earned sweat.

I could forget everything when I trained; good or bad, it didn't matter, it would all just melt away to the back of my mind. I couldn't have thought about anything even if I wanted too, nothing else mattered. I could have been anywhere in the world at any time or on any day, for when I trained the world consisted of only me, the coaches and the lads.

Growing up I had always thought that each day carried with it its own special atmosphere. Like Friday nights and Saturday mornings always arrived with an air of anticipation about them; people stepped lighter, they walked and talked with more consequence, every song on the radio seemed to be written for or about the weekend. Whereas, conversely, Mondays, no matter how sunny or bright they might be, were always tinged with a sepia-toned blandness, people walked around with the weight of the world on their shoulders. And the radio didn't seem to play anything but lovesick ballads and hollow disco songs that sounded as if they had been recorded in someone's bathroom and always seemed to remind me of people I didn't like.

But when I was out there training, whether I could gaze up at a cloudless blue sky from a bunch of sit-ups or had to close my eyes against the driving rain, it didn't matter. Not even if the ground was frozen bone-hard and numbed my knees and elbows, because of jarring pain more than the cold, the time or the day lost its meaning, faded into the background like the sound of Mum's kitchen radio.

At least by going to the ground for my treatment I was spared the frustration of having to see the lads out on the training pitches, or being subjected to the roars of their laughter reverberating from the changing rooms. Instead I had the lonely sound of my footsteps to accompany me through the strangely empty corridors of the stadium.

I had been down to the training ground a few times to see the lads, say hello and watch them go through their paces, good for team spirit supposedly, although it wasn't any good for mine. They were very nice and all, the lot of them, slapping me on the back, wishing me well and trying to write rude jokes and wise cracks on my plaster, but when you're not playing, when you're injured, well you're just not part of it, it's simple as that.

All the stories and the one-liners don't seem funny, it's as if you're a kid again, allowed to stay up and watch Dave Allen on TV but not having a clue what's so funny about stories about God or seeing him dressed up as a vicar. All the talk and debate about the last game have nothing to do with you, not if you didn't play any part of it, you nod your head thoughtfully or make the effort to crack your face into a smile at the right moment but it's no good, without the other faces to guide you you'd never see the punch line coming, your humour and your spirit are as strained and broken as your body.

Every day, as I made my way to the ground to see the club physiotherapist, as I sat staring out from the top of the bus watching the town slip slowly by - the park, Lui's, the train station, out past the Crown and into the maze of narrow streets - as we trundled ever closer to the ground, I wondered if the country would ever be the same again. The mountains of rubbish that seemed to be piled round every lamppost or down every alleyway didn't seem to be getting any smaller, even though there was talk of the strikes coming to an end.

I would try and comfort myself with the fact that I wasn't missing many games due to the fact that the pitches were frozen solid most of the time; the cold weather and the strikes, it was as if the whole of the country was seizing up. There was a rumour going round at the club that one of the lads hadn't been able to bury his granddad because the gravediggers were on strike but I reckoned that it had more to do with the fact that the ground was as hard as concrete.

By early February, by the time Ian Dury, of all people, had reached number one and Sid Vicious had been found dead in a New York hotel room, I was down to visiting the physio only twice a week. At first I had thought this was great news, at the very

343

least I wouldn't have to deal with the frustration of travelling up to a virtually empty ground every day. There was something almost haunting about being there when all the stands were empty and the place didn't have that match day atmosphere pumping through it, it was like going to a pub with your mates and not being allowed to drink. But it didn't take long for the reality of time on my hands to sink in, the very first morning that I awoke knowing that I didn't have to get up it dawned on me that I had the whole of the day to fill. Fourteen or fifteen long, unscheduled, unsupervised hours loomed ahead. It seemed as daunting as looking out to sea as a kid.

The first thing I did was to turn Mum's kitchen radio on. But not even the sound of Debbie Harry pining about her "Heart of Glass" could manage to fill the emptiness that seemed to hollow out every room in the house. It was if the silence was taunting me, I knew that there was nothing really there, that it was as real as holding up a seashell to your ear and hearing the sea, but still I couldn't escape the feeling of being mocked.

Inevitably I ended up at Lui's, although it was out of desperation more than choice. My last visit had unsettled me more than usual and of course I could just imagine what the boss and coaching staff at the club would make of me starting each day with a plate of eggs and bacon instead of the bowl of porridge that they would insist upon, and besides... I couldn't even hold a knife and fork yet! I had to ask Lui if he would take the plate back behind the counter and cut it up for me. And of course he had made such a big fuss, cursing and berating himself the way that only Italians seem to be able to do. I could feel the heat billowing like clouds on my cheeks as the rest of his customers, mostly builders, glanced enquiringly round in my direction. That had been the whole reason that I'd asked him to take it back, so that he could do it discreetly. I would have hidden behind my newspaper, I thought to myself, if I could have held the bleeding thing up with two hands!

As for Jenny, I hadn't seen or even spoken to her for nearly two weeks now, not since the night that she had finally demanded to know my true feelings for Elaine, I had stood at the bus stop and watched her bus melt into the night, staring like a moron, until the shape of the roof had finally faded from view and the lights from the top deck had slowly extinguished like the flame of a match. I could still taste the venom in her voice that night.

'Did you fancy her?' she had sniped.

I had rolled my eyes and groaned.

'Well did you?' she had ordered. As hard as I had tried she had begun to get to me. I regretted the words the second that I had said them.

'Yes.' It was as if they knew they shouldn't be out, tiny clouds of expelled air escaping from the safety of my thoughts, out in the cold night air where they could do damage.

'I mean no! I… Oh I don't know!' My hands dropped to my sides in an expression of defeat. Why is it so hard!' I thought to myself Why do I *make* it so hard!

'Oh, Johnny!' Her voice had meant to carry the threat of anger, I imagined, but it came out like some kind of childish squeal. I could feel her stare though, burning into my skull, from out of the corner of my eye I could tell that she was all puffed out, arms crossed over her chest in defiance. For a moment I had thought that she wasn't going to say anymore, that maybe she was lost for words after my stumbling confession. Part of me had even hoped that she might storm off and give me time to regroup but then I heard her exhale deeply, the kind of noise that a boiling kettle might make and once again she had squealed.

'Oh, Johnny, how could you!'

'But I haven't done… ' But she had cut me off.

'Did you really think she'd be interested in *you*?' She had spat. Although they had been designed to cut deep, her words had lacked that razor-sharp edge. I had looked up from my feet and seen her crumple a little but when our eyes had met she had regained her resolve.

'You think that because you're name's been in the papers lately and a few people recognise you, you're irresistible do you?' I had been waiting for that. She was referring to earlier that evening when a couple of boys had stopped us in the street, they hadn't asked for an autograph or been in awe of me in any way, they had simply wanted to confirm what they thought. 'You John Chalmers?' they had asked through a mouthful of gum and attitude. 'The Southfields keeper?'

Jen had found it amusing at the time, especially at my obvious discomfort, taking the piss, fluttering her eyelashes and pretending to swoon, but now the whole episode had lost its innocence now, was nothing more than ammunition to be used against me.

At the time, I could tell, that she had been touched by my awkwardness, at my lack of self-image. 'You'll have to get used to that sort of thing,' she had told me, her face creased with the kind of concern that girls wear when they come across a lost puppy or something.

But later, as we had walked the rest of the way to her bus stop in silence, I thought to myself, bus stops, it seemed as though most of the turning points in our relationship had taken place in bus stops. She had stamped her feet and hugged herself against the cold. 'Bet I've missed it now.' She had shivered, her words colder than the weather. I had peered down the street, almost willing the thing to appear as if by magic, but there had been no sign of a bus, just the odd car trundling by, and the sound of their engines meant that you could dismiss them as a bus long before they even came in to view.

Across the road from us a mountain of rubbish had lain in the opposite bus stop. Black bin liners and soggy cardboard boxes had spilled across the pavement and down into the gutter, it had seemed as if the whole of London had become one giant rubbish tip.

Whilst Jen had shivered I hadn't seemed to feel the cold, had been numbed by the frosty atmosphere between us. Why can't I say what I meant? I thought to myself, put my thoughts or feelings into words, why am I always left with this screaming voice ringing in my ears, the words that I want to say drowning out everything else, only no other bugger apart from me can hear them.

My arm had ached like nothing on earth, the tips of my fingers almost blue from the cold but I had made no attempt to warm them...what was the point? I couldn't feel the bloody things.

'Oh, thank God for that!' Jen's voice had cut through my gloom as a bus, with the lights of its top deck shining like some kind of approaching spaceship, had swung round the corner and, mercifully for both of us, into view.

Did that mean that it was over? I didn't have a clue, all I knew was that one moment I would have swallowed my tongue if she had phoned and yet half an hour later I would find myself fighting the urge to pick up the phone and call her. And of course it didn't help with Lui asking after her.

Bloody Hell, I thought to myself, I've come here to try and forget about nagging things like Jenny. I had come to read or talk about football or watch peoples faces as they trudged this way and that past the window, I hadn't come to try and work things out, have them plonked right in front of me in the shape of queries and questions, served up right under my nose along with my plate of artery-clogging bacon and eggs.

It was funny, he couldn't have been more proud if I had been his own son when he had first discovered that I was going out with Jen, relieved that I was seeing a nice, decent young girl with an admirable career ahead of her, a girl from the right end of town. Of course Jen or her friends didn't share the same intimacy with Lui as us, how could they? But like all the kids in town, he seemed to know all of them at some level or another, it had always amazed me.

He would sit there opposite me in the chair that Dave had always sat upon, tea towel folded in half lengthways over his shoulder with what I knew was genuine concern showing on his face. He looked older now, I thought, as if the years had finally caught up with him. The olive-coloured skin on his face was as creased and lined as a piece of old leather and his eyes seemed a little duller, as if the bulb inside was slowly wearing out. His hands too, they were, I noticed, the hands of an old man, thick veins protruded like worms just beneath the surface of wrinkled skin and I couldn't be sure but I thought I noticed them shake a little, nothing drastic, just a faint tremor, but it shocked me nonetheless.

A few days before we had had a conversation that I just hadn't been able to shake off. It was the reason I had returned so soon to try and prove to myself, and to Lui, that what he had said, what he had seen within me, hadn't unnerved me as much as perhaps he'd thought.

The truth, though, was something completely different. I hadn't been able to think of much else, his perception of me had been alarming. He had, as they say, read me like a book. But the thing that I had found so frightening was that what Lui had perceived had been so obvious to him, and yet I couldn't have seen it if I had stood staring into a mirror all day. If I had been honest with myself, if I had ever had the courage or possessed the integrity to look hard enough, it might have been different, I might have been able to see what was clearly so apparent to everyone else, that I was still just a boy pretending to be a man, playing a part that was simply too big for me to handle.

I had been sitting there on my usual chair staring out through the window, through the heavy condensation, at town; at darkest suburbia, at the passing traffic, at the passers-by, at nothing. When Lui had appeared like the shop keeper in *Mr Benn* and sat down opposite me. And it was weird because I would find that a part of me would groan inwardly at the intrusion and yet another part would welcome the comfort of attention. He would ask how I was and inquire after Mum and Dave, he would even ask after Billy despite himself. And his advice, when he chose to dispense it, was never anything more than obvious but I would appreciate it nonetheless.

'You know you-ah problem Johnny?' he'd asked rhetorically, 'You too nice is what.'

Confusion must have clouded over my face as I struggled to see how being too nice could be a problem.

'You think they all need a part of you.' He reached out, grabbing here and there at imaginary objects.

'Whenever you come in,' he had continued, 'you say to me that you gotta meet Dave or that you gotta to meet Billy.' He had held out his hands and looked from one to the other as if he had the pair of them perched in his upturned palms, like a couple of garden gnomes.

He had looked for a moment as if he were worried that he had said too much, sinking back into his chair with a heavy sigh. For a while we had sat in silence, I had stared, like I always did, out the window. A group of people had been looking down the road in the direction of town, craning their necks and standing on tiptoes to get a better view, the sound of a police siren had grown louder and louder, rising out of the distance like slowly turning up the volume on the telly. I had had no idea what they were looking at and the sight of the ever-growing crowd had aroused barely a shred of curiosity, I had been too busy trying not to see anything.

He had taken a moment and wiped already clean hands on his tea towel, drying carefully between each finger, and then leant closer, resting a hand on top of my plaster. 'I don't mean to upset you, Johnny,' he had said in a whispered voice.

I had smiled thinly. 'You haven't, Lui,' I had said reassuringly. There had been a crowd forming on the other side of the road as well by now, people pointing and talking to one another in animated voices. I couldn't be sure but it had sounded as if there may well have been more than one police car out there. Across the table Lui had attempted to stifle a cough, politely trying to recapture my attention. I had been aware of the change in mood, it was as if something had been tightened, the air almost squeaking from the strain. I hadn't been angry or upset with him, just shocked at how perceptive he was about my insecurities. Was I really that transparent?

He had shuffled in his chair and whipped the tea towel off his shoulder, I had sensed that he was about to say something else, that no matter how uncomfortable it may be for us, it was his duty. He had started to wipe the table down in great sweeping movements from side to side, gathering the courage, I had guessed, to continue. But just as he had looked up and cleared his throat for a second time, four workmen in donkey jackets had breezed through the door laughing and joking and calling over good-naturedly for Lui to get his "eyetie arse" back behind the counter and to put the kettle on.

Two days later there was a knock on the door. 'Sid's dead,' muttered Billy as he shuffled in. I closed the front door behind him and followed him into the kitchen. Without a word I busied myself with making the tea, I heard him pull out a chair and slump himself heavily down as if he'd been pushed.

It had been three days now since the death of Billy's hero, Sid Vicious, had appeared in the papers. He had slipped into oblivion in a drug-fuelled haze like so many rock stars before him, crushed by the very thing that had elevated him to such height... the weight of fame.

After that we sat there for a while drinking tea and joking around and making small talk, about birds, football, anything and nothing, with me trying to put off what I knew was coming, what had been building for months, piling up and festering inside him like the mountains of rubbish on the city streets. Each time I sensed that he was shaping up to say something I would come out with some other piece of irrelevance.

But I couldn't put it off all night and besides, Billy's thoughtfulness would only stretch so far.

'I'm gonna go at the weekend, J,' he told me, spurting it out in between bouts of my empty talk. I didn't respond at first, turned instead and stretched my legs lazily out across the kitchen floor as if he'd told me nothing more than he had finished his cup of tea. But in reality I could feel the panic rise inside, it took all my willpower to keep it down, like trying to swallow bile gathering in the back of your throat after drinking too fast, desperately trying not to puke in front of everyone.

I took a deep breath and ran the index finger from my good hand around the rim of my teacup. This isn't how it's supposed to be, I thought to myself, it wasn't how mates said goodbye, not blokes... not us! It should be hearty slaps on the back, getting pissed and sharing stories about the scrapes that we had been in since whenever, not all strangled feelings and delicate silences.

'I mean,' he went on, dipping his fingers in his cup and flicking the dredges at me in an attempt to get my attention as I stared vacantly into the darkness out of the window, but I knew that he was really trying to shake me, shake the pair of us free from this feeling of oppression that hung in the air, this feeling that had seemed to rise from inside, oozed from our pores like sweat. 'What have I got to stay 'ere for?'

Still I didn't reply, instead I pushed myself to my feet with a huff and busied myself with the washing-up in the sink. I stared out of the kitchen window at the tiny strip of garden but all I could see was my own distorted reflection looking back at me. If I were to turn the light out, I thought absurdly, and stand here in the dark, I would be able to see it clearer, not that it would be much to look at: a faded patch of grass that has never really recovered from the abuse it took when I was a kid, a shabby old fence at the back and an equally shabby coal shed to my left with maybe the shadow of a cat perched on its roof. Ridiculous thoughts like that always popped into my head at the most inappropriate moments, maybe it was a defence mechanism, who knows? My way of not having to face something that I knew would defeat me. And then, quite suddenly and without warning, even to myself, I turned sharply and snapped. 'And where you gonna go then?'

The ferocity in my voice shocked even me and for a moment we sat and stood staring at each other before I turned back and started slamming clean mugs and cutlery down upon the draining board in a shower of foam and bubbles. 'I mean the thing is,' I persisted, I was annoyed now, driven by fear, 'you keep saying you're gonna fuck off, but where the fuck are you gonna go!' I dried my hands on a tea towel and threw that down on the draining board with an equal amount of gusto. 'What the fuck are you gonna do?' I turned to face him, about as annoyed with him as I'd ever been in my life, even more than the time I had grabbed him by the throat, because back then I hadn't really been annoyed with him, only myself, and we had both known it, but this… this was different. I was angry, annoyed, irritated, but most of all I was *scared*… and, of course, we both knew that as well.

'Thumbing down the first bus and jumping off at fuckin' Stratford or somewhere, ain't running away you know!' I had gone too far and really didn't want to care but I turned back around and dipped my hands back into the bowl of dirty water and pretended to wash up non-existent crockery. I heard the fizz of his breath as he inhaled deeply, the sound of his own mug slamming down on the table, but still he didn't say anything, not a word. I could just make out, in the blurred reflection of the window, the rise and fall of his shoulders as he struggled to contain the retaliation that I suspected must have been seething away inside of him. Still, I knew that he wouldn't retaliate, wouldn't say a word and, of course, that only made it worse. For it meant that he cared, cared more than the pair of us were comfortable with, and that would never do, for what then?

I continued to stare solemnly out into the night, not wanting to turn round and put us both in an uncomfortable position, but the problem wasn't behind me, it wasn't with Billy or Lui or Jen or Mum, it wasn't the fear of losing my football, it wasn't even with Dave; it was with me, it was always with me. And if I'd only had the sense to listen to what I already knew instead of running round and round trying in vain, always in vain, to hide from the voice that whispered constantly in my head, my own voice, I could have saved myself and maybe everyone I had ever really cared about a lot of pain and grief.

And then out of nowhere I had an idea. Rounding on him once again, he must have suspected another volley of abuse, but instead I asked brightly, 'How do you fancy going to Wembley?'

Confusion stared back at me. 'What?' he snapped.

'Tonight,' I nodded, warming to the idea. 'England v Northern Ireland... the European qualifier.'

CHAPTER TWENTY - SIX

February 1979

I couldn't believe what a crowd there was, 92,000 was the official figure reported in the papers the next day. For a European qualifier against a supposedly inferior opposition I thought it was a pretty impressive turn out. You get a feeling for that sort of thing, I mean it's not as if you can do a quick head count or anything, you just know it in your guts. But then Billy had pointed out that half the "micks" that were there as he put it, probably all lived within ten miles of Wembley.

'How can you tell anyway?' he had said mockingly as we made our way slowly along Wembley Way. He was back to his usual self now, now that we had had a few of pints, at least three in The Torch on the corner, that promise of mayhem and mischief glinting in the corner of his eyes.

'You just can, can't you?' I had shrugged.

All the way up to the Twin Towers it was packed solid with shuffling bodies, I'd never seen it so busy, except of course in the year of Fulham's cup final. On the few times that I had visited Wembley, gaps would emerge sporadically created by the different speeds that people would be making their way up to the stadium, but on that night, just the same as the '75 final, you couldn't have slipped a lamppost between you and the person in front. Mostly it was a sea of red, white and blue hats and scarves on the move, the countries' colours wrapped around necks and pulled firmly down on heads keeping out the cold February night. But there was plenty of green on show as well, on the odd occasion you would see a solitary Irish hat or scarf but generally there was group of them together, weaving their way up the walkway like giant clusters of seaweed.

We didn't have any tickets but of course Billy had known just the man to see in The Torch and had returned from the toilets with a pair of tickets in his hand and a grin that looked as if it belonged on the face of the devil himself. A minute or so later, when the tout that had accompanied Billy had made his way back to his seat at the bar, he had looked to me a little greyer about the cheeks than before. I had tried to tell myself that it must have been the beer but I knew that I was only trying to kid myself.

'How much do I owe you?' I had asked.

But he had just waved his hand indifferently and told me, 'We'll sort it out later.' But I knew that he wouldn't want to discuss it again.

By the time Bob Latchford scored his first and England's second goal, most of the desperation that had filled me earlier had drained away and I was feeling a lot better. And we didn't even see it!

We were still in a bar below the stands, leaning against one of the many giant pillars that ran around the circumference of the stadium, supporting the stands above like the rib cage of a whale.

The roar from outside that resonated through the roof like thunder told us that we had missed an early second-half goal, and that it was obviously our second. There were a few groans and effing and blinding from fellow stragglers like ourselves but Billy just shrugged.

'We're gonna win anyway,' he said unexcitedly and returned to his pint. My first reaction was one of complete shock, like someone jumping out when you least expect it and scaring you half to death. This followed by a wide-eyed panic that wanted to drive me back up into the cauldron of the stands and catch the replay.

But of course there wasn't one. Despite the spine-tingling atmosphere, this was a part of experiencing a live game that I could never get used to, that and the lack of commentary.

'Betchya it's Keegan again,' proposed Billy.

I thought about it for a moment and was just about to suggest that it might well be Stevie Coppell when it suddenly hit me that it didn't matter one little bit, that it could have been Peter bloody Shilton, brought on and put up front, for all I cared. I mean the result was a forgone conclusion anyway, just a case of how many, surely? But, more importantly, watching the match, cheering on England, wasn't even the reason that we were there.

I had to admit that as went scrabbling around for convenient distractions, going to Wembley to watch England was a pretty good one. But still, it wasn't going to change anything, even I wasn't that stupid. It wasn't going to stop Billy from leaving town… from leaving me. It wasn't about to extinguish this sense of… *end* that seemed to be embedded within me. It had taken root so long ago that I could no longer control it now, like unwelcome weeds in a flowerbed it popped up in virtually every thought that entered my head; mysterious, shapeless shadows ready to cling to every thought or daydream that my mind was willing to produce.

So by the time Latchford grabbed his second, and England's fourth and final goal with just over twenty-five minutes still left to play, I had found, all to grimly, that the awe of the occasion could no longer hold me.

There would have been a time, not so very long before this, when the act of standing upon the open terraces of the greatest stadium in the country watching England would have been just about the best thing, other from actually being out there on the pitch itself, that I could have possibly wished for. But now they were yearnings that felt as if they belonged to somebody else.

I mean what could be better? Standing there among the crowd, with the Twin Towers looming above in the night sky, the floodlights shining down on the most famous pitch in the world, a playing surface as green and as flat as a snooker table. We had squeezed our way right down to the front, so that all that separated me and Billy from the pitch was the cinder running track and arc behind the goal. We were so low that you could actually make out the camber of the pitch as it curved ever so slightly away to where the goal at the far end reminded me of a ship passing by on the horizon. We could see the expressions on the players' faces, a feature that wouldn't have been a big deal if we were down at Fulham or at Southfields, where you were packed in so close to the action, but it was something that I regarded as a real treat in the huge spaces of Wembley. The same with making out the clouds of steam rising off their backs, watching their chests rise and fall as they recovered during dead ball moments, it should all have been enough to absorb me.

I wanted to let the roar of the crowd drown out the tide of insecurity rising within me, to let every drop of atmosphere wash over me. The walkway along the front of the royal box where so many great players had passed by, shaking hands with the Queen, and of course the steps. How many times as a child had I sat glued to the telly, watching in wide-eyed fascination as players had dragged their energy-sapped bodies up those steps to collect their medals; names and faces that were as familiar to me as classmates, as I saw them every day in the pages of comics and sticker albums.

But none of it seemed to be able to sink in, not even my greatest pleasure could hold me, the procedure of studying the goalkeepers' every move. I had been mesmerised at first. I was, after all, in the presence of Pat Jennings and Ray Clemence, arguably the best two goalkeepers in the world and two of my biggest heroes. And they made it look so easy with their handling, rising to collect crosses with what seemed an effortless elegance. To me they were as graceful as any of those ice skaters or gymnasts you would see on a Saturday afternoon sometimes on *World of Sport*.

Studying keepers had made me appreciate the strength and agility in other sports such as gymnastics and skating, but where they lost me by dressing in tights, vests and outrageously colourful and glitzy costumes, the likes of Jennings and Clemence epitomised to me what it was to be a real man. How could I ever possibly hope to compare with such masculinity and professionalism? You wouldn't see men like these passed out in the back streets of London at the crack of dawn.

'Shall we piss off before the rush?' suggested Billy with barely ten minutes left to play. Already people were beginning to file out in an effort to beat the rush at the final whistle.

'We can be first to the bar then before the rest of 'em.'

'What,' I rolled my eyes in boredom, 'The Torch you mean?'

He broke into a grin. 'Nah!' he said. 'Don't think we should go back there for a while.'

In other circumstances I would have protested, but the match was won, two more valuable points, and it wasn't as if I'd even paid for my ticket and I was pretty sure that Billy hadn't either, although I never did find out. So we turned and followed the growing line of early leavers back up and out through the exit, and at the last moment before we disappeared below the stands I turned and had one last look over my shoulder at the endless wide spaces of the Wembley pitch, with the ghosts of so many heroes scattered across it, and then we were gone, lost in the dispersing crowd and melting into the night. If only my fears could have disappeared so easily.

CHAPTER TWENTY - SEVEN

March 1979

I finally saw Jen again, although it was over a month later in some fancy new place in town, a wine bar, her choice of course, with its name, "Marseille's", emblazoned in a fluorescent green above, and a window basket running along the front. I could have told them that that wasn't going to last five minutes.

Not much had happened since Billy had gone. One day seemed to blend into the next, almost as if my life were on hold, just waiting for something important to happen.

Mum had told me that she was letting the house go, as I knew she must. I had two months to decide what to do, either move in with Dave up in town, which would please no one, not even Dave, or keep the whole world happy, or so it seemed, by allowing the club to find me digs close to it and under the watchful eye of the boss and his staff.

I knew it was the smart thing to do, sensible and professional, but it just didn't feel right, there was something in my guts, a voice as faint as a breeze, but there nonetheless, whispering around my head.

Dave had offered on more than one occasion for me to stay, there was plenty of space in his room, he had said. 'Just buy a lilo,' he had explained. 'Simple.' The others hadn't seemed to mind when we had suggested the idea to them. It was Dave who was actually against it, he knew it was a bad career move, ruffling the feathers of the club, but he'd felt that he had to offer when he'd seen my apprehension. 'I'm hardly gonna let you sleep on the streets, am I?' he'd said, rolling his eyes in that mock exasperation of his. And although I had made a show of considering letting the club own my soul, as I saw it, deep down I must have known for each time that I went to see him I left another bag of belongs there, some clothes and bits and pieces, as if I were trying to sneak the idea by myself.

Since Billy had gone I had felt almost fragile, as if I'd been hollowed out. It reminded me of a time I had been ill as a kid. I had virtually collapsed at the foot of the stairs. My legs had simply given out, I can still remember how they had felt like jelly, and it was the same unpleasant sensation that returned when Billy had clasped me firmly by both arms that damp, depressing Monday morning on the platform. 'I'll be alright, J,' he had said, smiling thinly at me, looking older than a boy of seventeen should ever have to. But his voice had lacked its usual conviction, I didn't think that it was bravado, it was just that for probably the first time since Billy had thought about or mentioned it, the cold reality of his actions had finally sunk in. And after I had watched his train disintegrate into nothing and turned to make my way back down the steps, I had found, frighteningly, that my legs couldn't be trusted to hold the rest of me upright. I had clutched the rail and, with every drop of blood in my body feeling as if it had all rushed up into my head, stumbled back out into what felt like nothing more than a game of my life now. The only difference being that there was another player missing.

My legs had just begun to feel as if they belonged to me again that evening when I made my way through town looking for Jen's wine bar. Still felt a little unsteady and a bit wobbly but for the first time in a long time I was aware of the sensation of my feet actually landing on the ground, of the pavement resounding through the soles of my brand new boots. And it was weird, for at the same time that my legs had finally begun to feel a part of me again, I had resigned myself to the fact that Jen no longer was, and then she had phoned.

It had caught me completely off guard, like being beaten at your near post or something. I hadn't even known that she was back. I'd heard from somewhere that she had gone on holiday for a week with some colleagues from work, other policewomen.

I'd just reached the point where I didn't think I could quite remember the sound of her voice, the way her tone would sound as if everything she said was a question, the gentleness of it. But it all had come rushing back, a volume knob turned up in my head the moment she'd said my name down the phone. 'Johnny?' she'd asked, as if it could possibly have been anyone else.

The tan made her look older, and the vest top that she wore, despite the chill in the night, showed off her brown back and shoulders effectively. It clung to her body in the right places, which only served to intimidate and unnerve me even further. The place was cast in semi-darkness, each table illuminated by a single candle wedged into an empty wine bottle, the necks of which were encrusted with dried wax, giving the impression of a waterfall or fountain frozen in time. I supposed it was all meant to be very Mediterranean, creating the effect that you would find in places abroad, the likes of Ibiza, where Jen had just spent a week, where the sun shone and the promise of mystery and romance lurked on every beach and in the shadows of every shady bar. I was pretty sure, though, that romance wouldn't be hovering in the air of "Marseille's" that night.

She sat alone in a booth against the far wall, a glass of white wine in front of her, and straight away I was aware of the changes between us; the Jen I knew would never have dreamt of entering a bar of any description on her own, never mind ordering a drink and taking a seat by herself.

'We didn't fancy Tenerife.' She wrinkled her nose in a show of distaste as if the very thought of the place filled her with disgust. It didn't suit her, this air of superiority. 'Not after what happened the other year.' She was referring to the plane crash that had killed so many holidaymakers two years before.

'Probably the safest place *to* go,' I muttered, more for something to say than anything but I was aware of the quizzical look on her face.

'What do you mean?' she said sharply.

'Nothing.' I paused then shrugged. 'All I meant was that they're not gonna let it happen again are they?'

Something close to anger flashed in her eyes. 'That's just typical you!' she snapped

I sat up, genuinely alarmed at just how quickly she had lost patience with me. 'What!' I protested 'I just meant… ' But what was the point?

I suppose I had expected her to be a little more sheepish, unable to look me in the eye, racked with guilt even, considering why she had asked to see me. I suddenly found myself thinking about the time in the reserves when we played up at Birmingham against Kenny Dennis. And the boss warning us how strong they would be if we let them. *'The best form of defence is attack,'* he had told us in the team talk. *'Get in first and don't let them play, first to every loose ball and put 'em under pressure when they're in possession.'* His words came flooding back for some reason.

'You think just because something bad has happened to someone or something that it won't happen again!' She folded her arms tightly across her chest and took a deep breath as if she were trying to stop her irritation from squirming out of her body, and when she was satisfied that she had contained herself she turned to me with a calm resentment that I didn't recognise and said coldly, 'Like your *arm* I suppose.'

Suddenly I felt very tired, like I hadn't slept for days. 'I just meant… ' But like before I couldn't muster the strength to carry on, the sheer weight of finding the right words defeated me. I had only said it in the first place to try and fill the awkward silence that hung over us. She pursed her lips and made a face that suited her mood.

'I mean just look at you!'

I made a brief inspection of my appearance. I still wore Dave's old denim jacket, over the top of a plain black T-shirt, a pair of jeans of course and, this was the funny thing, what I thought made me look really smart, *cool* even, a pair of brand new suede Chelsea boots purchased that very weekend from the King's Road.

Dave had let me keep the jacket, hadn't said so in so many words but since the morning I had awoken in Bowie's shadow in the doorway on Heddon Street, it was as if we had both assumed that it was mine. Sitting in the kitchen later that morning with an ominous silence growing deeper by the moment. I had suddenly become aware of the disgusting odour swirling around me. I had reeked of the streets. Cigarette smoke and stale beer had worked its way into my very flesh and every stitch of clothing. After I had picked it up from Kenny Dennis' mum at the laundrette I had just carried on wearing it and the next time I saw Dave he hadn't even asked for it back, had just joked that it looked better on him than me.

'Just look at you!' snapped Jen. 'Who do you think you are?' she continued testily. '*Dave* I suppose.'

I closed my eyes. 'No,' I replied flatly and lifted my arm, allowing the unbuttoned sleeve to hang from my cast. 'It's the only thing that I could get over my arm.'

As an explanation this seemed to satisfy her but she crossed her arms again and frowned deeply.

We sat for a minute or two in stony, awkward silence with me slouched across the table sipping at my fancy foreign beer and Jen sitting as stiff as a board like some officious school teacher, staring in the direction of the window or across the bar and into the gloom, anywhere but at me.

But her discomfort was all too obvious, I stole a glance and could see the tightness in her face, lips pursed and jaw clenched. I knew that she was trying to find the right words or the right way to tell me that it was over. I'd known that from the moment that I'd set eyes on her. Maybe she was annoyed with herself for all of a sudden realising that she lacked the courage to see it through. She had probably rehearsed this moment, I thought to myself, over and over in her head a hundred times, ever since our last date, maybe since our first date. Perhaps in her mind's eye she had imagined that I would be more distant, hostile even, but now, after all this time, to find me so subdued and tolerant, well, she must have felt as if she had been sent out to club a baby seal.

A part of me wanted to simply stand up and, without so much as a word or glance over my shoulder, walk out the door with as much dignity as I could muster, save us all the bother, but that would have needed a strength of character that I simply didn't possess. So instead I sat there defenceless and hopeless like the baby seal waiting for the final blow to reign down.

I deserved it, I supposed, for admitting that I had a crush on my nurse, for not calling her sooner, for letting the bad feeling drift on for so long, so long that the damage had become irreparable. If I had let myself it would have driven me mad, I mean we had seemed so strong together, like the brick viaducts behind the park, which, for some inexplicable reason, seemed to spring to mind so often.

But I guessed none of it would really have mattered, they were all just suitable excuses, my flaws. They merely served to confirm what Jen had always known deep down. If I had been honest with myself, although of course I never was, I had known it all along. For Jen was too much like Debbie… like Cindy, like my nurse even! Just liking each other was never going to be enough, I was no loose cannon like Billy but my foundations were just as unsettled. If I closed my eyes and lined their faces up in my head, Debbie, Jen and Cindy, like three cherries on a fruit machine,

I could see the same look in each pair of eyes. It might have been shaded by different colours, blue for Debbie, brown for Jen and green for Cindy, but it was the same nonetheless. It was funny because I could never see it at the time or, maybe I chose not to. It was almost sorrowful, as if they could see something that I couldn't.

I was pretty sure there was nobody else, I couldn't say for certain of course but she didn't have that way about her. I'd seen it before many times, in the eyes of other boys' girlfriends. They can't look them in the eye, the guilt won't let them, they shift this way and that praying for the bloke to get the message and end it for them. It wasn't like that for me and Jen, it wasn't that she *couldn't* look at me, it was that she didn't *want* to look at me! Just a glimpse of my lack of... anything, made her crazy.

Splitting up because she had met somebody else, I admit, would have knocked the wind out of me, like taking the full force of a volley right in the guts, a real pile driver. But the idea of losing out to *myself*, to my lack of maturity, I reckoned was even worse. And what made it even harder was that I knew that there was not a thing I could do about it, it wasn't a case of mending my ways or promising to be faithful or more considerate in the future, nothing could ever change who we were or fill the gap that yawned between us.

For weeks now I had tried desperately to avoid being alone, for whenever I was, the demise of our relationship rose, like bile, to the surface of my mind. Insecurity clenched at my guts and I couldn't put my finger on why. I tried to romanticise it, like trying to compare it to a film that, ironically, Jen and I had once seen, *Up the Junction*. It had come on late after I had taken Jenny home one Saturday night. We had been to the pictures and I wasn't really in the mood to sit and stare at another screen for a couple of hours but those late night films were always a good excuse to stay at Jen's on her sofa long after we had sat down and shared a cup of cocoa with her parents.

Although spending an hour or so alone cuddled up with her

always came at a price. Those few minutes spent making polite conversation with her parents were always the most awkward part of the evening for me, they had replaced those anxious, skin-crawling moments when I would walk Jen to her door, when the thought of kissing her goodnight would haunt my every step, right from the moment that we would step off the bus, climb the hill and turn into the tree-lined tranquillity of her street. But we were past all that, we had reached a point that we were both comfortable, we enjoyed being close and instinctively knew the level of intimacy, without saying a word, that the moment would reach.

And to think, after we had watched that film, *Up the Junction,* I used to joke about it. Tease her that it must have been based on the two of us, with Jen playing Suzy Kendall's role as the upper class girl forsaking her roots to see how the other half live. And she would roll her eyes in that playfully exasperated way of hers, as if she were trying to inspect her fringe, but the bitter irony of it all was that it had turned out to be true. What is it they say? Life imitates art. For just like Suzy Kendall's role in the film, she had found that the gulf between us was just too wide to bridge.

The mood between us grew darker with every passing minute, as if someone were creeping up and blowing out the candles on each of the tables around us in turn. I sipped at my beer tentatively, trying to make it last so that I wouldn't find myself in the unenviable situation of having to decide whether to order another drink or not. Jen was almost crackling with a mixture of frustration and anxiety and I was seriously wondering if she was going to able to stop herself from exploding when I suddenly felt a hand on my shoulder. 'Hello, Johnny, how's your arm?'

Jen's eyes rolled in frustration as I turned to look up at the first truly friendly face I'd seen all evening.

It belonged to Rob Sawyers, a reporter with the local paper. A middle-aged man who always appeared to me, no matter what the hour, as if he was coming to the end of a long, hard day: tie hanging loosely around his neck, shirt untucked, the buttons straining around his belly. The result, I imagined, of too many liquid lunches interviewing local celebrities, mostly South London footballers. Many a time I'd seen him board the first team coach early in the morning looking like he hadn't been to bed. On numerous occasions I had been warned by first team players to watch out for journos, as they called them. They were all, especially the seasoned pros, always very guarded with the ones that hung around at the training ground or up at the club but as far as I could make out they all seemed to have time for Rob. Indeed he was one of the selected few to be invited to travel to away games on the first team coach, joining in with card games and sharing a beer on the way home if they'd won. They trusted him, although he wouldn't spare anyone if they'd had a stinker. He was always fair in his match reports and he never twisted your words like some of them.

'Getting better thanks, Mr Sawyers,' I smiled politely. I knew that would annoy Jenny, answering him the way some kid would a grown-up. She was always telling to me start behaving like the professional that I was now, and it only irked her further if I pointed out that I was still only semi-pro. I had always found it secretly amusing that her gentle scolding was actually more belittling than my own behaviour.

She may have been cursing the interruption but I couldn't think why, the tension had grown so thick it swirled around us like a mist. Maybe it was because Rob had appeared just as she was steeling herself for the final moment, had thwarted her just as she was about to say what we both knew had to be said. But even though I knew it was only dragging it out, I welcomed the delay, and looking into a face that showed genuine concern lifted my sagging spirits more than I could have realised. After a time, when your team-mates see you day after day, week after week, walking in and out of the treatment room but never training, other than the odd lap round the field, never appearing to get any better and no nearer to playing, their sympathy and interest in your state wanes. I had become the kid with the plaster on his arm, they would ask how I was or how it was going but they were empty enquiries now, their minds somewhere else even as the words tumbled automatically from their mouths. I couldn't say I blamed them. What was the point of asking a question when you already knew the answer?

But with not being able to play I hadn't seen Rob for a while. 'Plaster comes off next week,' I explained, lifting my arm.

'That's great, Johnny.' He smiled warmly, patting me on the shoulder. 'You'll be back in the first team in no time, you mark my words.'

The sound of a barely concealed scoff came from Jen's direction.

'Anyway,' said Rob, sensing the atmosphere, 'I don't want to keep you from your good lady.' He acknowledged her with a friendly nod and smile which I was glad to see unsettled her as she squirmed a little in her chair and threw back a rather weak smile in return, as if to excuse the abruptness of her nature. But the serenity didn't last two minutes after Rob had left, only up until a couple squeezed past us on the way to a table and the man gave me a second glance and told me that he hoped I'd be back soon. It was as if she begrudged me the very thing that she was always telling me to embrace. I couldn't work it out.

'What now!' I exclaimed. 'It's not my fault the geezer's a Southfields fan, they are the local team you know!'

Jen stared menacingly across the table, as if she were trying to burn holes in me with her eyes. I slumped over the table and stared into my warm beer. I'd had enough now, just wanted to get the hell out of the place, out of that dark, cloying atmosphere. I felt as if I were sitting in a cave, a cave that was slowly becoming smaller and smaller each time I looked at the walls; it was like a bad dream. Suddenly, from the back of the bar, the gentle strumming of an acoustic guitar started up, accompanied by the soft crooning of a lady's voice singing what sounded like an old Joni Mitchell number;

a hippie duo. The bloke on the guitar had longer hair than the girl. I slumped even further across the table, my body language screaming that this was all I needed. People were beginning to look over now. Not blatant staring but rather furtive glances, the way people do when another couple are arguing.

Eventually she leaned across the table, her face inches from my own and hissed through gritted teeth, 'Can't you see?' I was close enough to have kissed her, wouldn't have had to move my head more than inch or so, and who knows, maybe it would have changed everything, taken the sting out of the moment, like frozen peas poured into a boiling pan, but I could almost taste the venom on her breath, she was no longer the Jen I had got to know these last few months, she was… she was every girl I'd ever known.

I shook my head. 'See what?' I could feel the old sensation beginning to creep across my skin beneath the plaster and up the backs of my legs. She rolled her eyes and exhaled so deeply she nearly blew out the candle on our table.

'Oh, I suppose you pretend that it's not happening to you, do you, *fame.*'

I sat up in wide-eyed bewilderment. 'Fame!' I said.

She looked quickly from side to side. 'Will you be quiet!' she almost spat.

'Is that what you think it is?' I said, ignoring her. 'Just because a few people who live round here and a local reporter recognise me!' I wanted to tell her that she should be the one to grow up and stop being so stupid, but I knew that I didn't bear that much animosity towards her, despite the fact that I knew it was already over. But I never had the chance to tell her that even if I had wanted to, for next she dropped the big bombshell, revealed the real reason for the bitterness simmering within her.

'Next you'll be telling me that you don't know anything about P.C. Collins being beaten half to death either, won't you?'

CHAPTER TWENTY - EIGHT

May 1979

What was it, I wondered, that led me to keep on raking my nails up and down the length of my puny-looking forearm; the warm weather perhaps? All around me, as I made my way along Oxford Street, people's clothes screamed of the summer just beginning. Capped-sleeved T-shirts and pullovers knotted around waists for the men, whilst the female population of London seemed to have this secret code where, no matter how young or old they may be, they had to reveal at least one piece of flesh; either legs, shoulders or mid-riff, sometimes even all three… and more.

I turned off into Regent Street, with all its fancy shops, following the road's gentle curve before me. If I scratched hard enough I could make the dead skin, which had been suffocated to death by the plaster, flake away like dust caught in the strips of sunlight through a closed curtain. Did it still itch anymore? I couldn't tell. I should have been used to it now, the amount of times it had been in plaster. The last time they had decided to slap a second cast on after some lengthy deliberations with the club physio, who hadn't been satisfied with something or other about my rehabilitation.

I should have been on my way back there now, the club. Instead of going to meet Dave in what would inevitably end in a long night of loud music and beer.

Still, it was Friday afternoon and I couldn't see the point. The season was over and I was nowhere near being able to train yet, had weeks of physio ahead of me before they would even let me look at a ball and what could they do that afternoon that couldn't wait until Monday, I kept asking myself. I'd just explain that things had simply taken longer at the hospital than anticipated.

I had become quite familiar with "up town" and especially around the West End area lately, adroit at slipping down back streets and alleyways, I found I didn't have to charge through the busy streets like a mad thing to keep scheduled meetings with Dave. I was beginning to feel that I *belonged* in the capital now, that it wasn't just a place I visited, like some sightseer down to see the Tower of London for the day. I no longer treated it like an enemy to be feared or an unknown opposition to be regarded sceptically, instead I had begun to let the character of the place spread through me, like the veins in a leaf, I looked up instead of down at my feet all the time, at the buildings, at the architecture that you never really saw; a world of pillars, scrolls and carvings, stacked layer upon layer above the fancy shop names.

Maybe that was the reason I had been mauling my arm, and nothing to do with the weather. That feeling of unease, that mad itching that would betray me whenever I felt anxious about something. For I didn't *need* to take a trip along Regent Street to reach my destination, in fact it was quite a detour. No matter which way I tried to look at it, the truth was that I wanted to go back to Heddon Street.

I couldn't remember when it had started or even explain it but all I knew was whenever I went there, I found that I was surrounded by this overwhelming sense of contentment, it was like waking early as a kid on a cold, wet morning and dreading the prospect of dragging yourself from beneath the warmth of the covers only to suddenly remember that it was a Saturday.

I mean I had always found the place fascinating, ever since Dave had first taken me there to act out the *Ziggy Stardust* cover. Of course I hadn't felt the same burning sense of passion that would ignite Dave but the history of where we were had sparked something inside me, like a tiny flame beneath a pile of leaves.

And heaven knows I had spent too much time up in Dave's bedroom, lying on his bed gazing at the album sleeve whilst he had sat hunched over his tiny desk in the corner, not to be aware of the almost mystic appeal that seemed to emanate from the very cover. But it hadn't been until I had paid my own type of twisted tribute to Bowie's alter ego, by sleeping beneath the K.WEST sign in the cold morning dawn, that I had found myself inexplicably drawn to its confines more and more.

I would simply slip in one end, on this occasion through the pedestrian passageway, and amble quietly out through the other, taking it all in on the way. Gazing up at the windows, trying to imagine what it must have been like to be present on that cold, damp January night back in '72. The strange thing was there was nothing to see, just a normal London street, unremarkable buildings that housed unremarkable offices, a monolithic cul-de-sac that lurked on a thousand London streets. But there was something about the place, it made me feel as if I were somehow walking in the footsteps of some kind of historical event, the way people feel about visiting ancient battlefields or famous buildings or streets. Of course I would take a good look at the famous K.WEST sign and the doorway beneath it, I would try and do this discreetly and not look too much like some wide-eyed Bowie fan, and in any case, more often than not that's exactly what I'd find there anyway. People hanging around in the doorway, having their photos taken, trying to work out where the phone box was. But if I stopped to think about it, that's exactly what I had become too. On those rare occasions at Dave's when there was no record playing I would always look for a Bowie album, despite the literally hundreds of LPs that adorned the place. It would always be *Hunky Dory, Aladdin Sane* or *Ziggy*. It was if I were trying to educate myself all over again from the beginning, and whenever I thought it might go unnoticed, I would look so hard at the place where he had once stood that my eyes would ache from the concentration. It was if I were trying to see something new, something that I might have missed the time before.

Such was my increasing fascination with all things Bowie, I had even got Dave to recreate his *Aladdin Sane* lightning bolt on the second plaster that I had had cast. Not that he had needed much persuading, it had almost become a signature for him, just another little thing about me that wormed its way under Jen's skin that night in the wine bar.

Still, I was doing my best to steer clear of anything to do with women. And my reaction towards a young couple who breezed straight past me hand in hand, just as I had stepped back out into reality and into the throng of Regent Street, spoke volumes for my frame of mind. The girl, all dolled up for a Friday night in skin tight jeans and high heels, had to keep breaking into a little jog to keep up with her boyfriend, who appeared blissfully unaware of her predicament. A laugh so short and sharp had exploded, like an unexpected burp, from deep within me that it had taken me quite by surprise, was out before the comic appeal of what I had just witnessed had even registered. The girl had looked so ridiculous, so subservient, as she allowed herself to be literally dragged by the hand through the streets of London, tottering like a drunken tart as she struggled to keep up. And I hadn't even flinched when she had turned and glared at me, in fact I had laughed even harder, throwing my head back in exaggeration as she disappeared into the crowd, arm outstretched before her. *Women… sod the lot of them.*

But the truth was that I had lived my life in their shadow. It was impossible to escape the influence that they had had upon me. Heaven knows, the country was even governed by one now!

The *Winter of Discontent* had finally thawed and the spring had brought with it a new prime minister; a conservative, a lady! Maggie Thatcher. The "Iron Lady" she was to become, but in my eyes they all seemed as tough as steel.

Debbie, Cindy and now Jenny; they had all, when the time had come, proved to be tougher on the inside than I could ever be. When it came down to it, none of them could tolerate my lifestyle. At first they had dropped subtle hints about the company that I kept until finally succumbing to growing frustration and perhaps not in so many words, challenging me to choose between my mates and them... between them or Dave and Billy.

And now, one by one, they had all gone, just like I knew they would.

But then so had Billy... and Mum, she'd gone too, and what's more, so would the house in just over a week. And all that I had left was Dave. But what they had never understood, not any of them, not Debbie, Cindy, Jenny or anyone else, male or female, who had been a part of my life, not even Mum, was that I had never had a choice. It had never been a conscious decision. For we had never *chosen* one another, me, Billy and Dave, life had chosen *us* to be together. Circumstances had propelled us into each other's paths; none of us could remember that far back, we just sort of knew. And we were so much more than just mates. Closer than brothers, closer than any family, and it was nothing to do with the blood brothers ritual that we had performed down the park one summer holiday, the scars from which we each still carried, like crude lifelines, on our palms. It was something more than that, something intangible that moved inside and between us like a shadow across water. For in so many ways we knew each other better than we knew ourselves. And something that I never understood, that none of them could ever see, not Debbie, Cindy or Jen, was that the thing that had brought us together, whatever the circumstances may have been, our bond of friendship, was the very thing that they had wanted me to break away from.

I crossed over and ducked down Brewer Street and past the Glassblower pub that sits at the split in the road, thinking of the first time that I had been in there, the time Dave and I had gone in for a quick one to get us in the mood for the *Ziggy* cover, but it had ended up too foggy. I had been there I don't know how many times since but whenever I passed it, or indeed came anywhere near Regent Street, the memories of that first, exhilarating encounter, sprang to mind.

I walked virtually the length of Wardour Street until I found myself, once again, back out on Oxford Street. A ridiculous diversion, I thought to myself, for what amounted to no more than a few moments of nostalgia, a glimpse into a past that I was rapidly feeling at home in. Five minutes later and I was standing outside the Dominion Theatre waiting for Dave.

'He'll be okay, Johnny.' Dave shrugged in that easy, laconic way of his. 'Probably lovin' it, working on some site, drinking his work mates under the table and beating them all at arm wrestling.' He took a swig of his beer and smiled at the thought, a wave of fiery orange hair breaking gracefully against his cheek. He put his drink down and pushed it back into place.

We were sitting in a pub tucked away round the back of the Dominion waiting for its doors to open and drinking with all the punks.

I sighed and stared out at the city, people passing this way and that, competing with the traffic, hurrying to catch the weekend.

It had been two weeks now since Billy had gone and I couldn't believe how much I missed him. Two weeks and not a word, not a phone call or anything. If I was honest with myself I hadn't really expected anything else but it was the not knowing that made me so damn restless, and Dave's insouciance only served to fuel my anxiety. I mean I knew deep down that he would be okay, he was that kind of kid, Billy, a survivor. And what Dave had said was probably all true and normally I would have let Dave's ability to see things for what they were calm my nerves, let his words, like dissolvable headache tablets, soothe my fears. But it wasn't a normal situation, the timing of his disappearance was just too coincidental to simply be a twist of fate, but the truth, from which there seemed to be no hiding, was just too appalling to face. So how could Dave behave as if I were fretting over nothing, how could he appear so untroubled by it all?

The sun broke through a gap in the clouds and poured into the pub, its heat magnified through the plate glass windows.

'But what about Collins?' I exclaimed. 'I mean is he… ' I stared disbelievingly out of the window, unable to find the words, scared to say them out loud. The sudden burst of light forced me to shield my eyes and it wasn't long before it became almost unbearable but I just sat there defiantly, ignorant in the full force of its glare. And then all of a sudden it vanished back behind a cloud, taking its heat with it, as if it had never been there. A glimpse of what things could be like if only life didn't get in the way. We sat there for a moment in silence and when I did turn towards him, Dave's eyes were upon me, and I could see the concern flickering in them, like frost dancing in the moonlight. He leaned across the table, and in an instant I could see the change in his disposition; it didn't fit the mood. 'He'll be okay, Johnny, I *promise*.' The earnestness that filtered through his words was nothing like I remembered, it held me for longer than one of his usual comments designed to pacify my emotions. 'They've got no proof against him, trust me, Johnny, he'll be okay.'

'How do you know!' I whined. 'I mean do they *need* proof to nick him?'

He closed his eyes and took a breath, exasperated, no doubt, by my anxiety.

'Look… ' he began.

'No!' I interjected. 'You don't get it, Dave,' I said through gritted teeth. 'Why did he go if he hasn't got anything to worry about, why…'

He leant across and squeezed my good wrist firmly. 'Johnny...' His words were faint, like a dying echo. I could feel the panic rising within me and, horrifyingly, for a moment I thought I was going to cry, could feel the stinging of tears surface in my eyes. Something crawled across my brain, like an itch on the inside, and then there was a roar of laughter from the bar and the rest of Dave's words were engulfed beneath the wave of noise.

The unsatisfactory ending of our dispute over Billy remained, lingered, like the promise of summer. The prospect of red-skied evenings hanging out with friends, wringing every last drop from the day should have lifted my spirits. But just lately every night seemed to be a night out with Dave, drinking and seeing bands, and of course there was no Billy anymore. It would have been easy to blame London or even Dave for transforming me from committed footballer to some sort of late night groupie, but the truth was, I knew I didn't have to look further than a mirror to face who was responsible.

The pub had begun to fill up now, mostly with punk rockers. There were the "Part-time Punks", the ones who played at it all, who used the scene as a kind of release, a vehicle to transport them from the boredom of their every day lives. You could see the decency at their core, it ran right through them like writing through a stick of rock, poorly hidden beneath the thin veil of their costumes. They were betrayed by the manner of their behaviour, the way they used ashtrays or were mindful not to spill their beer or bump into anyone around them. If you were to pull a comb or a stiff brush through the all too carefully spiked-up hair, it would most likely reveal a nice, respectable side or middle parting, the kind that you would find behind the desk of every bank manager or estate agent in town.

Then of course there were the punks that you would see everywhere, at all the gigs and in all the dives and haunts around town, no matter what night of the week it might be. Same faces, same clothes, a uniform of Doc Marten boots, tartan bondage trousers, ripped T-shirts baring band names and studded leather biker jackets, all this no matter what the weather. Only the hair colour would change, one week green, the next maybe red. They were the "Diehard Punks", they hadn't so much become punks as punk had become them. The ones who had given their lives over to it all, who had been there when it all began, they had seen the chance to grab onto something, had probably been as influential as the early bands. "The Great Unwashed" Dave would jokingly call them, but he would credit them with having the astuteness to see the havoc this rising tide would create, and, like surfers trying to catch a great wave, they were going to ride it all the way until it crashed and broke upon the rocks of oblivion.

I drained my glass, another pint nearer the end of my career. But I had gone way beyond that now. Somewhere in the back of my mind it had been accepted. There were demons of a different kind haunting my insecurities. I was just about to go and fight my way to the bar when this great brute of a punk appeared beside us, three pints of beer crammed between his hands. They looked ridiculously small there in his palms and it was a wonder he didn't crush them within his grasp.

'There you go, Bowie Boy,' said the giant, grinning through broken teeth and I recognised him as the bouncer from outside The 100 Club. 'And one for the keeper.' He nodded his great, scar-covered head in my direction.

'Cheers,' I smiled, feeling a little awkward.

Dave lifted his glass. 'Yeah, cheers, Mugsy.' He smiled appreciatively, 'I owe you one.'

Mugsy placed his great slab of a hand on Dave's shoulder and gave him a gentle pat, frowning a little as he did so, almost as if he didn't trust his own strength not to break Dave in half. Visions of King Kong staring stupidly at Fay Wray in the palm of his hand sprung to mind.

'Yeah, well,' he said, 'try and give us a mention in your review.' He nodded in the direction of a scary-looking mob laughing and drinking at the bar, they were busy throwing peanuts at the bar staff and cheering each time one of them managed to find its way down the front of one of the girl's tops.

Dave gave a little sigh of amusement, as if he'd seen it all before, which of course he had. 'Just try not to kill anyone, eh, Mugsy,' he smiled. 'You won't get any encores if you do, you know.'

Mugsy threw his head back and grinned manically, 'Try not to, Davy Boy, try not to.' He picked up his pint and turned to rejoin his mates at the bar. 'But if those stinkin' Mods or skins come down… ' He shrugged his huge shoulders 'Then I can't promise nuffin'.'

CHAPTER TWENTY - NINE

May 1979

I climbed back out into the fresh night air, the pollution of London never tasted so good. People were still spewing from inside the club. You could tell the genuine punks, the hardcore ones, they had been the first out. They were the ones baying for blood, frantic to track down the rest of their clan. As opposed to the ones just there for the ride. The "Plastic Punks", the kids just playing at being bored and frustrated with life, there was no way they were going to get involved if they could help it. They would watch the battle unfurl from a safe distance and then, when they were back at work or college, boast that they had been there.

I sighed heavily and stood back against the wall, watching the crazed grow crazier. Hands buried deep in my pockets, I came across Dave's flat key and held it out in the palm of my hand. It glinted in the yellow beam of the streetlight like a poignant moment in a film. 'Why don't I go back now?' I said to myself, just like Dave had suggested. It would certainly make a change to have an early night and heaven knows I could have done with it. My legs ached from traipsing through the streets and spending most of the evening on my feet. I started to make my way down the street, allowing myself to be pulled along in the swell of the crowd. I thought I'd go along until the first bus heading in the direction of Baker Street came by, I even started to actually look forward to going back to Dave's. I would probably be the only one in this early on a Friday night, I thought to myself. 'Make some tea and toast', isn't that a line from the Hunky Dory album? No that's *'Make some coffee and tea'*. You would think I'd know after all these years of having it drummed in my head.

Think I'll go to the training ground in the morning, get some of the youth lads or apprentices to fire a few shots in, sling a few crosses over, nothing too hard. It would just be nice to feel a ball in the palm of my hands again, work up a bit of a sweat… start to feel good about myself again.

These thoughts carried me further than anticipated, and before I knew it, and without really realising, I was turning into a side street off Oxford Street, the urgency of the crowd rising as paces and pulses quickened; past a pub struggling to get rid of the last of its customers, past a bookies with a hunched figure sitting in the doorway nursing a can of beer and surrounded by crumpled betting slips and empty cans of Hemling. He was moaning out loud and even though I knew he was nothing more than a pissed tramp, I felt an urge to help him… *'Have you seen the old man who walks them streets of London?'*

'What am I going to tell her?' he cried drunkenly. 'They told me it couldn't lose!' And it wasn't until I moved closer that I realised that he wasn't a tramp at all, he was dressed in a suit, tie hanging loosely around his neck, a pissed-up City boy who'd blown his mortgage payments on a tip.

I started to turn away when he looked up at the figure standing above him. 'Hey,' he slurred, 'aren't you that keeper?' But I had already moved off, recognition was the last thing I needed. I had received the odd second glance over a shoulder as we had been herded down Oxford Street, but the company that I had found myself in wasn't really the sort you'd find leafing through the back pages of newspapers or watching *Match of the Day* or *The Big Match* on a Sunday.

But it did make me suddenly aware of what I was doing, allowing myself, yet again, to get dragged into something that could only possibly end one way… badly. And where the hell was Dave? What did he think he was doing? I knew that he only wanted to get a report or whatever they called it, for his music paper, quite the journalist he had become, but he was bound to get embroiled in the heat of it.

I could just start to feel that old familiar feeling of anxiety swell up in my guts, the feeling that always followed the unbearable itching along my arms and legs, when the crowd began to emerge from out of every opening. Shadows spilling like oil from the alleyways and side streets. Casually at first, then with a little more urgency, some glancing over their shoulders, and then from somewhere in the distance came this almighty roar. My first impression was that it must be thunder, but then the sight of the punks rushing past me, scattering out into Oxford Street and beyond, made me realise that it was something even more foreboding… a police charge maybe?

Fear took hold and I started to follow the crowd but then something clicked inside me. What was I running for? I'd done nothing wrong! I wasn't even a punk!

But despite my show of bravado the panic wouldn't leave me. Nausea swam inside me, I felt dizzy, disorientated standing alone against the waves of charging punks, like staring at your feet in the sand as the tide floods back out to sea. And just then, from out the gloom, stepped Dave.

It was as if he had appeared from out of thin air, one moment I couldn't see for the stampede of spiked-up hair and leather and the next all I could see was Dave.

He stood in the entrance of an alleyway, his silhouette illuminated by the glow of a Victorian-style street lamp. It was like a scene from some science fiction film. *Dave… The Man Who Fell to Earth.*

His calmness in the midst of the mayhem seemed almost absurdly out of place. I was used to seeing Dave unflustered when whatever circumstances we might have found ourselves in demanded panic, but there was something else, I couldn't see his face clear enough to read an expression, but there was something about his appearance that unsettled me… it was almost supernatural.

The drunk from the betting shop stumbled over to me, 'What the fuck's going on?' he slurred as if he'd only just realised that something untoward was happening, oblivious to the impending danger like only drunks can be. 'And who the fuck's that?' he went on, following my gaze and waving an unsteady hand in Dave's direction. 'Who the fuck's he think he is, Gary 'fuckin' Numan!'

'Dave!' I cried, trying to keep the fear from my voice. 'What's happening?'

He didn't seem to hear me, just stood there like a mannequin, and if I didn't know every inch of him I would have thought that maybe I had been mistaken, that the figure was someone else. And just as I was about to call out again he began to amble, as if time meant nothing, over to where I stood.

'What's going on? What's happening?' but it was as if he hadn't heard me, the faraway stare in his eyes telling me his mind was somewhere else. 'Dave!' I shoved my face in front of his in an attempt to fill his vacant look with the growing apprehension overflowing in mine.

He blinked as if seeing me for the first time. 'Skinheads, Johnny,' he said calmly. I looked around at the dribs and drabs of still retreating punks. I didn't quite understand.

'But… ' I couldn't make sense of it, wasn't that the whole idea? Why would street-hardened punks turn and run from a few skins when it had all been organised? But as usual he seemed to hear the voice in my head and answered my thoughts.

'There are *hundreds* and *hundreds* of them, Johnny!' His use of the word hundreds told me everything I needed to know, Dave wasn't prone to exaggerate. 'There must be every skinhead in London… they just appeared… ' There was still not a hint of fear in his voice, even as the roar from somewhere down the streets grew louder... nearer. Any moment now we were about to be engulfed by more bloodthirsty skins than I could ever imagine and yet, incredulously, he seemed to have his mind on other things. Where the hell could his thoughts possibly be?

'Johnny...?' the drunk next to me slurred. He had stayed beside me all along, ever since Dave had appeared, but it was as if he wasn't even there. 'That's it!' He made an attempt at clicking his fingers. 'Johnny Chatterly, the keeper!' Confusion clouded his face 'No wait... Chamberlian... Johnny Chamberlain.' He puffed his chest out the way drunks do when they think they've done something clever. 'I knew I knew you!' He prodded a finger irritatingly in my chest. 'You're Johnny Chamberlain, that young goalkeeper,' he boasted as if he was doing me a favour. But I didn't have the will to even acknowledge him. He mumbled something else but it was drowned out by the deep noise resounding from the alleyways. I glanced over Dave's shoulder at the shadows moving closer, like black clouds rolling in from the sea. I could make out the shapes of so many bald heads, hear the resonating pounding of their stampede.

'Dave!' My voice crackled with terror. And then in the blink of an eye, and just in time, he was himself again.

'Here.' He spun me round and pulled me into the shadows, down a back alley that ran alongside the bookies, so dark that I hadn't even known it was there. And just in time, as the army of skinheads charged out into view and onto Oxford Street. The drunk hadn't followed us and now he just stood there bewildered, as skin after skin rushed by, almost identical with their shaved heads, in their DM boots and turned-up jeans with braces dangling in great loops upon their thighs. The only thing that told them apart was the different colours of their Fred Perry tennis shirts and the fact that some wore Harrington jackets, and despite the weather there was the odd Crombie in sight. It was obvious that he wasn't their prey, standing there stupidly in his crumpled shirt and tie, but unfortunately he was just too an easy target to resist. A gangly skinhead rushed past him with what seemed barely a second glance, but something caught his eye and he stopped suddenly. He took two giant steps backwards until he was facing the City man.

He lifted the drunk's tie off his chest with the palm of his hand, as if he was admiring the quality of silk. 'Give us it,' he ordered.

The drunk looked up at the shaven head with a look of utter confusion. 'Whaat?' he mumbled.

'Give me the fuckin' tie, nonce!' he snarled. And so with a shrug of his shoulders the man fumbled at the knot hanging loosely round his neck, pulled the tie through his collar and handed it over.

'Cheers.' The skinhead's grin reminded me of a kid on Christmas morning as he began to tie it round his own neck, tucking it awkwardly beneath the inadequate collar of his Fred Perry shirt. He smoothed it down, admired the crimson and white stripes that complemented his own red Harrington jacket and, just before he set off to join his clan he snapped his head back and, with lightning speed, crashed it into the drunk's unprepared face.

I winced at the sight. 'Bastard,' I said. Dave just shrugged dismissively with the eyes of someone who'd seen it, and much worse, all before.

'Come on,' he urged, and melted into the darkness behind us. We felt our way past black bin liners that overflowed with the names of a thousand badly chosen dogs and horses, through piles of discarded beer cans and empty glue bags until we came to a dead end in the shape of ten foot wall. Dave pulled two dustbins together and clambered up.

As I watched him busy himself with his make-shift platform, something suddenly occurred to me. 'Fuckin' hell,' I sighed, a little louder than I had meant to.

'What's wrong?' Dave asked, gazing down from on top the wall. 'Shit!' he rasped, suddenly remembering, and leant over and reached out an arm. 'I'll pull you up.'

I shook my head. 'It's not that.' Although now he had mentioned it, climbing over wasn't going to be easy. Little things like scaling walls, things that, as a kid, you'd do without a second thought, were things you had to consider carefully when you had an arm as fragile as a piece of old china.

'What then?' I could see the scar in the centre of his forehead deepen into a frown as he sat astride the wall, as if what we were doing was… was simply part of every day, a part of being us. How I envied him and Billy that. I mean I knew that something was up, and whatever it was had to be something so intense as to upset the equilibrium that balanced Dave's life so steadily, but there he was taking all this in his stride; finding a way out, leading us down the alley, constructing an escape, while I just went dumbly along, contributing nothing but negativity.

'I'm fed up of skulking down piss-stinking alleyways!' I moaned. 'We seem to have spent half our fuckin' childhoods in them!' We both knew what I meant and for a moment I wondered if I'd managed to dig up some dark memories that he had buried. I heard the deep intake of breath as he sat there, like a general aboard his steed. He looked up and down the street as if to make sure it was clear, and then he peered back down into the gloom of the alley where I stood. And I saw the contours of his face crack into that familiar thin grin.

'Come on, Johnny,' he cocked his head back, 'you wouldn't have it any other way, would you? You and me together, like always,' he rocked gently from side to side as if he didn't have a care in the world… '*And if the homework gets you down we'll throw it on the fire and take the car downtown*'… a couple of Kooks you and me!'

'Yeah,' I sniffed, 'everything's bleedin' *Hunky Dory.*' He laughed at that, threw his head back so far he nearly toppled over backwards, but still, there was something there, something hovering beneath the surface, I knew him too well; too well and yet not at all.

'Come on.' He leant over and took my good arm with a strength that I had always known was there but which belied his build and never failed to amaze me. 'Anyway,' he concluded as I swung a leg awkwardly over the wall, 'at least you had a childhood; me... I was born an old man.' And his smile grew a little wider. But like so many of his smiles, there was no humour behind it.

I hadn't a clue where we were, slipping and skulking this way and that through the back streets of the West End had left me completely disorientated, but Dave seemed to know. All the shops looked expensive; affluence seemed to ooze from every building in this part of town; extravagant dresses draped over beautiful mannequin dolls, trays of gold and diamond jewellery on view behind caged windows and giant oil paintings of ships below sinister-looking skies with clouds scudding across them, set in swirling gold frames covered the walls of refined little galleries perched on street corners that were barely wide enough for a car. The smaller the property, it seemed to me, the more exclusive the place looked.

The narrow streets were virtually deserted, just the odd couple sauntering along, holding hands and gazing in the shop windows. The endless stream of traffic that flowed like water through London day and night could still be heard but it was no more than a dull drone coming from somewhere beyond the towering rooftops.

'Where we going?' I groaned, almost pleading. The words seemed to leak from me, the night's events had caught up with me so much so that even speaking no longer came easy. All of a sudden the act of even placing one foot in front of the other seemed too momentous.

'Home,' he answered. The weariness in my voice caused him to look over his shoulder. 'You okay?' he asked.

I forced a smile. 'Course.' But every step grew heavier than the last, like walking through treacle.

'We'll just cut through up here onto Regent Street and you can catch a bus home.' He pointed in the direction of a dimly-lit alley ahead but I wasn't really paying much attention, happy, as usual, to let him guide me. The rumbling sounds of the traffic grew louder as the Regent Street lights came into view. I remember the feeling of relief, as if we were explorers stumbling from out a wild jungle and back into civilisation or something, when all of a sudden the sound of running footsteps rushed up the alley behind us. And as we turned together in unison, the sight of a dozen skinheads spilled round the corner to greet us, their elongated shadows folded at sinister right angles across the cobbled alleyway and halfway up the walls.

And from out of nowhere Bowie's *Young American* clean cut face had popped up in my mind.

I looked across at Dave and there was no fear there, the skinheads had slowed down, bumping into one another as they came, one by one, to a sudden halt behind their leader, the tallest of the bunch. In fact, if I detected anything in his face it appeared to be something close to relief, a sense of inevitability, as if he had been expecting such an intrusion.

For what seemed an eternity, we stood facing each other, Dave and I and the skinheads, with nothing but a few yards of cobbled no-man's-land between us. And then fear kicked in.

'Dave!' I said through gritted teeth. 'Come on!' I reached out and grabbed his forearm with my good one. 'Let's go!' But he didn't seem to hear me, had been away in one of his trances where the only thing that he sees is whatever's running through his mind. He simply stood there, it seemed as if he were puffing out his chest, head slightly tilted, chin up to the night, arms moving slightly away from his sides, palms turned out as if he had been almost offering himself to them, like a sacrifice. And then it hit me. That was what he'd been doing, saying, 'Look at me… Don't mistake me!'

And then, as if somebody had clicked their fingers in front of him, he sprung into life. 'Come on!' he called, and turns sharply and made off down the alley, where a cat and mouse chase unfolded through the back streets of the West End, me and Dave pursued by a half a dozen ranting skinheads, out into the lights of Regent Street, straight across the road without even breaking stride, ignoring the sounds of screeching brakes and blaring horns, before we had dived back into the darkness by the Glassblowers pub. At first that was where I thought we were heading, for the sanctuary of the pub, but even though Dave knew the landlord, who, like everyone whose life he seemed to touch, had an obvious affection for him, I couldn't imagine he would welcome us bringing a gang of bloodthirsty skinheads to his door. But just as I was about to protest he turned right and ducked into the gloom of Warwick Street. We had put some distance between us and the skins now, solvent abuse and tobacco no match for a childhood built on football.

But then he seemed to deliberately slow down. At first I thought he kept glancing over his shoulder to make sure I was keeping pace but as he took another sharp left, back on ourselves towards Regent Street, I realised that he was making sure that we hadn't lost them, that they were still close enough not to lose interest in their prey. And then it suddenly dawned on me. That he knew exactly where he was going and what he was doing, that these were no last minute, spur of the moment twist and turns he was making in a desperate bid to shake them off. That instead he was leading them on, reeling them in, into the comfort of *his* zone; trapping them in *his* safety net… Heddon Street.

And the reason he had led them round on such an elaborate route, for he could have easily turned left the minute we had burst out onto Regent Street from the alley, was so that we could disappear out of sight long enough for me to make an escape.

He looked round twice again, to double check that we were on our own, and then stopped suddenly. He grabbed my shoulder and froze, listening out for the skins, making sure they were still chasing us. The drumming of their DM boots on the streets told him they still were. 'Quick, Johnny!' he said hurriedly. 'Go!' He pointed across the narrow street into the shadows in the direction of Oxford Street. 'There's an alleyway between those buildings,' he explained. 'You can get back onto Regent further up,' he went on. 'Shoot up to Oxford Street and get back to the flat… I'll see you there later.'

I just stood there in the dark, staring at him, in disbelief. 'Go!' he shouted, shoving me towards the darkness. I couldn't even *see* the path he meant it was so dark, but, of course, that wasn't the reason that I didn't move. He glanced nervously from the direction that we had come and the pursuing skins, more nervous than I can ever remember him, the thundering of their boots growing louder with every second. They were nearly upon us. 'Johnny!' he said through gritted teeth. 'You've got to go! *Now*!' I couldn't see his face clearly in the gloom, just a dark patch on his forehead where the scar deepened from his frown, but his eyes glistened and sparkled like glass. It was the gleam of a mad man; wide-eyed… frantic. But this was Dave's face I was looking into, the sanest, coolest boy that there ever was, that there ever was likely to be.

'I'm not leaving you,' I said. I was almost crying, sniffling like a little boy, not because I was scared of getting beaten up, had happened too many times for me to care, and besides, I knew that if we wanted, they could never catch us. But it was for that very reason that I was crying: he wanted to be caught! I didn't fully understand why but something in the back of my mind grasped the enormity of the moment. Realised that the final scene was about to unfold and that Heddon Street, an integral part of Dave's life, was to be the backdrop. It was as if it had all been staged. I had this crazy image of Dave sitting in Lui's, a cold cup of tea beside him, hunched over, feverishly scribbling it all down in one of his dog-eared notepads that he always carried in his pocket.

He leant closer, and there was genuine anger in his face, I could see it in his eyes, could feel the heat of it on his breath. 'Johnny, I'm telling you… *fuck off*! I don't need you here… I don't *want* you here,' he hissed.

'But…' He didn't let me carry on. There was no time, for the skins were at the end of the road now, bumping comically into each other as they ground to a halt again, not knowing which way to go. He hit me hard in the chest. I felt the air rush from my lungs as I struggled for breath. Gasping in hissed tones, I staggered forward and reached out blindly for his arm. He stepped neatly behind me and dragged me, like a corpse, across the street and sat me down in the entrance of the alleyway, far enough along to be shrouded in darkness, unseen from the gloom of the street.

'Sorry, Johnny,' he said, patting me on the shoulder. 'But I haven't got time to argue with you.' He glanced down to where the skins were still arguing amongst themselves over which way to go. 'Just stay there till they're gone, don't move till then, okay!' he told me. 'I'll see you back at the flat… and for God's sake don't follow me!' I was still wheezing hard, the air creeping slowly back into my body. 'There's nothing you can do in your state.' And then he slipped out into the shadows and crept along the wall before stepping out a good fifty yards or so along from where I sat, out into the middle of the street, directly into a tiny pool of yellow light from a street lamp. He stood there scuffing his feet along the floor like a bull readying itself to charge, and he didn't stop until they were roaring after him again.

A number of thoughts raced through my head as I sat crumpled in the alley, my head between my legs, desperately trying to suck great mouthfuls of damp, piss-stained air back into my breath-starved body.

Why? What was he hoping to achieve? Was he just taunting them, leading them round and round on some wild-goose chase, knowing full well that they could never really catch him, not if he didn't want them to? But it seemed more than that, I had never, never, seen him so animated, so determined as he had been before he had momentarily knocked the life from out of my body. He didn't want me with him, that was for sure, no doubt worried that I'd slow him down or that maybe I'd trip and fall, really fuck myself up.

But still something wasn't quite right, I couldn't put my finger on it, something kept nagging me, something right in front of me that I couldn't see kept rebounding back at me from the floor, like talking with your face in a bowl. And then when it hit me it was as if the wind had been ripped from my sails again. Another sacrifice!

Panic tore through me like a hurricane. I stood up so fast I nearly fainted, the lack of blood and air in my body coupled with the sudden realisation of what Dave intended left me reeling and dizzy. By the time I had managed to stumble back out into the street I could just make out the diminishing figures of the skinheads disappearing into the shadows of Heddon Street.

Fuck... oh fuck... what was I gonna do? I looked frantically up and down the street for somebody to tell, but what good would that do? As if rushing up to some tramp or a couple wandering hand in hand through the back streets of the West End was going to help. Unless I came across a gang of punks or a couple of coppers, I wasn't going to find any help on the streets. I went after them, sprinting as fast as my body would allow, every breath I took felt as if I were swallowing fire, out of the gloom and straight over Regent Street, which was eerily quiet, the banks of white-stoned walls rising like a great wave before me. In fact it was as if the whole of London had suddenly gone to bed, there wasn't a car or a person to be seen in either direction, the yellow glow of the streetlights illuminating the famous sweeping crescent shone down on a ghost town. The rumble of the traffic could be heard at either end, and I knew if I waited probably no more than a minute, everything would spring back to life: cars, buses and black cabs rushing by, late night tourists and night clubbers appearing from every which way. But I didn't have a minute, and besides, who was going to help? *Excuse me... my mate's being kicked to shit by a gang of skinheads in that back street... fancy helping me?*

I was just about to charge headlong into the fire when I had a change of plan and decided to enter by the other entrance, the footpath further up that led to Ziggy's phone box at the end. In truth, I had no plan at all, hadn't had long enough to form any idea other than to get in there, but what use was I going to be? Only one of me, and a virtual cripple at that, against eight or nine glue-crazed skinheads, which led to the question, what did Dave expect to achieve on his own either? I didn't have time to think of answers, in fact I tried to put all thoughts and ideas out of my mind, I would never find any anyway, and plunged into the shadows of the alley.

I couldn't see anyone at first, the beacon of light from the famous K.WEST sign momentarily transfixing me. Then something on the opposite side of the narrow street dragged me back, further down. In the shadows there was movement... voices, not shouting or blood curdling screams but raspy voices, it sounded like the venomous hissing of so many snakes. From somewhere inside instinct kicked in and I managed to collect myself for a moment. There was no fighting going on, they weren't jumping all over and kicking the life out of him, that was clear. I edged a little closer, sticking to the shadows of the walls. The closer I got I could start to make out the taunts, threats spat out into the night of what they were going to do to him. Dave was standing in a doorway surrounded by bald-headed figures. I couldn't imagine how he had let himself be cornered in such a fashion unless it had been deliberate.

'No way out this time, *freak*,' hissed the leader. He stood a few feet beyond the circle of skinheads, prowling around the man-made ring.

'But why would I want to go anywhere?' Dave replied with what looked like a nonchalant shrug, as if he were discussing how to spend an empty afternoon with a friend. 'Thought I'd spend some time with my big brother!'

The world seemed to slide out of view and I reached out blindly for the wall. 'How *is* our Daddy these days?' Dave went on. 'Still a twisted, murdering prick?'

Dave's words stopped the tall skinhead in his tracks, he was no longer stalking around, but stood, a few inches taller, face to face with Dave: identical bodies, identical framework, like bookends… like *brothers*.

'He ain't no murderer!' spat the skinhead. He jabbed a finger at Dave's chest. 'He didn't kill *your* stupid mother, the mental fucker killed herself!'

My head was spinning, I felt as if I'd been punched in the chest again. I leant in a doorway unable to breathe, unable to move. It was the skinhead from *The Kick In*. How had I not seen it? But more than that, he was… he was… Dave's brother! How had I never seen *that*? Not ever, in all the years that the unwelcome images of that dreadful summer's day had crept back into my mind, had I once imagined that the boy who had inflicted such a terrible, humiliating beating on Dave had been his brother… Christ almighty.

The ground seemed to shift beneath my feet. They were brothers! Half-brothers, or so it appeared from the way the skinhead had referred to Dave's mum as "your" mother. They stood there inches away from one another, brothers… strangers.

The skinhead was at least an inch and a half taller and I had always assumed that it must have been about the same in years. Was it like staring into a mirror I wondered to myself, could each of them see something so strikingly familiar but yet so faintly subtle that you had to know what you were looking for to distinguish it?

'He fuckin' hates you, you know?' the skin sneered. He was trying to taunt Dave, hurt him inside, he knew with all his mates behind him that it was a forgone conclusion that he was going to hurt him physically, but after last time he knew that he couldn't break him, and now with barbs about their father he was attempting to cut Dave deeper than any rusty old compass could. 'Says you're a friggin' weirdo,' he went on. 'A *freak*.'

Dave clasped his hands on his cheeks and let out a dramatic gasp. 'Nooo! Really?' And then in a flash replied in a deadpan voice, 'Why's that then? Because I can spell my own name or because I can count up to four on my own perhaps?'

There was a moment of silence between them, as I stood mesmerised in the shadows, a silence that almost hummed from the tension surrounding them. It hung over the whole street, suspended from roof to roof like some giant oppressive canopy. Dave's refusal to bite was beginning to frustrate his sibling, I could see it in the way that he had begun to shift restlessly from side to side, backwards and forwards and the way in which he kept clenching and unclenching his fists, as though he were trying to relieve himself from a bout of pins and needles.

'Reckons fuckin' your mum was the worst day's work he ever did.' The skin was bouncing up and down on the spot now as if he needed a piss, a demented, crazed look in his eyes. The light from the street lamp bounced off them as if they were glass.

'Now I know you're lying!' Dave cried out. And for a moment his brother thought that he had finally nailed him, that he had found a way through Dave's defences; he could see it in the change in his body language, the slight drop of his shoulders, the way he rolled back onto the soles of his feet. And then, just as he had mentally let his guard down the closest thing I had ever seen to a sneer broke across Dave's face, and as he spoke he seemed to find that extra inch and a half that he lacked. He stared directly into his sibling's eyes as he spoke. 'Because the useless, lazy little fucker never worked a day in his life.'

I think at that moment the skin realised that he was never going to win. Somewhere behind that tattooed mask of evil it finally dawned on him that he was out of his league, punching above his weight. Why was he even bothering with this war of words, I wondered. Surely if he knew Dave at all, which he obviously did, he must have known that he could never have realistically hoped to win. Much quicker and better to simply end it right there, finish it the only way he knew how, by him and his cronies jumping all over and kicking the living crap out of him. So why the hell wasn't he? Why had he bothered at all with this one-sided slanging match?

But at the very moment that this thought was rattling around in my head the skinhead, unwittingly, provided me with the answer.

'You gonna fight back this time, you little shit?'

Dave took a moment then casually glanced over his half-brother's shoulder. 'Not a lot of point.' He shrugged. And I realised that he had him exactly where he wanted him, if you didn't know any better and had happened to stumble into the scene unfolding it would be easy to think that it was indeed Dave who was trapped, cornered by his nemesis and his bloodthirsty gang. But the more I saw, the more I realised that Dave was in control, pulling the strings; the puppeteer of the whole sick play.

'As soon as I start beating the shit out of you,' Dave explained, nodding in the direction of the huddle of bald robots behind him, 'your little gang there will join in.'

The skin afforded himself a fleeting look over his shoulder

and then turned back to face Dave, his eyes narrowing into sinister black slits as he appeared to be considering Dave's point. The childlike crucifix and teardrops stained on his face seemed to rise, like embossed paper, from his skin as the pale light from the street lamps painted his flesh a ghostly-white.

'Nah they won't,' he said finally. 'Just you and me.'

Dave tilted his head back. 'Huh,' he laughed mockingly. 'They'll be on me after the first punch!'

'No!' his brother insisted, a hint of desperation in his voice, worried that once again Dave wouldn't properly fight back, robbing him of the respect gained from victory. 'I'll tell 'em.' And he shouted across to the mob lurking in the distance, 'No one jumps in, right! Just me and my little brother!' Then he sneered lecherously through the half-light at Dave. 'Right, little brother?'

Dave could barely keep the grin from splitting across his blank expression. 'Fine,' he shrugged and allowed the faintest of smiles to creep up his cheeks, a nervous, twitchy smile, more for show, I reckoned, so his adversary would think he had seen through his bluff. But it was a grin like nothing I had ever seen before. I was used to that smile of his that carried not a trace of any real happiness, but this was different, somehow even darker; storm clouds, like omens, raged behind his glazed eyes. It was as if his whole being had become possessed by something more evil than I could imagine.

His half-brother edged closer, his whole manner more aggressive. I tried to picture him with hair, a greased-up quaff, and suddenly he was transformed into his old man… Dave's old man.

'What you waiting for, Bowie Boy?' He spat the words out with such disgust as if he were labelling Dave a ponce or a pervert. The menace in his voice reverberated around the street like thunder. He closed in, his shadow swallowing Dave like a black wave. I felt the taste of sick in the back of my throat, and he was just about to speak again, I just caught the hiss in his voice, when all of a sudden his head snapped back and forth twice in quick succession, as if it were being worked by a string, snuffing out the words in his mouth. Like a gunslinger in a draw, Dave had thrown two lightning jabs into his face and had replaced his arm by his side before the dazzled skinhead had even known what had hit him. He touched his lips and inspected the blood coating his fingers, rubbing it between the tips and his thumb as if to check that it was genuine. He looked up at Dave and was met with one of his impassive shrugs, as if to say, *'Well, what did you expect?'*

The skinhead licked his lips and spat blood on the floor by Dave's feet. Gurgling, guttural noises escaped from somewhere deep inside his chest, his whole body seemed to rumble from the force of containing it, like an earthquake ready to explode. 'Right then,' he growled and leapt forward, arms raised, hell-bent on destruction. But once more he was stopped dead in his tracks, as Dave's left fist again crashed in and out of his unprotected face, three, four times, like a piston, each jab landing with unerring accuracy, in exactly the same spot as before. The skinhead's whole mouth was just a mass of red now, as if he'd been stuffing his face with jam doughnuts. Blood dripped in great globules from his chin and lay splattered across his cheeks and nose.

This time Dave stepped out into the inky-black street and any hint of his casual persona had vanished, there was nothing languorous or carefree about the way he stood facing the root of all his nightmares now. The slightly sideways stance, fists tucked in around his chest, there was a ruthless efficiency about him. He didn't say a word, just stood there waiting patiently, for what were a few more seconds, when you've been waiting four years? His hair, even in the pale streetlight, seemed to gleam a kind of robotic metallic orange: *The Man Who Fell to Earth,* the transported alien; *Ziggy* in his back street. I realised how much he must have been waiting for this moment, planning it even.

Again the giant skinhead put a hand up to his mouth, but he

didn't need to look at his palm this time to know what was on it, he simply flicked the blood off his hand and sent it spraying across the tarmac, where it lay glistening black in the glare of the streetlights, like puddles of oil. The rest of his gang began to shift restlessly in the background, unsure what to do, whether to ignore their leader's orders and simply jump in or stand back obediently. They looked anxiously around at each other for any signs of authority but it was in vain, they all lacked the courage or confidence to make a decision. And then, literally as one, as if the night were suddenly full of a million beady eyes, their heads turned in my direction, like a pack of startled hyenas, their senses heightened as I let out a sudden gasp of air.

I had been holding my breath from the fear and hadn't even realised it, and now I had unwittingly given myself away. I pressed myself further between the angle of the doorway and wall, trying to melt into the shadows. They couldn't see me, I was sure, and the way their eyes continued darting up and down the street searching for signs of life encouraged me to hold my breath again and remain where I was.

A young couple, full of innocence, giggling and holding hands, strayed in from the main entrance of the street. The sound of their laughter punctuated the air like shards of broken glass tinkling down upon the cold, dark tarmac. They stopped to kiss and cuddle in the shadows when they suddenly became aware of the drama they had stumbled into. For a brief moment the two acts stood staring at each other: the two main characters duelling in the street and the rest of the assembled cast in the background against the pair of lovers. Each invading the other's private ritual, before the young couple wisely decided that they didn't belong in the scene that was about to unfold before them and turned and scurried, hand in hand, back into the noise and safety of Regent Street.

Fortunately the distraction had shifted the attention away from me, heads turned back towards the main entrance of Heddon

Street, but Dave had been the only one who had had to turn and look over his shoulder and the skinhead was determined to take full advantage of this. Whether or not Dave sensed him coming, caught a glimpse of his shadow elongated along the street, closing in on him like a dark mood, or it was all part of his plan, I will never know, but just as it seemed as if he was upon him, Dave ducked out to his left, turned sharply and thundered three more punches into the left cheekbone of the flailing skinhead. They were knockout punches, *thud, thud, thud,* like the sound of pounded meat. On top of the punishment he had already received he had every right to stay down where he fell, not even the rest of them could have blamed him. He had been totally and utterly outfought. But there was more at stake than just a loss of face, something stronger than pride to win. He dragged his gangling, long frame back to its feet, staggered from side to side - he looked like a baby giraffe taking his first steps, slowly unfolding its newborn body - and then managed to find his balance and stand up straight. Unbelievably I began to feel something close to sympathy stirring inside me and shuddered, the way people do when they say someone's walked over their grave, from the thought that I could waste even the slightest, sliver of a thought on the boy who had caused me and my mates so much grief, the person who, more than any other, had shattered the simplicity of my little world.

But any thought that he had been broken, cowed into submission, soon evaporated when I saw the hate that burned in his eyes. He hurled some threats and insults at Dave, it was all he had left to fight with, but they were unintelligible. His mouth was full of blood and the side of his face had already swollen grotesquely out of shape. He had begun to wheel around in circles, cursing and pointing erratically all around as if he couldn't really be sure where Dave stood. In the distance, the lights of Piccadilly Circus tinged the underbelly of the clouds. Dark clouds gathered overhead, especially, it seemed, in the confines of Heddon

Street, as if the cold weight of menace had sent the warmth plummeting into submission.

The skinhead wasn't making any progress in Dave's direction, he just sort of stood there, knock-kneed, legs, astride like a broken tripod or a crippled oil platform, his bony fingers jabbing the air. It was pathetic. Once again I had to fight back any feelings of sympathy. But Dave had no such problem, he emitted a kind of impatient sigh and, for the first time during the fight, took a forward step. He stood above him, arms hanging loosely by his side, peering down as if he were examining a crippled bug. He wanted his half-brother to see how utterly useless he had become, how he, the lean, mysterious Bowie fan who repulsed him, who stood for everything a skinhead detested, had beaten and broken him, in front of all his friends, into a dribbling, bloody mess. For the ultimate humiliation I thought perhaps Dave might extend a finger, as if he were about to call for an elevator, and simply push him to the floor. But Dave hadn't finished, was nowhere near, he had yet to rid himself of the pain; of the rejection. He had inhaled the smoke of humiliation for so long that it had formed layers inside, it clung to the walls of his heart, clogging his arteries like tar.

Three more blows smashed into the face of the buckled figure in front of him, blood sprayed everywhere now, as if Dave were pounding a sodden sponge. In a pool of light I could just make out the skinhead's eyes rolling dangerously in his head before he crashed to the floor with a sickening thud, but the danger didn't seem to register with Dave, he sat astride his back and, with no hair to take hold of, gripped an ear in each hand and began to systematically drive the skin's head into the ground. It was too much for the rest of them, as the sound of braking teeth rang out, they surged forward.

'Dave!' I yelled out, but my words were drowned out by the sound of the charging skinheads, and he hardly needed me to tell him of the danger. He jumped off the prostate figure of their leader just as the first skinhead to reach him aimed a twelve-holed boot at his ribs. He managed to avoid the brunt of the kick but was still sent sprawling across the road. The skinhead closed in and swung another boot at Dave's head but Dave was ready for him this time and with his reflexes unaffected by the first kick, swept the reckless skinhead's standing leg from underneath him, sending him crashing to the ground on his back, as if he'd slipped on a bar of soap. He lay there struggling for breath, the wind knocked out of him. As Dave jumped to his feet, he planted his own foot in the hapless skinhead's face, as if to show him how it should be done.

But that still left five, maybe six more and it was too many, even for the fully-charged, fighting machine that Dave seemed to have morphed into. The next two had reached him now, but after witnessing the result of their mate charging in manically, they showed more caution, they stalked him from either side, and as Dave picked off one with a couple of well-aimed jabs, the other tried to land a few haymakers of his own, but Dave managed to protect himself from most of the damage by deflecting the blows with a raised elbow. With blood pouring from the nose of the skin he was facing, he turned his attention to the one trying to smash his skull open, but just as he bobbed and weaved his way into range and landed a thumping uppercut, lifting the haymaker skinhead off his feet, the other four piled on top of him like a wave crashing over him. I was no more than a second or two behind, none of them, not even Dave, had seen me slip from the shadows and I intended to take full advantage of the element of surprise, it was the best weapon I had. For when that had gone, one arm wasn't going to be much good.

In the briefest of moments it took for me to reach them, a lifetime of unlived memories spun like a roulette wheel round in my head. They reckon your life flashes in front of your eyes before the moment that you think you're going to die, but to me it's just the opposite. I couldn't say for certain that I thought I was going to die, didn't have the time to think anything, but I knew that whatever was about to unfold would be final, the irrefutable feeling that nothing would or could ever be the same again, and something close to relief began to creep through me, a sense of liberation almost. For since - I didn't know when - I had been haunted by the certain knowledge that it was all going to end, that I was never going to make it as a goalkeeper, I just never knew how. Two broken arms hadn't even finished me off but now the cobwebs of premonition that hung in every corner of my mind had finally gone; braking from my hideaway, like a soldier out and over the trenches, had blown them away.

I saw myself between the goalposts of famous pitches that I now knew I would never play on: Elland Road, Highbury, Old Trafford, Maine Road... Wembley. Cheered on and applauded by crowds that would never see me, for saves that I would never make. I saw me and Dave laughing on a beach someplace, older now, the lines of maturity playing round eyes, creasing our features like paper; and around our feet, splashing in the surf, two children, the sea breeze whipping spray into their tiny faces, forcing them to turn away from the lens of my mind's eye. I wanted desperately to see their faces, search for familiarities, to know if they were boys or girls... but I knew I would never be able to. Like a dream that you wished you hadn't woken from and can't, no matter how much you try and squeeze your eyes shut, force your way back into. The moment had gone, the spell broken, for I was upon them, and, just like a dream I knew that all those moments would never come true.

They had formed a scrum around him, DM boots flying in everywhere. I took a running kick of my own at the first skinhead I came across, aiming deliberately at where I judged the base of his spine to be, the coccyx. I knew from bitter experience how painful it could be, from the time a stray boot had embedded itself into the top of the crack of my arse. I had felt physically sick from the sheer agony, the weirdest sensation of pain I'd ever known, as if the marrow had been scooped out from inside my bones. I was hoping my victim felt the same, it would almost certainly be one less to worry about in the scheme of things. And the second he froze, body rigid from the shock, and fell to his knees clutching the cheeks of his backside, I knew he wouldn't be getting back up. His mates hadn't seemed to notice, too busy trying to kick the life out of Dave, and even as the boots crowded above him and the kicks reigned down, even in the heat of this war with no rules, I felt the stomach-churning discomfort of what I'd just done, of how, in the law of the playground, it used to be frowned upon if you resorted to kicking in a fight; considered cowardly. The sensation of the skin's spine, hard at the end of my foot, reverberated through my body, rolled like seasickness in my guts. It proved what I had known all along of course, that I lacked the will for a fight. It wasn't fear, in fact I felt bizarrely at ease, as if a hymn were being sung in my head.

From somewhere to my left a fist suddenly flew through the night and thudded into my eye. I hadn't even seen it coming but its landing certainly brought me back to reality. I no longer felt sick, just a blinding pain in my eye socket, as if a firework had exploded in my face. Instinctively I took a step back, narrowly avoiding a second bomb from detonating on top of me. I was suddenly aware of him closing in, my attacker, his shadow snuffing out the light, it was almost claustrophobic. But still I reached out and grabbed him with both arms and pulled him down even closer. It was a move borne out of survival more than retaliation; with me hanging round his neck, I reckoned it would prove virtually impossible to throw any decent punches. It provided me with the few precious seconds I needed to gather my senses. I could smell the cider and glue on his breath, dredging up the memories from times before; I could feel the distinctive fibres from his Fred Perry shirt rubbing fiercely against my cheek as we grappled like confused magnets, him trying to escape my clinging body. But there was something else... an extra accessory to the skinhead uniform, something dangling in my face. It was a tie. And I realised I was wrestling with the bully from outside the bookies.

The realisation lit something inside me, justice for the poor drunk. I reached blindly out gripped the tie and yanked it up with all my strength, twisting and turning it as I went. The result was instant. His body snapped up straight, eyes bulging as he omitted strange gurgling cries. I stood on tiptoes, lifting my arm as high as I possibly could. I started to run a little from side to side, tugging in and out in a bid to tighten the knot cutting into his neck. His stare grew wilder, his eyes like two cue balls about to pop out from his skull as he clawed at his neck like some crazed animal on a leash. What with his writhing and bucking and my own efforts, between us we managed to pull it even tighter; a silk noose choking the life from him.

But I couldn't hold on forever, Dave still needed help. Although, since my arrival, there were two less skinheads for him to contend with, and with two less DM boots flying around his head, he had somehow managed to scamper far enough out of range to enable him to find his feet.

So with the muscles in my good arm fading fast, I could feel them beginning to twitch and wobble, I summoned the last of their strength and gave one almighty tug on the thread of silk in my hand. The move caught the choking skinhead off his guard, had been too busy trying to tear the constricting garment from his windpipe, and as his body came rushing towards me I dipped my head and slammed my forehead into his unprotected face. *An eye for an eye*, I thought. White light exploded before my eyes, even though I had instinctively squeezed them shut. The collision rushed down the length of my face, stabbing like needles into the roots of my front teeth. I was fairly sure that I had broken my nose, it felt as it had landed up somewhere in the back of my skull. I staggered backwards, blinking away the tears and stars, and gingerly put a hand up to my nostrils. To my surprise there was no blood, but I could still taste it, that unmistakable metallic tang, as thick as syrup upon my lips. And when I traced its flow my fingers felt the puckered skin of the wound I had opened up in the centre of my forehead. *I'm a sitting duck* I thought to myself. Doubled over, eyes overflowing with water, I couldn't have defended myself if my life had depended upon it. But fortunately I didn't have to, for when I eventually managed to flush out the last of the salt water and lift my ringing head, I saw the hazy figure of the skinhead lying spread-eagled across the street, his nose, truly broken and bloody, twisted across his cheek.

Dave appeared to be holding his own... *just.* With their leader lying utterly destroyed at their feet and Dave back on his, they trod cautiously. They stood side by side, a few feet apart, in a sort of half circle around him, unsure what to do next, and Dave didn't give them a chance to work it out either. He ducked sharply to his right and unleashed a ferocious jab into the mouth of nearest skinhead and had stepped back to where he had stood before he or any other of his bewildered companions had realised what had happened. It bought Dave time, a few precious seconds, but how long would it be before their hatred reached boiling point again and they found their will? I could make out his eyes darting from one to the other as they slowly began to edge forward like zombies from some crappy B horror movie. And then I saw him do a double take in my direction, as if seeing me for the first time *'What the fuck are you doing here?'* shot like some telepathic message through the night. In that moment the darkness seemed to intensify, the few tiny squares of light from the buildings above appeared more distant. The space around us was closing in, Dave was running out of room and only a few feet remained behind him before he would come up against a wall of blackness. The situation seemed to register with the thug in the middle, and the split second Dave took to acknowledge me was when he made his move; he took one giant step forward and hit Dave squarely on the jaw. The sheer ferocity of the punch sent him reeling backwards and if it hadn't been for the wall he would probably have ended up on the floor. He looked completely stunned as he sagged against the brickwork, the events of the night were beginning to take their toll. Since I had stepped into the secluded confines of Heddon Street and up to the moment Dave stood surrounded against the wall, not more than ten minutes had passed, I reckoned. But that was an awful long time to be living on a knife-edge, fighting with your wits as well as your fists, protecting your body whilst all the time you're ripping open the barely-healed scars from a torturous past. Sensing that this was their moment, the three skinheads leapt as one upon Dave's exhausted body in a flurry of fists and boots.

I was there in a heartbeat and once again attempted my "kick in the back" approach. I no longer felt it to be cowardly, anything that would gain an inch of advantage was acceptable for this was a street fight with no rules or conscience. I had just slammed my head into another person's face for heaven's sake! Something I never thought I would ever have the stomach for. But the violence permeating the street, through the walls of the buildings, had simply taken me over, I was a part of it now, a cog in the machine, no longer just a victim caught up in it. But just as I swung my leg, too late to change direction, my intended target swivelled round, resulting in my boot deflecting off the top of his thigh and becoming entangled in the loop of his red braces. Whether it was instinct that made him turn or he had heard me approaching I didn't know, I was only aware that the motion of his body had me frantically hopping about in a bid to stay upright as I was sent spinning to one side. I tried to kick and pull my way free but succeeded only in tying myself up further. He was spitting and cursing, twisting this way and that like a hooked fish.

'Get the fuck off!' he snarled, thumping my shin in frustration. The muscles in my calf were turning to liquid, the tips of my toes on fire. I couldn't stay up for much longer so, in a move reminiscent of my fight with the "tie" skin, I summoned the last of my strength, took one almighty hop forward and braced myself as our bodies slammed together. He hadn't been expecting it, or even been looking, too busy pounding my shin, so at the moment of impact I was able to raise a forearm into his face and send him crashing to the ground before he even knew what had hit him. I no longer had any morals left to wrestle with, nothing to tug away at my sense of what was right, simply stepped out of the red loop spread out upon the floor and then back down onto the face of its prostrate owner and didn't take my foot off until, like crushing ice, I felt the rubbery contours of flesh and bone give way beneath the sole of my boot.

Is this what I had become? What certain teachers and people in authority always said I would: *scum*. Drinking and fighting like animals down back alleys… stamping on faces! Two skinheads I had left lying there, very possibly scarred or marked by broken bones for life. In truth they had defeated themselves, I reckoned. If the first thug hadn't been wearing the tie he had pilfered as a trophy and the latter wore his braces over his shoulders instead of as a fashion statement, as part of a uniform, then in all likelihood I wouldn't have stood a chance. But I had chosen the wrong time to dwell on such things, for as I turned to see how Dave was faring all I saw was a giant fist crashing straight into my face.

Later on, lying in hospital, when the whole grisly nightmare began to slowly unfold in my mind's eye each night, piece by piece, like prizing open folded paper, I could actually make out the word LOVE branded across his knuckles, seconds before they crash-landed somewhere deep inside my brain. And I remember thinking that he'd hit me with the wrong hand, it should have been the other hand… HATE.

But at the time it took several seconds before I realised that I'd been hit. When I was finally able to sit up and look around I couldn't tell my left from my right. In fact, so disorientated was I that if it hadn't been for the ground beneath me I reckoned I would have struggled to work out up from down. I had never been hit so hard in my life, the sheer strength of it had poleaxed me. There was a ringing in my ears that couldn't have been louder if I had crept beneath the bell of Big Ben and I could feel my left eye closing by the second as the blood pounded beneath the battered flesh. I clawed desperately at the wall behind me, like a drunk trying to find his feet, until a thudding boot in my side buckled me in two. And it was then that I made one of the biggest mistakes of my life.

I could have crawled up into a ball, protected my face and head as best as possible and simply waited until he had kicked himself out or until Dave, if he was still on his feet, had intervened or someone had come along, probably wouldn't have felt a thing by then anyway, or I could have laid on my side and shielded my arm from the brunt of the punishment. But I did neither of those things; instead I made the critical, career-ending, life-changing error of shuffling round on my backside to face my attacker.

I can still remember the scratchy feel of the brickwork against my back as I leant there, then the flicker of a memory ran, like water across glass, through my mind, sparked off by the sensation of brick against my back and a box of white light that glowed somewhere high up just outside my peripheral vision... *I had been here before*. Slouched against this wall, slightly detached from reality. It was like returning to a dream. Then two more kicks brutally assaulted me, finding their target easily against my useless body. The first in exactly the same place as the last, in my side at the bottom of my rib cage; the second landed firmly in my guts, nearly cutting me in half.

I began to feel everything drift away from me, the visions in my head became distorted and the voices grew distant, it was as if I were melting from the inside. I lay there doubled over and fighting for breath, it was the second time within the hour that I had been winded, only the first time had been nowhere near as brutal. My left eye had closed completely and I had to keep blinking away thick globules of blood in my right from the gash in my forehead. More kicks reigned in, wilder and less accurate now, frenzied blows deflecting off my shoulder and my legs. I couldn't really feel them but the direction of one or two forced me to instinctively put my left hand down to stop myself from thudding into the ground.

I can still recall the cool smoothness of the well-worn pavement beneath my palm, the very one that Bowie, posing in outrageous purple boots, had stood upon. It was the last thing my left hand ever felt against its skin. If I had been given a choice, I suppose I would have opted for the feel of a leather ball as I made one last heroic save, or perhaps even the softness of Elaine's cheek as my fingers caressed it, not a slab of concrete. But then Dave would have loved it for what it represented and, as ridiculous as it was, I took a strange comfort in that.

I was aware of the danger, even as I struggled for breath, of leaning on my damaged arm but, try as I might, I just didn't have the strength to push myself back upright. Somewhere outside the fog in my mind I heard a voice. I never did see his face, the face that robbed me of a football career, who was responsible for nearly killing me… *for virtually saving me.*

I heard his voice though, slurred and full of hate, something about a "fuckin' goalkeeper", and then the world exploded.

I was aware of a loud crack and for the briefest of moments I thought it was the sound of gunfire bouncing off the walls and around the confines of the dead-end street, that maybe one of the remaining skinheads had a pistol tucked away somewhere down the waistband of his bleached jeans, that maybe Dave had been shot! But then the crack disintegrated into a sickening splinter and I was blinded by unspeakable pain. Glaring, white-hot light burned in my brain, I wanted to scream but felt paralysed, bile stung the

410

back of my throat but I couldn't throw up either, it was a if my whole system had shut down. I was spinning from the inside out, round and round in a vortex of pain; faster and faster, deeper and deeper, until there was nothing but darkness.

And then I'm floating, above the cars, the black taxis and buses, looking down on the rooftops of the buildings and landmarks of London, the Thames sparkling green and blue below like a silk scarf. And then I'm honing in on Heddon Street, drifting down like a parachutist upon the tiny ant-like figures below. They are littered, like dead flies, up and down the street; beaten and broken bodies in billowing pools of blood. There are only two people on their feet, one bald, his pink head showing like a beacon as he runs back out in the direction of Regent Street, and the other is Dave, standing above a hunched figure in a doorway. The pair of them illuminated by the square of white light attached to the wall above them, the words K.WEST etched across it. I can't see Dave's face but can tell by his body, the shape of his shoulders, the way he runs a hand through his mop of hair that he is agitated. He tilts his head and shakes it to get a better look at the body in the doorway. At first it looks nothing more than a passed-out drunk, bent over double, lying on his side. But his face is a distorted mess of blood and bruises, and there is also something poking into him, as he has been stabbed with a thin white jagged object; the blood seeping across the step proof of his injury. But as I drift closer I can see that it isn't something sticking *in* the crumpled body on the ground but something sticking *out*. Broken bone from his forearm, snapped like the branch of a tree, protruding through the ripped skin, and then the full extent of the horror hits me, and I am no longer bouncing along in the air, but plummeting to the ground like a stone, heading straight for the corpse-like figure leaking life in the doorway… on a collision course with myself.

CHAPTER THIRTY

May 1979

Dave moved closer, wavering a little, unsteady on his feet, but still that familiar gait, unmistakable. Somewhere in the background a streetlight projected the length of his shadow across the road, engulfing me like a wave. He stopped a few feet from where I lay against a wall, crumpled like a broken doll. And for a moment or two, before the world began to swim in out of focus, he looked like some kind of futuristic spaceman, a shadow cast in the light as he stepped out of his spaceship, a scene from *Close Encounters...* ' or *Ziggy* back in the street where he had landed seven years before.

But it was hardly the time to tell him and besides, the pain I was in had become so excruciating that I couldn't even speak. It wasn't only my arm, it felt as if my whole body had been shattered, as if I had been paralysed. The sight of Dave began to blur, as if my eyes were a windscreen in the pouring rain and my wipers had stopped working. I'd been here before, on more than one occasion. I was about to pass out, but I had never experienced such pain in my life. I tried desperately to fight it, to blink myself back into a state of consciousness. I tried to focus on Dave.

How long had I known the boy standing before me? This *Starman* this *Ziggy*, this *Thin White Duke*... this *Space Oddity*. All of my seventeen years for sure, but it seemed longer. There had been times when he had almost felt a part of me, like he flowed with the blood through my veins, and yet the air of mystery that hung around him at times transformed him into a stranger.

Blood dripped rhythmically from the wound on his head, *drip, drip, drip,* streams of red flowing through the contours of his face, running along the line of his jawbone and forming a dark, sinister puddle by his feet. For a moment it was all that could be heard, the sound of his blood splashing on the tarmac as we stared up and down at each other in crazy, stunned silence.

But the numbing waves of oblivion began slowly to wash over me, and it seemed so appealing: sleep. To pass out, somewhere to hide from the agony that ripped through my arm. It was as if it were clamped between the jaws of some kind of terrible wild animal, tearing and ripping through the flesh and into the very marrow of the bone and all I could do was lie there and watch, already half dead.

'Johnny?' The familiar, reassuring sound of Dave's voice hovered somewhere outside my head, I forced my eyes open but the glare of the streetlights felt like needles in my eyes.

'Johnny!' he moved close. 'We've got to get out of... ' he stood over me staring, transfixed, down at my arm and gave a short gasp as if he had had the wind punched out of him. 'Oh, *Johnny*... what have I *done*?' Something inside me registered the change in his voice, the shock curling the edges of that usually soothing tone of his, like the heat of a flame too close to paper.

What seemed like an eternity, but was probably no more than a moment, passed by. 'All right, Johnny.' He had regained his composure now, the cool Dave I had always known, relied on, it had only betrayed him for the briefest of moments but it was enough. I hadn't actually looked at the damage yet, each time I tried to manoeuvre my head in that direction it felt as if my brain would shatter like glass.

'All right, Johnny,' he repeated soothingly, and it could have been the loss of blood from his head, but he looked a little unsteady on his feet now. 'It'll be all right.'

But of course I didn't know that he had been looking down at the broken wreck of my arm, the bone sticking out, torn through the skin as if it were a paper bag. 'I'll call an ambulance, hold on.'

Terror ripped through me now as the sound of his footsteps faded back into the night. I knew he would never leave me and that he had only gone to the phone box, the very one that Bowie had been photographed in. But his presence pacified the panic that welled inside me. Crazily I thought of trying to move, of trying to haul myself to my feet. I felt like a child, scared and lonely in the dark. And that was when I heard the sound of the sirens, growing louder with every heartbeat. And it was just as well, for I couldn't hold on any longer. Even the gentle vibration of the air in my lungs racked my whole body with pain. I wanted to die. If it meant being rid of the unspeakable agony that I had never thought possible, I began to will it upon me, to release me. I wanted to scream out, purge; but I was already dead inside. I saw myself from above, lying in the doorway, a broken shadow in the half-light of the lamplight and the K.WEST sign. Couldn't life be sicker and more twisted than any fiction or any damn TV programme that they could ever make? For there I was, about to die like any Bowie fan would *die* to die. And I could see it all from my extraordinary place above, and the last thing I remember seeing before I slipped into unconsciousness was Dave, hobbling into the phone box that his hero had "landed" in. And for a crazy moment I wanted to laugh, for a twisted thought came back to me. I remembered that we had never taken that picture, the one on the back of the *Ziggy* cover where Bowie's standing in the phone box. We had run out of film. But he was going there now, if only I had a camera... if only I could move... and then darkness.

CHAPTER THIRTY - ONE

May 1979

Everything is white, as if the infinity of space is one giant cloud and I'm floating endlessly through. Everything is a blur, going round and round, and when it begins to clear it takes only a moment to realise that I'm not dreaming at all, but staring up at the blinding white washed ceiling of the hospital. From the corner of my eye I see shadows flickering faintly but the effort of trying to roll my eyes in the direction of the window exhausts me and sends my head spinning until I have to close them, until the feeling of nausea passes. My body is too weak to take anything in yet: light, smells, food, even the sipping of water makes me feel sick, it's as if I'm as fragile and empty as an eggshell.

The dizziness has passed but I still don't want to open my eyes, don't want to face the reality, the appalling truth. No, no it can't be! How do I possibly return from this?

I'll never play again, there will be no coming back from this, not this time. If I manage to walk out of these hospital doors with two fully functioning hands it will be a miracle in itself; a miracle perhaps, but just one catastrophe too many… To never play again, for my league debut to be my last game. If there is a God, he has one twisted, sick sense of humour. In time, when the stark reality has embedded itself in the foundations of my mind, where it can't be shifted, I'm sure the prospect will leave me horrified beyond belief. I'll probably even wish that I'd lost the damn thing, for what use will having two hands be if I can't play football again? It will taunt me every day, hanging there uselessly like an exposed appendix, but if it were no longer there, just a stump at the end of my arm, playing again could never be an issue.

I drift back inside myself, squeeze my eyes shut and try and step off the edge of reality and fall into an abyss of dreams. I can see myself hurtling down, down, down through the years:'79,'78,'77,'76 whiz past, each year a blur of memories, a spinning newsreel of my life;'75,'74,'73,'72,'71… and there I am, I can see myself, safe and sound in my own bed. Surrounded by pictures of Gordon Banks, George Best, Gary Glitter, T-Rex, cocooned in the safety of childhood. I want to stay here forever, where the only worries I have are which side will I be on at play time and will I have sausage and chips for tea tonight?

But, try as I might, I can't seem to stay here. The image starts to distort, like ripples running through a reflection in a pond. And I'm rising now, climbing the ladder of years, hurtling towards the light. I try desperately to stay submerged, but my imagination lacks substance, I lack the strength of mind to weigh myself down and instead I break the surface of my dreams and open my eyes to the stark horror that is the rest of my life.

'Dave!' I tried to move but my feet were caught up and twisted in the sheets. 'Dave… Where are you?' I knew I was asleep but couldn't seem to open my eyes. 'Dave!' I called louder. I could hear the sound of footsteps running down the corridor towards me. I kicked and bucked but ended up nowhere, my useless arm refused to move, suspended in a mid-air sling like something from a slapstick comedy. It no longer hurt, didn't even feel a part of me. I felt gentle but firm hands upon me, guiding my body back down into the mattress.

'Easy, Johnny, easy,' a soothing voice told me. I felt the warmth of a hand upon my forehead and the voice moved a little closer, 'Easy now, take it easy now.' I recognised it instantly, the delicate lilt in the tone, it worked like a sedative and helped to pacify me almost immediately.

'There you go now, Johnny, there, there,' she purred, while all the time stroking my hair. And for a moment there was no place I'd rather have been than lying there in the care of my very own angel. But the thought of Dave wouldn't go away and I forced my eyes open and blinked the sight of Nurse Wallace… Elaine, into focus. 'Dav?' I tried to speak his name, but the word seemed to die in my throat, as if it had been sieved through shingle.

'Just relax now, Johnny,' my angel whispered. 'You've had quite a time of it.' I gazed into the kindest smile I'd ever seen and could feel myself beginning to drift away again, nothing I could do to stop it. *But I'm going to take that smile with me…*

I awoke again with a start, chased from sleep by disturbing, grainy images in the shape of Dave disappearing out of my view in Heddon Street… out of my life. The naked, white light still hurt my eyes, so I drifted off again. And when I awoke I had no idea how long I'd been asleep or even if it was night or day, time had lost its meaning. I couldn't even begin to guess how long I had been there; days, weeks… months perhaps.

I'd been there before, of course, lying in a hospital bed with my arm and dreams in tatters. But in the past, both have managed to be stitched back together by the sheer brilliance of surgeons and the sheer insouciance that can often protect a seventeen year old, the way a coat of veneer protects a table. But this time, even with my distorted grip on reality and my veins full of painkillers, I knew that the damage had stripped it all, hope and healing, down to the very bone.

The walls and ceiling were both brilliant white, the familiar sound of footsteps squeaked upon the linoleum floor, the unmistakable odour of disinfectant hung in the air, that smell of efficiency. I glanced out of the window, at the square of blue sky with the crest of a tree creeping above the sill. From somewhere along the ward I could hear the tinny resonance of a portable radio: 'Britain's Number one… ' the jingle chimed… 'and still at the number one slot, here's Tubeway Army and "Are Friends Electric?"… ' And of course I thought of Dave. Tubeway Army, I thought to myself, from obscurity to the nation's favourite. That will make Dave squirm, I wonder if he knows?

He had been rattling on about this figure Gary Numan for some time now. *'It's cold outside and the paints peelin' off-a-my walls…* ' I could hear his mechanical voice clinking away a few beds down. And I could see the attraction for Dave for there were certainly similarities between him and Bowie's *Thin White Duke*. This Wharhol-esque, robotic figure with his striking bleached white hair, I can quite easily imagine him singing *Heroes* or anything from the *Berlin Trilogy*. Perhaps he too was influenced by Bowie… hell, perhaps he was influenced by Dave!

I keep having the dream, over and over, running through my muddled mind so many times that I can't tell if it is a real memory coming back to haunt me or just a tortured illusion.

Dave dropping from the top of the sails; but this time, as I lean over to watch him fall, I fall too… and Dave, he's like some Russian gymnast dismounting from those two giant rings that hang from the sky; all elegance and finesse, twisting and turning like a ribbon in the breeze. But me, I'm all arms and legs, flailing limbs slicing through the sky, the wind ripping the air from my lungs. And what had begun with me fearing for Dave's life ends up with me fearing for my own as I plummet to the floor, for I am going to end up smashed and broken, drowning in a sea of my own blood. In my mind's eye I see my body splayed across the deck; dreaming within a dream, the past and the future in perfect symmetry; like standing in a hall of mirrors. And all the while Dave is slowing down, floating like a falling leaf, arcing his lithe body to land gently on his feet. I catch a glimpse of his face, and there is that serene, easy smile upon it, as if he is savouring every moment of his descent; for he knows he is going to be safe, has known it all along, going exactly where he wants to be.

I want to scream but, of course, nothing comes out, and just as I'm about to die, the deck rushing to meet me, I see Dave grinning up at me, his arms outstretched, ready to break my fall… his ultimate sacrifice.

It always ended the same way, awakening with a start; Dave's waiting arms and smile burned into my brain. But when I tried to sit up I found that I couldn't move, like Gulliver tied and staked to the beach, I couldn't even raise my head off the hospital pillow.

Then once as I lay in a pool of sweat trying hard to focus my hazy vision on the white squares on the hospital ceiling, I heard a voice in the air. At first I thought it might be part of the dream, tricking me into believing that I was really awake, that it was just the drugs blurring the lines of reality and sleep. But I could sense a body stirring, adjusting in the seat beside me, and the words when they came were very real, piercing the fog that had grown around me.

"You could have saved him!" I could feel her squirm in her chair.

"You should have known!" Jenny hissed. She wasn't alone, and I knew it was Debbie, I could smell her before I heard her mumble something to Jen.

"Why couldn't you look after him the way he looked after you? Just once!" she cried.

"Just once! When he needed you!" Her voice tore through my brain like the raking of nails down a blackboard.

And there was another voice now; calm but firm, in control.

'Jenny!' Elaine said sternly. ' I am going to have to ask you to leave, Johnny's lost a lot of blood, he needs rest... not to be shouted at, to be... accused." The air crackled.

'Debbie,' Elaine continued with authority. "Please take your friend outside to get some fresh air.' There was a moment's silence, and as I lay there gazing stupidly at the ceiling, I could sense the two girls' shock that the nurse knew who they were, and I could almost hear the pieces being put into place in Jen's head.

"God, it didn't take him long did it?" She sneered with such venom that didn't do her justice.

"Please leave... now!" demanded Elaine, and as much as Jen

would think otherwise, it was spoken by the nurse in her, ingrained professionalism more than sentiment.

And as I lay there, willing myself back to sleep, to forget - the coma patient in reverse - I found myself wishing for the father I never had. Every bit as violent as Billy's and as shameful as Dave's... for I wanted something to hate... someone to blame it all upon. But it was no good, like trying to squeeze toothpaste back into a tube... and besides, Jenny's words kept ripping through me, tearing at my skin as if I were lying upon a bed of thorns.

CHAPTER THIRTY - TWO

June 1979

I thought that it would be the worst day of my life, Dave's funeral. All week as I lay there, staring at the patch of sky in front of me with everything and nothing running round and round in my head. It was almost as if I were dead myself... but then, in many ways, I suppose I was.

He had been found at the park at the end of our street. The park where we had grown up, blitzed through our childhoods like whirlwinds, played in from morning till night and then gone back home through the gap in the railings in a haze of grass stains, mud and bruises but always with a smile on our faces. Row upon row of football pitches; from the passing trains over the viaduct it had always, to me, looked like a giant croquet lawn, but when they told me Dave had been found hanging from a crossbar I knew exactly which pitch it would have been.

He had been wearing one of his old Bowie T-shirts, the one with the *Aladdin Sane* album cover on it. I couldn't erase the scene from my mind, every time I closed my eyes it was there, printed inside my eyelids: frayed sleeves pulled tight around his arms, torn at the shoulders to fit over his head, cotton wearing thin from all the years, and Bowie's face moulded across his chest. Of course they would all turn to me for an explanation, to put an end to the gossip and the theories that floated like ashes through town. But there was no point, for at the funeral I was no more than a dead man walking myself... and who speaks to ghosts?

The imminence of its arrival haunted me with every breath that I took; how could it not when all I could do was count down the minutes? And even if my daydreams did manage to slide something over the top of my thoughts for a moment or two it still never really went away, it was always visible, like a picture through tracing paper.

I was scared to go to sleep, kept seeing myself standing alone beneath a thundery-looking sky at the foot of his grave, the rain drumming relentlessly upon his coffin. And I wanted to cry, could feel the anguish welling up inside me, could see my head slowly start to inflate with the trapped tears, but still they wouldn't come. I closed my eyes and tried to force them out, but not a single drop came, nothing but the feel of the rain running down my cheeks. And then, just as I was sure my head was about to explode from the pressure, I would notice the lid of Dave's coffin slowly beginning to open, I would watch in fascinated horror as the screws slowly unwound of their own accord and pop out into the mud, and just as a bone-white hand crept out and started to push back the lid, I would awake with a start, never screaming, or even scared for that matter, but drenched in a pool of sweat and freezing cold, so much so that in the end I would have no option but to press my buzzer and call for a nurse to come and change my sheets. The first time it happened I could see that the nurse on night duty, not one that I was overly familiar with, doubted my explanation of a nightmare, thinking it was more likely that I had wet myself and I was so embarrassed that I begged her to put her face to the material and smell it, and after that, as it quickly became a nightly ritual, I could see the sympathy cloud her face, but I couldn't meet her gaze, I didn't think I deserved it.

But when the day finally arrived it was in complete contrast to my nightmares, for as I mind-numbingly watched the sun slowly rise, it shone so brightly in the blue, cloudless sky that it was hard to believe that such a beginning to a day could offer nothing more than an end to a life. Dave was going to be buried on what turned out to be one of the hottest days of the year. He often commented to me that life was a bit of sick joke, one of his "wiser than his years" philosophies, but I could see the truth in it now.

How, I wondered as I lay there watching the dawn slowly dilute the night, can the sun shine today? And the more I thought about it, the more I realised that the day would be just like any other day; the sun would shine, the shops would open, people would go to work, the papers would report on politics, taxes, strikes, babies would be born and old people would die. The day would unfurl just as the day before had and the day before that and Dave's funeral would pass the rest of the world by. Gilbert O'Sullivan's "Nothing Rhymes" started to drift through my head and I realised that my mind had performed its masochistic trick of conjuring up a song that could have been written for my mood, and as if to prove the point, after spending the entire night, with my whole body crawling with the fears and insecurities that life without Dave promised, I fell into a deep, unforgiving sleep.

They had tried to stop me from going, the doctors. Had reasoned that the last place I needed to be in my state, both physically and mentally, was at my best friend's funeral.

'You lost a considerable amount of blood, Mr Chalmers,' my surgeon had told me, as if he were talking to grown, mature man! 'These things need to be monitored.' And with a weary shake of his head he added, 'amongst other things.'

For I had since discovered why it felt as if lightning was splitting my head in two every time I opened my eyes, especially when I awoke. My skull was coloured black and blue and so many blood vessels had burst in my eyes that the blood had flooded across the whites like ink across blotting paper.

'But I have to be there,' I had insisted. 'He's my best… was my best… ' But I found I didn't have the will to correct myself, to speak of Dave in the past tense.

423

He had taken a deep breath, sucking in over his teeth the way that only *real* grown, mature men can. 'Very well,' he had said without a shred of sympathy in his voice, as if I'd been a drunk or football hooligan dragged in from the street; nothing but a drain on his time and the hospital's reserves. 'We shall see what we can do.' And without another word or even looking up from his clipboard he turned and strode authoritatively back along the ward, a nurse at each of his heels, scurrying along to keep up, like obedient puppies.

But it was just typical of me that, for all my determination and defiance in the face of my surgeon and his posse of young trainee doctors, who nearly always seemed to be huddled around him on his visits to the ward, hanging on his every word, I found that when the time came, I couldn't go through with it. The realisation of being there, dressed in an ill-fitting suit with a white shirt on and black tie around my neck, one that Elaine had lent me, suddenly made it all so real. I don't think that I had fully taken it in, like hearing of really bad things that happen to other people, I never really thought that it could happen to me.

Being helped by Elaine from the back of her car, standing at the gates of the church; it all of a sudden became clear to me why my surgeon had been so insistent that I didn't attend. I needed her full support the moment that we stepped through the old wooden gate. I could feel myself begin to waver. It was as if the alien blood still finding its way cautiously around my body had suddenly taken a wrong turn or something. Everything was blurring around the edges, the sound of the gravel crunching beneath our feet sounded distant, as detached as an echo. For they were lining the path, three deep at least, dotted between the gravestones, overflowing out of the double doors. It seemed to me as if the whole of town was there; there were faces that I knew as well as my own, faces that I hadn't seen for years, faces that would probably never again have crossed my mind, faces that I didn't even know that I knew. They belonged to shopkeepers, bus drivers, landlords, schoolteachers, school friends, work colleagues; people from all walks of life. It was amazing how many worlds he had touched, age was of no consequence, and he hadn't even had to reach out. They had bowed to his touch.

And it felt as if every face was on me, knowing that whatever pain they were feeling that it would be nothing compared to the pain that was ripping through my body. I felt their sympathy, it hung so heavily in the air I could almost taste it, but it only served to turn me further inside myself.

I took a deep breath and muttered to Elaine, 'I don't think I can do this.'

I felt the warmth of her breath, the softness of her hair tickling my face as she lent a little closer. 'It's okay, it's okay,' she whispered and tightened her grip around my good arm, and it gave me the strength to step into the forebidding gloom of the church. And once inside the faces grew even more familiar, as if we were making a journey through Dave's body itself, meandering along the arteries and veins of his life, and we were close to his heart now, the place where he kept all these people, and there was a seat for me... right at the front.

I sat at the very top of the hill beneath the giant oak tree that overlooked the whole of the cemetery, with Dave's freshly-dug and unfilled grave no more than ten feet away. I had been foolish enough to think that I could walk up the hill unaided, despite the fact that I hadn't even been able to make it to the church doors. But my reasoning had been that without what had seemed the weight of the world upon me, I would be able to move a little easier, but of course I was wrong. It had nearly killed me. I hadn't even been halfway up, the dates on the gravestones still somewhere in the last century, when my legs had begun to feel hollow. Nothing more than empty chambers beneath me, as if the blood had drained away through some undetected wounds in them, running in rivers down the cemetery path and evaporating into the sun-baked earth.

Elaine had wanted to escort me of course, fearing that the climb would be too much, but I had insisted that I'd be okay. I had needed to be alone.

'You sure?' she had asked, her voice thick with concern, as we had sat in her car outside the cemetery gates.

'I'll be fine,' I'd said. I had tried a sort of half-smile, being in her company seemed to warrant that at least, nothing dramatic, just revealing enough evidence to show her that I was capable of being left on my own for a while. But it was no good, it had been so long that the muscles in my face no longer seemed to move in that direction.

We had sat in silence for a moment, basking in the heat of the summer sun as it poured into Elaine's little mauve Mini, and without a word being uttered, something had passed between us. I couldn't put my finger on what it was exactly but I hadn't imagined it, that much I was sure of. It was more than just sympathy or even worse, pity. It had filled the car like smoke, engulfing the pair of us, and if it had been at any other time I can't imagine that I wouldn't have stayed there and allowed nature to take its course. But I had been in no fit state of mind to deal with it; to deal with anything. We had talked for a few minutes after that, nothing deep, she was concerned about my arm and whether I'd be okay to walk up to the top of the cemetery and I had assured that I would be fine. But the truth was that as much I was grateful for her companionship… and maybe more, I just needed to be alone for a while. As much as I had wanted to enter the church and mourn with people who were closest to me and Dave, I had found that I just couldn't do it, it had been as if there was something powerful preventing me, as if trying to make myself sit in the space left vacant for me on the front pew would have been like trying to connect two identical magnets; the force between us had been too strong to overcome, it would have taken chains to drag me onto it.

The thing was, since the *Aladdin Sane* night I had found a kind of comfort in the old church, looked upon it as a sort of monument, a solid reminder of everything that was strong and dependable about town. Whenever anything bad had happened or anything had changed in town, the church had always remained the same, like St. Paul's during the Blitz, it stood stoically amongst the rubble of life. But that had all gone now, evaporated in the sun. It had felt as if every pair of eyes in the place had been upon me when all I had wanted was to be left alone, I couldn't face the commiserating looks, the sympathy, I just wanted to be left to wallow in my grief. I couldn't imagine ever living without it now.

I'd seen the look on old Browny's face, the sadness welling in Kenny Dennis' eyes and his mum beside him, almost drowning in her tears, and it had all been too much, all those people, all that pain, it had hummed and echoed off the cold stone walls like so many trapped bees.

And then of course there had been Jenny and Debbie. I had felt their eyes burning into me before I had even stepped into the cool, heavy silence of the church; even as Elaine had guided me with strong, reliable hands along the gravel path flanked at least four deep with mourners, I could feel the weight of their stares crushing my will, as if they were somehow blaming me for the predicament that we all found ourselves in.

I had begun to drift off, not into a sleep but more of a trance-like state, the warmth of the sun on my face permeating my eyelids, transporting me for a brief few minutes into a void of reddish-orange, where nothing mattered and nothing could touch me. When all of a sudden the light went out and I was brought back to earth with a thump. I opened my eyes to find a face from my childhood blocking out the sun; a little fuller in the cheeks and heavier under the chin perhaps, but still that lazy warmth swimming in the eyes, still the same old Ketchup.

We sat side by side beneath the tree, the dappled shadows of the sun, as it edged slowly through the cloudless sky, dancing across our outstretched legs. Half of me was surprised to see him there and yet it seemed as if the other had been waiting expectantly for his arrival. I hadn't seen him in the church, indeed I hadn't even been sure that he knew about Dave. It was strange in a way because when I'd started to swim in and out of the shallow waters of consciousness after my surgery, Ketch's face had been one of the first things that I can recall seeing, even though he hadn't even been there, the minds way of protecting you I suppose, wrapping you in a kind of mental security blanket, dredging up images that you can always rely upon. Come to think of it, maybe picturing Ketch hadn't been so strange after all.

I hadn't been in touch but then, of course, I had been lying, half-dead, in a hospital bed for nearly two weeks. Although I knew that however injured I may have been, it amounted to nothing more than an excuse, albeit a very good one, for I doubted whether I would have had the courage to tell him. Would rather have placed the other arm under the wheels of a bus, I thought to myself, anything rather than have had to pick up the phone and dial his number. But God, it was good to see him!

I turned my head to look at him. He had sat down beneath the tree beside me, placing a firm hand upon my shoulder when I had tried pathetically to get on my feet. 'Stay there, Johnny,' he had told me soothingly, the years of living in Scotland curling his words at the edges. And as I took it all in, everything about him came flooding back: the downward arc of his eyes, the contours etched in his face, it was all there just as I always remembered it, as familiar as the touch of a well-worn banister.

We sat there, the two us, side by side in our black suits with years to fill but nothing passed between us but silence, it was enough to simply be together, everything else could wait.

The sound of the town's traffic hummed in the distance, monotonous but soothing and every now and then the rattling of a train took over, you could see it for a second or two as it rose into view above the gravestones at the bottom of the cemetery, passing over the viaduct before it disappeared back into the patchwork of the suburbs.

'They'll be here soon,' he sighed, checking his watch. He hadn't been able to stand it either, it transpired. When he had seen me turn round and walk back up the aisle, like a groom having a last-minute change of heart, he told me that it was all the excuse he had needed.

'Did you see Billy?' I asked after a while. I had started to drift off again, the painkillers they had given me mixed with the emotion of the day made for a pretty exhausting cocktail. *'Can you hear, I'm floating round my tin can, planet earth is blue and there's nothing I can dooo…'*

'Nah.' He shook his head. 'From what I've heard I wasn't surprised.' Then he went on, 'But then again, I was still half expecting him to walk in any minute… who knows, perhaps he did.'

It wouldn't have surprised me either. I couldn't imagine Billy missing Dave's funeral, not even if it meant him being arrested somewhere along the line. I still worried about him, even now. The toughest kid that I ever knew, out there in the big wide world all on his own and after all that had happened to Dave, to me, there was still a part of me that wondered where he was each night, if he was fighting drunk in some pub, or where he was going to spend the night. At least I knew that he knew. He came to see me in the hospital one night. I don't remember it, didn't even see him, but when I came round after the operation one of the nurses told me that they had discovered this scruffy blonde lad,

429

about my age, by my bedside about two o'clock in the morning, just sitting there as quiet as a mouse, looking at me. They had no idea how he had got there. And when the nurse on duty had demanded to know who he was and how he had got in he had simply looked at her as if she were the intruder and, ignoring her questions, asked one or two of his own: if I was going to be alright. If I would ever play again. And when the nurse had insisted that he leave and come back in a day or two when I was up to seeing people, and preferably during visiting hours, he had just upped and left; 'Without so much as bye or leave,' she had told me. 'Honestly,' she had shaken her head as she'd busied herself untucking and tucking my bed sheets back in, 'some people.'

There was so much we had to talk about, things I needed to know if Ketch knew; *'From what I've heard… '* he had said, but what *had* he heard? The gossip in this town could erode the truth until it was smooth enough for anyone to handle and pass around easily. I wanted to make sure that Ketch knew only the facts and I was the only one who could give him them.

'How *is* your arm?' he asked after a while of sitting and listening to the breeze slowly flutter through the leaves above. It had started to pick up a little, the breeze, as if we were caught in the wake of something powerful thundering past.

I shrugged and lay my good hand upon the plaster. 'Okay I s'pose.' I know he was only concerned but it just felt so trivial talking about my arm when the whole reason that we were reunited, sitting there beneath the tree at the top of the cemetery, was to bury the best part of our lives.

The canopy of leaves and branches wavered even more violently, exposing us to the glare of the sun. Ketch squinted, shielded his eyes then finally stood up and looked down in the direction of the entrance to the cemetery. 'They're here,' he said and held out a hand to help pull me to my feet.

I still didn't trust my legs to hold me but took Ketch's hand

and saw the procession of black vehicles below, followed by a stream of bodies that snaked behind and all the way until it disappeared around the bend in the road. It was a breathtaking sight, like some giant black centipede shuffling through the streets of London.

The wind whipped up tiny clouds of dirt around our feet, its presence on such a baking hot day was completely out of place. But then what the hell was right on such a day?

'There weren't that many at the church,' I said, staring disbelievingly at the gathering crowd below.

'They were still arriving after you'd left,' explained Ketch.

All of a sudden I could imagine everyone gathering around the freshly-dug grave beside us, all the faces that I had seen at the church, hustling for position, but standing to one side, opening up a path for me to take my place at the front, where I would teeter on the edge. I felt a sharp tug in my guts, as if they'd been tied in a knot and pulled viciously at either end.

'I don't think I can watch it go in the ground… ' I mumbled, my words seemed to get lodged in my throat.

Ketch looked at me as if I were about to keel over and die there and then on the spot. I tried to pull myself up and not appear so useless. 'The coffin I mean… '

He squeezed my shoulder, concern clouding his eyes. 'You gonna be alright, Johnny?'

'I dun… I dunno.' My attempt to not be such a burden was failing badly. Since I'd got to my feet everything had taken on a dreamlike quality. The cluster of black bodies that had begun to swarm through the gates below, headed by the pallbearers carrying Dave's coffin, seemed to me so far away. As if I was peering down at them from the crest of a mountain, looking at them through a magnifying glass. The wind echoed hauntingly through the empty rooms of my head, even Ketch's voice sounded a little distorted, out of tune with the movement of his mouth.

'He wouldn't mind, you know.' His words ached with compassion. 'If you wanna go... ' He shook his head, 'Dave wouldn't want you to go through this, Johnny.'

I closed my eyes and took a deep breath in a bid to steady myself.

'No, I gotta be here, Ketch.' But shutting out the day was a big mistake. The ground lurched like the deck of a ship caught in the eye of a giant storm, I could sense the ground rushing up to meet me, split second thoughts of crashing to the earth on my shattered arm before Ketch's arms caught me.

'*Whooah*, Johnny!' He led me back into the shade and sat me back down against the great oak tree. 'You need your nurse,' he said and turned to look down the path. 'She'll probably be here in a minute.'

Just then there was a movement behind us, at first I thought it must be the rustling of the wind or a stray dog roaming through the hedgerow for scraps but it sounded almost like footsteps, and then the look on Ketch's face made me turn awkwardly over my shoulder. And I saw the reason for Ketch's surprise; it was Billy, brushing off the bits of twigs and leaves, cursing beneath his breath as he made his way towards us.

And it might just have been the moment, the fear of what was to come, what we were all about to lose, but I couldn't stop the tears from coming. I reached out for Ketch's arm and this time he didn't object but hauled me to my feet as I reached out and buried my face in Billy's neck, my body heaving from the emotion pouring out all over him. And there was no caustic remark, no quip about acting all "poofy" he just put his arm around my shoulder and held out the other to greet Ketch.

'Alright son,' he said, 'how are you? Showing them Scots bastards how to play football I 'ope.'

And the next moment we had all come together, a human tepee, me with my arm sticking crazily out at the side, the three of us, Billy with a strong arm wrapped around the both of us in a fierce embrace, and I still had my face pressed into his shoulder, the musty smell of his black jacket mingling with my tears, but I could tell that we were all crying, weeping the uncontrollable tears of the lost, I could here it in the cracking of Billy's voice as he told us both that it'd be all right.

'But what now, Billy?' I cried. 'What the fuck do we do now?' And maybe he couldn't here me, mistook my strangled words for cries of anguish, but he didn't answer, simply held the pair of us tighter. But then again, what else could he possibly have done?

CHAPTER THIRTY - THREE

June 1979

The crowd of mourners shuffled wearily back down the dusty path, not so clustered together as before, but now that the coffin had been slotted into the ground like a wooden peg and the service was over, people found comfort in their little groups. There was no one particular place that they were heading to. Some were going to the Crown to drink to Dave's memory, not that many of them would need much of an excuse. Lui was going to open up and make tea for some of the older ones. Ketch and I watched them all go, rolling like black beads into the distance, whilst Billy lurked back behind the oak tree just in case, feeling a little too exposed now that the crowds had gone. When everyone had taken their place around the grave and he was relatively sure that it didn't hold any plain-clothed coppers, he had squeezed his way up to the front and huddled in between me and Ketch, where the three of us had just about kept each other standing.

And now there was just one lonely figure making her way up the hill, swimming against the black tide. 'Bit old for you, ain't she?' Billy called as he watched me watching Elaine weave her way through the great puddles of mourners.

'What do you mean?' I sniffed, head still full of tears. 'She's just the nurse from the hospital.'

'Bollocks!' he grinned. 'The same one that looked after you last time… the one that pissed Jen off.'

I smiled despite everything, I'd forgotten that Billy would

have seen her before. I never could get away with anything with Billy or Dave, and besides, it was good to see some of the old Billy again, the childish devil back in him. God knows we were going to grow up quickly enough now.

Later that evening, just as the sun slipped out of sight down behind the viaduct and melted into the heart of London, tinting the skyline the way the distant West End lights faintly illuminate the backdrop of the *Ziggy* album cover, I think was the moment that I fully realised that I would never lose Dave. I knew I'd never forget him, of course, but that past week, lying hopelessly in my hospital bed, I had started to worry that maybe some of the memories of him would fade, lose their clarity as I grew unavoidably further away from their time. So concerned was I, it had been one of the reasons that I had been scared to sleep, the fear of wakening and finding that some other part of Dave had been ever so slightly erased, like a rubber across a drawing.

But as the four of us sat in the park sipping from cans of beer, with me, Ketch and Billy regaling Elaine with stories of Dave, I finally realised that he could never go, not unless I were to lose my mind completely, for he was there, all around, in everywhere I'd been and everything I'd ever done.

We weren't the only ones in the park of course, for all the people that had chosen to remember Dave at Lui's or in the pubs, the majority of his own age had decided to honour him at the park. There were at least another ten groups huddled together and dotted around each and every corner of the playing field. Virtually every kid from our year was there I reckoned, even the gimpy kids. And it was odd, time standing still, for they were just the same as I would've imagined them to be, hanging out with the same friends, ignoring or sneering at old enemies.

Clusters of girls like Debbie and Jen, the exclusive club, passing round and swigging cheap white wine or Babycham, the boys sitting around not really knowing what to do or say, some of them supping from beer cans, uncomfortable with their emotions but just knowing that they should be there, for he didn't have an enemy at school, Dave, there had been nothing to dislike, nothing to fight against. He could be a friend to the bully boys and befriend the bullied, more often than not dispelling a situation before it arose, just by being there.

Most of the girls had cassette recorders with them, and although I did manage to pick out some Blondie and even Elvis Costello, nearly all of them, as a tribute, were inevitably playing Bowie. There was the *Aladdin Sane* album blaring out, *Ziggy, Diamond Dogs,* I even heard *Low,* more for the dedicated Bowie fans, much less mainstream. All of them filling the summer night, layer upon layer, the different textures of Bowie's voice mixed together, swirling around until, if you lost the thread of one particular song that you were following, the park became a cacophony of electric guitars, drums, saxophone, synthesisers and, of course, Bowie's distinctive voice.

'Time I got you back,' remarked Elaine. 'Dr Murdoch will have my guts for garters keeping you this long.' I didn't want to go back to the hospital. Even though my arm had begun to ache; it was a dull, throbbing pain, like a headache in my arm, and the idea of lying down beneath those crisp white sheets did hold a certain appeal, but it wasn't enough to outweigh the thought of being back in that ward. I wanted to be out in the night, in the park, drinking recklessly with the people who knew me best, who I knew best. Not breathing in clinical, stifling air and surrounded by strangers and competence.

'Looks a right bastard, that one,' said Billy to no one in particular. He was lying staring at the night sky, hands clasped behind his head as if he were sunbathing.

'He's okay,' said Elaine, but her voice lacked conviction. Billy's frankness in front of Elaine jarred me, although I didn't know why.

'Bullies,' he sneered. He lit a cigarette took a long, deep drag and ejected smoke rings up into the night sky with such force that they were still in a perfect O by the time they faded into the darkness. 'They love the power,' he continued. 'Get a kick the moment they sense a weakness.' He turned his head in Elaine's direction. 'I bet he gets a hard on bossing you lot around.'

'He's not that bad!' she protested, a little taken aback by Billy's assassination of a man he could barely have seen for more than a few minutes.

'I've seen his lot before,' he continued, unimpressed by her defence. He sucked violently on his cigarette and stared blankly into space as the memory of a thousand tyrants that he had spent his life standing up to came flooding back. The profile of his face looked as if it had been carved out of marble, eyes narrowed, jaw clenched as he faced up to the intimidation in his mind. 'My old man's the same.' His voice was distant now, brooding. 'So is Dave's… they think can intimidate you just by… ' He turned to face us mouth frozen in mid-sentence as the realisation of what he had just said hit home. For a moment I thought he was worried that he might have unwittingly offended any of us, which of course he hadn't. It just hammered home the reason why we were all there, sitting about and getting pissed in the park. The silence that followed had more to do with the fact that Billy's remark had made us all aware that this kind of thing was going to happen a hundred times every day, the realisation that Dave was dead. Dead and buried. And that tomorrow morning, when we awoke, because we had no choice, we would have to face the rest of our lives without him, growing inevitably, uncontrollably, further away from the time when he was a part of us.

By the time the night had finally taken over, most of them had left, but maybe the cloud that had hung over them all day didn't hang as heavy now. For as the night had drawn in and the beer and the wine had taken hold, old barriers had been broken down, they had begun to realise that the law of the playground no longer reigned out in the grown-up world. Driven by drink, unlikely friendships had been forged, the cassette players, one by one, had gradually been switched off and everyone had slowly begun to congregate round Debbie and Jen's group.

From what I could make out, they had some self-made compilation playing, all well known songs but they spanned the whole decade, from singles to album tracks. As we lay there watching them all mingle, old reputations and attitudes dissolving in the night air, I wondered vaguely whose tape it was. Had Dave made it for one of the girls? I pictured him, eagerly selecting tracks, searching for songs to educate and nurture the budding Bowie fan. A smile I didn't think possible at the time weaved its way across my face. More because of the fact that whoever's it was had probably only feigned an interest in Bowie in order to get close to Dave. And then something remarkable happened.

"Heroes" began to play. And the whole group started to sing. By the time he was remembering *'that time at the wall'* they were all singing at the top of their voices, heads thrown back, arms round each other's shoulders, swaying from side to side. You couldn't hear the cassette player in the end, it was completely drowned out by the drunken voices. It was as if they had finally found a way to let out all the anguish and confusion that had built up inside. Elaine was sobbing uncontrollably, and she had hardly known Dave. But I didn't cry. Nor did Billy or Ketch, for some reason it didn't feel sad, didn't feel like a time to mourn, in fact I couldn't *stop* smiling. And when I looked across at Billy and Ketch, I found that they were smiling too.

CHAPTER THIRTY - FOUR

June 1979

I never did spend another night in the hospital, despite all of Elaine's protestations (probably the reason why my arm never did heal properly). I mean I went back for treatment and further X-rays, but even my attendance at my appointments began to dwindle, which tested the patience of all who were involved, even Elaine. But the thing was, deep down, in the bowels of someplace unreachable, I knew that none of it mattered. It had nothing to do with Dave's death, though that was what all concerned tried to blame it on. It was just that somewhere in between passing out in Heddon Street and coming back to life in the hospital, I had finally lost all self-delusion. Even with everything that had happened I had discovered, unwittingly, a kind of inner peace. I hadn't been aware of it at first, what with the turmoil of Dave's death, had put it down to the drugs and painkillers flowing through my veins. But as the reality of it all was there to greet me each day, I slowly came to realise that there was this undercurrent of calm. Even when the dosage was low and my system was fraying at the edges, there was this inner contentment. I would never become a professional footballer.

In the scheme of things it hardly seemed to matter, but the difference now was that I was fine in the knowledge of it. I would never again have to shoulder that great unbearable burden, that gut-burning feeling that I was going to let everybody down. I already had. But the worst thing, I guess, was that I no longer cared.

I awoke in the armchair back home, with a pain in my head that felt as if it was too big to be confined inside my skull. It buzzed like fury trying to escape, forcing itself against the back of my eyeballs until I thought they were going to pop out of their sockets from the sheer pressure. But none of it, not even the unquenchable thirst that I couldn't seem to satiate, no matter how much water I drank, could compare with the pain drilling its way through the bones in my arm. It was greyish dark outside, I tried to focus on the clock on the mantelpiece but the hands were just a blur. They seemed to be somewhere around the four-thirty mark, but I couldn't be sure, too early whatever it read. I slumped back down in the armchair. And no matter how I tried, I couldn't stop my thoughts from whisking me away from the relative comfort of home, back to the night of the concert, back to the last time I had two good arms… to the last time I saw him…

I stood quietly in the kitchen, shaking, sweating and drinking tea, long before I was really awake. Everything still took on a blurred appearance, as if I were looking at the world through cling film. I ached for sleep but couldn't face the images that came with it; better, I reasoned, to bask in the heady glow of insomnia. Besides, it was morning. And of course there was also the fact that there was a nurse asleep upstairs in my bed. At least I hadn't had to stutter and explain that I couldn't share the bed with her. Not that she might want me to of course! Thankfully I had avoided that little episode, which I would have made ten times more awkward than it should have been, I'm sure. It had been obvious to Elaine that the sofa would be more comfortable and offer the best support for my arm.

I took my tea and returned to the sofa, gazing dumbly at my dim reflection in the blank TV screen. My legs and arms were visible, hands either side, one clenched round the handle of my teacup, the other cased in plaster, but the rest of me, from the chest up, was shrouded in darkness, lost in an opaque cloud, as if a fog had settled across me. And to my mind it could have been real, not just a trick of the shadows, if I had stood up and walked down the street, I reckoned that I would have been cloaked in that dusty, grey gloom. The thought appealed. To shut myself away from it all, from all the shit, entrenched in my own cocoon, in my own private hell.

Finally I tore my eyes away from the screen and averted them to the ceiling, as if I could see through the floorboards and the plaster to where Elaine lay sleeping in my bed. *My* bed! Imagine it! A nurse in *my* bed! Wait until I tell Da… I sank deeper in the chair. I guessed it would always be like this.

I thought I heard a noise, a sudden movement from out of the room somewhere; Elaine stirring perhaps? But it was only Jack the milkman delivering next door. I heard the faint tones of his familiar whistle, the gentle tinkling of his crate as he bypassed our house and entered the gate on the other side. It was another telling reminder that Mum was hardly ever here, no milk delivered, no paper through the letterbox, a house slowly fading from view, like a drawing hidden beneath tracing paper. Who would eventually move in here, I wondered, when Mum finally handed back the keys to the council?

I found myself trying to imagine the house with somebody else living in it, without the presence of our sofa, our armchair, telly, pictures and souvenirs dotted above the fireplace. Surely they would strip down and re-paper the walls? The tiny flower patterns looked old and faded, dated even, styles you would find in re-runs of *Bless this House* or something. And would it lose its smell? A smell that had always reminded me of… well, home. A female smell, with not a trace of a man. It consisted of cooking, of Mum's perfume, of hairspray and washing, of overbearing bath salts and the drudgery of the hospital. I felt a pang of something from my past but I wasn't sure what, a bit like I did when I threw my Action Man into the Thames.

I hoped it would be a family that moved in. The place needed to be filled with laughter again. Lately, whenever I had been there it seemed to be full of nothing but silence. It erupted in every room, covering everything like dust. I hadn't thought of it until then, but I wondered what Elaine had made of it all last night, stepping into this stagnated world, like stepping into a painting.

I couldn't seem to get comfortable, in mind or body. I felt the need to go out, to wander down to Lui's, to go and see Billy, drink in the air of the suburbs that I knew so well instead of the stale odour that circulated through the house. But I couldn't just very well up and leave Elaine on her own.

But the urge to step outside was too strong. If I could walk the streets that walked inside of us, if I could turn myself inside out almost, surround myself with everything that we were, had been, then maybe I could hold on to *him*. For it was ridiculous but I was scared that I was going to forget him still; the way he looked, already it felt as if his image had begun to fade from the pages of my mind. If I closed my eyes tight, squeezed hard until the beer rose up again and clenched my brain like a sheet of paper in a fist, I could sort of make out his face but it was as if it were stepping away through a mist. The dark butchered scar losing its shape, those piercing, cool eyes became dull, swirling away like water down a plug hole, all I could still see clearly were the waves of bleached orange hair crashing down over blank cliffs.

The thing was, I hadn't seen it coming, not any of it: the anger, the hatred that burned inside him, the relationship between him and the skinhead... how could I have been so blind?

Along with the crushing feeling of life without my best mate came the heartbreaking feeling that I had never really known him at all. There was a song... a record of Mum's, no doubt buried beneath the pile of LPs in the sideboard, unless of course she had already taken it with her. "Empty Chairs" it was called, off Don Mclean's *American Pie* album. How did it go? '*Never thought you'd leave until you went'* … The lines from songs… Sometimes it felt as if my life had already been written and sung about, I just needed to piece it all together.

I crept up the stairs with, for some unaccountable reason, a different perspective on everything I saw and touched. Suddenly conscious of the smoothness of the well-worn banister rail as it caressed my palm, aware that I had to step over the fourth from top step so as not to make a noise and wake Elaine with a start, rather than just doing it automatically. I found myself really taking in the painting hanging on the wall halfway up, the one I had seen a million times, maybe more, seen but never really looked at, the one of the side view of the young girl standing with her feet in the sea, holding up her frilly white dress with one hand whilst the other stopped her hat from blowing out to sea. It had been like a window all through my childhood, the same view everyday, but instead of overlooking rows of houses or lines of narrow gardens, it had opened out onto the same pocket of beach. Where was that, I wondered, for probably the first time in my life, who was she? Was she on a day trip? That would certainly explain the lack of swimwear. What year? Victorian, I reckoned, judging by the clothes…

I peered through the open door, not wanting to enter my own bedroom. Elaine was fast asleep. She looked strangely out of place amongst the shelves crammed full of football books and organised mess of a typical boy's room. I wondered how she would feel waking up with pictures of muddy footballers surrounding her. I had intended to slip straight back out again but something stronger than embarrassment pulled me further in. It had something to do with the way she lay there; the way her hair fanned majestically out across my pillow and the length of her eyelashes resting on her cheeks. I had never realised how long they were. She looked so peaceful, completely relaxed in the depths of her sleep. I doubted I had ever been that contented in all the nights that I had spent in that bed. The whole room smelled of her, she clung to the walls, pervaded the air… it was intoxicating.

Eventually I retreated back downstairs and into the front room and was just about to flop back into the armchair when I saw myself trying to struggle back up again. It was enough, and I decided to go out for a walk after all. I left a hastily scribbled note on the kitchen table explaining that I had just popped out to get some fresh air, milk and bread and added that she was more than welcome to help herself to an egg and black coffee if she couldn't wait. But just as I was about to leave I noticed something sticking out from the letter box. Too early for the postman, I thought, must be something hand posted. I released the white envelope from the shutter, gently closing it so that it didn't slam. It had my name on it written in blue ink but no stamp or address… *but there was something about it, couldn't put my finger on it*… a sympathy card or note from some friend no doubt, shoved through the door the night before. I couldn't deal with it now. I was so full of sympathy that I didn't think I could suffer anymore. So I laid it on the telephone stand, slipped out and closed the front door behind me with barely a sound, a trick honed in my youth.

It was still early but life in town had already begun, people on their way to work, the sound of their existence drowned out by the rumbling of cars, buses and distant trains. The only thing to distinguish it from any other time of day was the crisp early morning smell and the position of the rising sun. I almost let myself get carried away in it all, that vibrant, new day feeling, that feeling of… expectancy. But nothing, it seemed, could enter me, I'd been left too hollow, so much so that the sound of my own footsteps reverberated through my guts.

There was so much to get my head round, to try and face up to. The world without Dave… it would be like trying to face up to the sun. And then there were other things that kept nagging away at me, it annoyed the hell out me that they should even be *allowed*

444

in my head when I wanted it to be filled with nothing but Dave. But despite my best efforts, like a draft, they crept through the cracks in my mind; the world without football… or football no longer *my* world… replaced with Elaine maybe? Oh how the heck did I know! And then of course there was the biggest revelation of all, my conversation in the early hours of the morning with Billy! I kept going over and over it again and again in my mind, how he had revealed to me over cups of stewed tea and burnt toast that he was going to give himself up.

'*Should* get three or four years,' he had told me as we'd sat, like a million times before, at the kitchen table, tired and pissed. He had said it as listlessly as if he were considering which pub we should go to for drink.

'I could do that standing on me 'ead,' he'd shrugged as I'd sat there, face pressed into the palm of my good hand as if the weight of living was too much to keep it from crashing into the table top.

His toneless, indifference had defied me. It was as if in his head he were already behind bars. I hadn't thought that I could take it. 'Why the hell did you have to nearly kill him for?' I had cried.

'Eh?' Confusion creased his face.

'Why couldn't you have just given him a slap or something?' I had gone on. 'Instead of putting him in hospital!'

For a moment he had stared across the table at me. 'What the fuck are you on about?' he'd said impatiently. But before I could answer, he'd said, 'It ain't for *fighting* that I'll get put away… it's for *thieving*.'

He had shrugged his shoulders wearily. 'Come on, J, you knew I was nicking from sites!' He had smiled. 'Or tipping others off. You know, leaving doors unlocked or windows ajar, a man's gotta survive, ain't 'e?' His acceptance had seemed out of character.

It was my turn to be confused. I hadn't understood. 'But… '

'Thing is though,' he had continued, staring at his teacup, 'the job they nicked me for, I had nuffin' to do with.'

'But… Collins!' I had stammered.

Billy's eyes had opened wide. 'I know!' he had exclaimed. 'Fuckin' scumbag set me up!' He had clicked his tongue and shaken his head. 'The day you played up at Birmingham against big Kenny,' he had explained, 'I was meant to be working over at a new factory in Croydon, remember?' He had smiled thinly at the memory. 'But there *weren't* no fuckin' work! It was a set-up! He stitched me up over a staged break-in and nicked tools!' He had nodded his head, satisfaction playing in his eyes. 'Deserved all he got,' he had mused.

My heartbeat had quickened, I couldn't comprehend what I *thought* I had just stumbled upon.

'But I thought *you* beat Collins up!' I had cried.

He had looked at me as if he were seeing me for the first time, as if, for moment, the boy that met his gaze wasn't the one he had known forever, whose shadow lived within his, but instead a complete stranger.

'J!' He hadn't seemed able to find the words. 'He didn't tell you, did 'e?' he'd finally said.

'Tell me what? *Who* didn't tell me?'

He had shaken his head. 'Typical,' he'd muttered.

'Billy!' I'd pleaded. 'What are you talking about?'

'J,' his voice had been almost a whisper now. '*I* didn't beat up Collins… Dave did!'

I had stared dumbly into his face, his spiky blonde hair falling tiredly across his frowning face. Something masquerading as pity had reflected in his eyes. He had been hurting for me.

'But… ' I had stammered. 'But why didn't he say something… why didn't he tell me?'

'Trying to protect you,' Billy had reasoned.

'Protect me!' I had exclaimed. I had laughed harshly, without a trace of humour. 'If he was trying to protect me then why did he ki… ' I couldn't say it, just couldn't.

Billy had leaned back in his chair and surveyed his surroundings, gazing round a kitchen that he must have sat in a million times, in the same chair, across from the same face, and for a moment it had been as if we were looking through a time tunnel: I had seen him aged six, seven, eight, nine, ten… the years screaming by; a catalogue of T Rex T-shirts and muddy football kits.

Eventually he had sighed heavily, thrown an arm over the back of the chair and said, 'Reckon he thought it was about time he let you grow up.'

I had slumped across the table, chin resting on splayed out arms. I had wanted desperately to cry; to feel the blissful sting of release, but I hadn't been able to. I hadn't had the strength.

'Thing is,' Billy had begun, waiting for my attention, 'without Collins to testify, the case will probably get thrown out.' He had sighed heavily. 'So I reckon, like always,' he had smiled thinly, 'he was protecting us both.'

Then all of a sudden the sound of snoring had reverberated down from the bedroom. We had looked up at the ceiling in unison then at each other and burst out laughing.

'We should tape it,' Billy had suggested. 'Use it as blackmail for hospital drugs.'

I had smiled back at him. 'Yeah,' I'd nodded. 'Could go into business, become dealers,' I'd joked. 'And there was I, worrying about my future!'

With the rising tension that the conversation had built deflated by the thunder of Elaine's snoring, we had relaxed a little, I could feel the enormity of the day beginning to take its toll, the heavy fingers of sleep creeping through my veins. I knew it wouldn't last long when it finally had me in its clutches, so felt I needed to take advantage of it when I could.

'You'll be all right with her you know,' he had said with as much reassurance as someone like Billy could muster. I had tried

447

to smile but my face wouldn't let me. Is this what I had reduced us to? How… *pathetic* I had become, unsettling the people around me to the point that they felt the need to pity me, transforming Billy into someone he wasn't comfortable being.

But I had seen where he was going. He had shaken his head sagely.

'Too much history with Jen,' he had pushed the chair neatly back beneath the kitchen table. 'Even Debbie, they're like sisters.'

Oh Billy, I had thought to myself, how clearly my world shone in his eyes, just as it had in Dave's, they knew what played on my mind or tugged away in my heart by simply being in the same room. And he was right, of course, how was I ever to forge a relationship with some girl I was always petrified of letting down? They were just too close, as close as Dave and Billy in their own way… it was almost incestuous.

He had pushed his chair back and made to leave. 'Better get off,' he had sighed

'Stay here,' I'd suggested. 'You missed the last bus ages ago.'

He had screwed up his face. 'Nuh!' he'd said. 'Don't wanna cramp your style with Florence Nightingale up there,' he'd smirked, rolling his eyes in the direction of my bedroom

I had clicked my tongue. 'Shut up!' And for a moment it had been the old Billy, ribbing me, mockingly trying to reel me in. But he could see the insecurity seeping out of me, I had reeked of it, I hadn't wanted him to go, didn't want anyone I cared about to ever go again. He had picked up his cup and drained the remains.

'Fuckin 'ell, J!' he'd exclaimed, screwing up his face and spitting the dregs back into the cup. 'You gotta move in with her soon.'

'Why?' I had asked, taken aback by his sudden show of anxiety. And then a smile as sinister as anything Jack Nicholson had ever revealed had split his features in two.

'Cause you can't even brew a pot of fuckin' tea properly, that's why!'

I had walked him to the door, two shadows standing in the gloom of the landing light. He had placed a hand on the door handle, paused as if he had forgotten something, and then turned to me and said, 'I don't think he was ever truly 'appy you know.'

'Why!' I had mumbled. 'What do you mean?'

He had peered at me through the darkness, searching out my eyes. 'He was too clever for the life he was given,' he'd sighed.

Billy had this almost beautiful way of simplifying everything that seemed too complicated.

'Well… how would he 'ave put it?' he'd whispered. It was as if the house itself was asleep, our voices rumbling through the walls like creaking pipes. '*Reading between the lines.*' He'd smiled for a moment at his impression. 'Not only was there his old man's resentfulness and that psych- half brother of his,' he'd said, 'but he met Bowie when he was eleven or twelve, didn't 'e! Went round his 'ouse! had a cup of tea and talked about fuckin' music!'

I hadn't thought about that night when we had stood outside the Café Royal in the longest time; the night after the last *Ziggy* concert. Strange, considering my head was full of nothing but Dave and the way he had filled my life. That night, and meeting Bowie of all people, simply hadn't risen to the surface yet.

'I mean… ' he had continued in more hushed tones. 'What else was there for 'im?' He had sighed so heavily it had seemed as if he had been deflated. 'Except of course to look after the fuckin' pair of us.' He'd nodded. 'And I reckon 'e thought it was about time *we* did that ourselves now.'

Lui's was open, thank God, a reassuring sight of steamed up windows even at that early hour. I could just make out the blurred image of Lui wiping down tables, tea towel draped over his shoulder.

449

'Johnny!' he gasped as I shuffled thought the door, 'Johnny!' He moved across the floor with surprising speed placed a hand upon my shoulder and guided me towards the table we had always occupied. 'How are you?' he flustered. 'Should you be out hospital yet? You look tired.' He wiped his hands nervously on his trusty tea towel. I could tell his heart ached for me but somehow it made me feel worse. Perhaps I shouldn't have come. I hadn't deliberately set out with Lui's in mind, the street had just led me there... but who was I kidding? And I had to admit, the thought of his bacon sandwiches and endless cups of tea were very appealing.

As I rested my chin in the palm of my hand and watched the morning gradually unfold, my thoughts drifted back to Billy. Anyway, I tried to console myself, I could always visit him if he does go down. Probably only be up at the Scrubs. I smiled to myself; funny, but in a weird sort of way it would be almost comforting to know where he was every night, although I doubted he would see it that way.

Lui appeared with bacon sandwiches and piping hot tea. He smiled fatherly, nodded and left me in peace, sensing that I needed time to myself for a while. I gazed idly about the room; there were the usual mix of builders and lorry drivers tucking into full plates, laughing and joking over mouthfuls of eggs, bacon and chips, agreeing and disagreeing over football, slobbering tea over the horses and page three birds. And there was Lui behind his counter; like a judge at his bench, joining in the conversation when invited but always just on the edge of the banter, shrugging his shoulders or lazily waving a hand in that continental way whenever the jokes began to lose him.

It felt good to be in that environment, despite the fact that I was nothing more than a spectator. To simply immerse myself in the easy familiarity of it all was enough to lift my spirits off the floor, and as with the park, I felt close to Dave, could see him sitting opposite me, staring pensively out of the window or hunched over the table scribbling feverishly away in a notepad. I could see him every time the door swung open, every customer's frame transformed itself into his. Gliding languidly across the floor, I could see his finger doodling etched into every rainbow shape left on the table from Lui's cloth, and if I closed my eyes for more than a few seconds I swear I could hear the faint whisper of his voice floating through the air.

As I reflected upon all this, a part of me glad that Dave seemed to be haunting my mind whilst another worried that I was going crazy, I caught the glimpse of a figure across the road just before they disappeared round the corner of the street that led to the train station. I didn't have a chance to see his face but he was a lean man dressed in black pegs and a denim jacket. His hair was a kind of bleached blonde, or it could have been more ginger; strawberry blonde... *more orange*, it was hard to tell in the early morning sunlight. I was out the door and halfway across the street before I even realised it.

... and somewhere behind me somebody leans on a car horn, cursing my stupidity as I run across the road. But I don't even turn my head, I don't see them, don't see anything other than the shape ahead of me. I round the corner and see the back of him shuffle unhurriedly across the street, the gait of a ghost drifting towards the station entrance. My heart is somewhere near my throat, and rising. By the time I cross the road it's pounding in my head... feels as if it's everywhere, pounding, pounding, pounding. The man just a few yards in front of me slowly runs his fingers through the waves sweeping over his head, but I am close enough to see that his hair isn't orange; it's not even blonde, but bleached milk bottle-white. And the black pegs carry the same colour piping down the seams; more Numan than Bowie. In fact, the closer I get, it begins to dawn on me that the only thing the stranger has in common is the denim jacket. But still I approach, driven on by I don't know what... ghoulish fascination maybe.

'Excuse me, mate,' I hear myself say. 'Have you got the time?'

The stranger turns his head. He is much older than I... than I imagined. His eyes blue not brown. They appear to me as the kind of eyes that you could read if you had a mind to, not the unfathomable pools of mystery that I was so used to staring into, a set of eyes that would too easily reveal the feelings of the mind and body they shared.

He looks a little startled from the manner of my approach; I didn't mean to appear so zealous, and besides, there is a clock above the station entrance. He glances at his wrist. 'Half seven,' he reports.

I nod appreciatively. 'Cheers, mate.'

He shrugs in acknowledgment and turns back towards the station. I watch him disappear up the steps that lead to the platforms and keep staring at the arched entrance, long after he has gone, long after the rumbling sound of the train above has been soaked up by the soot-stained buildings lining the rails, staring at nothing but empty stairs, seeing nothing but this insanity for the rest of my life.

I didn't return to Lui's, didn't have the strength of mind to explain my hasty departure. I would have had to lie and I didn't have the wit, and besides, he would have seen right through it. His concern would have weighed heavier than my own self-pity.

I stayed on the opposite side of the road to Lui's and passed by just as a dirty big coal truck pulled up outside and allowed me to skip past unnoticed. The cleaner of the bookies nodded a "Good morning" to me as she busied herself with the lock on the door, her gaze fell to my arm and I noticed the frown creep across her brow. She was a friend of Mum's; the concern, though it was unspoken, felt comforting. This town was home, I thought to myself as I made my way back past the row of tiny cottages before the park, and the sudden realisation that Elaine would be waiting for me back at the house filled me with a kind of tingling warmth that took me by surprise. Although how much longer I could call the house "home" I didn't know. Elaine had said that I could move in with her and her flatmates *'for as long as it takes'* was how she had put it. And there would be no grey area concerning the sleeping arrangements then, for she shared a terraced place with two other nurses in Croydon… and there were only three bedrooms.

The sun was surprisingly warm for the hour, it had burnt away the last of the early morning haze and evaporated the dew that had sparkled like shattered glass across the wide expanse of the park. Of course I could move in with Derek and Mum, that's what she hoped for after all. *'Derek insists,'* she had assured me but as much as I knew he would never object, I seriously doubted that that was the case. Anyway, having Mum clucking about me and forever under Derek's watchful, disappointed eye was my idea of hell. I could just imagine his face, caught somewhere between seething and sympathy, as Mum fretted herself silly over my broken arm and shattered heart. Bless her, despite her nursing experience, she had never been able to do anything when *his* leaving had fractured it, so how in hell could I expect her to fix it now Dave's death had picked it up and smashed it, like dropped china, into a thousand tiny pieces?

I stopped by our old entrance and found myself ducking between the railings and making my way through the long grass and weeds before stepping out onto the boundary of the park. The gap in the railings was lower and narrower than I'd realised, hard to imagine us skipping through now, barely breaking stride, bubbling over with the exuberance of childhood. I stood upon the outskirts of my past, shielded my eyes from the glare of the sun bouncing off the top of the viaducts and saw the memories unfold before my eyes. Football matches, fights and awkward kisses popped up like moving targets across the range of the park.

I had to fight the urge to turn round and go and see Billy. I had told him that I would go to the police station with him but he had refused my offer of course, just as I had known he would. I had to admit to a sense of relief although my proposal hadn't been a hollow one. But the thought of accompanying him to the station and then leaving without him was, I reckoned, more than I would be able to bare.

Will he really get sent down? I tried to convince myself otherwise. But his past was like a weight around his neck and down was the only place it could really take him, despite his almost flippant attitude. *How will I find my way through with the landmarks of my life removed?*

The thought of the day alone crept into my head. Elaine would be at the hospital by mid-morning and then there would be nothing but hours of emptiness stretching into the distance, like standing on the brink of a wilderness. There would be no one for me to hide behind then, nothing to stop the fear of the future from capturing me, smothering me to death with the weight of its uncertainty. I knew I should go back to the hospital, my arm hurt like hell, but the thought of lying there in those beds and every one of the appalling memories that the place represented and nothing to do but think... well, it seemed as if I had spent half my life in hospital beds.

I don't think I had ever felt so alone. After Billy had gone there would be no one left who could... could truly *fill* me. Elaine and I... we didn't know each other well enough yet... not yet but I was sure we would get there. But what was I going to do *now*? Like an addict I couldn't see beyond the next hour.

I found myself stumbling back through the long grass and leant heavily against the thin black railings. Lui's tea rose like siphoned petrol through my guts, acid hit the back of my throat and I spewed into the undergrowth.

I looked up and gazed into the distance, blinking away the stinging tears that blurred the image of the viaducts. Was I a man now? Did it mean that all the vile poison that had been poured over us, all the grief that had been suffered, all constituted "Real Life"? Had we passed through all the passages of childhood?

Up to then I had always thought of myself as, well... lucky. I had been acutely aware, like a sly kid, I suppose, that I was regarded, albeit in different degrees, with sympathy, because I came from a "broken" home. And I had learnt from an early age to use it to my advantage, we all had had learnt to play it as a kind of "Get out of Jail Free" card when we had sailed into deeper waters than we had intended. If I was honest, it had never been a hindrance. It *should* have been, but, for me anyhow, I couldn't honestly say it had been. The thing was, I had never known any different. Billy and Dave, well… their situation had always been different, in a sense more *real*. That's how it had always felt anyhow. As if I was somehow pretending to be going through the same level of grief as them, just because I was their mate. I had always felt almost ashamed of the ease of my home life. But I was paying for it now.

A tall, dark figure stood outside the entrance of the park. He leant against the heavy iron gates, arms crossed, head bowed so you couldn't see his face, just his mousy-brown hair, as if he were trying to hide inside himself. There was nothing odd about him but he just seemed… *out of place*. Something fluttered in my chest, I turned to move closer, to see him clearer, to… *Oh not this again please!'*

I forced myself to stop, closed my eyes and took a breath. I shook my head and even allowed myself a little laugh now that I had managed to kerb my frantic delusions. And when I looked up, the figure had gone anyway.

I didn't have a choice, I supposed, as I started back along the street; I would *have* to move in with Elaine. *Living with my girlfriend;* I couldn't exactly take my annuals and scrapbooks and cover the bedroom wall with football pictures, could I? I sighed deeply; the end of my childhood. Mind you, it had died along with Dave.

I was nearly home now, turning into my street… *my* street? It was no longer mine. I had thought I did, but I didn't own anything of this town anymore, it had somehow moved away and left me without actually going anywhere. It suddenly occurred to me that I didn't know hardly anyone who lived along here anymore. Old Mr Harrold, he had died the other year and I had never even seen the people or person who had moved into his house, the Indian family that lived in Dave's old house, the old neighbours on my side... they had moved up to Nottingham with his work, Bowie himself could be living there now and I wouldn't have a clue! The thought of it made me smile despite myself. Perhaps I would take the club up on their offer to send me on a coaching course, the boss had said it could be the making of me, had said he reckoned I would thrive on the... *shit!* I had forgotten the milk! I stood in the middle of the pavement, head bowed and shaking my head, not quite believing the level to which my stupidity could stoop. I would have to grow up quick if I was to make a realistic go of it with Elaine, I reckoned.

I continued on up the street, eyes still fixed on the ground, walking without looking, moving forward without seeing, the way I had always progressed in life.

Anyhow, I carried on deliberating, I would still be involved in the game, only this way I wouldn't have the pressure of playing, that crushing feeling that I was always about to let somebody down.

My eyes never left the pavement, dodged round a lamppost without even seeing it; instinct borne out of a lifetime of traipsing the same street. It suddenly occurred to me that I had been avoiding the edges of each paving stone, careful not to step on any line; the way we had always done as kids. I was moving at a pace now, positively gliding over the tarmac, moving from side to side, in, out, across and up, as if I were playing some manic game of hopscotch with myself. The pavement began to melt before my eyes as the tears welled. But as they rolled down and dropped off my cheeks I couldn't help but smile; laugh even. Because the thing was, I knew... I just *knew*... that if I made it home, back to the house, back to Elaine, without stepping on the cracks, then everything would be all right. It wouldn't be today or tomorrow or heaven knows when... just certain in the knowledge that everything would eventually be okay... if I just keep off the cracks.

Johnny,

I want you to know how it is. I want you to know that it's all right, that everything is okay. I can't explain it better than that but for you I will try.

You'll be all right you will, Johnny Chalmers! Don't worry about your football, it's going to be your life, I just know it. It's who you are.

Billy as well, he'll be okay, but you'll need to keep an eye on the little git!

The thing is, Johnny, I don't feel right. Inside, like there's some sort of gap or something. I've always felt it, ever since I can remember. It's not like it hurts or anything it just makes me feel... echoey. At first I thought every one must have it, this hole that don't mean anything, like that useless bit in your guts, what's it called, the appendix? But as we grew up I came to realise that it was just me. I thought Mum could maybe take me to the doctors and all I would have to do is take some medicine or something. But every time I said anything she would just look at me the way she does, you know, like she's not there and I would just forget all about it.

But then I actually started to quite like it, the way I didn't feel like other kids, it made me feel like I was floating or something. You know how we lie on our backs in the park after football sometimes? And stare up at the sky and the tops of the viaducts look like their moving but really it's just the clouds floating by that are moving, well that's how it felt. As if I was somehow living in a Bowie song. And I knew I had to get away, I started to feel trapped, Johnny, the park, the town, they all felt like they were closing in on me, like I couldn't breathe. I knew I didn't... belong. Shit, Johnny! I wish I could explain it better, and you think I'm all clever with my big words!

Anyway one day I decided to leave, run away I guess. It wasn't like I was frightened or anything, I just knew that I had to leave. I had it all planned, I was going to go to Beckenham, see if I could see Bowie and then... just go. But as I sat on the wall outside Haddon Hall waiting for him to appear I thought of you, and of Billy, and it's not like I'd miss your ugly faces or anything! Just that as I sat there staring up the road and down at the pavement and I started to think of our games and our races home from school and the stupid stuff we do like not being aloud to step on the cracks, and I thought who's going to look out for you if I go? And I knew I couldn't leave you, not yet anyhow.

But if you're reading this then things are different now and I know its time. I left this letter with Bowie one time when I gave him some of my writing and stuff, that night outside the Café Royal. He was… **is** so cool, Johnny! We would just talk music and stuff and he would listen, I mean **really** listen, and he read my writing, he told me that I seemed to **get** him better than any of the music critics that he read and was amazed that I was so young! And he asked me about my life, about home and stuff, and it all just sort of came out, about Mum and **him** and other stuff that I just never seem to have the words to talk about. One day you'll know. I think Angie thought I was a bit weird but she was kind. I put a note with this letter, Johnny, and I told him all about you, and I asked him that if anything ever happened to me, I don't know what, he would get it to you, because I couldn't think of anyone else I could leave with. Couldn't exactly ask you or Billy to look after it could I!

I just want you to know that I'm okay, Johnny, that I'm not **sad** or anything, like I said, I never really fitted. Put the Ziggy album on sometimes, and think of me, but never get sad. I didn't, listening to it was about the only time I didn't feel mixed up inside, I would lay there, close my eyes, and picture myself in nearly every song, that first time Johnny! I can't explain it, but it felt as if… well, like he screams on the last track, that I was 'Not Alone'. I hope this makes some kind of sense, but by the time you read this you'll understand a whole lot better. That's all I've got to say, Johnny, you'll be okay though, I know you will. Just remember, boy! Keep off the cracks now!